SISTERS

SISTERS

Chinese Whispers Book I

Mark Whitworth

Publicaciones Ili Pika, (Ili Pika Publications)

Patzcuaro, Michoacan, Mexico

For my wife, Andrea Kidd, who is one of three sisters. Thank you for putting up with me!

Contents

Contents

Preface

Living in China for six years opened my eyes to the wealth of its history. Iconic structures such as the Great Wall and the unearthed extent of the Terracotta Army made the Chinese past come alive. Residing on the delta of the Yangtse River (Cháng Jiăng) and travelling into the mountainous interior made apparent the physical constraints under which Chinese history unfolded. My working speciality has always been geography, but my passion is for ancient history. These books are a result of those twin interests.

Each year, a veritable army of Chinese archaeologists supplement the enormous variety of extant historical items and structures. Their discoveries have been such that histories, once considered myths, are increasingly found to have much truth in them. It is unfortunate that, just as the National Trust in the United Kingdom tends to glorify specific periods, the Chinese have often been similarly one-track. Re-creations frequently focus on a style that is inappropriate to their actual antiquity.

The written work of Sīmă Qiān in the second century BCE has been the focus of much speculation. He identified the existence of the Xià Dynasty, coming before that of the Shāng, and existing in China at the start of the second millennium BCE. It is a misfortune that both Sīmă Qiān and later commentators ascribed to the Xià the attributes they saw around them some eighteen hundred years later.

More recent historical adaptations have seen the need to apply even more modern characteristics suited to viewing audiences. Therefore, the populist view of this period of history not only includes the pomp associated with the Hán Dynasty (202 BCE – 220 CE), but the inclusion of fantastical martial arts has further compromised it. In many respects, the modification of some ancient Chinese history is akin to Shakespeare's re-writings of the life of Julius Cesar or Sir Thomas Malory's Le Morte d'Arthur. Well-intentioned but anachronistic.

I intended to write a story based on the times of the Xià that set the record straight. This tale is a fictional account, but nothing within it could not realistically have occurred. I have attempted to paint a picture of real people living through this period using myths, archaeological evidence, and a degree of speculation.

Acknowledgements

In writing **Chinese Whispers - Sisters**, there are many people to whom I am indebted. However, any errors and omissions are entirely my responsibility, and I know that some individuals mentioned below may not approve of aspects of my story.

My dear friend, Ian Self, was the first to read this book. To him, my most grateful thanks for providing feedback on the storyline and suggestions regarding grammar and punctuation; he was immensely supportive.

Sue Scott, in New Zealand, whom I have known since my time in China, has done an excellent job of proofreading my novel. She executed the task superbly, for no remuneration, and at great speed; sometimes, I could not keep up with her. Sue also gave me content feedback at various points and reassurance that the story was worth reading.

Petrina McGregor provided a mix of proofreading and content advice on the first of the two books. Her advice was invaluable and given for no reward.

My good friend, Peter Barker, advised me on various medical aspects, such as wounds and scarring. He became so perplexed at the questions I was asking that he requested he read the book himself. Having done so, he gave me further input regarding anachronisms. Cheers, Pete!

My sister, Susan Swanston, conducted the final proofreading of both books accurately and rapidly, exhibiting skills way in advance of my own. Thank you, Sue.

My eternal thanks must also go to my wife, Andrea Kidd. She has been there for me throughout and was the third person to read this novel. Sometimes, you wonder, when writing about violence, sex, drug-taking, and death, how much your partner might go off you. Andrea has not done so yet, although I keep reassuring her that the characters are a product of my imagination, not alter-egos!

It was intended that a section at the end of the book would identify all the sources I used. Unfortunately, this proved a little lengthy. Instead, in the section titled Sources, there is a link to my website on which I give much greater detail. However, below, I identify those people or organisations that have influenced me the most and, in some cases, those who contributed to telling these stories.

The first is an extensive group of individuals, Chinese archaeologists. Without them, I could not have told these tales. Their work from the middle of the Twentieth Century to this day has been incredible. In the earlier years of the People's Republic of China, they focused on proving the Yellow River as a single origin point for the Chinese people. Their findings demonstrated the opposite: that Chinese culture had influences from its furthest flung reaches. There are far too many of them to thank individually, but two stand out, people whose work has enthused me enormously. They are:

Professor He Nu of the Archaeology Institute of Chinese Academy of Social Science, primarily for his work and many research papers on Taosi.

Professor Li Liu, whose books cover a wider field, examining the transition from the Neolithic to early Chinese civilisations.

I would also like to thank Astro Pixels. They provide data concerning the moon's phases right back to 2000 BCE. These phases were critical to people living without modern lighting. This information is freely given through the Moon Phases Table, courtesy of Fred Espenak at www.astropixels.com. It is an excellent resource for writers of history. Thank you, Fred.

Finally, thanks to the great Scott Taylor, who contributed artistic flair to the cover design and the map. Without Scott, the world would not be quite as fascinating.

Introduction

The stories in *Chinese Whispers - Sisters* occur between 1926 and 1905 BCE. At the commencement of each chapter, the location is given; this can usually be found on the map on page xv, but an atlas or a modern mapping package like Google Earth would also help you find them. In addition, the year in the Xià dating system[1], the animal assigned to that year by Chinese culture, the day of the year relating to the solstices and equinoxes and the date in the Gregorian calendar.

Historians assign various dates to the commencement of the Xià Dynasty. There are also different interpretations of how this may have arisen from the Lóngshān cultures. I have chosen a later date than suggested in the "historical myth", one more aligned with archaeological evidence. It was a time of momentous change in China. Before this era, centuries of climatic change and disaster had occurred, undoubtedly leading to a massive reduction in population. Humans were already impacting their environments negatively, and some changes had come back to bite them.

This period also represents the commencement of the Bronze Age. Although bronze had been in use for at least a millennium, particularly in western China, it was not particularly significant prior to the Xià Dynasty. Just as in Western history, stone has continued to be the raw material most of the population has used for thousands of years.

The locations are authentic and well evidenced through archaeology; I have visited many of them. I have attempted to ensure that the descriptions of the period's landscapes, structures and vegetation align

---

[1] This is only fully explained in book two, *Sisters*, but for it is basically sequential and ascending with each new year commencing at Chinese New Year, not on 1st January. (The BCE dates are obviously descending.)

with the findings of specialists in these fields. However, applying a heavy dose of conjecture is necessary after four thousand years. The physical events, such as flooding, reflect actual events. However, there is difficulty accurately dating these; I have tried to apply them as logically as possible in my story.

In my use of speech patterns, I have deliberately avoided conforming to the preconception that Chinese culture has persisted unchanged. In any account of the pre-dynastic period, or indeed any historical analysis of the pre-Confucian Chinese culture, it is necessary to suspend what some regard as certainties about Chinese society. There is no evidence that an imperial cult existed four thousand years ago or that there was gross stratification of society. Although the role of females was undoubtedly changing in this period, there is no evidence for the complete suppression of women, nor was automatic filial piety known to be prevalent at this time.

So many of these misconceptions are based on Confucian ideals, albeit ones that were honed by Confucius rather than invented by him. As the Neolithic morphed into the Bronze Age, it is more likely that Chinese society had greater similarities to other cultures undergoing massive changes, such as those in western and southern Asia or Europe. It is doubtful that their culture even approximated that of Confucius, fourteen hundred years later, or that of his biographer, Sīmǎ Qiān, another five hundred years after that. We unknowingly derive our preconceptions from these two individuals; at the very least, they are distorted, if not wholly incorrect.

My characters' names have been drawn from Chinese mythology and often fulfil roles akin to those in the myths. Others have names that describe their characters, albeit in Pinyin, the official Romanised system for standard Mandarin Chinese. In scrambling around for minor characters' names, for one, I used that of a cleaner I employed in Suzhou and for another, that of the Terracotta Warrior who sits on my terrace; clearly, the fictional characters are not representative of either!

At the end of the book are sections on history, mythology, and characters' names. The information included is often fascinating, but it is unnecessary to commit it all to memory to appreciate the tales.

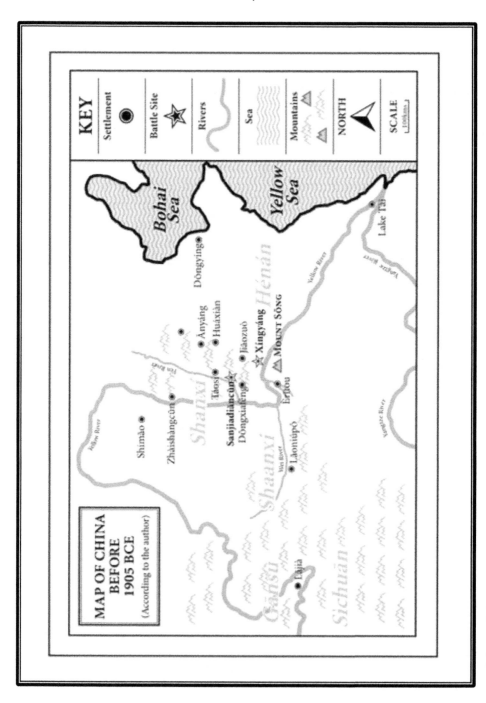

One: The Lesson
Táosì, Shănxī: The Palace Hall
Year 69: Year of the Hare
The spring equinox
22nd March 1926 BCE

There were upwards of thirty women chained along the ledge overlooking the hall. Finding enough anchor points to hold them in place had been a struggle. If they were now silent, the state of their clothing and dishevelled hair clearly indicated that this had not previously been the case. Closer examination would have revealed bruises and cuts from the beatings they had taken as they had been forced into the room. All strained forwards to observe the spectacle unfolding in front of them. Even if they were coerced into attending, not one could turn away from the dreadful scene.

It was a large hall. Stout tree trunks ran up through the rammed earth walls, their prime purpose being to carry the weight of the cross members supporting the roof. The room was surprisingly well-lit. Sunlight streamed through significant gaps in the compacted soil, evidence of both weather damage and a disinclination for repair. The state of the palace hall reflected that of the city, which suffered from a surfeit of neglect. Once it had been the pride of the Lóngshān, now the damaged architecture quite perfectly mirrored the damaged culture which it served.

There was little in the way of decoration. In more normal times, the hall may have been strung with army banners, and weapons might have lined the walls. Men would have sat cross-legged on straw mats while they pretended to listen to their sovereign between mouthfuls of meat and gruel. Small boys would have flitted from mat to mat, ensuring the males had ample food, warily approaching in case fault was found and they were cuffed for their shortcomings. But then, in normal times, no woman would have been seen inside the hall. It was taboo.

1

But these were not normal times, and this was certainly no normal gathering. Such an auspicious day; a full moon coinciding with the spring equinox deserved a special show. It seemed it was to be a double execution, mother and child, that the audience was here to be taught a lesson. In the hall's centre sat two young men dressed in black robes with black rope belts and black caps. Everything about their clothing had an almost intense, absorbing darkness. In stark contrast, their faces appeared whiter than white.

The pair lounged as best they could in uncomfortable and bulky wooden chairs, idly chatting while waiting for the audience to settle. Despite facing the unwilling women, they both toyed with the tools of their trade lying on the small table between them. There were three short knives: one of decorated bronze, one of fancifully carved jade and one of simple stone. Accompanying the weapons were two pottery beakers containing *jiu*[2].

Only one other piece of furniture remained in the hall, positioned in front of the two men and closer to the gallery. It was a table so big and strong it could have held two enormous men lying side by side and still left room for others to sit around the edges. Chīyóu's eating table was four strides long and two wide, more than a handspan thick and cut from a single piece of downed cypress. Four stout legs had been formed from younger trees, but each was so wide that no man could wrap his arms around a single leg. The table was several centuries old and bore the scars and stains associated with regular feasting.

Wrapped around each table leg was hemp rope. The multiple twisted yarns ran over the tabletop and around the limbs of the diminutive female form lying on its surface. The woman's ankles and wrists stretched to near breaking, formed her body into an imperfect cross. Four further bindings extended across the width of the table. The first lay just above her kneecaps, the second across her pelvis, and the third above her breasts. The fourth rope had been tied, forcing her jaw open and pinning down her tongue. It was evident to all in the room that the woman was completely immobile.

---

[2] An alcoholic drink.

2

The victim herself was less convinced. She had some control over her fingers and toes, although it hurt to flex them. She had total mastery of her eyes, although her view was limited. She could see the women chained on the ledge, her mother central to the group, and large cracks in the high ceiling, but glancing sideways brought nothing but the empty areas of the hall into view. Attempting to self-examine her own body was futile, her vision blocked entirely by the bindings tightening in and over her mouth. It was downwards she most wanted to look, for it would have provided what might be her last view of her child, as yet unborn.

Immobility meant it was difficult for the woman to clear the saliva running down her throat. She sensed a real possibility that drowning was a likelihood before anyone could commit further physical damage. Her hearing and sense of smell seemed more acute than usual. After hearing the scrape of a chair, the sound of a man rising, and a shuffle of footsteps, the acrid smell of stale sweat hit her hard.

She knew his identity before he spoke and knew he was not alone; he never was. Both these men had pressed themselves against her time and time again. She would know their gross stench anywhere. She also knew that the consequences on this occasion would not deter them. This time, they had reason in law to do with her what they wished. It was a relief that they were obviously not planning to rape her. The dire alternatives rotated through her mind, but not a single option left her or her child alive. Ultimately, it amounted to a palpable release when the men first spoke.

"Ladies. We are together in this sacred place to celebrate our skills and share them with your Sisterhood." It had been Hú who spoke first, as usual. "You see before you one of your own, a shaman, or should I say a false shaman, who until recently attended the observatory and was your choice of palace soothsayer. I say your choice because she was certainly not ours! Prince Xí, you should speak about her misdeeds."

"You may wonder why we hold her here in chains..." The second man directed his remarks to the audience, although he gazed lasciviously at the prone form on the table as his face reddened slightly, "...but it will become clear that we do indeed intend that this be a lesson, in more ways than one. This witch has transgressed. She has wronged us all. She has wronged Táosì. There is only one punishment available to us for such

3

treasonous behaviour." Xí paused, directing a twisted smile towards his comrade.

"It has come to our attention that there is a technique that you have used to save the unborn children of women in their death throes, and we intend to demonstrate that we have brought this technique to perfection."

"But she's not dead!" shrieked the victim's mother from the balcony.

"Dear Lady, I assure you that she will be. Of that, there is no doubt. You should know better than most that today, yes, this very day, both she and you will lose your right to protection. It is the law! Therefore…therefore she is an ideal example for us to show you how to get this procedure right. Is that not true, Prince Hú?"

"We have little doubt that this will be a lesson you will never forget. None of you will allow this newfound knowledge to slip from your minds. Not one! Prince Xí, would you like to explain?"

Xí approached the smaller table and picked up the first of three knives.

"We have a sharp jade knife!" He paused for effect, holding the weapon up and displaying it to the gallery before returning it to the table. "We have a sharp bronze knife!" He tossed it in a lazy circle. Momentarily, he caught the blade inexpertly in his palm before dropping it to the floor with a clatter. Instantaneously, bright red fluid trickled from his hand, and someone in the audience giggled surreptitiously. Xí wiped the blood on his robe and picked up the third knife, ignoring the pain. "And we have our very own…Táosì mined and crafted…a wonderful stone knife! Which would be the perfect knife for our lady of Liángzhǔ? Jade? Bronze? Stone? Hú, what do you think?"

"A stone knife would suit us best, Prince Xí." Hú smiled at the assembled women. "A dagger made from rock makes pretty, jagged patterns, does it not?"

"I think it would. I think it would." Xí bowed playfully to the watching women, only wincing when he felt his face was hidden from them. "But let us not be hasty, Hú. What do you think about some sample cuts to test the blades?"

Xí lifted the bronze knife and approached the main table.

4

"Now, ladies. Prince Xí is going to demonstrate the wrong cut first. Prince Xí…"

At this point, the prone figure closed her eyes. She was powerless. Best to try to blackout. She tried and tried, but the mist of unconsciousness did not come. As her eyelids flickered open again, she took in the chained audience, now in almost as much shock as she was herself. Quite suddenly, her view was eclipsed, and the odorous wine-filled breath of Xí filled her nostrils as his stare met her own.

"And now we start. Remember, ladies, this is what not to do!"

There was a sudden, sharp pain between her breasts, which swept downwards across her swollen belly. Every nerve ending in her body screamed for her to react, escape, and flinch. It was a battle the expertly tied bindings won; there was no escape. The rip stopped short of her pelvis, and even through the pain, she realised Xí's blade had only been prevented from going further by the knotted rope. It was an instantly excruciating pain, although it quite oddly dulled as swiftly as it had commenced. She felt her blood welling from the incision, trickling down the sides of her belly. A severe cramp knotted her diaphragm, where she had tensed against the blade.

Xí had cut her flesh but had taken care not to cut into her breastbone or muscle.

"Ladies, I said, a demonstration of an incorrect cut; this is it! Wrong! Please do not do it this way. We should clean this gore up."

Xí spat three times onto her belly and rubbed his saliva into the wound. Consequently, the blood flow increased; the two men were clearly unprepared for the resultant mess.

"Rags!" hollered Hú, directing his call to the open doorway. A scurrying noise followed, and shortly, a young boy arrived carrying a bundle of filthy rags. "Clean it up!" ordered Hú, and the boy set to on the table, having had to climb onto it to reach the woman. "And her! Clean her!" The lad shook in fear as he wiped out the wound. The girl's skin was stained with blood, spittle, and from the soiled cloth, what appeared to be the remnants of a tar barrel. Fresh blood streamed through the dirt as the boy scrambled off the table.

The short break enabled the woman to strain against her ties once more. It was to no avail; the only tangible result appeared to be increased blood flow. Absolute desperation had absolutely no beneficial effect.

"Enough! Prince Hú, would you like to demonstrate the correct cuts? If you attend to the lateral, I will attend to the vertical. You take the jade."

Hú picked up the jade knife and displayed it to the women on the ledge. He took his time, probing with his fingers to locate an area between the victim's breasts and swollen belly. He paused.

"You know, Prince Xí, I would have preferred the stone knife. Not only does it make a better fit in my hand, but such a blade also reminds me of my precious state, my exalted sovereign, and this woman's sins! Still, I will allow you the pleasure!" Having glanced at Xí and grinned, he returned to the job at hand.

"Here!" The knife sliced in an arc across the upper abdomen, bisecting the first vertical cut. Her explosive scream was silent but transmitted waves of agony throughout the hall as her eyes screwed tightly shut. "And here!" His second cut curved under her swelling. At this point, his victim passed out, although neither Hú nor his audience knew.

"Good job, Prince Hú! I will now demonstrate the vertical incisions with the stone knife." Xí found himself having to lean awkwardly to access the woman's side. He grabbed her thigh with his left hand to support himself, using his right to wield the blade. "We take a line from Prince Hú's upper cut to his lower." As the duller stone knife dragged across the flesh, a more ragged arc opened around the left-hand side of her belly. The blood flow was such that it pooled, only gradually dripping from the table and onto his boots. Irritated, Xí moved to the other side of the table, leaning towards the woman's face.

"How are you doing, my dear?" He asked playfully. "Only one more, and then we can begin for real! You're not asleep, are you? Prince Hú, some wine perhaps. To wake her?"

Hú grabbed the wine glass from the low table, throwing its contents into the victim's face. There was a soft, chesty moan. Xí had rounded the table; he made little pretence of focus when administering the incision down the woman's righthand side. His last contribution overlapped Hú's original lateral cuts. The woman did not even feel the final incision in her semi-conscious state. Agony after agony after agony had now caused a shutdown of her pain register. The irritating trickle of blood running down her sides was now the primary sensation.

"Now, we are done! Perfect." Hú moved toward the audience. "I am sure you are aware, ladies, it is not for us to slay…sorry…cause the death of a shaman, even a false shaman. Therefore, one of you will follow our guidance and cut this wretched child from this woman's belly! Do I have a volunteer? Perhaps her mother?"

The absolute silence from the tamped earth shelf on which the chained women stood spoke volumes. The victim's mother, central to the group, required support from those on either side of her. No woman should have to endure this treatment, no woman should have to watch this torture, and indeed, no mother should have to witness her daughter sliced in such a fashion.

"He said, does he have a volunt—"

"A volunteer for what? It looks like you are having fun. What's going on?" Chīyóu stood in the doorway, his shoulder resting on the door jamb. Their king's presence was entirely unexpected. He should have been on a three-day hunting trip and had only left that morning.

"My lord!" If there was a time for obsequiousness, this was it, but Hú struggled to manage quite the right path for his deference. "My lord. Are you hurt? What…what…what has brought you back so early?"

"A pain in the arse is what brought me back. A pain in the arse!" Chīyóu waddled towards his eating table. "I have piles!" He turned toward the women in the gallery. "Witches! Who will find me a cure for these damned piles?

"It seems, Princes, that they are struck dumb, but please explain why they are here?" The king waved towards the gallery. "It might be convenient to gather our best medical knowledge together in one place, but I doubt they are here to tend to my arse. In fact, my arse wasn't here when they were first gathered? Why are they tethered?"

"It…it…it is for a lesson, Lord Chīyóu. It…it…it is a lesson for an auspicious day. The equinox and a full…full…full moon."

"So, you are now teachers as well! This shamanic stuff seems to suit you well! And you seem to have a whole class of entirely focused students." Chīyóu was in a good mood for a change. Despite his condition, he was disinclined to condemn their excesses in bringing a host of women into his hall. He stared up at the gallery, appearing to take in one pair of eyes at a time, although if the truth be known, his sight was only sufficient to make out that they were female. "You lot must understand it's time for you to learn some true science... it's to us men you must now look for guidance...your time is gone!"

Chīyóu turned and, for the first time, took in the cypress wood table.

"Princes." Xí and Hú bowed before him. "You will tell these ladies to clean up this mess. I will eat tonight from this table."

"We will, my lord," Xí mumbled.

"Ye...ye...yes, sir," stuttered Hú. "Do...do...do you see on whom we practice? It...it...it is the witch's birthday!"

Chīyóu lowered his face toward that of the woman pinned to the table. It seemed an eternity before he gathered himself, and then he only raised himself upright with his arms. He turned. That night followed day was accepted, but it was widely understood that dusk came in between; there was no such gradual change in the countenance of the sovereign of Táosì. Thunderous would have been an expression of momentous understatement.

"Guards! Guards!" Ten armed and leather-clad men ran into the hall as one. Chīyóu barked orders.

"You four, take these two fools...No! Stop! Strip these robes off these two imbeciles, then put them in the cells. You four, unchain those women up there!" He turned to the last two guards. "And you two - cut the bounds on this" He pointed to the table. "And be careful!"

Stepping towards the women shaking in the gallery, Chīyóu raised his arms to them.

"You had better save her! You had better save her, and you had better save the baby, for that lump right there is my first and only son! Do it and do it right!

8

Two: The Yáodòng
Táosì, Shǎnxī: Hòutú's Yáodòng
Year 83: Year of the Snake
Four days to the spring equinox
18th March 1912 BCE

There was nothing special about her loess cave. The dwelling could have been described as one of the poorest in the city and undoubtedly needed considerable repair. The cleft in the loess behind her opened onto a damp, cold, poor home. Carved into the escarpment and barely high enough for her to stand upright in the centre, the back and sides tapered off to less than half her height. She may have only been a small woman, but she certainly lived in a tiny abode. How anyone could call this a *yáodòng*[3] she could not conceive, but it had been her home for over thirteen years.

Located at the head of the Da Nan Gully, her dwelling was just three hundred paces from the cemetery of the rich and the same again to the observatory. However, her view of the city was compromised by the gully walls. To the northwest, towering over the gorge, she could see the crumbling tamped earth walls of the palace but little else.

They could not keep her here much longer; there was change in the air. For Hòutú, it was a signal that her lifetime of hard work was coming to fruition. She made a mental list of improvements that would have to be made to render her home habitable for a few more years but ran out of fingers. She had to move. Life had to change.

Living in the worst home in Táosì was one thing, but it was quite another being systematically excluded from what could laughably be described as the society around her. An invisible line extended around her home, passing along the clifftop, then forming a semi-circle on the floor

---

[3] A house cave carved in the loess.

9

of Da Nan Gully, over which no one should cross on pain of death. Only a few braved that perimeter, then only with subterfuge and under cover of darkness. Even passing vagrants knew to keep clear. She believed they had expected her to die before now or certainly hoped that would have been the case. Only her pigeons and a few of the local Sisterhood kept her on track. The wait was interminable.

Life had not always been this way.

The yáodòng's entrance faced almost due east, where Jīnxīng[4] and the summer triangle dominated the sky, even as it brightened. Hòutú perched outside the cave on one of her only two pieces of smoothed stone. It had the benefit of keeping her backside dry, raising her just a hand's span above the morning dew. It was cold enough for her to remain wrapped in the vast bearskin she had worn while she slept. She ran her hand through the fur, appreciative of its warmth, and fondly remembered it as the last gift she had received from Niúláng. He had left her two presents; the bearskin was probably her greatest luxury, but the other was of even more significance.

When Niúláng had been sacrificed, his soul was given to the star Altair as a gift. Her lover's sin had been killing the bear and failing to offer its skin to Chīyóu. Hòutú's mother, Zhi Nü, had been taken much later, blamed for the indiscretions of her daughter, blamed for saving her child's life and cruelly sacrificed to the star Vega. Hòutú would ensure that when it was her turn, her life would be given to the third star of the triangle, the least bright of the three, Zeneb. Her daughter, Tú, who would surely live many years, would eventually wander the morning and evening skies as Jīnxīng, for she was now the one of prophecy.

Taking ownership of a star seemed so much more than being buried in a rich plot surrounded by the accoutrements of one's life. Who would gaze at an unnamed tomb other than graverobbers? How temporal. Many eyes would touch the stars throughout all the histories yet to come. While the sun and moon still shone and rivers ran, no one would forget the stars or planets. Almost eternal!

The pin-pricks of light faded more quickly as the rising sun promised to warm her face. She allowed the bearskin to slip from one

---

[4] Venus

10

shoulder. Her hemp tunic was stiff and badly needed a wash, as did her long skirt. She wished for the silks of her youth, not for the fancy living that accompanied them, but more for the warmth they would impart and the fact they would keep her skin from the roughness caused by the tunic she now had to wear.

Hòutú warmed her face and hands with her breath, but it was still cool enough to remain well-wrapped. Leaning forward, she placed each palm on the sides of the copper pot and promptly yelped. It was the same mistake she made every morning. At her age, she should know better.

"Tú!" she called into the cave. "Tú, it is time. Come on."

From the back of the *yáodòng* came the sounds of her daughter rising. She had been sick in the last few weeks and was only now gradually recovering her health. Unusually, she bore the same name as her mother, although she answered to Tú – when she answered at all. The name had passed down through the generations, generally alternating, but the Sisterhood had insisted the child carry her name. She was, after all, taking Hòutú's place in their design.

Tú appeared, her tunic rumpled like her mother's and her hair flying all over the place. She was still beautiful, even with sleep barely having left her. Unlike her mother, she wore trousers, which demonstrated their age and were far too short.

"Will you watch the pan, Tú Tú?" Her mother rose to her feet and headed for a section of the cliff face that afforded some shelter. Half the city might be able to watch her urinate, but at least she could not be seen from her own front door. Having finished, she scratched her clog through the loess in a vain attempt to cover the damp ground. She was unsuccessful and sighed before returning to the small fire.

Tú may not always have been the most cooperative of children, but she was practical and wanted breakfast just as much as her mother. She had drawn herself up the second stone, onto which she had dropped her buttocks before stirring the millet porridge.

Hòutú yanked on a hemp rope that extended into the cave, at the end of which curled a cantankerous nanny goat. Making a sustained effort, she pulled the creature towards the fire as the animal groaned in displeasure.

"Milk this morning, Tú?"

Tú nodded, returning to the cave to retrieve a bowl and two plates. Each of the three pieces was brown earthenware, and each displayed a snake wrapping itself around the inside. If anything above all else could be regarded as their family symbol, it was the trapped snake coiled within the confines of the pottery.

Hòutú gazed at her daughter across the fire. They were both as ensnared as those snakes and Tú, in what was now nearly fourteen years, had never been further than a minute's walk from their home. For it was not a home; it was a prison. If her daughter had been Niúláng's gift, he had paid for it with his life, but she had paid with her freedom. It was now time Tú broke free. The sacrifices would all be worth it in time.

Chīyóu was the culprit, but he was also a saviour, with Hú and Xí his failed executioners. If Hòutú considered carefully, she could not come up with the name of someone who would have made a worse leader than Chīyóu, and she could not imagine two less competent advisors than Hú and Xí. Before the plan was derailed, there had been lengthy discussion about the suitability of all three, and all had agreed they were demonstrably the failures that the Sisterhood required. Táosì's recession worsened by the day.

Remembering those names took her back to that morning spent on Chīyóu's table. The whole situation had run away from the Sisterhood; those two sadistic bastards had almost gone too far. Some of the sisters believed the entire thing had been miraculous; it had not; there had been some careful planning. There had been no miracle about the set-up; falling pregnant with Niúláng had been a pleasure. Again, there was no miracle. A similar act had been far less fun, in fact, one committed with gritted teeth, to have had to bed Chīyóu once she knew she was with Niúláng's child, an act that still distressed her to this day.

Chīyóu's haemorrhoids were also a long-term project, the work of a lifetime by both his cooks and those unfortunate enough to find themselves commanded to his bed. She could be considered lucky that Chīyóu had returned precisely when he did, although a little earlier would have saved a great deal of pain, blood, and panic.

The only miracle was that the sisters managed to save Hòutú and her daughter. Her wounds had been deep and had become severely infected. The cuts were treated with garlic, onion, and honey, but the scars

12

would never leave her. Only two weeks after her torture, the child's arrival had caused the wounds to open again. Hòutú would only ever regard childbirth as an agony she never wished to repeat, even if it had produced a single positive result.

After the birth, when it had turned out to be the girl the Sisterhood had planned, Chīyóu had lost interest. He lost interest in Hòutú and lost interest in punishing the two princes. He may have fifty female children for all he knew, but he had no male offspring. That was his only focus.

As it turned out, Hú and Xí had not lost interest in Hòutú. Whilst they would have loved to have had her erased, they were bound by the law. The mother of a child should not be killed until that child comes of age. The only concession they were granted was that the mother and child should be confined to an area defined by a stone's throw distance from their prison. If the pair broke confinement, they were then fair game. The two princes had personally chosen Hòutú's home in Da Nan Gully as they had believed it would be impossible for her to avoid breaking the conditions of her imprisonment.

That had not been the case. Only twice had Hòutú stepped outside her safe area, and then only on a technical basis, as floods had twice raged down the ravine, forcing her to cut steps in the gully wall to escape the torrent atop the cliff. She had known that neither of her tormentors nor their henchmen would be out in such inclement weather. On both occasions, she had returned sodden to the safety of her *yáodòng* well before they had pushed their noses outside the palace doors.

It was Chīyóu's stupidity that kept him in power. He was held in place by two forces: a few powerful men, none of whom wanted each other to have control and the concerted efforts of the Sisterhood to ensure he did not stumble around too randomly in his reign. The latter acted as a lever to reinforce the former.

Many years before, Táosì had been a robust Lóngshān state with strong leaders, but there was no way the city could survive the changes that were coming. Chīyóu and his scum were simply the catalysts to speed the process of decline. Undoubtedly, the Dàgùduì quarry had more stone than could have been used in a thousand years; there was no supply problem. The problem was demand.

It was more than three hundred years since the great drought had commenced, and, whilst in living memory, the rains had returned, they were still uncertain and limited. Today, the population was stable. Even without seeing them, Hòutú could count the empty homes simply by the lack of noise. Táosì had been home to as many as fifteen thousand; today, there were fewer than a quarter of that number. There had been jobs in the lithic industries, in pottery making and jade carving. There had been massive demand for carpenters and builders, let alone all those who fed and watered those craft workers, and then there was the palace and the army. Hòutú had only personally observed the very end of the decline. All that she knew from previous times had come from her mother and other members of the Sisterhood.

If the earlier population peak had not managed to degrade the quarries, it did cause significant damage to the local farmland and forests. Hòutú had learned that today, gathering firewood alone involved a day's walk. The cypress trees were gone; the supply of beams and supports for grander houses and the palace with them. Yields from the fields of millet and wheat were so low that, in many years, the farmers did not even bother planting. They were keeping herds of goats instead, which added to the destruction of the vegetation. Hunting was hardly an option anymore; the bearskin on Hòutú's back, the cause of her lover's death, had been from one of the last bears ever seen in the vicinity; it was no wonder Niúláng had been put to death. What would they have done to him if they had found he had killed not only the last bear but also impregnated the king's last virgin shaman? It was a matter that one would not wish to consider for longer than necessary.

Hòutú shook her head. Her task had not been a simple one at the start. Its derailment meant that the burden must fall on her daughter instead. It had involved her in extreme risk managing the switch. Her preordained role, one for which she had been specifically trained, was passed to her daughter. She would not experience the glory that she had earned. Instead, she was forced to adapt.

Her sacrifices would not bring about her redemption. Those sacrifices were now made entirely on behalf of her daughter and Tú's role in the Sisterhood's plan. That is why she became pregnant by Niúláng yet bedded Chīyóu. That is why she had lain on that butcher's table and then

14

accepted the ignominy of her prisoner status and her role as a part-time whore. While Chīyóu, Hú and Xí still lived, her life was over if she stepped out of her confinement. The confinement would not have been important in itself, but the same conditions applied to Tú. For that reason, the chains must soon break. Tú was now ready to take on the role initially her mother's own; her fourteenth birthday loomed.

Only two skills remained to be added to Tú's already impressive list of accomplishments. The first was easy: mastering the observatory. Hòutú had taken her daughter through the technical aspects with a hastily manufactured model, but she desperately needed the actual observatory to demonstrate she knew what she was doing. It was not complicated; a few simple rhymes to remember at what time of year the sun would rise against each gap in the observatory wall and the use of the correct *bi, cóng*[5] and staff. The information was crucial to the farmers. Without it, they had become lackadaisical about their annual routines.

The second skill was a different proposition; Tú had to learn to socialise. Not simply to mix but to persuade, convince, manipulate, and do all these things without looking the slightest bit out of place. There had been little opportunity to develop these skills. Their only visitors had been a handful of members of the Sisterhood and the few men in the town who had been brave enough to take up Hòutú's offers of sex, for which they paid with a contribution to her cooking pot. It was an indication of the success of her whoring that they managed to eat well at least twice a week. Tú had to remain hidden during these encounters with the men. The limit of her education with the opposite sex had been observing her mother rutting from under a blanket. It was not the schooling she might have expected.

Hòutú's thoughts returned to the present. Yú was coming – or that is what the pigeons had told her. Yú from Bǎodūn. Yú from Mount Sōng. Yú was the prophesy, even though he was as much a part of the derailment

---

[5] Carved jade. A bi is in the form of a disk with a central hole. A cóng is a more elaborate structure but has a square outer section with a circular inner tube through its length, they may be short or tall. Presently, their use is completely unknown, although there is speculation that they are ritual objects as they are found in many graves.

15

as Tú. If the original plans had worked out, it would have been Gǔn, Yú's father and she, Hòutú, who would have been the hammers that drove in the pegs supporting the new Motherland. Instead, it was to be Yú and Tú.

When Gǔn had insisted on trying to help the remaining Liángzhǔ people as they tried to escape the devastation of flooding, it had thrown the sisterhood's plan out by a generation. It had been an excellent scheme, but there had been no allowance for independent thought. Gǔn was responsible, and one knock-on effect had been Hòutú's need for a child, thus guiding her into the arms of Niúláng. That tryst had been the cause of her long-term incarceration. Everything was linked. Only the pigeons had prevented the precarious structure from tumbling.

Tú passed the plate of gruel. Her mother noticed she had added only a little fresh goat milk to each bowl. Tú seemed to be saving the rest for herself.

"That's selfish, Tú. You should share the milk equally. When will you learn some manners?"

"It's not for me!" Tú scowled. "It's for the pigeons." It was the first time she had spoken all morning.

"Just remember, the pigeons should not have milk regularly, only when they are sick."

"Hu Zu is sick and walking in circles in his cage."

"Hu Zu is an incredibly old pigeon. We will probably end up eating him by the end of the week. He certainly cannot do the job anymore. He's walking in circles because he wants sex, not because he is old!"

"I won't eat Hu Zu; he was the first one I remember hatching…and what about his wife?"

"Look, xīngān[6]. In the wild, they would have died years ago. We have kept them fit and healthy, fitter and healthier than us, in fact. There comes a point when it is kinder to kill them than let them fade away. I will want the same for myself..." she caught Tú giving her the evil eye, "…eventually!"

"We could sacrifice him!" exclaimed Tú. "That would be better than eating him."

---

[6] Heart and liver. It is used as a term of endearment for the most important person in your life.

Two: The Yáodòng

"Sacrifices do not fill your stomach. Sacrifices are to make an impression."

"On the gods?"

"What gods? Sacrifices are to make an impression on the people. Don't you forget that."

The pigeons were an open secret. They were impossible to miss as they wheeled across the sky and occasionally descended on the odd millet field. But they were a secret within a secret. It had taken many decades for the Sisterhood to circulate the myth that eating pigeons made you both infertile and mad. They had sown the seed by surreptitiously poisoning high-profile figures and pointing the blame. It was now common knowledge amongst the populous – no one would kill them, and certainly, no one would eat them. Now, only the shamans would tame and keep the birds. It had been more challenging to persuade people to persecute the eagles, goshawks and sparrowhawks, those species that systematically culled the pigeon flocks. The message that eating the predators made you faster and more potent had not overridden the fact that they did not make for good eating.

The birds' pen was just inside the entrance to the cave, where an ingenious flue rose through the loess; it had a trapdoor the birds could enter but not exit. Designing it had been a nightmare as the duct immediately became a conduit for the rains. Hòutú had to construct a second tunnel to act as a spillway. In the end, that had been fortuitous because, in the rainy season, they used it as a supply for their domestic water. In another life, Hòutú could have been a water engineer, a thought that entertained her as she found it odd that Gǔn, the man initially intended for her bed, performed just such a role. Those fleeting moments were enough for Tú to rally and raise her voice again.

"What if—?"

"No!" It was a mother's exasperation that had taken hold of Hòutú. She was generally placid, but the forthcoming events had begun making her tetchier than usual. "Sorry, love. I'm thinking about things, just like you are, and it's starting to get to me."

"What if he doesn't like me?"

"What? Hu Zu? Of course, he likes you; I sometimes think that he thinks that you are his mother. Like most males, he's never really

17

grown up, just grown old." She chuckled to herself, relieving a little of her anxiety.

"Not Hu Zu! Yú!"

"Ah! So that's what is worrying you. That I understand, it's grown-up thinking. That is something on which we must work. You'll have to stop wearing those old trousers - and smarten up your hair - and wash - and something even more important."

"What's that?"

"You are going to have to learn how to smile!"

Tú scowled, jumped up, picked up the jar of millet grain and headed back into the cave to tend to the pigeons.

"I said…smile!"

Hòutú was comfortable with her daughter's love of the birds. They were their lifeline and had been essential to the Sisterhood for several centuries. Once they had learned of their homing instinct, it had not been a great leap of faith to appreciate that they could use them to send messages. Those messages had initially been binary in nature; a dark pigeon meant 'yes' and a light one 'no'. It was a start, but not enough to coordinate several thousand women from the mouths of the Yangtze and the Yellow Rivers to the Sìchuān Basin and the western deserts.

It was believed that the Sisterhood of Lake Tài had first considered the problem and proposed a solution; the trade routes had spread the idea by word of mouth. Eventually, a coven descended on the foothills to the south of Mount Sōng, and a format was agreed upon. Astonishingly, the Sisterhood had developed writing, which was the secret within a secret within a secret.

The pigeons themselves only carried a tiny copper band. On that band were scratched some numbers. As many as six numbers could be etched on the metal, which meant quite complex messages could be relayed. Each number referred to a list held by the pigeon keepers, a numeral equating to a full or partial sentence. The reference list had regular additions but was only updated for functional purposes during the new year when groups of the Sisterhood could meet. Only a few physical copies of the list were kept, and those only in nodal settlements. Most pigeon-keeping shamans were expected to memorise the contents; rhymes made rote learning easier.

18

It was in this manner that the grand plan was implemented. It was in this way that Hòutú had learned of Gǔn leaving Bǎodūn, that he had perversely veered off towards Mount Sōng, and now, fifteen years later, she had found out they were back on track. Yú was heading for Táosì.

Thinking of the messages reminded Hòutú it was time for her daughter's lesson. She rose and passed her hands over the two *ménshén*[7], which stood on either side of the cleft in the cliff, causing her to cross-step left and then right before she entered the *yáodòng*.

Tú had already started. She was kneeling in front of a square of sand, wielding a short stick in her left hand. In the sand, one symbol had been neatly scratched.[8]

Hòutú swiftly brushed out the figure using the ball of her foot.

"We may be close, but we are not there yet. Give it time, Tú, give it time. It would help if you remembered that many are frightened of that symbol, many who would kill you for daring to use it. They do not know what it means, but many of our despot rulers have seen it before, and they fear it means their end. I always think they see it as a dagger through the heart!"

"But it's a good word!" Tú protested. "It's for all of us, for the good of everyone."

---

[7] The guardians of the threshold into buildings. Over time the characters of the *ménshén* have changed. It is assumed that at the beginning of the Bronze Age they would have been mythological demons.

[8] The symbol is courtesy of the website Chinese-Word.com.

"I think you forget, Tú. You forget how many will die before that symbol flies on every flag across the land. It would help if you also remembered it will be us who are responsible for those deaths. Some might see our role as worthy, but those who suffer will not, and the ghosts of those who die will haunt your dreams. Remember that. This is not an easy life we chose."

"I didn't choose it! You chose it for me. Why should I take the blame for all the many acts of the Sisterhood? You keep saying, 'We are just the hammer that bangs in the peg.' Well, I am not sure I want to be the hammer when I am held in the hands of the Sisterhood."

"The Sisterhood is the only reason you are alive, Tú. You owe them everything. Why do you think I did not succumb to sacrifice, and you along with me before you were born? The Sisterhood saved me, and they saved you. The Sisterhood stopped the princes from killing us and manipulated Chīyóu into protecting us. The Sisterhood protects you in this cave!"

"And nothing but a little yard around it as a safe zone! We are prisoners, *Māma*[9], prisoners."

"And prisoners find ways to escape. That is what is coming, Tú. Escape. And for you to fulfil your destiny."

"It's my destiny that I—"

"Enough! Recite the list and draw the words as you do it. Now!"

Tú gave in and commenced her lesson. It was easy enough, and she did not believe she had made an error for over a year. Whilst drawing, she also sang the words and pondered whether to make a deliberate mistake to test her mother. Perhaps another day.

Hòutú watched her daughter with pride. Fewer than a hundred of the Sisterhood had mastered these skills, and she had been Tú's only teacher. If only she could have stopped her using her left hand. Not that it mattered, although some characters she produced had a slightly different flow. Tú could have done it with the stick between her toes for all she cared, but it had made it much more difficult in the early years. The instruction, 'copy me', had meant her watching a reflected image of her own technique, and getting used to it had taken some time.

---

[9] An informal name for one's mother.

Two: The Yáodòng

When the time came to reveal the Sisterhood's secret writing, there would have to be teachers. Hòutú was unconvinced that her child would slip into that role quickly; being left-handed would complicate everything. Tú would have to use her innate intelligence to get her through.

With the lesson over, Tú kicked the sand and scraped it flat. No image, character, or writing remained – it was as if they did not exist. If the truth be known, they did not.

High above was a click followed by a flurry of feathers as wings flapped somewhat pointlessly in the long flue. Most birds had mastered the concept of a slide, but Háng had not. Háng was a dependable pigeon, although it was clear he was not particularly smart. Hòutú considered him to be on par with Tú's father. As the incoming bird stepped around his mate, head bobbing and cooing expectantly, his keeper reached inside the pen and, holding him firmly in her right hand, quickly uncoiled the copper ribbon from his leg. The process was over almost before it had started. Háng went back to his posturing as if there had been no interruption.

Hòutú carefully passed the copper band to her daughter, who studied it intently.

"He's coming." Tú glanced over at her mother. They both knew that Háng had only flown in from Dōngxiáfēng, little more than a two-hour flight for the bird but three day's walk for the average human. "Yú. He's on the Fèn River. He's coming with an army of two men! What?"

"Read it carefully, Tú. Context. You see the word army, and you think that might apply to a group of three people? Think! It could be twenty, two hundred, two thousand or twenty thousand, which is it? Context. Do you have an army with twenty people?"

"No!" Tú spluttered. "Twenty thousand is an impossible number. It must be two hundred or two thousand, but which one?"

"Remember, Tú; he has been kept well-informed. The Sisterhood is with him, and he has probably been inundated with information from people leaving this dying city. With that information, how many would you bring?"

"If I could feed them all, I would bring four thousand." Her remark demonstrated careful analysis of the general situation, but Tú clearly had no experience of warfare.

21

"So…how many do you think he has brought, two hundred or two thousand?"

"Two thousand." Tú beamed, the first time she had smiled all morning.

"Correct. Pass me the band." Hòutú checked the markings and engaged her memory. Tú was right; Yú was on his way and nearly there. She watched as Tú returned to the sandpit and drew the forbidden character again. This time, she did not scold. "Yes, it will soon be time for the flag, but we can expect visitors before Yú arrives, and they will not be friendly. Let us hide the dream for a few more days. Yes, Tú Tú?"

Tú stood and exaggeratedly wiped out the symbol with her toe.

Three: The Sisterhood

Dōngxiáfēng, Shǎnxī: The back of a stationary cart.
Year 83: Year of the Snake
Three days to the spring equinox
19th March 1912 BCE

The three women took their responsibilities seriously, very seriously indeed. They were guardians of a principle, not one that mere temporal issues would sway. Their meeting site was inauspicious and somewhat uncomfortable but suited their needs. To all intent and purpose, it would seem they were three old friends taking a break from their daily chores.

It was a rare meeting, supposedly a regular annual event, although it had now been over two years. Since the last conclave, one of the three was new to the group, but it mattered not. The newcomer was nervous but also excited by her inclusion. There would be slight differences of emphasis, perhaps, and more nuance on the agenda. However, the three women were fully aligned regarding the bigger picture. If collectively, their minds were focused on the grand plan, each internalised their personal circumstances, which were somewhat akin to heavy but unseen chains. Deep in thought, they sat for a moment in silence, dwelling on their private thoughts, some of which were the stuff of nightmares.

The debutant, the youngest of the trio, had been forced to watch the torture of her mother and brothers before watching them slowly die. When she was little more than a toddler, her family's Lóngshān assassins had chained her to the wall above the killing pit. The monsters had gagged her in such a manner that she could not turn away from the scene. Closing her eyes had been an option, although that tactic had merely thrown her mind into overdrive, and her imagination created even more despicable horrors. She had been but a child yet would never forget, never forgive,

23

and would allow no diminishment of her energies in support of the Sisterhood. Her views regarding the destruction of the Lóngshān were shared just as ardently by her two companions.

"You're drifting, Girl!" Their leader's astuteness sometimes made it seem like she could read your mind. "Focus!"

"Sorry." There was little more she could say, but a smile from her superior helped her forgive herself.

Their objective was to remove the obstacles to parity; almost any collateral damage was acceptable in achieving that. It was always the bigger picture, the longer-term, a determined search for a final solution. No matter how many heads were trampled in the process or how many lives were lost.

The Sisterhood's ambition had contributed to Táosì's present state, as the town descended into the same disorder into which the Lóngshān to the east had plunged centuries before. The lower Yellow River valley was now their target, Táosì simply a tool to interfere with its workings. They would move people and take new lands. They would apply technologies that had advanced far ahead of those achieved by the Lóngshān. They would re-establish a culture that had once been integral but was now, for many, only a myth, a tale or folklore, a nirvana.

In truth, the woman in charge had worries of her own. Whereas those of the youngster were primarily historical, her supervisor's concerns were for the coming ten years. Already, she was battle-weary, not from fighting with arms, but from the persistent, ever-present unpleasantness and danger she faced at every turn. She had long since stopped counting the number of times she had been raped, forced into servitude, or degraded and damaged in all manner of ways. She had put it behind her, for thinking about such atrocities only increased her fear of those to come.

If it were not for the cause, she would be insane by now; she had seen many friends take that particular route. Whether it brought the battered and abused any relief was a moot point; madwomen were treated with even less regard than sane ones. Although she could now see the light and had a spark of optimism for the future of their people, she had no such confidence as regards her destiny. She had no long-term. She would die and knew, with certainty, she would die horribly, in agony, never to learn if her death had been in vain. A successful outcome would finally be in

24

the hands of others. They would enjoy her triumph; she could have no personal satisfaction. Her body would rot, probably in some random ditch, with no one inclined to say a few words or build a memorial. No matter. She knew her fate.

"Is it you now daydreaming?" The youngster summoned up the courage to playfully turn the tables on her mentor, "What I want to know is if what we have achieved at Mount Sōng and in Èrlǐtou is sufficient, and are they prepared in Táosì?"

"We've tipped the balance enough for the process to snowball. It can take on a life of its own now, but you must drive it in Táosì and Mother in Èrlǐtou. You are both essential. My work will continue deep in the heartland of the Lóngshān. We will each take direct action, although only as much as necessary. We do not want to push too hard and come undone."

For such an august body, they seemed preternaturally young. Grandmother was in her twenties, Mother in her thirties and Girl in her mid-teens. Their titles did not reflect their genetic relationship, only their seniority within the Sisterhood. If they topped the pyramid, Hòutú and Tú could be thought of as in the top third.

However, theirs was a reasonably egalitarian institution, although the disparate locations of their members had forced them into forming this decision-making council and stratifying their organisation over the years. The pigeon fanciers were the second tier, now comprising fewer than eighty, as the geographical extent of their influence had shrunk. Whilst keeping no ledger, the reports from their lieutenants indicated there were perhaps as few as two thousand remaining in the Sisterhood as a whole. In the organisation's entire history, it could only have been in the first few decades their numbers had been as low. To some extent, it paralleled the decline in the general population, although there was acceptance amongst the leadership that their actions had not been sufficiently evident. As a group, their activities had become more covert. Such was the nature of a longer-term project; their planning had already consumed two centuries, and few had yet to see any positive results.

The Sisterhood traced their lineage back to the great Nüwa, the mother goddess, who had held the sky from falling. Their present task may have seemed less significant, but they saw themselves as the guardians, preventing humanity from falling into an abyss. Their social transformation required control of the Lóngshān, and unseating the overlords of the Yellow River could only be achieved by manipulating the physical environment. The ends may be popular with the masses, but the means would harm many innocent victims. The Sisterhood had to tread a fine line; its members might accept the price, but many people would suffer and die before they saw any benefits.

Whereas the lower reaches of the Yellow River were presently lost to the Lóngshān, down south, the problems had been entirely environmental. The inundations of the Yangtze had caused regular and extreme flooding from Sìchuān down to Lake Tài and the delta. The refugees still streamed north today. Jiǎngsu had also suffered the full force of Yellow River flooding. It had now been two generations since the yellow beast had diverted, spilling its sediment-laden waters southwards, destroying the Sisterhood's cultural and symbolic home.

To imagine only the Sisterhood had suffered was ignorance. Hundreds of thousands, if not millions, had died in the devastation. In the first years, homes and lives had been swept away in one huge rush. The survivors found their lands laid waste and their granaries destroyed; many more lives were taken by starvation. As the people searched for food, new diseases spread through the once bountiful lowlands, and the curses of cholera, yellow fever, and malaria inflicted many more deaths.

The Yellow River was temperamental. It seemed the cycle repeated only haphazardly with each annual flood. If one year seemed to offer hope, the next would take it away. The choices in Jiǎngsu were death by flood, starvation, or terrible sickness. The only alternative was to leave, although the newly impassable terrain and the Lóngshān warlords to the north stood in the way. At times, death at the tip of a spear seemed preferable to other dire options.

As a policy, the Lóngshān killed all male migrants and enslaved the females. The term enslaved took on many meanings. Like Táosì, the eastern Lóngshān were not only a male-dominated society but also imbalanced in terms of gender. In principle, they preferred that women proliferated, undertook all the manual labour and serviced every man's needs. Their ideal was a society with a male warrior class and a female working class, but their rule had only resulted in disharmony, discord and a host of women attempting to escape their lands.

26

Three: The Sisterhood

Now safe from the annual floods, the Lóngshān slaves had extended the croplands onto the drying flood plains of the old courses of the lower Yellow River. The need for labour mounted each year to feed their growing armies and sustain their elite, whose lifestyle demands grew disproportionally. The Lóngshān were poised to proliferate in political influence and their geographical sphere; however, the limited growth of their workforce was a restraint. Only fools would think that their society was sustainable, but by and large, their leaders were fools, albeit bullying fools.

That the Lóngshān had been unable to sustain Táosì and control Shǎnxī was, in large part, due to the Sisterhood. Although decimated in the lower Yellow River, the Sisterhood had maintained a limited presence in Táosì. It was a fine thread that could easily have snapped; that presence now consisted only of Hòutú, Tú and a handful of willing helpers.

Mother was responsible for the Sisterhood's control of Èrlǐtou. Hers was a significant responsibility, although she would eventually pass it on if they successfully destroyed Táosì. On the surface, her burdens did not appear to match the horrific experiences of her two colleagues. Hers had been a peaceful life. In Sìchuān, she had avoided the worst effects of the flooding and earth movements. Whilst living beneath Mount Sōng, she may have been frustrated by her husband's escapades, but she had been in no danger. Her safety had improved further in Èrlǐtou; only a direct attack from the Lóngshān would unsettle their growing community.

However, it seemed Mother's heart was heavier than her two comrades. All three had secrets, many of which they even kept from each other. However, Mother's biggest and most terrifying secret was known to both Grandmother and Girl, although she hoped no other living being knew of the facts. It had been a dirty business, the consequences of which could unravel. Mother's guilt surrounded the sacrifice of her own family for the Sisterhood. If unearthed, the details of that sacrifice would lead to wide-scale repugnance. It was a heavy burden, one that became heavier by the day.

"You know, it is not just us," Grandmother spoke again, interrupting Mother's chain of thought. "Much also depends on the Xīwǎ peoples. They were once an agricultural people, as you know, Girl. They may be semi-nomadic herders now, but they understand the

27

incompatibility of their way of life with the farmers, so they actively seek agreement and defined borders. They see the mutual benefits of a trading relationship with those who till the fields."

Kànménrén, the Xīwǎ leader, vehemently detested all that was Lóngshān. That he had been captured and tortured by them was not the prime cause for his feelings; the loss of his wife and three sons to that same torture was. He had experienced what his family had been through yet had survived. It was as livid a scar on his soul as were the welts all over his body.

"And how is your father, Girl?" Grandmother's sympathetic expression demonstrated understanding of the family's loss. Now, Kànménrén's sole living relative was Girl. That the Xīwǎ leader was amenable to her suggestions had proved invaluable to them and was quite typical of their operational methods.

"He is as well as could be. He misses my mother and brothers. Extinguishing his hatred will only come from eliminating the Lóngshān. He will do all in his power to assist Yú and ourselves."

"He's a good man." Mother was the wife of Gǔn, the father of Yú. If Girl was the controlling influence on Kàn, she performed that role for Gǔn. All three knew the weakest guiding hand was the one that influenced Yú. It was not that the man's life partner did not have the ability or control; they were concerned about how she might end up using that power.

The fact that the Sisterhood's source of power came from manipulating male leaders was an issue that was put aside for a while. It was, however, never far from their thoughts that the situation was untenable in the longer term. The parity they strived to achieve would only stabilise if as many women as men were leaders amongst their people. For the time being, and perhaps for the remainder of their lifetimes, there was a grudging acceptance that manipulating male leaders was the only course open to them.

Gǔn's impulsiveness had almost derailed their plans. When leading his people out of Sìchuān, he had responded to the pleas for help from Mount Sōng, thus bypassing Èrlǐtou. The delay led to a later-than-expected relocation, forcing the Sisterhood to modify its plans. Just as Tú was to replace Hòutú, Túshānshì was to take over from Mother, whilst Yú stepped into the role intended for Gǔn. It was the delay of a generation and the substitution of experience for inexperience; it had been a tough call. The decision had caused considerable unrest amongst the sisters.

However, securing the southern slopes of Mount Sōng from the Lóngshān had its advantages. For one, it acted as a reception centre for those unfortunates still escaping the south. Their numbers were now vastly reduced, but still, they came. Mount Sōng would eventually provide a way back for these people. In addition, Kāifēng, once a conservative and outrageously cruel Lóngshān centre, was now slipping towards them. Its new young leader, Yúntóng, had recognised the need for change and, if not fully supportive, was undoubtedly not the roadblock his father had been. It helped that the Sisterhood had provided his new partner, an alliance guided by Grandmother. Once the Lóngshān were defeated, Kāifēng and the mountains provided the gateway back to the south.

Grandmother had been one of the earliest refugees and had seen it all. She was a distant cousin of Hòutú, although they had never met. Both hailed from the shores of Lake Tài and considered themselves Liángzhǔ, who, before the great floods, had been one of the most advanced societies in the Motherland. The Motherland was now a shrunken thing. No longer did the peoples regard themselves as one. They were disparate and, in many cases, desperate. The Lóngshān inspired the dog-eat-dog philosophy and the female subjugation that now predominated; their influence had grown as the Motherland had shrunk.

Members of the Sisterhood were rare amongst the eastern Lóngshān. A few hung on but with shattered morale. Hopes for a better future had dissipated; their numbers grew fewer each year. Grandmother was the principal emissary to the Lóngshān lands, and hers was an unenviable task. The risk of capture and death was one she accepted, but the dreadful conditions she witnessed on each of her trips left her completely drained.

If there was one overarching driving force in the Sisterhood, it was Grandmother. It was she who finally broke their contemplation. "Mother! Girl! Your thoughts?"

"My biggest concern is this battle. It might seem like a minor issue, but everything hinges on Yú winning. What if he loses?" Girl trembled slightly at the enormity of the task.

"Any battle is always about stacking the odds. There is an art in war. It is not simply a matter of two forces on a battlefield. It is about supply lines, the condition of the participants and choosing your ground. There is also the question of motivation." Grandmother grinned, "Chīyóu's generals may be motivated, but the forces they command rarely see any benefits other than an early death. Anything you can do to have the opposition in a weakened state is beneficial. Wiping out their leaders will leave the foot soldiers rudderless; their only ambition will be to save their own lives. Take every step to reduce the odds; poison is always an immense tool. Think about it!" Grandmother smiled at Girl. This seemingly nervous creature would one day lead the Sisterhood; she was clever beyond imagination. All she needed was confidence.

"I will. I will." Girl's scrambled thoughts were coming together. "It does seem it comes down to me. Yú is a good man; others will follow him, but he is tactically inept. Túshānshì is great. She has him eating out of her hand. I swear she whispers in his ear while he's asleep, and he does anything she asks the next morning. Anything! But, you know, sometimes there is no time for them to spend in bed to come to a decision! An idea comes from me, then to her and on to him. Then, it must be implemented. It can take time."

"And there is little time in battle. That is why you need careful preparation." Grandmother worked on turning her protégé around. "You have the site. Yes?" Girl nodded. "You have the tactics. Yes?" Again, a nod. "Everyone is briefed. Yes?" A third nod. "Then the implementation is key; if you can worsen the opposition's preparedness, the odds of successful implementation increase tenfold. Yes?"

"I suppose so." Girl's doubts were easing.

"They do! Think about it. Think of any edges you can add." Grandmother turned. "Now, Mother. Your task is less urgent but of even greater scope and importance. What news?"

"Gǔn's work continues unabated in Èrlǐtou. Everyone thinks he's insane, but that is one way of keeping the Lóngshān off his back. It has increased his motivation to see himself building a city-state for Yú. I swear he has always been fonder of his son than me. Now, it is Yú first, water second and me a very distant third. Having him around long enough

30

to ensure he is fully under control takes some effort. Remember Mount Sōng! He did his own thing. I have to tread carefully."

"And the timeline…if Gǔn behaves?" Grandmother enquired.

"Eight years will do it. At some point, someone will ask why we are protecting, draining, and irrigating enough land for fifteen thousand when we have only a tenth of that number." She paused. "There is a proviso, though. Those eight years depend on stopping jealous eyes shining in our direction from the Lóngshān towns to the north. If they can organise themselves to put together a joint force, there is no way we could hold them back."

"And that is how I spend my time," Grandmother leaned towards her co-conspirators. "Spreading disharmony amongst their leaders and persuading them to focus their attention on each other. Their kings have become so anxious to maintain their lordships that their attention to external issues has diminished. They have even eased up on persecuting the people around Mount Sōng. It seems they are now focused on retaining those they have, but doing so by force will only worsen their circumstances. There are now only occasional slave raids to keep us on our toes. We must watch the situation closely, particularly as more female refugees end up in Èrlǐtou. Don't drop your guard."

"I'll not be doing that!" Mother appeared somewhat upset by the implication.

"Please don't take that the wrong way." Grandmother's arm snaked over the shoulders of both her comrades. "I need your help—both of you. We will need another lever amongst the Lóngshān. We need a lever of disinformation, and I believe we may have found that lever in Táosì. It will be a matter of relocating the lever. Girl, Mother, you will both play your part."

"What is this lever?" Girl queried, "And does it involve more work for me? I'm not sure I can take on much more at present."

"The lever has two parts, and I think you'll find they will be more than willing to cooperate when they see the course of the battle. Their names are Lord Hú and Lord Xí. They have played the role of soothsayers to Chīyóu but are clueless. We want them to escape."

"It is more work!" Girl exploded.

31

"A little, a little. Your father will do most of the work. All you must do is allow them to escape from the battle, probably in the river, and make sure your father's men pick them up. It is nothing you cannot handle.

"Mother. You come into this to ensure Kànménrén gets safe passage down the Yellow River for the pair. We wanted them embedded with one of the Lóngshān lords within a year."

"How is that going to help?" Mother looked concerned but curious.

"That is where I come in." Grandmother smiled broadly. "I'm planning to feed them accurate information. I'm planning to make Hú and Xí indispensable to their masters. I'm planning to build them so high and then..."

"Then?" Both Mother and Girl whispered together.

"Then I'm going to pull the rug from under their feet so hard they'll bounce off the stars!"

Four: The Congress

Ānyáng, Hénán: The King's Palace Hall
Year 83: Year of the Snake
Three days to the spring equinox
19th March 1912 BCE

There had been pomp and ceremony aplenty as the warlords had arrived. Banners and streamers extended the length of the street from the city gate to the palace compound. Under pain of death, citizens were instructed to cheer and clap each party as they arrived and continue until they passed from gate to gate. They were to do so on their knees. The expectation was that they would immediately clear the horse dung from the roadway before the next party rolled in. Over two days, fifteen separate retinues had arrived. The city had reached the point where resources were strained, reaching a breaking point. Many townsfolk had fainted from their exertions, having gone without food or water. Fainting resulted in immediate execution at the hands of the supervising troops and a further expectation that the people on either side would clear up the mess. As a result, many citizens were propped up between neighbours. Whether they were dead or alive became a moot point.

Upon arrival, each party had been taken to their rooms by slaves, whose instructions included one that insisted they should not make eye contact with the visitors; it made for awkward communication. Very soon, news had reached the king that the visitors were executing his slaves for minor indiscretions, something he had to accept but was extremely inconvenient. As the system began to fall apart, King Léigōng, the host and Ānyáng's warlord had been forced to allocate men from his crack fighting squads to act as ushers, a role that caused much discontent.

If their meeting had a clear agenda, it had an even tighter guest list: only the warlords themselves would attend. Their retinues were to remain outside, where they eyed each other aggressively and hurled insults. Inside, there were to be no supporters, no advisors, and no attendants. It was a challenge for a group that was used to being waited on hand and foot. On a large cypress sideboard stood several flagons of wine, plates of bread, fruit and ròugān[10]. They would have to serve themselves if they wanted to eat or drink.

In this, it was fortunate there were no others present. Whilst each of them signed up to rigid protocols in public and expected to be treated as gods, they were coarse, ill-educated and rowdy in private. It was a room of equals only in one regard. As every member of the sixteen believed he was superior to each of the other fifteen, there was no opportunity for the development of stratification. Equality could only be broken on the edge of an axe, and as weapons had been banned from the room, they could not put their fighting prowess to the test.

This group had fought. It was only due to geographical happenstance that they could not say they had all fought each other. It was simply too much effort for little reward for Ānyáng to pick a fight with Yáowángchéng. Those in closer proximity had experienced battle with each other, occasionally an alliance and more often than not, the death of their father, brothers or sons at the hands of another warlord. To describe the atmosphere as friendly would have been impossible.

The only semblance of some priority was that the assembled men all accepted that King Léigōng would speak first. If nothing else, his offer to feed and house them and upwards of eight hundred of their supporters deserved a little recognition.

"Welcome. I will not ask you to greet each other individually. I do ask that we treat each other with some civility and that you should continue to do so until you have departed my city." He tried to meet the eye of all present to receive an affirmation. In time, and with apparent reluctance, fifteen heads nodded agreement.

"I have asked you all to attend this meeting to discuss the problem of the Southerners. There has been too much pressure on our borders. There are too many people moving. There are too many for us to take in

---

[10] A dried meat similar to jerky or biltong.

34

as slaves as they would eat us out of house and home. There are too many to kill as we do not have the time or the weapons.

"It seems they have started to take land on the great river to farm in the last year. In addition, there has been no recent contact from the King of Sānménxiá. We no longer have messengers coming from the Wèi or Fèn Rivers. It has to be supposed that even the mighty Táosì may have fallen. King Chīyóu is a notable absentee from this gathering."

"But isn't that your problem, Léigōng? It's you and your little kingdom here that is exposed to them. We have no such problem in the east." Lord Fēngbō's state was coastal, although quite southerly.

"You say you have no problem. That may be the case, but I suspect it is that you have no eyes in your head. This thing started in a rush, and we coped with it. The additional women were useful. We all have new fields opening up as the weather has improved and the river flooding has stopped. But once the immediate rush slowed, I suspect we thought the migration would stop. It has not. There are more and more of them. They keep coming."

"What is at stake here?" Yú Shi was from the area north of the Tàishān Mountains. "What will I lose in Chéngzǐyá? Nothing! It is you to the west who are struggling, and it sounds like you're simply not dealing with these people forcefully enough."

"My point is that I am not powerful enough to defeat them. Have you ever heard this from me - that I am not powerful enough? Never! Look around you. Ānyáng is more powerful than any of your states. My armies would beat any of your own in battle. Yet—"

"Yet you are coming to us and saying you have a fight on your hands that you cannot win. Is that right?" Yúntóng was younger than most in the room. His base in Kāifēng had been more exposed than any to the flood of refugees from the south. "Perhaps you are taking the wrong approach entirely. Have you considered integration rather than confrontation?"

"We've heard all about your idea of integration, Yúntóng. It seems you've integrated the Southerners into your bed!" Raised voices came from many in the throng.

"Taken a Liángzhǔ whore for his queen, I heard!"

"Talk about sleeping with the enemy!"

35

"No good will come of it—"

"You'll end up with piglet babies!"

"Who's going to take the throne in Kāifēng then? King Pig?"

"It's not like that." Yúntóng realised he was alone in his opinion and, rather than defend his position, fell quiet. "I will play my part." He whispered but resolved never to return for a further meeting as he said the words. These men were no longer his kin.

The arguing went on for the remainder of the day. The question was quite simple, and the answer even more straightforward, but each warlord found a reason not to wish to answer it. In truth, they were much more interested in smash-and-grab raids on each other's properties than in a wholesale communal defence.

The Lóngshān leadership replicated the ideals held by Chīyóu in Táosì. As long as their personal wealth appeared to increase, they cared not one jot if their citizens became poorer. In fact, for many years, their private wealth had been decreasing, but they could not see this because the gap between them and the poor in their communities was widening, thus making them appear to be more prosperous. As they were all in the same boat, their belief that there was an improvement in their own situations was reflected by every other warlord. Thus, their apparent wealth viz-a-viz their peers had not changed. As there was no way to quantify the problem, no one was any wiser.

The only people who understood the decline in wealth were those slipping into food insecurity and starvation. The warlords had no interest in the peasants at the bottom of the pile. Only insurrection would bother them, and the lid was firmly shut on internal revolutions.

Only King Léigōng appeared to have grasped the potential danger, and although Yúntóng had perhaps shared his analysis, it was clear from the exchanged glances that they disagreed on a response. The Kāifēng monarch had decided to pre-empt the matter with an approach that would have proved wholly unacceptable to the others at the table in accepting externally led controlled evolution. Yúntóng was effectively signalling an end to what the Lóngshān laughingly called their culture.

The meeting resumed the following morning. There were now only fifteen at the table, for Yúntóng had left. If the numbers had changed, then so had the agenda. King Léigōng was privy to more information than he had shared, although he had no intention of admitting it. He was the most powerful warlord at the table, but not through his military acumen, a larger army or better weaponry. Léigōng was the most powerful of the warlords because he was the only man around the table who knew when to stop.

"It seems we have not reached an agreement. I understand and sympathise with each of your positions. If I were in your shoes, I might hold the same views.

"Therefore...therefore, I will put one other point to you and let us see if we can agree on this. Could we agree to reconvene this meeting in two years? By then, we will have more information and will be better placed to determine whether we might wish to take any joint action.

"I know this is alien to you, but could we put it to a vote? Who agrees to meet here, two years from now, to discuss the question of the Southerners? It will be the same arrangements. Hands, please!"

All members of the meeting somewhat reluctantly raised their arms in agreement. It was a watershed moment. It was the first time any Lóngshān gathering had resorted to any form of democracy.

Five: The Soothsayers

Táosì, Shǎnxī: The Palace Hall
Year 83: The Year of the Snake
Three days to the spring equinox
19th March 1912 BCE

"Who are they?" It was a fair question.

"We have learned only that they are on the river, my lord. Perhaps a thousand or so in number. One of the shepherds said they were led by a man named Yú. That is all we know. Oh, and they appear to be planting trees, sir."

"You don't just march a thousand people into my valley and start planting trees. It makes no sense. And I have not given my permission! The Fèn River valley is mine from the great Yellow River to Tàiyuán in the north. I'll have their necks before they plant as much as one more tree. Planting trees!

"And what's that supposed to mean, a thousand or so?"

Three men sat around a low table. The chairs had not been designed for their present use; all three teetered on the edges of their seats. In front of them was a crude map; a piece of thread stood in for the Fèn River and a large pebble for Táosì, although a smaller stone to the south, adjacent to the river, provided the focus of their attention - the approximate location of the tree-planters.

Two men wore long black silk robes, pulled tight across their ample bellies and held in place by black cords. Their long sleeves interfered with their gesticulations, and both periodically tugged them back to free their hands. Their untidily cropped short black hair made the onset of baldness clear; both appeared to be making up for it with the length of their wispy and straggly beards. Dead white skin indicated they were unused to either manual work or spending much time outside, but

38

both might be excused their apparent long-term idleness as they were only now coming to the end of a long winter. It was cold in the hall, although both men were perspiring freely. One could be forgiven for thinking that they might be twins, an impression they were anxious to encourage, for they believed such a state would only enhance the aura surrounding them.

If they had an aura, it was recognised only by the townspeople or any wandering unfortunates who had crossed their paths. It was an aura of fear, not respect, for the two had the absolute backing of the man sitting with them. Chīyóu commanded Táosì and its surroundings. He was an absolute dictator with not an ounce of benevolence. It was widely believed that his trust in his two lieutenants was both a serious threat to the state and a danger to the life of any individual who crossed them. People ran scared of the pair everyone knew as Hú and Hum, renamed as such by the confined Hòutú, although to their faces, they were always Prince Hú and Prince Xí.

The king was a larger specimen than the other two, not fatter, but carrying more muscle bulk and half a head of additional height. His face and arms were browned, his fists like hams, and his unkempt hair reached down into his thick, matted beard. Chīyóu could have been mistaken for a quarry worker if not for the smart leather jerkin and the quantity of bronze weaponry lashed to various parts of his outer clothing. It may have been clear that he was an outdoor type, but it was even more evident that he was a warrior. In every sense, he demanded and commanded respect from his two underlings. He had only allowed them to sit in his presence because it made it easier to discuss their plans.

Chīyóu was fully aware that it was his power the two henchmen wielded over his people. He was also aware that they were the closest thing he had to soothsayers since the witches had abandoned him so long ago. It would surprise many of his people, but their commander feared his two thugs, not for what they did, but for what might befall him if he lost them. He might bully them, but he had to keep them on his side. Providing decent food, luxurious shelter, and a string of victims for sacrifice or torture had done the trick so far; Chīyóu saw no reason why it should not continue to do so.

He had denied them only once, and that denial had led to catastrophe. Not only had the witches refused to prophesise, but it also led to a gradual migration of females from Táosì, something he had been forced to outlaw over the past few years. The pity was that stopping the women meant killing them, which had the same effect as their leaving anyway. Men now dominated the city, perhaps two to one; it was a society that was failing and failing badly.

"So…we send the women and children to the quarries," muttered Chīyóu, "but they'll need guarding, so we need men as well."

"My…my…my Lord." Hú always adopted a stammer when speaking to his superior; he felt it gave him a subservient image, although the affectation greatly irritated Chīyóu. "In…in…in the quarry, there is a narrow entrance. It can be guarded sufficiently by the bowmen."

"Yes! What age should the children be?" Their commander sometimes shifted quickly between seemingly disparate issues, and it was necessary to have rapid answers even if they proved wrong. Generally, if the bigger picture worked out well, Chīyóu would eventually forget most of their mistakes as long as they convinced him that one of their foretellings may have been correct.

"Our prophecy is that the battle will be won with the help of boys, so make it only children of seven years or less who may join their mothers." Xí had joined the conversation.

"Se…se…seven. That will do."

"So, every male of seven years or more will come with us to the river?" Chīyóu looked around for assent, unaware his error would increase the army's numbers with boys unable to keep up or offer anything of value to its fighting capacity.

"We might agree that, my Lord, but it will leave the city empty. Unguarded. Open to thieves and vagabonds and to—"

"To what? All the thieves and vagabonds will be with us or in the quarry. Are you planning on making magic to produce some more?"

"No…no…no, my Lord."

Both Hú and Xí feared leaving the city, not for the safety of the people, their leader or even the place's infrastructure. They feared someone gaining access to their private rooms, in which, over many years, they had stashed looted pieces of value, primarily jades and bronze. They had removed objects without anyone missing them or laying the blame on the two men; many graves had been emptied. On odd occasions, when someone had noticed, the pair had been swift in conjuring up a likely suspect and putting him to death before anyone had the opportunity to believe the truth.

"You could leave the two of us in the city, my Lord; that would make perfect sense. No one would dare do damage—"

"Or…or…or theft!"

"…while we are here."

It left Chīyóu in a quandary. It made no sense for him to leave the two men behind when their advice may be needed in the south. It made no sense that the city required guarding; his reputation would ensure that. However, it did not make sense to go against their wishes. It was once bitten, twice shy. He would have to persuade them by other means.

"Princes, if you do not go, you will not be entitled to the spoils of the battle. I will take half; the remainder can be divided amongst the warriors. If you go, I will take half; you two will take a quarter between you, and the remainder can be divided by the rest. What about that?"

As ever, greed would win out with Hú and Xí. However insincere it might be, flattery was a weapon Chīyóu used sparingly; he hated calling them princes. While he may not have been fully aware of the pair's considerable stash, he knew from experience that they were greedy slugs and always allowed a tasty little lettuce to be left out to tempt them.

"Yes."

"I…I…I suppose so." Greed had not only overpowered their desire to protect their ill-gotten gains but also their natural cowardice. They would now have to consider how to keep themselves out of any real action.

Chīyóu rose. "Right, I need to know the weather for the next five days, when the moon will rise and set, and I need to know if those peasants are staying where they are. I want fog, and then I want a storm. Sort it!" His final order was barked over his shoulder as he left the room.

Hú and Xí remained seated. It was not protocol, but they had little chance to move, and their reactions were slowed somewhat by the thoughts running around their heads regarding the realities of going into battle.

"We will have to change our clothes," mumbled Hú.

"And take weapons."

41

"We have those aplenty, but we don't want to take anything of value. No point wasting items that could later be traded."

"That's true."

Both sat with their chins in their hands, moving their heads from side to side. It was as if they might attain an improved perspective on the two stones and line of hemp on the table.

"He wants a prophecy, Hú. You know what that means."

"I do. I wished dearly that I did not, but I do know."

"We have to pay her a visit."

"I know."

Both men sighed. Being princes had brought its rewards; there was no doubting that. Being soothsayers was something of a risky occupation. Neither of them had a clue about making any prediction other than outright guesses, but they did know someone who did. The only problem, and it was a significant problem, was that she was as uncooperative as any witch could be. If that had been the end of the problem, then so be it; they could have tortured her into a prophecy, but it was not. It was fourteen years since they had sworn an oath to Chīyóu that they would never touch her, and it had been made clear that retaining their positions was reliant upon that promise.

Hòutú's final public prophesy, uttered with venom from what had appeared to be her death bed, had been that if she or her daughter were to be harmed again, Chīyóu would die. Hú and Xí needed Chīyóu and therefore required that Chīyóu live. Now, Chīyóu needed an accurate prophecy to ensure he lived. Thus, both Hú and Xí needed the best soothsayer in town.

They must visit Hòutú.

Six: The Prophesies
Táosì, Shǎnxī: Hòutú's Yáodòng
Year 83: Year of the Snake
Two days to the spring equinox
20th March 1912 BCE

It was well past nightfall when a barked order woke them.

Apart from her regular customers, there were only two men who were stupid enough to come within a stone's throw of Hòutú's *yáodòng*. Their stupidity masqueraded as bravery, but that bravery came only from the protection they felt emanated from their lord. Prince Hú and Xí, the king's henchmen and would-be soothsayers, had come calling. Hòutú had renamed them Hú and Hum what seemed a lifetime ago. Now, the names had stuck, but only she felt able to use them to their faces.

The pair's only claim to fame on the soothsaying front had been to predict a storm of shooting stars in late summer and to forecast a landslide just south of Dàgùduì Quarry. In the former, everyone, including the stray dogs, knew there was always a shower of stars at that time of year; everyone, that is, except Chīyóu, whose position derived from his strength rather than his intellect. As for the landslide, every resident of Táosì, including those same stray dogs, had seen Hú, Xí and a troop of soldiers hacking away at the top of that slope; they had been at it for weeks. It was only a matter of waiting for the first heavy rains.

The pair had celebrated in advance by placing the town's petty criminals below their preparations. When Chīyóu heard that the prophecy had been fulfilled, he promoted them. He advanced them again when he heard that all but one of the prisoners had died in the resultant mudslide. He celebrated further by cooking the survivor alive and feeding him to his hunting dogs. Hú and Xí were unpleasant individuals, but the state's ruler was equally odious.

Hú and Xí were now the second and third most powerful men in Shǎnxī, and if Chīyóu's decision-making was poor, theirs was even worse. The three men were not responsible for the city-state's terminal decline, only for what had gone wrong in the last fifteen years, but those years would have been considered a disaster by anyone's standards.

"What do you pigs want?" Hòutú hollered from inside the cave, knowing they dare not touch her.

"Pigs! Pigs? It seems, old crone, that you mistake us for your Liangzhu brethren."

Hòutú emerged entirely naked. She had considered her actions carefully, and the thought of stepping out in near-freezing conditions was not one that she would have preferred. To reduce the impact of the frigid soil, she stood as close to the embers of their dying fire. Still, she desperately missed the bearskin.

She shivered slightly before pulling herself erect and facing them squarely, hands on hips. It was a deliberately provocative act. The last time they had seen her unclothed was when they were carving her up alive. She was still a good-looking woman with a taut body, one that was entirely inaccessible to either of them. It was not as if they had not tried when she was younger, in those days before she was scarred. Before her torture, she had repeatedly fended off their advances. Back then, she had often resorted to physicality to rid herself of them. Now, she relied on their belief in magic and archaic rules.

For the moment, she stood in near darkness.

"My birthplace may have been on Lake Tài, but you seem to confuse our people with our diet. I doubt you have eaten pig in years!" The faintly mocking double-entendre went way over their heads. She pushed harder. "I had heard that neither pork nor woman has passed your lips since you were weaned." And harder. "It's not usual for piglets to come in pairs. Your mother must have been an extremely old and disease-ridden sow. Was she slow of thought? Is that why she named you Hú and Hum?"

The half-moon emerged from behind a low cloud, and quite suddenly, her form was illuminated. The two men stared. The scars they had incised in her body years before were vivid. The vertical line between her breasts and her tuft of pubic hair had been Xí's cut; it remained in situ,

44

slightly puckered and whitened. The near circle they had created with four vicious slices around the mound of her pregnancy had taken on a new shape as her body contracted after the birth. It was the first time either man had seen the wounds since inflicting them, and their surprise was very evident. The scars had morphed into something else entirely. Across Hòutú's flat and firm belly was a distinct rectangle bisected by Hú's vertical slice.

The shock was palpable. Neither man was capable of speaking. What they saw was not what they had carved on Hòutú's body. Their incisions had morphed, and the cuts around her pregnancy were still apparent but were no longer curved wounds; they clearly showed the symbol of the Motherland. It was as if magic had occurred. Both cringed and pulled away. It took all their powers to remain in this woman's company. Eventually, Hú managed to draw himself together and speak.

"I never cut that mark on you! Witch! You are a witch!"

"He should have let us cut it out back then!" growled Xí.

As the moon slipped once more behind a cloud, it was difficult to see if their faces were reddening or had whitened further in fright, although Hòutú suspected she had achieved both and silently laughed at the thought of their mottled features.

"Enough, crone! We will have information from you." Hú was undoubtedly unsettled, but he had to speak, as it seemed his brother had temporarily lost the use of his vocal cords.

"Ah, Hú. That would be so much more preferable to sex. I won't have to touch you." Hòutú took three steps towards the pair and chuckled as they shuffled back the same distance. "Still scared, boys? Still scared of this 'old crone'?"

As the moonlight returned, it became clear their disquiet had increased further. Hòutú could almost count the drops of perspiration forming on their foreheads. If she was cold, they must be freezing. As she stepped back onto the warmer earth by the fire, she sensed that her child had joined her before she felt a bare shoulder gently kissing her own. Tú was coming to terms with her adult body; she had not yet grown into it, and Hòutú was impressed that she had chosen to face down these two idiots by emulating her mother; it had taken guts. She glanced down at Tú's naked form and was stunned to see the bloody daub on her belly, tracing the same pattern as the scars on her own.

"Tú, I had not realised it was your time of the month. These gentlemen will be even more amused." It amounted to a thunderous whisper; she felt a need to further disgust the two men.

The shock in their visitor's expressions was now more clearly visible than the marks on the face of the moon. If protocols had been broken with her nudity, it had been broken in half and thrown in the bone pit when they realised they had ended up carving the symbol of the Motherland on her form. Now, looking as if she had cut the same pattern onto her flesh, her daughter had taken those protocols, casting them into a ravine where they were smashed to dust.

"Filth! You stand there naked and flaunt your menstrual blood! You are animals!"

"Yes," exclaimed Hòutú as she touched the tips of her fingers across the stain on Tú's belly, "we are animals." She raised her fingers and placed them on her tongue. "That is what this is all about."

There were so many ancient protocols that the two women had broken down in their show of defiance. Uninvited, they had flaunted their nakedness in the open, but it was the sight of menstrual blood that hurt the men's misguided sensibilities more. The offence caused was such that the pair appeared set to retreat. They may not be permitted to harm her now, but Chīyóu might change his mind. It was time for Hòutú to ease them back onto the purpose of their visit.

"So, now, you've seen the freaks, and you have seen our tits. Is there any more of this show you might want more of? Hú? Hum? What is it you want?"

"If you insist on standing naked, we will turn our backs. Our ears will be open, but our eyes will be less offended."

"Offended? What I can see is rampant lust, not offence. Are you sure you are here for information, or have you been told there might be something else on offer?"

The two men were now arguing amongst themselves. It was clear that Xí wanted out of there, clear he wanted nothing to do with what he considered their expression of evil. Hú was more circumspect.

"Prince Xí, it is magic, although we are protected. They cannot touch us." Hú desperately wanted his kinsman to stay, not wishing to face the two women alone.

"You should ask yourself this question. Who would want to touch you? Not I! Not my daughter! Why would we taint ourselves by touching you?" Hòutú was trying to bring them back to the discussion. She needed to feed them information. Her daughter broke the moment.

"Besides, if you turn your back, you'll be unable to see the magic spells we weave around you."

"Shush, Tú. No more. Let them ask their favour."

The men shuffled from foot to foot, looking this way and that, expecting demons to appear from any stone or crack in the loess cliff, but they did not turn. They had been scared when they came here and were now terrified, but they could not let it show too much. The fact that they were trying to face down two witches was bad enough. That one was wearing the hated symbol carved into her body, by what it would appear had been their own hands, took them to the edge. That the daughter flaunted the same sign, painted on with menstrual blood, pushed them over a yawning abyss. It was already apparent they were here on orders because otherwise, they would not be here, and now they were balancing on the edge of reckoning, the threat of their master or the danger of the witches. The choice was unhinging.

Hòutú had quickly realised why they had come; they had been unable to satisfy their commander with their made-up predictions. Chīyóu must be in trouble, which meant the princes were in trouble; they were primed to believe anything they were told.

Hú collected himself once more. It seemed he was now focussing firmly on the women's feet. Xí had taken to staring into the cosmos, anywhere but directly before him. Their embarrassment became more evident as the moon peeped through a gap in the clouds. However, this time, it was Xí who spoke.

"There is an army on the Fèn River, just three days south of here. Who are they?"

Hòutú's heart leapt, but her face remained expressionless.

"On the river, Hum? Are they swimming or skating? To my mind, it's too cold for swimming and too warm for skating. Perhaps they are drowning?"

"Perhaps they are." Clearly, Xí would not rise to any more bait she might throw his way. His face wore a murderous expression, and just for a moment, Hòutú's confidence was slightly shaken. Maybe it was time to be more cooperative. "Perhaps they are, and perhaps they are not. They are camped on the river, a big force, maybe a thousand. Who are they?"

"You probably hadn't noticed, but we are confined to this small, damp cave. Perhaps you could tell us who 'they' might be. What have you told Chīyóu?"

"That we should send a fog and attack them when they are blind. Then he should send a massive rainstorm to sweep them into the river. Oh! And that he should let the young boys fight. That's what we have told him, and that's what he should do." Hú had re-joined the discussion.

"Well...there's a fog every morning on the Fèn at this time of year, so he shouldn't have any problem with that one. But..." Hòutú looked skywards, "If it rains in Shǎnxī before the next full moon, I think that those Liangzhu pigs might just fly all the way here for your next meal. You are idiots. Do you know what happens at the next full moon? Do you even know when it is?"

"Seven days, or...." Hú was indecisively triumphant. "A beautiful full moon in six days. A time to hunt!"

"Oh!" Hòutú stifled a chuckle, "So...you can count. Well! When the full moon does not appear, what will you tell Chīyóu? A dragon ate it! And what will you hunt, stray dogs or billy goats, because there's nothing

48

much left here? What will happen to you when Chīyóu trips on his spear because the moon does not appear at your command? Perhaps you can tell the sun to rise at night?" Hòutú paused, and Tú stepped in.

"You will not see a full moon in a week."

"Even you cannot change the phases of the moon!" Hú interjected.

"No, I cannot. But I can change the possibility of someone seeing it!" Tú was magnificent. Even her mother was taken aback.

"I will make a prophecy," Tú paused, awaiting their full attention. "There will be fog if you take on these strangers by the river in the next few days. Another prophecy is that you will need every citizen of Táosì to help you but that the young boys will come out as the winners. My third prophecy should be that there will be no storm. However, that is so obvious, as my mother told you, that it would not amount to a prophecy." Tú raised her voice and was joined by the unexpected howl of a lone wolf from the distant hillside. "So, my third and final prophecy is that you are going to lose this little fight, and you two," she pointed with both arms horizontal in front of her, "You two…will not know if there is a full moon in seven days, for I predict that you will both be dead."

There was silence, dead silence. There was no movement. The two couples faced each other, not ten steps apart. All knew the awfulness of the moment. Yes, a prophecy was made, but in that third prediction had come something that could leave Tú dreadfully exposed and unprotected by the law. The two men grew visibly taller; they would have their meat. It did seem they were perhaps too focused on celebrating a broken ordinance to understand the details of the deadly prophecies.

"You have cast a death spell, witch! The matter will end badly for you. Chīyóu's dogs might find you stringy and tasteless, but they'll have fun tearing you apart while you plead with them for your life." Hú turned to Hum. "At the party of the full moon, perhaps?"

"I think so. I think so. Let us go, Hú. We can watch from the terrace and raise a beaker to soothsayers and the death of all witches. They cannot escape."

The two turned and strode off until Hú tripped on his long black robe, causing him to stumble further on the broken ground, which offered him a far less splendid exit than he would have hoped.

"It's not time for your period, Tú. Where did this come from?" Hòutú turned to examine her daughter's belly.

"Well…you said Hu Zu was getting old!"

Both Hu Zu and his partner pigeon, ended up being sacrificed, but he only from necessity and his mate only for that minor deity that also doubled as a cooking pot. After a middle-of-the-night feast, consuming a well-fed pigeon each, accompanied by the remaining millet gruel, Tú was replete and went back to bed to sleep it off. With full stomachs and the fire's embers transported into the cave, it was warmer, the warmest evening of the year so far, but there would still be a frost in the morning. Hòutú sat still as a stone and weighed the potential outcomes of her daughter's prophesy and their dramatics. She bowed and prayed that the ordinance would hold until after the forthcoming battle.

Seven: The Observatory

Táosì, Shănxī
Year 83: Year of the Snake
The spring equinox
22nd March 1912 BCE

It had been a noisy morning. The commotion had begun in the early hours. The screams from the northwest acted as an alarm call, dragging Hòutú from her sleep. As the screaming diminished, it was replaced by an ever-growing grumbling. Hòutú guessed it must be the womenfolk being moved. For as long as it took for her to encourage the embers back to flame, the voices had risen. They were now fading into the distance. She guessed the procession had passed the southeast gate on the way to the quarries of Dàgùduì. It would not take them long. She could only hope the women cooperated fully and avoided any injury at the hands of their gaolers.

Hòutú had received information from the local Sisterhood and, in turn, had passed on what she knew, telling them to cooperate, urging them to go to the quarries, and to take enough food to last a week. They should be fine. All they had to do to survive was to avoid conflict, but if they could ensure the men were also well-fed and well-bedded, a positive outcome would be both sooner and happier. Hòuyì, the master archer, was a good man at heart, and whilst he would follow orders, he would not do so inconsiderately.

It was fortuitous that the sisters held her in such high regard because they had not been entirely keen to submit, mainly because so many of their partners and sons were headed off down the Fèn River. It had been necessary to remind the elder sisters that the rule of fourteen would soon come into effect, that her own life and that of Tú were way further out on the line than theirs. After the initial discussions, it took an additional day before she received an affirmative response. It was clear to

51

her that they had only just reached a consensus. She prayed that the screams and grumbling were only for show.

As the noises from the Dàgùduì procession began to fade, another hubbub replaced them, but this time from the north; the palace was astir. A few supplies were still stored in the compound above her cave. Periodically, there were the sounds of lifting, hauling, and dragging accompanied by shouted orders and men swearing. Soon, these sounds faded as the men lifted their burdens and staggered off to what she suspected would be the parade area inside the palace compound's wall.

It would be a while longer.

"Tú! Get up!" How her daughter had managed to sleep, she knew not, but she had, and she was now grumbling.

"Not again! It's too early to exercise. I won't!" If a sheep had bleated, it could not have sounded more pathetic.

"No, Tú, not exercise this time. Well, it is exercise, but not as you've known it. We're going for a walk. A real walk!"

Tú propelled herself from the cave mouth.

"Now? We can go now?"

"Listen and wait." Hòutú gestured towards the palace. Tú's hearing was more acute than her mother's; she would hear the orders more clearly.

"They're leaving…by the northeast gate…and down the gully of the Na He." Tú was excited, "They're going to overnight in the cave scrapes west of Jing Cungou! That isn't very far. Why there?"

"No, it is not. It means the following day, they'll have a long march as they have to be as close as possible to Yú's camp." Hòutú was muttering, almost to herself, "They've not got enough boats or wood for rafts to dare float down the river. There must be another overnight stop in the plan, and it must have caves or at least scrapes. It's too cold for them to be exposed. The trouble is, I know nothing about this area around the lower Fèn River. Nothing!"

"That's fine, *Māma*. It doesn't matter. They will know. Your message must tell them to find the caves where Chīyóu will hide. It's not as if you need to know where they are."

"True. You're right, Tú. Now, you think about it. If Chīyóu plans to attack in the morning fog, he will want to be in position before dawn. How far would he want to march in the dark before the attack?"

"Not long; he would want to be fresh. But he would want to be far enough away so that Yú doesn't know he's there. He needs to be hidden and—"

"And Chīyóu needs to know about these caves already. He must have used them before. We tell them to look for caves that have been used as temporary shelters before. But how? Tell me how Tú? How do we get a message like that onto a piece of metal like this?" Hòutú held out the thin copper foil. "Even then, we can only get a pigeon to Dōngxiáfēng. We—"

"They're on the—"

"Boats!" Hòutú screamed out the word she had only muttered earlier. "Is the fisherwomen's pigeon here? Tú, go check!"

Having returned from the pigeon's pen, Tú confirmed the bird was there. Hòutú scratched carefully on the copper band, and within minutes, the bird was freed and in the air.

"I told her to meet us by the southwest gate by noon. Give it a few minutes, and then we'll let the others out for a while." Hòutú smiled. "Now we will do what you have been asking to do since you were about two years old. Let's go for a walk."

Hòutú turned and strode towards the southeast, towards the upper end of the Da Nan gully. Tú followed warily. She was free, but the immediacy of the proposition seemed daunting. As they climbed onto the plateau, she realised that everything she would see from now on would be seen for the first time.

"We'll not spend long here," said Hòutú, "But you need to see your grandmother's grave."

Tú looked around, "Where is it?"

"You're standing on it." Tú leapt to one side. "Oh, Tú Tú, don't worry, she's dead. They put her here as an additional punishment for me. I believe they hoped a flood would wash out the loess, and we'd have her floating past our *yáodòng*. It never happened.

"I have not spoken to you about your grandmother before. I'm sorry. I thought it would be unfair to introduce you to her story as a child, and then I failed as you became a young adult."

"How did she die?"

"They killed her, Tú. I don't know how, but it would not have been pleasant. It is not the fact that they killed her that is important. It is the reason they had a right to kill her. That is what you need to understand."

"They needed a reason?"

"Well, yes, or to be more precise, they needed there not to be a reason for not killing her…it was the rule of fourteen. Until a child is fourteen, it is protected. This rule has saved you. Also, until a child is fourteen, the mother is protected. The law has saved me because of you. I had just turned fourteen when I was tortured with you inside me. As you were not yet born, they could have killed me because I was overage. And because of that, my age was the same reason my mother became exposed.

"When I was on that table…when I was on that table, they actually planned to have my mother cut you out of me. They were not going to select someone at random. We were fortunate that Chīyóu interrupted. You being born then meant I had the protection of the rule of fourteen." There were tears in Hòutú's eyes. "Sorry, I have not stood here since you were born. These scars across my belly might remind others of the promise of the Motherland, but to me…well…to me…they are just a reminder of my mother, Tú."

Tú threw her arms around her mother, comforting her as best she could.

"She was called Zhi Nü. She was a good woman, Tú, and a wonderful mother. I have missed her every day." Hòutú wiped her sleeve across her face. "Enough…enough! The rule of fourteen was good when there were good rulers, but now it is abused. Many women have fled, and many have been massacred. We need new rules! It is only one reason for our fight, but a good reason.

"We will return here, Tú, and dig up your grandmother. I am not so fussed about her body, but I want something that is buried alongside her. It's important.

"Come…Enough! Let me show you around."

54

Seven: The Observatory

Hòutú took her daughter by the hand, turning her toward the east. In the distance, the city wall formed the horizon - a ragged, tumbledown line. The rising sun threw shadows towards them, making the spaces at the foot of the ramparts look deeply forbidding. Closer to them, only a few paces away, was another much lower structure, across which it was easy to see the jumbled expanse between it and the outer perimeter. This area had once been one of the city's most important: the stores. Everything had been kept there, and everything had been well-guarded, but that had been years ago. Few buildings were still standing, and most of the storage there appeared to be in the caves dug closer to the palace.

"There are things of interest here, Tú, really there are, but it will take a lot of turned loess to dig up something worthy." She rotated through one-hundred and eighty degrees, dragging Tú with her. "Now, on the other hand…this is actually where your grandmother should be."

The area to the west of where they stood formed a rectangular compound comprising a space of perhaps four hundred by three hundred paces. Again, it was a chaotic mass of upturned slabs, gaping holes, and surprisingly broken and fallen tamped earth. The deterioration surprised Hòutú, and a frown appeared on her face.

"This, Tú, is the old cemetery of the wealthy. I'm a little taken aback that it has changed so much since I last laid eyes on it, for it has been unused for many generations and should have remained untouched." She shook her head. "Perhaps we might find the contents of some of these bedrooms of the dead where they should not be, perhaps in the bedrooms of the living. We will see!"

Tú walked with her mouth and eyes wide open. There was nothing that was not new to her. It may as well have been another planet. They ambled further to the southeast, where Hòutú had to hitch her skirts to crawl over a low wall of tamped earth. Again, it was in poor condition, pieces breaking off as they scrambled over the top.

"And it looks like more of the same here! This, Tú, is the graveyard of early ancestors, who founded Táosì when there was wealth, happiness, and fairness. It must have been a golden age."

"There are bones, *Māma*, bones sticking out of the earth! All around us!"

"Should it be like this, *Bǎobǎo*? It should not! Once again. Once again. I sense the days of the living disturbing the nights of the dead. Look around you; look around. In this spot, no one can see you dig. No one will see the jades and the bronzes you might retrieve. All that remains would be to transport them to a hiding place. Let me tell you, Tú, a little bird has given me a good idea where one of those hiding places might be."

Hòutú suddenly realised that her daughter had spoken for the first time since leaving the gully. She turned, catching her stare and how it shifted from object to object. All this was new to her. She was struck dumb, and all she had seen so far were two decrepit graveyards and a half-abandoned storage area. What came next would open her eyes even further.

The views began to open up as the pair turned to the southwest. After walking some two hundred paces and up a slight rise, they were not only upon the observatory platform but also afforded a three-hundred-and-sixty-degree vista. To the south, from east to west, they could look out over the walls for the first time. In the foreground lay the unworked fields where once vast swathes of millet had been grown. The southeast gate bisected the fortifications directly below them. A road leading to the Dàgùduì Quarry wound off into the distance, only disappearing as it entered the low hills. Glistening in the sunlight, where there was still water standing, the bed of the diverted Nan River turned sharply eastwards below the wall, evidence of the determination of the city's builders to achieve as much of a moat as possible. To the west ran the Song Cun River. With a greater flow, its stream bed rarely dried up as it ran along the southwestern walls.

Tú turned to look back across the expanse of the city. She was familiar with the palace walls, visible from their gully home, but all else was new to her.

"So, that is the palace compound and...there in the distance...there is the northwest gate. So that must be the people's village, over there, in the direction of my shadow. But what is this area here?" She pointed westwards at the collection of buildings inside the walls. "Here, Māma, I mean, where all the piles of debris and rock and earth are? What is this?"

Seven: The Observatory

"The crafts area, Tú. It's where the workers work! That is where the stone is cut, the jade is carved, and the furniture is made. Some bigger animals are slaughtered there, and, perhaps every blue moon, it's where they make bronze!

"We'll head around the wall toward the southwest gate, for that is where I said I would meet the fisherwoman. We can take our time. If we walk along the wall, you'll have an unobstructed view all the way around." Hòutú stumbled on a large crack in the tamped earth. "That is if the thing doesn't fall apart as we walk! But before we set off, Tú, this is the observatory. Do you remember me showing you how it works?"

"I do, but I imagined a much grander place. The way you described it gave it an otherworldly feel. This just looks like some lumps of mud."

"And that is what they are, Tú, that is what they are. However, they are unusual lumps of mud and are carefully aligned. To the layman, they do magic, but to you and me, they are a calendar. Until we can be open about our writing abilities, we need these places to assist the farmers. Do not forget this remains a magical spot; even if you do not believe it is and I do not believe it is, we must ensure that they believe it is. Our power, Tú, is not magic, spells or soothsaying. Our 'magic' is based on information, whether it be the pigeons, our writing, or this observatory. To us, these are tools, but to all others, they must and will, for the time being, remain magic. Just as we must and will remain–"

"Witches?"

"Call us that if you must. Call us shaman, call us soothsayers, yes, call us witches. But we must maintain the mystery of these powers if we want to shape the future. If we lose the mystery, we lose the power, which one day might be fine, but right now, our lives and even your children's children's lives depend upon everyone believing you are a witch. Even if you are a very pleasant one!" Hòutú's smile cracked wider than it had in years. "Just not first thing in the morning, eh Tú?

"We will be back in this place within days, Tú. Do not forget what I have said here. Now, let us continue our stroll."

Describing their journey as a stroll stretched the term to the absolute limits of its definition. The city's outer walls resembled a set of broken and worn teeth. Tamped earth structures needed regular

57

maintenance, and the ramparts appeared as if no one had as much as shored it up in a lifetime. Instead, what should have been a relatively flat track along the walls provided an exercise in scrambling and, at points, climbing. When they reached the southernmost point, the wall curved ninety degrees towards the northeast.

"Which way?" Tú was ahead of her mother. It took Hòutú a moment to catch up, gather her breath and reply.

"Along the wall, of course!"

Eight: The Industries

Táosì, Shǎnxī
Year 83: Year of the Snake
The spring equinox
22nd March 1912 BCE

"Sometimes, I wonder why you should think I can work out which direction we're supposed to go. How am I supposed to know?" Her mother seemed to be flagging a little. "Do you want to stop for a bit? Here, explain these." Tú pointed down to the rough shacks on the inside of the wall.

"These are rough cave entrances used by the workmen when it is too cold or wet to work outside. The whole of the outer wall has these caves. Originally, they would have been quite fine chambers, but as you can see, many are now just too dangerous and have been abandoned. The wall should be as strong as the loess cliff where our *yáodòng* is cut, but they have not looked after it. I fear the outer wall is now an empty shell. It is certainly no longer a good defence."

"And what about those...those hut things." Tú pointed again towards the centre of the craft area.

"Now, those are cut into the loess. They dig out a square or rectangular pit about as deep as a man is tall. Then, they put a post in each corner and erect the roofs you see. It is the same design used around the town, and we will go and investigate one later. However, caves are dug off the pit for storage or bedrooms in the homes. It is an expensive design. Most of these are very old, built when Táosì was much wealthier than today."

"Don't they flood when it rains?"

"You'll see the roof overlaps the edges of the pit and that the pit itself has a raised lip. If they're built properly, the rain does not get in unless there is a hole in the roof. Like that one!" Hòutú indicated a collapsed roof. "Look, you can see what they were working on…this is a jade carving shop! Let's go down and have a look."

The pair slid down the smoothest part of the encircling wall, which had an incline of around forty-five degrees. As they approached the workshop, a large sandy-coloured and dusty hound scrutinised them, lifting its nose before slumping back, jaws settled over its front paw.

"Is that a dog?" Exclaimed Tú. "Is it? I thought they were smaller. That's a big dog!"

"It is, *Bǎobǎo*, it is, but they will rarely harm the women of the town. It's there to safeguard the jade workshop, but it does not see us as a threat. Now, if we were men," Hòutú laughed, "If we were men, we would probably have got no further than halfway down that slope. The dogs are trained that way."

"Who trains them?"

"Women! It makes life a little bit easier from time to time, particularly when you want one of them for the cooking pot." Hòutú ducked under the shading roof, carefully manoeuvring down six large rough-cut steps. "Be careful, *Bǎobǎo*. You'll need time for your eyes to adjust to the light."

Tú followed her mother. The steps led them into the centre of the sunken pit, in which stood a low but sturdy wooden table. On its surface were two stone discs, a series of oddly shaped bronze knives and some smooth stones to the side of them.

"You have heard the saying that 'workers must first sharpen their implements when they want to do their best.' Well, this is where it comes from, Tú.

"They sometimes try to use bronze for the carving now, and these two wheels can be turned. They place the jade on…" Hòutú knelt at the table and looked around for a precious stone piece but could only find splinters and other tiny broken parts. "I was going to show you, Tú, but it seems the jade master is a little short of jade! I wonder where it is?"

Tú had poked her head into one of the caves leading off the pit, returning rapidly with her hand clenched across her nose.

"It stinks in there!"

"I should have told you. In most of these structures, the cave on the northernmost side is usually used as a latrine. They'll have built a short tunnel through the loess to let the waste drain away. Every few days, they flush it down with some water. In this case, I suspect the tunnel has collapsed, and now they don't want to fix it because of the shit build-up. In Táosì, Tú, you will see a lot of shit.

"If there was one stroke of luck we had when they condemned us to our *yáodòng;* it is that our home is to the south and east of most of the settlement. We might get the north winds in winter, but the winds are from the south in the summer; it takes the dreadful stench away from us. No one has taken care of sanitation in the city for years. It's as if they don't understand. Not only is it unhealthy to be surrounded by this crap, but it also attracts flies and—"

"And what?"

"And it's a waste. A waste of good shit!" Hòutú beamed at her daughter. "We'll store that one away for another day. There are two birds that could be downed with just one stone. We'll see!"

"See what?"

"Another time. There's too much missing in here; there's no real work going on. No raw materials. Except..." Hòutú paused and then stood. "Except..." She moved towards a small ledge and scooped up four tiny jade pieces, "...look at these." She held her palm outstretched towards Tú. "I've not seen this before. Look at the tiny holes that have been drilled through them. This is the work of a master. The question is, where is the other stuff?" Shaking her head, she replaced the jade earrings on the shelf and headed for the steps.

Usually, just after breakfast was Tú's lesson time. Her objections were a thing of the past, mainly because she had been unsuccessful in persuading her mother there were better things to do. There were not. There was little else to do. Today, in Tú's mind, she had escaped the daily learning, although that was not quite how her mother saw it. At least there was to be a change of emphasis; this morning, her mother could not ask her to sit at the writing pit. Even so, Tú was poised for something.

"Tú, I think we've found an ideal place for this morning's lesson."

"But m—"

"No buts! Look over there. It's one of the bronze foundries. Come!"

"But...I'm tired after all this walking. Can't we have a sit-down?"

"And so we shall, Tú, and so we shall!"

Hòutú headed towards a similar building, although the stains of smoke heavily coloured this one. Crouching to enter the structure, she dropped down the steps quickly. When Tú caught up, she was sitting on a raised platform surrounded by many objects that Tú did not recognise and the odd one she did. She slumped in front of her mother.

"Not more writing?" She whined.

"No! Enough of writing. You have mastered all that is required for now. It is time for you to learn about metals." It was a new subject but a crucial one to grasp, one that would have been difficult without the tools and the foundry to demonstrate. It was an ideal opportunity. If anything now happened to Hòutú, her daughter had to fill her shoes. "I think this is best told as a story," said Hòutú, "But this is a story you will have to both memorise and understand. One without the other is not enough. This is a new story, one I have not told you before.

"To this point, you have been living in what we might call the age of stone. That is about to change. The signs of change are all around us. They have been for a thousand years. I am talking about metals. Men and women will not stop using stone; they will be using it until the end of time, but the metals are about to assume new importance across this land. More specifically, they are going to assume absolute importance in your life. This is what you need to understand."

Tú settled on the floor, sitting with a foot twisted underneath her. Her mother wondered briefly when the pins and needles would start before brushing away the thought. Tú would learn. That was what both their lives were about; she would learn.

"This is copper." Hòutú twisted a tiny pigeon band in her fingers, "It comes from rock, a special rock, but a rock, nonetheless. They have lots of this rock in the hills between here and Dōngxiáfēng at a quarry called Xīwū."

"Not here in the Dàgùduì Quarry?"

"No."

"Why not?"

"To be honest with you, Tú, I do not know. I can only tell you what I know and will not make up stories to fill the gaps. Some places on this earth have copper ore, and some do not."

"Ore?"

"It is the rock that contains the copper. There are other ores, as you will learn." Hòutú settled back against a vertical chimney. "What happens is that you break the copper ore from the ground, then heat it. You heat it very much, and eventually, an orangey-red liquid comes out of the fire."

"What, flying all over the place?"

"No. It is guided into moulds, usually rectangular shapes. Here they are." She pointed to a row of clay moulds. "After some time, it goes hard, and when it is cold, you can pick it up."

"And they do all that so that we can make the message bands for the birds?"

"No. Look around you. Can you see anything else that might be made of copper?"

Tú searched in vain, looking for anything similar to the copper ribbon her mother still held. She shook her head.

"Now, look at this cooking pot." Tú picked it up. It was brand new. At home, their own was still in need of cleaning.

"What? This one? It's not the same; it's more of a dirty colour, doesn't look like the pigeon ribbons, and doesn't bend." Tú twisted and turned the pot in her hands, enjoying the feel of new metal.

"All true! But this one is copper. Ours is dirty from much use, and you'll see greenish patches, but that's because our pans are so old. You've washed that green stuff off before, and when you do, it will look a bit more like the one you're holding. And it does bend. Just look at that dent in the side. I think that's why this pot is still here. It needs fixing. Is that not a bend in the metal?"

"Yes." Tú nodded and sighed. She had washed their pan every day for more days than she could count; the depression in its side always annoyed her as it made it more difficult to clean.

"The men who make the copper do not make the pans. They're all specialists. They have men who dig the ore from the ground, they have men who drag the ore to the furnaces, and they have a man who melts the copper ore into copper blocks. Then, they have a man who hammers the copper into a sheet on a hard piece of stone that has been perfectly flattened. Then, there is another man who makes the pots. He also uses a hammer and a rock bowl to form the shape. Another specialist makes the copper foil you see in my hand. However, that is done in secret, and it's done by one of the Sisterhood."

"I have two questions." Tú had suddenly become more interested.

"Just two? That's unlike you, Tú. I must have done a good job of explaining."

"The first is that you keep saying a man does this, a man does that, what about women? And…" she gazed earnestly at her mother, "where do the handles come from?"

"They are both fascinating and very different questions." Hòutú smiled. "The handles are made in moulds when the hot liquid copper is poured off the fire." She looked around and came across a series of moulds designed for various purposes. "You know what a mould is because we use something similar with animal fats. What happens when we put animal fat into a bowl and leave it overnight?"

"You get brown jelly at the bottom and white fat at the top."

"Correct! It acts as a mould. The jelly is a weak solid, and the fat is a stronger one. I find it strange that the stronger solid sits on top of the weaker one, but I have no idea why, although I suppose ice floats on water. Obviously, they were both liquids when they went into the bowl."

"So, both of them are moulded by the shape of the bowl." Tú had seen the same thing most days of her life but had never considered it once.

"True. When they make metal, some metals are stronger than others."

"Why is this important?" Tú was beginning to find the subject less interesting by the minute. It seemed they were going to talk about cooking. "And what about the women? Why is it all about men?"

"Wait a bit! Let's finish learning about the process before we start on the workers. Anyway, the handles are made in a mould and are pinned to the pot with copper nails." She searched around, finding a couple of bent examples on the ground. "Here…here are two old ones. They're the weakest bit. They heat them, so they hold, but you know we keep having to have the handles fixed. Here's a question for you. Do you think you could use copper as a knife or as a plough or for an axe?"

"Well, it sounds like you could make a knife or an axe, and I do not know what a plough blade is, so I can't say."

"A plough blade is what farmers use to turn the earth before planting."

"Maybe they would work, but copper does seem a bit soft. Wouldn't stone be better for knives, axes, and those plough things?"

"Yes, it is!" Hòutú smiled at her daughter's insight. "But there is something you can do with copper that makes it harder." She pulled out a small knife, a permanent fixture on her belt, and handed it to Tú. "What's that made from?"

Tú scrutinized the knife. She had never held it before. It did not feel like the copper pot; it felt heavier and had a strong, sharp edge.

"I don't know," muttered Tú.

"This is bronze. It is made from copper and something else. Here in Táosì, they make it by melting the copper ore with arsenic ore, which answers the first of your questions."

"What? About the women?"

"Yes. There is a problem with arsenic. It is poisonous. Over time, the people working with it become sick, and some die. We stopped the women working in the metal sheds to stop them from becoming sick. If anyone has to do it, the men can. There are too few of us."

"But—"

"That sounds unfair, and it is, but we need all the women we have right now. Táosì is dying. It has been dying for years. The reason Táosì is here is because of the stone. They have a monopoly on stone manufacture across the province. No tools are made of stone across Shǎnxī except here and perhaps in the odd cottage. Táosì's power was its control of the stone industry. But stone is not the future; bronze is."

"But it kills the people who make it!"

"Making arsenic bronze kills people, and Táosì only has arsenic. However, making a tin bronze is a different proposition. It is much cleaner with no deaths, and few, if any, get sick. Therein lies a problem, for Táosì has no tin."

"What is tin? And where will the tin come from?"

"Where does Yú come from?"

"Mount Sōng!"

"No, before that, before his father was stupid enough to trip over Mount Sōng."

"They came from Bǎodūn, in Sìchuān."

"Yes. So, where do you think tin comes from?

"Sìchuān?"

"Sìchuān. All the tin we could ever need comes from mines on Mount Tú, and Yú's wife's father runs the mines."

"But you said I was to have his baby!"

"That, my little *Bǎobǎo*[11], is quite another story.

"Time to go, Tú Tú. We should have a guest waiting."

The pair headed northwards across the craft compound, zigzagging between the huts, many of which were in a severe state of dilapidation. After crossing a small culvert, they approached a gate in the wall surrounding the industrial area.

"Why are there walls around everything?" Asked Tú.

"The leaders would have it that they are to protect what is inside, which is absolute rubbish. The walls and gates keep the workers in until they have completed their daily work. They are checked in and out by a guard. For many of them, it is little more than slave labour. All they get in return is somewhere to live and their food. If they're lucky!"

---

[11] A term of endearment meaning baby.

Nine: The Fisherwoman

Táosì, Shǎnxī: Southwestern gate
Year 83: Year of the Snake
The spring equinox
22nd March 1912 BCE

They exited the gate, which was already swung open in a low arch-like structure in the wall.

"Where now?"

"To the main gate, Tú, the main gate. To the best of my recollection, it is the only city gate that can still be called a gate. It could even be defended if it weren't for the fact that any attackers could just come around it over these broken-down walls. We're to meet the fisherwoman just outside the gate. She won't dare come in. None of the fisherfolk will; they're clearly scared of something, but only their gods know what."

"So, this lady lives on the big river? And they live off fish?"

"It's only the River Fèn, Tú, not the Yellow River. Yes, she lives on the banks of the Fèn. They catch fish, snails, snakes, toads, frogs, and just about anything you can eat that lives in or around the river. Each day, one of them comes up to this gate to sell their catch. Same place, same time, every day. Just outside the walls."

"And you know her? How?"

"She is a keeper of pigeons, Tú. She is Sisterhood. I may have met her; I may not. It is not knowing her that is important; it is knowing I can trust her."

They had reached the great southwestern gate. It was not in as good a state as Hòutú remembered, but it still stood. The tamped earth rose in two towers on either side, bridged by a series of tree trunks. To each side of the opening, large cypress trunks gave the gate a semblance of solidity, strong enough for two plank gates to be suspended from them. A considerable bar hung in brackets across them, giving them an air of impregnability.

"And we get out...how?" Tú had her teenager look on again, at which her mother smiled benevolently.

"You think I cannot get through, don't you? Well, young lady, you go and scramble around and over that section of the broken wall. Off you go!" As Tú left, her mother shouted, "And I'll use my magic!"

When Tú finally made it around the gate towers, it was only to find her mother sitting and waiting patiently on the other side.

"How did you do that?" Tú was still puffing from the climb whilst her mother appeared to be eating an apple, and a pitcher of water stood between her feet. And where did you get those?"

"I told you, Tú, it's magic! I think this one can wait for your birthday. Until then, you will have to profess ignorance! Look, here she comes."

The fisherwoman was also blowing when she came into sight. It had been a formidable challenge to meet the deadline, and she welcomed the water that Tú offered her.

"What's all the fuss, Hòutú, dragging me up here at a moment's notice? You know, I'm not as young as I used to be." The fisherwoman looked around. "And where is everybody? It's like a ghost town."

The three settled on tumbled blocks that had once been part of the city wall. Tú stared at the visitor, examining her clothing, hair and bare skin whilst listening intently. It was not often she heard a new voice.

"Well," said Hòutú, "It's quite a long story, and we'll need you to go on quite a long fishing trip."

It took a while to brief the fisherwoman. Much of that time was spent convincing her that two boats should go with two messages. She was so utterly confident that her skills would be enough that Hòutú had to bring out all sorts of imagined problems to convince her. Apparently, it would take them less than a day on the river, so if they set out early, the message could be with Yú's group shortly after noon. That should give him the afternoon to discover the likely caves and prepare his forces.

Before they parted, Hòutú scratched in the dirt, duplicating the scars on her body.

"If they have any doubt, show them the symbol. They will trust you."

The fisherwoman nodded before marching off down the slope, westwards towards the Fèn. She had been warned to avoid Chīyóu's army, although she had not seemed unduly worried.

It was the first time that Tú met anyone from outside the city. In her nearly fourteen years, she had got to know fewer than fourteen people and those not well. She had been fascinated, just watching the woman and imagining her home, boat, river and fish. She had never eaten fish. She was intrigued that this woman had walked from the river some two hours distance, her mother said, and was planning to take a boat down the river faster than Chīyóu's army could walk in three days. She had only the vaguest idea of what a boat might look like and none whatsoever as to how it might move. The concept of a river was based on today's views of the two Táosì streams. Nothing made a lot of sense.

She stared after the departing fisherwoman, realising she was becoming smaller as she increased the distance between them. Tú knew the woman could not be shrinking, but the concepts of perspective and vanishing points had not been required in their tiny space in the Da Nan gully; people did not disappear into the distance. They only ever vanished around a corner or over the cliff. She had to be brave in this new world. When she turned back towards the gate, her mother had disappeared. Tú scrambled back the way she had come. When she reached the top of the wall, she spied Hòutú, walking away from the gate along the straight road towards the palace compound. She was already halfway there. Tú slid down the inner side of the ramparts and jogged after the fast-diminishing form. Like the fisherwoman earlier, Tú was breathless when she caught up.

"You...you...have to...show me how...you did that!" Matching Hòutú's stride, she tried to peer into her mother's face but only ended up tripping on the broken surface.

"Show you what? Show you how to use a gate? They open! Sorry, Tú Tú, I shouldn't laugh; you haven't seen a gate before, have you?

"Now. What's that commotion?"

Ten: The Pigs
Táosì, Shǎnxī
Year 83: Year of the Snake
The spring equinox
22nd March 1912 BCE

The two women were closing on the palace compound. To their left and right were somewhat larger copies of the workman's hut they had examined earlier. Hòutú ducked into an alley to her left, where the noises could be heard more clearly. There was snarling and barking and squealing, loud and confused. After another twenty paces, they rounded a corner where six dogs, similar to the one they had spotted earlier, were barking and scratching at a door. It seemed the squealing emanated from inside the building.

"Sit!" Hòutú hollered the order. Tú was surprised when three of the dogs promptly sat, remaining stationary except for the wagging of their tails and uplifted heads. Two younger dogs quietened, although they seemed unsure about what should happen next. Eventually, one tried to emulate its elders while the other rolled on its back. The smaller sixth dog simply cowered, looking for all the world as if it were to be beaten.

"You see, Tú, these dogs look for all the world as if they are feral, wild things that would rip you apart. Although that is sometimes the case, they would rarely attack an adult. These are domesticated dogs. They are simply hungry and confused, with no humans around. It would help if you remember - it was not humans that domesticated dogs - it was dogs that domesticated humans. They like us, and now they need us. They like being told what to do, a bit like men!" Hòutú laughed uproariously at her joke.

"What about that one?"

"I think, my *Bǎobǎo*, that poor dog has suffered too many times from a heavy hand. Would you like to adopt it? Would you like a dog?"

"To eat?"

"No, not this one. Let's save it from whoever has been mistreating it and keep it as a pet. What will you call him?"

"Dog?"

"You cannot call it dog! It is a dog, the same as you are a human. Well! Sometimes. Do I call you human? Make it a simple name."

"How about…Tú!"

"If you think that's a good idea, you are completely mad. I should sacrifice you to Jīnxīng right now! Imagine if I go around calling the name Tú. Every single time, I'll get the dog followed by you - when you decide you will get up! No!"

"Jīnxīng!"

"Alright! This is a young girl dog, and Jīnxīng is a girl star, so I think we can cope with that. Jīnxīng!" Hòutú held out her open palm to the cowering bitch. "Now, this is the hard part. We have to get rid of these five and keep this one." To the far north, Hòutú could hear a bitch on heat howling. Reaching her arm around Jīnxīng to keep her secure, she pointed toward the howl and whispered to what appeared to be the alpha dog. After leaning toward him and patting his head, she shouted, "Go!" At once, the pack of five disappeared down the street in the direction of the noise.

"How did you do that, Māma?"

"Well, Tú, that wasn't really me. That was the power of a female in action. That noise was a girl dog who was ready for them. This little girl will not be ready for a few months, but we must be careful.

"Now, let's look inside. Pick her up." Tú lifted Jīnxīng into her arms, gently stroking her head. The bitch's tail wagged in a somewhat undecided manner.

Hòutú was struggling with the door. It was clear why the dogs had been unable to gain entry; it took all her might to push against the dead weight.

"I thought you knew how to use these things," piped up Tú. "Magic, you said! It doesn't look like magic to me; it looks like brute force!"

The door came away from its upper hinge, taking Hòutú with it as it fell inwards. Her daughter was about to make her second new acquaintance of the day, but there would be no discussion this time. As she lifted the door, the extensive pool of blood made it plain that whoever was blocking the door was no longer in a position to indulge in dialogue.

"He's dead. Careful." A length of twine tied to a large stone appeared to have caused the man's demise. "This place was booby-trapped. They did not want surprise visitors, it appears."

The corpse was short, middle-aged, and poorly dressed, although he had recently added a layer to his clothing, a fine cloak. Close to his face lay a half-eaten flatbread, and closer examination showed half of it to have already been stuffed inside his toothless mouth. Nearby lay a bag, from which the contents had spilt, small jade objects mainly.

"He was deliberately killed?" asked Tú.

"Yep! It's hard to work out how he fell against the inside of the door, though. Perhaps closing it behind him yanked that rock from the ledge, but it smacked him on the head alright."

"I wonder how he managed to avoid going with the army?"

"You'll always find one, Tú. You'll find one in every community. There's one in every small town, let alone a city like this. This is not the first house he has ransacked. Just look at his bag. You only realise how damaging these people are when they are locked up or thrown out of the town, and the theft and the trouble come to a complete standstill. The problem is, after a while, another one pops up with all the same attributes. I have no time for this man."

Hòutú pressed herself against the wall inside the room as Tú peered into the gloom from the outside.

"Don't come in; there might be another one, and…block that gap with your legs…quick!" Hòutú screamed at Tú as a piglet darted towards the opening. "Stop it!"

Tú pinned the piglet between her calves, where no amount of wriggling and squealing would free it.

"You've got it! Well done, Tú. Hold still." Hòutú pulled the twine free from the murderous rock and tied the porker's legs tightly, forming a carrying handle. "Well, we now have dinner. You've never eaten pig before, have you? We'll have a suckling pig, and perhaps…" she looked around the room, "You know if the owner of this cave does not come back, I think we should have a proper look around." She reached for a pottery flagon and, feeling it was full, hefted it under one arm. "Perhaps we shall have some wine with our pig!"

"But that's stealing, *Māma*. You said that—"

"It would be…but it isn't. Besides, I've not had wine since you were born. I deserve it. And before you start going on about stealing, remember that the owner of this house just killed someone. Stealing, my foot!" She glanced at Tú and realised there would be no convincing her. "I'll compensate the owner in a few days if he returns. I promise. Tú?"

It made quite a sight to watch the two of them waddle off. Tú with the bitch in her arms, Hòutú with the flagon encircled by her left arm and the piglet dangling from her right hand, its snout dragging along the ground. Da Nan gully widened here, running below the palace compound walls, and the sides were lower and easier to descend. It was then not but five hundred paces up and along the gully to their *yáodòng*. However, an alternative option was available.

"Tú?"

"Yes."

"Let's have a night on the town! I'll be exhausted carrying this pig back to our *yáodòng*. Let's use someone else's. Here, perhaps?" Hòutú halted at an open doorway, peered in and then entered. "Look, there's wood; there are plates and pots…and a fireplace with embers in the centre…and chairs! Chairs, Tú! We can sit in chairs."

If Tú's head was swimming from processing all the new things she had seen today, it was becoming decidedly worse. They had visited some of the more substantial buildings in the town. The thought of returning to their home had made her realise the extent of their poverty. However, it was still home. Now, in addition to theft, her mother was proposing they light someone else's fire, sit in their chairs, and use their pottery.

"And…there's a full water butt! Ours will be empty. That decides it. Hey, Tú! There are even torches on the walls! Come on in and close the lower half of that door. It'll keep the dog in. And the pig, if it escapes, come on!"

Tú reluctantly entered the unfamiliar home. Hòutú was dealing with the piglet, which squirmed this way and that against its bindings.

"Are you sure you wouldn't prefer to eat the dog, Tú? This piglet is feisty?"

"No! You're not to touch Jīnxīng! I'm never eating dog again!"

"You will if you're hungry enough!"

Hòutú looked around for the slaughterhouse wall; most eating areas had one. A sharpened rock protruded from the tamped earth, and a stout notched plank was fitted above. She stood and lifted the piglet by the bindings around its back legs. Eyeing up a spot, she moved across to the wall. Raising it higher, she swung the animal in a wide arc, aiming for the stone protrusion. The piglet's skull crashed into the rock; immediately, consciousness deserted the animal. She hooked the back legs over the plank and slipped her knife out in one fluid movement, slashing it across the animal's neck. The lifeblood gushed from the wound into a small gully below, which exited the home through a short, bored tunnel. Tú looked on, taking in the process.

"Is it dead now?"

"It will be in a moment." The animal flinched slightly before returning to its flaccid state. "It'll only take a few minutes to drain. This is a small pig; imagine the process with a full-size one.

"Usually, I would use this," explained Hòutú, indicating the blood, "but we haven't got time to mess around. We'll have plenty of food for me, you, and the dog. So, what about a drink of wine while we wait?" She waved at the flask propped against a small shelf on the left-hand side of the tunnel leading to the *yáodòng* door. "Come on, Tú, it's more training for you! How to remove a wax stopper from a flagon of wine. If we're lucky, it'll be *jiu* wine, maybe with honey added. If we're unlucky, it will only be *lao*[12], which tends to have all sorts of bits in it. Let's see. Do you need the knife?" she asked, wiping the blade on her skirts.

"Ow! Yes, please." Tú had been attempting to remove the wax with her fingernails and ended up breaking one. Taking the knife and using the blade as a lever resulted in a satisfying pop as the wax stopper gave way and looped into the air.

---

[12] A less refined sweeter and sticky wine often used in cooking.

"Don't lose the wax, Tú. It's always useful for something, including sealing the flagon again. If we have to!" She smiled at her daughter. "Go on, take a sip."

Tú had never consumed alcohol of any sort, and for her mother, it was so long that she could hardly remember what it was like. Having taken a gulp, Tú placed the flagon between her legs, her features contorting into a grimace.

"What's that made from?" Tú handed the pitcher to her mother using both hands. The pottery vessel was heavy in itself, but she guessed there was enough liquid in it to double the weight. Lifting the pottery to her lips, Hòutú took a short sip.

"Rice, my love, rice wine! Just imagine having enough rice to be able to make wine from it. This is *jiu*. We are lucky today! *Jiu* and pig! Maybe we should celebrate both our birthdays! I was your age when I last drank alcohol. Imagine!"

"If you think you're lucky drinking that stuff, I don't think you know what luck is…It's horrible!"

"Ah, Tú! Let's see if you say the same thing after a few more of these. Go and find some beakers, *Băobăo*. Our arms will fall off if we keep drinking from this great thing."

Tú was keen to explore the house. The square central area was roofed, although there was a gap the size of half a man around the sloping planks, which let in sufficient light. They had entered through a cave tunnelled in the west wall, which was featureless other than the door, not even a *ménshén*. She determined to investigate each of the other three caves.

The first, in what she guessed was the south wall, although she was a little disorientated being inside, proved disappointing. There was straw, bedding, and little else, although stout carved tree trunks supported the walls. The second was a smaller version of the first; she guessed it may have been where the children slept. Strangely, the two *ménshén*, who should have stood guard at the door, lay on the bed. She concluded they had been placed inside for safekeeping. The third proved to be the storeroom, and immediately, Tú felt she was in another world.

The owners of this *yáodòng* must be wealthy beyond compare. Notched between the upright trunks were what she would later learn were shelves. On the floor under the shelves was firewood, but what was on the shelves focused her attention.

One had a set of storage jars; another shelf held pottery plates and bowls; yet another was reserved for beakers. Tú had never seen such a quantity of personal belongings. On turning, she discovered a ham wrapped in cloth above which some dry *ròugān* hung in strips; she broke one off and chewed on the dry meat. Turning again, she saw bowls of dried beans and lentils. On opening one of the storage pots, she found a grey/brown flour in which weevils churned. There was food for thousands.

Suddenly remembering her allotted task, Tú picked up two beakers. After a moment's thought, she grabbed two plates from which a handful of sharpened sticks fell. After scooping them up, she returned to her mother in the central area.

"What are these, *Māma*?"

"Those? Those are eating sticks. I'll show you later. Was there firewood in there? If so, could you bring some? Quite a lot!"

When Tú returned, her mother was attacking the corpse of the piglet.

"You have to be careful with pigs, Tú. You have to cut around its arse first," which was a job she had already finished. "Then tie up this hole…It's full of shit, so you don't want that squeezing out." She had pulled the twine from the beast's front legs. "Then you slit its belly and whip out all the guts…making sure this bit with the string tied comes out in one piece." It was a slick operation, clearly a skill she had once learned and practised. The guts fell to the floor with a slop as she slit the internal section of the throat.

"Right, get the dog in here; she'll clean this up faster than you and me." Hòutú smiled, "We can leave everything else on. There will be too much to eat for the two of us, but we know where we can find refuse collectors!" She nodded at the dog that had begun to feast on the unsightly pile of offal. "Now, get me a bowl of wat…No, I'd forgotten; fetch a roasting stick. You'll see them in the storeroom, blackened, tough wood. That's them."

Ten: The Pigs

Hòutú rammed the shaft through the baby hog's mouth until the other end exited what remained of its anus. Then, taking a shorter stick with a sharpened end, she rammed it laterally through the pig's rib cage.

"A few of these will stop it slipping on the spit. Now. Help me lift it. See that hole in the wall? That's for the one end, and this," she kicked a bronze stand across the floor, "holds the other end. Now, all I need to do is wash my hands, and you can light the fire."

Within minutes, the flames were licking up the sides of the piglet. The two women settled into the chairs that had been conveniently positioned, not too far from the fire and not too close, which was an excellent job because they were heavy.

"Let's have another drink. Beakers this time, Tú. It'll taste better." And it seemed, slowly and surely, Tú was enjoying the new drink more and more. She felt warmed from the outside by the fire and warmed from the inside by the liquid; it was a good feeling, keeping her going while they waited.

When the hog was ready, her mother sliced chunks off the animal, which they ate with bare hands. Hòutú had demonstrated the use of the sharp sticks, which seemed to consist of jabbing one into a piece of meat and raising to your mouth. It was hardly complex, but it was easier than burning your hands.

As they ate, Hòutú indulged in a monologue. She was only interrupted when a piece of pig proved too large for her to talk around, or she reached once again for her beaker.

"I can only remember the names of the last twenty generations of keepers of the pigeons in Táosì, but they go back much further. When I was young, we lived in a cave like this one. It was a grand affair, almost palatial, with a central, open area more extensive than this and huge chambers extending under the loess. Beautiful! It was cool in summer and warm in winter.

"You know...where we live...the *ménshén* are poor pottery figures, and the weather had taken its toll. When I look at them now, they resemble little more than a pair of stone phalli. You know that they fall over in the highest winds. That reminds me of the lack of births in Táosì. The disparate state of the men. The dwindling intellect of their leadership. The decline of the state.

"I hated my masters, Tú, but loved my job. Since they caged me up, I only have half a job, but it's…it's an important job…Tú…looking after you and the pigeons and the messages and whatnot. Eeees im…port…ant, Tú. You listening?

"You know…you know…when…they were scared of me, Tú Tú. Scared. They still are…keeping me prisoner…they think it's a spell that means things have gone terribly wrong…They just don't realise…they don't realise, Tú…it's been going wrong since before it started. Throwing me in a cell isn't going to save them…the master plan will not save them…but it will save our culture…what we have left…it will be saved for our children…You will save it, Tú. You!"

The fact that she was slurring meant little to her daughter. Tú had taken beaker after beaker of wine, and her head was now swimming. She would never know how long her mother continued, for as the fire began to die back, she slumped sideways onto the arm of the chair and fell fast asleep. A while later, after continuing with her incontinent rambling, Hòutú's head fell back, and she began to snore loudly.

Eleven: The Hangover
Táosì, Shǎnxī
Year 83: Year of the Snake
The day after the spring equinox
23rd March 1912 BCE

Tú's head lurched forward, vomit spewing from her gaping mouth. The banging and banging and banging stretched from the top of her cranium to her neck. She retched again. Never in her short life had she felt so ill. It was a shock to find she was now on her hands and knees, the floor swimming below her as she attempted to orientate herself.

The final straw was coming face to face with half a piglet's head, hanging and inverted on the spit—another heave. Most of the bitter contents of her stomach arced through the air, although some surged through her nasal passages. The shock of the latter brought her to some semblance of painful consciousness, or at least the closest she would get to it that day.

Across the embers, having slid half out of her chair, her mother continued her sleep, mouth wide open and snoring like a pig. She did not look sick. Turning as slowly as possible to avoid further nausea, Tú spied the large water pot. Dragging herself towards it, she began to lift herself with her hands on its rim. It was a mistake. Unable to hold on, the vessel toppled from her grasp, dousing her clothes with freezing water. As it jarred against the hard floor, the breaking pottery proved to be the straw that broke the camel's back; her mother suddenly awoke.

"Don't waste it, Tú! Save the last of it." Hòutú made a double-take of her surroundings and her daughter's condition, quickly realising neither approximated what any sane person would have regarded as normal. A little water remained in the base of the pot. Rising and moving swiftly around Tú, she righted it and moved what was left to safety.

"What a mess, Tú! You can only blame yourself in these circumstances. It would be best if you did not start drinking on an empty stomach. You should not eat half a baby pig like you haven't eaten in a year. It's too rich, you know. And you should always, always drink enough water with your wine.

"It's a good job we have today and the next day with nothing to do…I mean, look at you; you're good for nothing. We'll get you washed and watered and put you in your own bed for a while. Come on, girl! Let's go!"

Notwithstanding the awful mess and the even worse stink, Hòutú led her daughter by the hand out into the cool alley. Jīnxīng followed. Tú winced in the bright sunlight, gasping in lungful after lungful of crisp, clean air, while her mother looked this way and that for a water butt. On finding what she needed and ensuring its opening was one of the larger varieties, she led Tú to the butt and, without any advance notice, dunked her daughter almost to the waist in its frigid waters. As Tú's head cleared the surface, her scream could have been heard down by the river. Their day could only improve.

After dragging Tú back to the *yáodòng* and making her somewhat comfortable on her bedding, Hòutú went in search of more fresh water. It proved a frustrating search. Either the containers were too big to carry, or they were empty. In her brain-addled state, it took her a while to figure out that transferring the water from the larger to the smaller containers was an option. Eventually, she returned to her cave with two medium-sized pottery jars clasped under each arm. By the time she made it back, half the liquid had spilt. It was of no matter.

It took a little time to wake Tú. It took even longer to convince her she should drink. When the girl had finally achieved a conscious state, having rehydrated sufficiently, Hòutú instructed her to wash. She stank.

More water was needed. The only remaining possibility was to move Tú towards the source. Her mother was damned if she would move the water to her daughter again.

The pair retraced their steps down Da Nan Gully toward the palace walls. Once they had hauled themselves up the western side, they were again surrounded by housing. Hòutú stopped at each water pot, instructing Tú to drink first, then to dunk her head. By the time they reached the westernmost point of the palace enclosure, Tú would have been regarded as human by some, if not all. It was the first time she had spoken since she had screamed.

"*Māma*, is that supposed to be fun? It feels like someone poisoned me."

"You have been poisoned, *Bǎobǎo*. Alcohol is poison."

"So, why did you let me drink it? I thought mothers were supposed to try to look after their children, not to murder them!"

"You're being silly, Tú."

"No, I'm not being silly; I feel like I'm dying!"

"You should think of last night as a lesson, like the writing. You need to know about these things. You need to know that if someone is plying you with wine, there is a time to stop, and there are things to do to disguise the fact you've stopped. Drinking alcohol is considered a social activity, and you need to be social."

"It doesn't seem very social to me. I feel as anti-social as it's possible to be right now. I know I smell, for one thing, and I'm struggling to keep up with you. That's a change from yesterday."

"You don't smell half as bad as you did a little while ago. There's another water butt. Go on. Drink and dunk!"

"But what about the people this water belongs to? When they come back, they'll be thirsty and need the water. You're making me taint each container we pass. It's not right."

"Look around you, Tú. Look around. Do you think these homes are those of the rich or the poor?"

"The rich, I guess. They're big homes."

"They are. They are big homes, the homes of Chīyóu's elite. Not only are they the homes of the rich, but also the homes of men. There's not a woman who could lay claim to one of them. On any day, you'll find women here, cleaning, cooking, and washing clothes. On any night, you'll find girls dragged unwillingly into these beds. But they are thrown out when they have been used, or the men have grown tired of them and want a new plaything. If there is any place on earth that demonstrates the wrongs of Táosì, it is not the prisons; it is not the whorehouses; it is not the slave labour in the quarry. It is here, Tú.

"You ask about them returning and needing water. My greatest hope is that not one of the owners of these homes returns from battle. I earnestly hope they will all die."

"Are they all bad?"

"Yes!"

Twelve: The Army
Guo Yǐ, Fèn River, Shǎnxī
Year 83: Year of the Snake
The day after the spring equinox
23rd March 1912 BCE

Chīyóu was feeling relatively pleased with himself. By his reckoning, they were just shy of two thousand when they left Táosì. Now, around halfway between their two overnight camps, he had lost only a hundred or so of his men. Most of the missing had been from the bronze working teams; they had been unable to keep up. Another fifty-odd had gone ahead, not to scout, although they could be expected to perform that role if required, but to set up the kitchens near the caves they would occupy at the end of the day. If nothing else, Chīyóu understood that an army marched and fought on its belly rather than its feet.

The track they headed down followed the Fèn River for much of its length. In places, the river swept away in wide bends, although when it did, their route cut across the base of each loop. The going underfoot was firm. There had been no flooding yet this season, and even the footsteps of a force this size failed to churn the surface. It was fast going.

There were mixed feelings among the troops, mainly dependent on their previous experiences. The leakage in manpower occurred primarily from the column's rear, where the oldest and the sickest stumbled along. Chīyóu and his henchmen were all in the vanguard; it did little to restrict the numbers dropping by the wayside.

The hardcore of Chīyóu supporters was buoyant enough; they knew they would benefit one way or another, be it in wealth or women, and one could always buy the other; their expectations were set high. Only a hundred or so could count themselves in this elite. It was a group rarely added to and had seen a significant reduction over the years. Two factors could account for their falling numbers. Their inherent desire not to share their spoils was first, but the second was mainly due to the fruitless and often dangerous hunting trips forced upon them. Just a couple of weeks ago, ten of their number had been swept away as Chīyóu tried to ford the Fèn River to find game on the other bank.

Each of the elite carried two spears, crisscrossed on their backs and a large axe in their belts, each weapon bearing a bronze blade. Each wore a thick leather waistcoat over the top of their tunics, many of which were highly coloured. The latter protected their torso from a frontal assault, but the rear straps provided little protection for their backs. It was an armour designed for attack; it offered little protection if you were to run away.

At the rear of the column were the adult workers. Again, each carried two spears and an axe, but there the similarities ended. Most weapons were stone-bladed and held in men's hands: two spears in the right, the axe in the left. Close examination revealed that the shafts of the spears and their axes' hafts were highly variable. Lucky was the man with one straight spear, and he was blessed if he had two. Their axes were regular working tools designed for hacking at roots and branches, but many lacked the edge required even for those simple tasks.

The workers had been promised bounty, although the older amongst them had previously been cheated. It would have been hard to find more than a handful enthusiastic about the forthcoming battle, and their hatred of the forced march was evident. It was not a question of if they would run off; it was simply a question of whether they thought they could get away with it. They all knew that mass desertion would result in a mass execution; therefore, each man would have to act alone if he were to slip away. As the day wore on, the perceived personal risks of staying increased, and deserting became more inviting. However, whenever an opportunity presented itself, someone else seemed to act first. If the march were to go on for four whole days, very few of this group would remain.

The boys were in the central phalanx of the untidy column. They followed behind their leaders and in front of their elders, positioned as such to ensure they kept up. Although most did, they were a raggle-taggle band, poorly equipped and dressed. They comprised almost a third of the total numbers and ranged from seven to thirteen years of age. Anyone fourteen or more was considered an adult and marched with the workers.

Boys who had turned up with a weapon of any standard had quickly lost it to one of their elders in a forced swap. There was some enthusiasm among the younger lads, but those old enough to realise what was going on knew they would be offered up as fodder to the enemy. The level of discontent was highest amongst these boys, although they were too scared to run and too afraid to object. Last night, they had been freezing and hungry, as many had found their food stolen before they had even shovelled a mouthful down. Most of them had a father present, either in the group of leaders ahead or with the working elders behind, but their paternity offered no protection. Maybe a handful of boys had any idea who their fathers might be, but this was a handful more than the number of elders who knew who their sons were.

If there was a group more content than the rest, it was the cooks, not that they deserved the name. They were promised dispensation from the battle and a share in its spoils in return for charging ahead. Running in pairs, they utilised their spears to carry pots and grain for the porridge, in addition to their axes. Leaving the army's main body was a further reward, for every one of their comrades would happily have slaughtered them. The entire military now hated them. The food they had served the previous night had been only partly cooked, primarily cold, tasteless, and insufficient. The cooking party were not particularly interested in rectifying the bigger picture as long as they ensured their leaders were adequately fed.

The cooks had attained their goal at surprising speed. It seemed they might be half a day ahead of the main army. The proposed campsite consisted of several short tunnels dug into a loess outcrop, although it was unclear why they had been constructed. There was evidence that one of the caves had been occupied, but probably not since the end of autumn.

The previous night had made it very evident that the group responsible for preparing food could only be termed cooks if one took a peculiar definition of the term. Their selection had been made based on their ability to carry heavy pots and food stores rather than any previous culinary experience. Back in Táosì, they had been used to having their

85

food prepared and served by women; their mastery of cooking was mostly non-existent.

A brief discussion between the mess crew resulted in a swift division of labour. Whilst some gathered firewood, others with large pots searched for water from a nearby stream. A third group scavenged for anything they might add to their leaders' meals to make them more palatable and perhaps more filling. Not one of the three groups had more than limited success until two hunters arrived. The opposing forces first met at this point, although only one side knew this was the case. The hunters ambled up as the second group of cooks filled their water jugs. It was not rare to see the odd hunter, and the greetings were amiable.

After the pleasantries, it seemed that there was a possible trade. The cooks desperately wanted the two sika deer and the string of plump winter rabbits the hunters carried. It did not occur to them that just one fat rabbit at this time of year was as rare as a snowflake in summer, let alone seven. The hunters were anxious to acquire a copper pan in return for their prey, but as was typical, the negotiations proved long-winded. Even though it took ages, in the end, it needed only one of the larger pots to suffice as an exchange for the meat.

During the meeting, the hunters proved exceptionally well-informed regarding the supply of firewood, freshwater, and additions to the cooking pot. Conversations ranged widely. At one point, it seemed the two strangers might wish to join Chīyóu's army. They certainly passed on helpful information about the size and deployment of the force down by the river. However, they pulled out in the end, citing the difficulty of recrossing the river with the copper pan in time to join the rest of their band before nightfall. By the time they left, everyone was in the best of spirits.

Thirteen: The Xià

Sanjiadiǎncūn, Shǎnxī
Year 83: Year of the Snake
The day after the spring equinox
23rd March 1912 BCE

To say that Yú was concerned was a considerable understatement. Not one fisherwoman had appeared bearing tidings but two, and this in less time than he had taken to dress appropriately. It seemed the Sisterhood, or more specifically, their pigeons, may have been bearing misinformation. The messages were identical in their content and the grave concern they inspired.

Yú's force certainly did not number twenty thousand, but they did not number two thousand either; he had only two hundred men and women at his command, and they were a mixed bag. They were undoubtedly keen, motivated to some degree by ideology but to an even greater extent by their leader's charisma.

Whilst Yú was ruefully contemplating the error, Túshānshì, his wife, was desperately trying to find out what she should say to him. The actual brains of the operation were a cabal of the Sisterhood who were currently discussing the possibilities, which were far too intricate and long-winded for Yú's wife to get her head around. It seemed that there were only two options left on the table. One involved running away as fast as possible and massively reformulating a strategy involving several generations. The other option was staying and fighting, sticking to the plan, and keeping their fingers firmly crossed.

"We don't have long. What is it to be?" Túshānshì, like the others, was exasperated, but more with their messaging failure than anything else; the pigeon code had failed them.

"We stay!" Girl looked little more than a teenager, but it was on her to make that final call. Túshānshì was no more than a message carrier, and Yú would simply do what he was told, although he would never really consider it was anything but his own idea. The multiple considerations that had been processed were as far beyond Yú's understanding as they were Túshānshì's. The odds of winning this conflict had to be balanced against the odds of reshuffling the genetic pack. If they succeeded in battle, the need for producing a Yú-like replacement within a couple of generations was removed. It was the fact that the second option was so complicated that it had led to the Sisterhood choosing the precarious notion of pitting two hundred against two thousand.

Túshānshì was beautiful. Not simply good-looking but alarmingly so. When she passed by, both men and women stared, even those who had seen her a hundred times before. It would have been enough if her advantages had stopped there, but they did not. She was also charming. It was said that Túshānshì could persuade the sun to come out on a rainy day and the moon to rise on her command. Of course, as a mere mortal, she could do neither, but she could convince people of almost anything, and more specifically, she had Yú wrapped around her little finger. Her attributes were so balanced that no one took offence or held grudges against Túshānshì's manipulations. Often, it did not appear that there was manipulation. Objects of her attention simply believed they were doing what they wished for themselves; such were her skills.

They say that every scale should balance. In Túshānshì's case, the result was that she did not appear to be exceptionally bright. However, it was not a fault that anyone ever noticed, as her other attributes tended to disguise it; this was also the case with her husband. Like his wife, Yú was charming. He was also handsome, rugged, lean, fit, and adventurous. Many women had thrown themselves at him over the years, although Túshānshì's persuasive powers had ensured he had remained firmly in her bed. Yú always appeared decisive and in control, whatever the circumstance, although this simply reflected how the Sisterhood's power operated. When Yú had to decide, he would do so immediately; only Túshānshì understood that the decisions had been made in advance on his behalf.

If people were in awe of the pair and their relationship, the respect was boundless because neither displayed airs and graces. It was understood that Yú was the leader and that Túshānshì was his wife. It was also known that either could be approached about anything at any time. They wore the same clothes, ate the same food, used the same bedding, and suffered the same privations as everyone in the band.

Notwithstanding the respect in which they were both held, it was beyond the imagination that Yú and Túshānshì were to become leaders of a new nation. It was beyond the reasoning of their supporters to consider any overarching plans for the new Motherland. For the time being, Yú was the leader of the Xià clan, and with fewer than two hundred members, it looked as if any plans for the future would be erased before they commenced.

Sanjiadiǎncūn was simply a bowl on the outside bank of the Fèn River, where the waterway curved back on itself in a giant loop. The name was given to the spot by Túshānshì and meant the village at the point with three sides. It was a valid name in that the bowl provided three landward sides and the river the fourth. At this point, the band had constructed a palisade, a circle of rough-hewn planks the height of two men and roughly thirty paces across. It was a cramped and uncomfortable temporary residence. The fort sat atop the river cliff, about fifteen paces from the edge, encircled with clear flat land before the slopes rose steeply on the three landward sides.

It could be argued that the place was undefendable, but the slopes leading down to it made this an understatement of massive proportions. Animal tracks came down the escarpments, perhaps as many as twenty of them, zig-zagging between thorn bushes towards the water's edge. Even the fisherwomen, still resting from their morning exertions, found it hard to comprehend how such a place might hold out against Chīyóu's army. With much headshaking, they returned to their boats for the long haul back upstream.

As the fisherwomen retreated into the distance, Yú's scouts appeared carrying a copper pan between them. Their appearance caused much merriment as they had been sent out posing as hunters.

"How did you catch that, then? Spear or arrows?"

"Did it struggle?"

"I see you've already gutted it!" The comment came from one of the women whose head was already deep inside the pan.

"Have you eaten the legs already?" jibed another.

"Yú, we need to talk urgently. Very urgently!" one of the hunters managed to sidestep the joshing and get down to business.

"Túshānshì, Girl, elders! Here! Now!" The response to Yú's call was immediate, and they swiftly arranged themselves in a seated circle. "Right, lads. Talk!" There was total silence as they commenced their debrief.

The first hunter explained what they had learned of the size and whereabouts of Chīyóu's army. Notwithstanding that much of the information tallied with that received from the fisherwomen, they were allowed to continue. It became clear that the total numbers in the force were diminishing quite rapidly during the march, that they had been poorly fed the night before, and the troops were tired and cold. It was estimated that they would turn up at their overnight encampment by sunset, but many would have to spend the night under the stars as there were not enough caves.

It was then the turn of the second hunter, and as he kicked off, broad smiles widened on both their faces.

"The first thing we did was to make sure the water they were using was from what appeared to be a single spring. It seemed like the freshwater came straight from the earth, but it's a bit more complicated. We traced it back some hundred paces where the original stream had pooled, then entered a culvert and tunnel. It was the source of their spring water. Being trained by the great Gǔn," a laugh went around the group at the mention of Yú's father, an inexpert hydrologist. "…we knew exactly what to do. We found as much carrion as we could—"

"The deader and the rottener, the better—" The first hunter could not resist.

"…And dropped them all into that pool. We even pissed in it and would have done worse if we had eaten better at breakfast. We did leave some sacking in place to stop the bigger bits from going through, but first, we tested it with a little stick. We reckon their 'spring' would have been deadly well before they drew their first water."

"My turn!" The first hunter chimed in. "Now we saw that the area was covered in these aloe vera bushes, you know, the spiky ones. Well! We told them how to prepare them to bulk out their food."

"Cut off the sharp bits—"

"…and discard!"

"Chop the rest into little cubes−"

"…being ever so careful to keep all the skin−"

"…and the gel−"

"…and the latex…and to pop them all into the pot to simmer for thirty minutes or so!"

"The latex?" Túshānshì interrupted, "But that's poisonous! Why? Oh!"

"That should stuff'em for the morning. They'll have the squits comin' out their ears!"

The guffaws from the group brought widespread interest from the rest of the clan. Soon, there was a circle of all two hundred, splitting their sides with laughter. Yú took the opportunity to lean forward for a quiet word with Girl and Túshānshì before addressing the crowd.

"Friends! We all know what we have planned, and I think we all know our individual roles. If you do not, ask before sunset tonight. There will be no time later. Remember that two things are deadly important for those of you allocated to remain in the palisade. Firstly, the attackers will come in fog, but it will be time to make sure they think the fort is beginning to awake when you hear the first wolf signal. Fires must be kept going, but there should be the sounds of people stumbling to the toilet and the odd guard's call. Those sorts of things. This isn't easy. You must convince them of these activities while remaining safely under those carts. You get under them as fast as possible and stay there. Questions?

"No. Alright. The rest of you. If your foxhole is not big enough yet, you have until sunset to dig it deeper. You must keep those thorn cuttings in place while Chīyóu's force comes down those slopes. We must keep them on the paths. They must think they are avoiding real thorns, so let's not make any mistakes with this. We are doubling the number of arrows for each of you to twenty. Listen for the signals, then use them wisely. Shoot the closest target. Always! Aim at the heart and lungs. Always! If you see a target that already has three arrows in him, well, then leave him. He's as good as dead!"

The Xià bows were handmade, often by the archers themselves, to allow for their individual height and strength. Around two-thirds of the archer's height was regarded as the optimal length. Each was recurved, comprising five strips of bamboo and silkwood thorn, glued together and bound with silk and the tendons of hares. The strings were formed from twisted bamboo fibres; each archer carried several replacements. The arrows, likewise, were works of art. Duck feather flights and barbed bronze heads lay at either end of a dead straight shaft of hardened bamboo, an arm's length from tip to tail and narrower than a little finger.

"By my reckoning, each one of us needs a direct hit with each of ten arrows to stand a chance of winning this battle. We will go to those foxholes before sunset. Take food and drink, keep your hands warm and stay silent, particularly those of you with more than one in your hide! They will have scouts out tonight, probably at the top of the cliff, but they may come down.

"When it all kicks off, you start firing only on the second wolf's call. And what does the third wolf's call mean?"

"We've won!" The response was raucous and instantaneous.

"Yes! We have won!" Yú's eyes ranged across the band. "Got it?"

A nod of assent rippled around the entire group. Their training had been first class, but camaraderie made them such a formidable force. They would die for each other if necessary. Not happily, and it would be best avoided, but their lives belonged to each other. Every man and woman linked their fingers and raised them in a cry.

"Xià!"

Fourteen: The Battle for Shǎnxī

Sanjiadiǎncūn, Shǎnxī
Year 83: Year of the Snake
Two days after the spring equinox
24th March 1912 BCE

Chīyóu had briefed his leaders as best he could. That there was discomfort amongst those he addressed was clear, and his own condition was something less than tolerable. Reports were that the men were also in a poor state but that many of the boys seemed as fit and ready as they ever were. Nobody bothered to ask who had not eaten last night's food, but the younger lads had been bullied into handing over their shares for the second night running.

Although it was a few years since his last pitched battle, the King passionately believed in his ability to have this one over swiftly. The tactics were simple; even the most challenged of his troops should have no problem following the instructions. First would be the spear throw over the palisade, spear one followed by spear two. Next, the charge and the axe attack on the wooden wall would begin. Then they set about whoever remained alive inside.

Chīyóu had sent out twenty pairs of scouts the previous evening; one of each pair had stayed put at the top of the river cliff. The second scout returned to guide each company, leading them to the trails and taking them down the encampment and the river's edge.

If there was an element of genius in the plan, Chīyóu felt it was the disposition of the spear throwers. The youngest and weakest would be closest to the palisade fence to ensure their throws would clear the barricade. The oldest and the strongest would be further out. There was also an outer ring, which would comprise his elite. They would stand behind and around his army to prevent them from running away. The only weakness in the encirclement was on the side of the barrier facing the river, where the shortage of space meant there was only room for the boys between the barrier and the fast-flowing waters.

Only two of his leaders had questioned their role in proceedings; as was expected, they were Hú and Xí. After reminding him of their prophecies regarding the fog and the boys winning the battle, they were now asking to be positioned furthest downriver.

"And what about this bloody storm you were going on about? There's no sign of that, is there!"

"Yes, but Lord, the storm is to be the storm of spears descending on this pitiful camp," Xí answered.

"And…and…and the storm of your wrath against the foe!" Hú added.

"The prophecy was fog…storm…boys win. That's what you said, and I heard nothing about a storm of spears. Not once!"

"Sooth…sooth…sooth–"

"Spit it out, Hú!"

"Soothsaying is a fine art, my lord, and many prophecies may have more than one meaning."

"So, when you say the boys win, you might just mean the girls win?"

"We have no girls, my lord." Xí attempted to rescue the situation.

"I know we have no girls! I was trying…I give up! Why do you want to be on the downriver side?"

"To…to…to stop the boys escaping downriver." Hú stammered.

"To stop anyone escaping downriver, my lord. It would be an honour to serve you this way, regardless of the risks." Xí added.

"Alright! Agreed! Now go away!"

The march from the caves passed over flat land that was only lightly wooded. It was remarkable that everything had gone to plan, notwithstanding the dreadful noises and smells emitting from the behinds of most of the men. A few had stumbled into a stream; others had walked straight into trees; unbeknownst to Chīyóu, a few hundred more had taken the opportunity to slip away.

The lowest land was intermittently lost to sight with fog on the river. However, the scouts did their job. After slipping and sliding on the downslope, the King's force was in place in the bowl. The dense thorn bushes between the tracks had proved their most significant enemy so far. Most of the men quietly complained of cuts and scratches but did so in hushed tones. Chīyóu's army now surrounded the palisade. The structure seemed to slip in and out of the thick fog for all except those boys closest. Even more remarkably, the king's army was nearly silent, the stillness broken only by the sounds of flatulence. A far-off wolf howled, breaking the hush. Through the muffling effects of the fog, they could hear sounds of life stirring from within the fence.

Chīyóu's troops were close enough together for instructions to be relayed by touch. Gradually, his entire body of men and boys raised their first spear to a throwing position. Within a moment, the barked order came.

"Throw!"

At this point, it did appear as if a storm had descended on the fortification. Spears were launched from as little as ten paces and up to fifty. They rose and seemed to coagulate as a solid mass to plunge into the fort's interior. With unfortunate effect, only a handful of throws failed to reach the barricade. Some of the youngest children, those closest to the palisade, were struck from behind. Boys began screaming, but there was to be no break.

"Second spear! Wait for it!" Yet again, the wolf howled. "Throw!"

As the second bombardment of spears was launched, a sheet of arrows flew into the rear of the King's army. Thud! Thud! Thud! Screams erupted as man after man took a hit. Blood pumped from those few whose necks were punctured. Those taking shots to the back fell to their knees whilst those unscathed turned their heads, incomprehension written across their features as they peered into the semi-darkness.

The second sheet of arrows sliced through the throng almost before the second hail of spears had reached its objective. Of the outer ring, the elite force, not a man remained standing, the second volley of arrows having found their marks with remarkable accuracy. The archers remained in position, their lower halves protected in their foxholes. Not that there was any returning fire. The poorly equipped and unarmoured Lóngshān farmers were now exposed to the onslaught. Armed only with axes, they were disinclined to throw them back through, or over, their leaders. They were sitting ducks.

As the Lóngshān's second spear volley dropped behind the wall, the third flight of arrows thudded into the backs of more troops and the fronts of those who had turned. The Xià's bronze-tipped missiles were designed with sharp barbs, making them almost impossible to remove and slightly blunted tips, maximising internal damage. Their targets were well-defined - lungs and heart. Anything else was either a mistake or through necessity. A single well-directed arrow, fired from fewer than forty paces, could penetrate a torso from back to front, the tip coming to rest on the inside of the frontal leather body armour of the elite troops. One hit to the heart would kill, one through the lungs would disable, and a pair would put the victim on the floor and render him unable to fight back.

In some respects, those Lóngshān troops closer to the palisade were more fortunate; they at least had the opportunity to lie down before being hit. It saved a few, but for most, the carnage around them mounted higher and higher. There was not a man or boy present who did not have the taste of a comrade's blood in his mouth before the slaying began to slow. As the sky lightened, the devastation became fully apparent. The king's attempt at a hail of spears had hit its target, but the few Xià within the protective fence had been well-protected.

The storm of arrows created by the Xià had far surpassed the intensity of the Lóngshān tactic. Most of Yú's archers had gone through twelve of their twenty lethal darts before the wolf howled for the third time. They had fired over two thousand arrows in the time it would take to count to one hundred. Many of their opponents lay dead or dying with three sets of flights jutting from their backs.

As the sun rose and the fog dissipated, the palisade gate swung open to reveal twenty armed and unharmed defenders. A ring of one hundred and eighty Xià men and women holding aimed and loaded bows descended the slope, joining their colleagues and forming a tight circle around those attackers remaining on their feet. They now comprised only some five hundred boys and perhaps as few as one hundred men. To approach the defeated, Yú's clan had to clamber over the twisted bodies of the injured and slain. The stink of blood and guts and piss and shit was suffocating.

Those who were damaged but not already dead were despatched, heads clubbed with blunt axes or a dagger slashed across the throat. The screams of the injured men and those calling for mercy gradually diminished as they were released from their pain by the swift death. It was a mercy killing for most of the victims, and while it was not immediately welcomed, it hastened what would have been a long and drawn-out passing from blood loss or infection.

Of the encircled boys and men, those still living dropped to one knee, casting their axes aside. A few attempted to scramble up the bank, but several arrows simultaneously took them out. One boy ran towards the river and received the same treatment. Terror was etched on every blood-splattered face, and several of the youngsters were weeping. The majority were in shock; all knew their lives were no longer in their own hands if they ever had been. Wary eyes watched as the encircling archers closed in on them, watched as they despatched the wounded and watched for any possibility of escape. It seemed there was none.

As they waited to die, from the riverbank to the southwest came the sound of two bulky objects falling into the river. Hú and Xí had succeeded where no others had dared. To the astonishment of the defeated, the archers allowed them to escape without fuss.

Sanjiadiăncūn had been turned from a pleasant bowl on the side of the Fèn River to a killing field. As the skies cleared completely and the sun lightened the area further, the true extent of the slaughter was apparent, as were the odds that had been overcome. The Xià had only suffered the odd injury, whereas over a thousand Lóngshān had died.

No one counted the corpses, and it seemed that no one considered the individual deaths worthy of investigation. However, there was one corpse the Xià wished to identify, that being King Chīyóu. When they found what they suspected was his body, a pair of the Lóngshān men quickly confirmed it. His death had been undeservedly swift; a single arrow had entered the back of his neck and into his brain. Not a single member of his own army would have wanted him to die that way; a grislier end would have been preferred.

Fifteen: The Aftermath

Sanjiadiǎncūn, Shǎnxī
Year 83: Year of the Snake
Two days after the spring equinox
24th March 1912 BCE

Yú had to address the defeated as quickly as possible. He ordered a cart drawn out from within the palisade. It was little more than a two-wheeled trolley set against the external wall for him to stand on. He was aware of the risk, which was higher than he considered acceptable, but Girl had urged him forward, insisting it would work.

The contrast between the faces of his clan and those of the defeated army was stark. There were smiles, grins and handshakes from the Xià and only sullen scowls, grimaces, and genuine fear on the visages of what was left of Chīyóu's army. It was a fear Yú wanted to remove, for a scared beast remains dangerous. Much better to disarm them mentally rather than physically.

"I want you..." He raised his voice to a shout. "I want you, both men and boys, to pick up your axes and come here." The defeated looked around apprehensively. "I want you to pick up your axes. I want you to come and form a close ring around me. I want you to come and listen!"

"How do we know it's not a trick?" A boy's voice hollered back from the mass.

"What's your name, boy?" Yú aimed his question in the approximate direction of the shout.

"Bóyì!"

"Well, Bóyì, you come here with your axe. Come and stand on this platform with me. Come on!"

The lad slipped through the crowd, approaching Yú with unusual confidence.

"What if you kill me?"

"I am unarmed. You have an axe. Come on. Come up here."

The boy paused for several moments before striding toward the cart, taking Yú's hand and leaping onto its load bed. There was little room for the two of them due to the number of spears embedded; it had proved an effective shield a little earlier.

"Bóyì. Well met. I am Yú." He dropped his voice to a whisper. "All I want to do is to talk to these men and boys. I want them to join me. I do not want them dead. I know that life in Táosì has not been good; in fact, I know it has been awful. I am not your enemy, Bóyì. I am your friend."

"Say you!" The boy shifted from foot to foot, avoiding direct eye contact.

"Yes…say me! I will ask your people what they want, and then I will offer them more than they want. Let's work it out. I need to talk to them, and I need them closer than this. You can get them to do it." Yú gently placed his hand under the boy's chin, looking him directly in the eye. "You can. It's simple, really. What do you want most right now?"

"Some food."

"And then?"

"To sleep…to sleep safely."

"And what do you think they want?"

"The same…they're hungry, and they're tired, and they're fed up with being bullied!"

"Well, in that case, tell them we're going to get them fed, tell them they will have the chance to rest and tell them that no one will bully them. You can say all that."

"I can?"

"You can!"

Bóyì turned to the mess of boys and began passing subtle messages into the gathering, signalling for them to come in and sit. He followed up by doing the same to the remaining adults from the army, and although it was with a great deal more reluctance, they eventually joined the semicircle arranged around the cart. Yú's troops formed an outer ring, still alert with weapons at the ready, each grinning from ear to ear.

"First, I would like to introduce you to someone." Yú beckoned his wife to join him. "This is Túshānshì, my partner. She will speak to you first. Túshānshì…"

Shock rippled across the seated mass. There were several aspects to the surprise, although one key to it was that they had never heard of a woman addressing a crowd of men. When the female ascended the temporary stage, the defeated men and boys fell dead silent, stunned by her absolute beauty, so stunned they momentarily forgot they had even been in a battle. Each leaned forward to stare and catch any word that might be cast in their direction. In addition, it was clear that this woman had been in the thick of the fighting, like themselves. She was smeared with dirt, blood and sweat, her long hair matted and unkempt, but even in such a state, she possessed an aura that radiated.

"Gentlemen." Túshānshì's voice was clear and loud enough to reach even those at the back. She oozed confidence. There was no doubting when she spoke, it was with command. "Gentlemen. Yú has something to say to you. When he is done, we will have a break." There was a small cheer at which she smiled. "Unfortunately, after that, when the sun is highest in the sky, we have some work to do. We will have to ensure we have food, bedding, and fire, and we will have to dispose of those poor comrades of yours who have fallen in the battle. We will speak again at midday when you again gather around this point with me."

Túshānshì jumped from the cart, winking at Yú as she passed him. "Your turn, Yú!"

Yú firmly believed that this would be the most important speech he had ever made. If he was nervous, he also knew it was essential to maintain a confident demeanour; he glanced at his wife to gain confidence before commencing.

"Friends! I call you friends, for that is what we will be. Just moments ago, with spears and arrows flying, you may have considered us your enemy, but we were never that. We are friends you have not seen for a long time. We are the friends who have come back to whisper in your ears and help you overcome your problems. We are the friends who will walk hand in hand with you, and in doing so, we will create a new future, a brighter future, a future where every one of us may hold our heads high.

"It is not the role of friends to simply laugh and pretend there are no problems. It is not the role of friends to agree with all your views. It is the role of friends to make you happier, not just today, not just tomorrow, but for all your tomorrows. That is why we offer our outstretched hands right now. And…" Yú laid his bow and dagger on the cart, "To demonstrate what I mean, in real terms, I would ask the ladies and gentlemen who have fought with me and against you to lay down their weapons." Yú's clan complied immediately, without any sign of dissent, although it left them outnumbered three to one, with the force they had been fighting still holding their weapons.

"Now…please be seated. If you wish to keep your axes in your hands, you may do so. If you wish to lay them beside you, you may do that instead." Although there was general unease, eventually, the remainder of Chīyóu's army, boys and men, were seated with their weapons by their sides. There was no sense of panic; in fact, there was a growing interest in the circumstances. The man addressing them had something they had not come across before. His charisma kept their attention, not the fear of a lash, which was the more usual circumstance.

"Friends, the first thing I would like to address are any complaints about this morning's battle. I will need some of you to speak up, but you may do so through Bóyì, here, if you wish."

An older man towards the rear stood.

"You fired into our backs. I have two questions. Where did you come from, and is that fair?" He remained standing whilst awaiting the answers.

"In response to the first of your questions, my troops were hidden in foxholes they had dug. After your army passed them, they removed the cover and had perfect shots at the rear of your army. You asked if it was fair. Yes, it was. We were outnumbered ten to one and would have lost a head-to-head battle. We could not afford to lose.

"However, what I would ask you to do is to look around. Admittedly, you were one of the lucky ones, but of your army, who was saved and who died?"

The older man did not need to look. "The children were saved. Many of us workers died. And it looks to me as if all our leaders were killed. Wiped out."

101

"Indeed! If you could have asked for one of those three groups to be protected, which would you have chosen, the leaders, the workers or the children?"

Now, the older man did look around him. "I would have saved the children." He sat promptly, not wishing for more attention.

"Now, I have a question for you." Yú was warming to his task. "When you set out from Táosì, which group would you have most liked to see hammered into the dirt? Would it be us, the Xià? Would it be the kids? Would it be the workers? Or would it be your leaders? Who has inflicted the most harm on you during your lives?"

A murmur started from the centre of the area where the children sat. Very swiftly, it became louder and rhythmic. Soon, it became overpowering, two words repeated over and over again. By the time the older men had joined in, it was a roar.

"Our leaders! Our leaders! Our leaders!"

Yú allowed the chant to continue, but before they reached the point where their volume would naturally diminish, he raised both hands. The noise subsided rapidly until only the single faltering voice of a little boy could be heard, until he, too, was encouraged into an embarrassed silence by a hand on his shoulder.

"Bóyì. In your experience, have your leaders ever stood before you, unarmed, when you all carried weapons?" Yú placed a protective arm around the young man's shoulder.

"Never."

"And why would that be?"

"Because they believed we would kill them."

"Would you have done so?"

"I don't kn...possibly...maybe." He looked for encouragement from the gathering.

"Yessssss!" It was a whisper, but one emanating from some six hundred mouths. It took the shape of a wraith as it wrapped around the natural bowl.

"Boys, you are the winners of this battle...the real winners. To the winners go the spoils and the rights.

"Bóyì. I will kneel here unprotected. Hold your axe ready to strike. That's it. I am a leader; I will be your leader if you give me a chance. So, here is the question. Are you going to take this chance to kill me?" Yú bowed his head, exposing the back of his neck. "What is it to be, Bóyì?"

"Noooooo!" This time, it was more of a groan from the gathering, but it dramatically increased in volume until Bóyì allowed his axe to slide to the floor. Yú stood and offered his hand to the young man, which was grasped firmly. A faint smile crossed Bóyì's countenance, although, within seconds, it had become a grin.

"Sir?"

"Bóyì, my name is Yú; please use it!"

"Yú. We have many grievances in Táosì. May we bring them to you?"

"You may, Bóyì, and we will ensure everyone's grievances are heard. However, this must wait until after we have travelled back to your city, and we have something of a mess to clear up here before we can head in that direction.

"Men of Táosì! I am going to make you three promises. These are not prophecies. These are promises." There was absolute silence within the bowl. Around them, the crows had begun to find their voices in the trees atop the slopes.

"Firstly, in a few years, you will never go hungry!" There was an appreciative roar.

"Secondly, you will be living in warmer climes!" Whilst there was some slight confusion, another cheer followed.

"And thirdly, you will live in a society where there are as many women as men, and if you live good lives, you may just find a girl who wants to marry you!" The third cheer bounced around the bowl, sustaining itself as if it would never end until Yú raised his arms again. Quite out of the blue, a single voice pierced the now silent air.

"And what do we have to give you?"

"You give me nothing." Yú stepped into the crowd. "It is not for me to take your gifts. You will give to yourselves, your culture, and your society. I come to take nothing. I am here to give. Together, if we are all giving, no one needs to take. Is this not true?"

There was nodding amongst many in the crowd, although some of the younger boys appeared somewhat bewildered.

"If you had asked me what you might have to give up, I might have given you a different answer. To rid yourself of hunger, to rid yourself of cold, and to rid yourselves of this ridiculous male-orientated and woman-hating society you have found yourselves in, you will have to give something up. You will have to give up Táosì."

"Who should we give it to?" Another lone voice piped across the gathered heads.

"You will give it to the gods. You will give it to your families. You will give it to your ancestors. For after you, no one after you will call Táosì home. History has run its course for that city; its race is run; it has no future.

"Your futures will be forged in a new settlement to the southeast of here, some twenty days march. Your future will be in your own hands. To choose a job, choose a home, choose a lifestyle, choose a partner, and choose whether to have children.

"To achieve this, Táosì must end, both as a city and as a way of life. It is a disgusting, debased and diabolical society. You have always deserved better, and now you will have the choice!"

Yú allowed the noise to rise to a sustained crescendo. After waving and smiling broadly at the assembly, he backed out of the crowd as they began to stand. As he entered the palisade, he turned to his wife.

"How did I do?" was his first question of Túshānshì. Her only response was to kiss him gently on the forehead and run her hand through his shaggy hair.

Between Yú completing his oratory and the sun hitting its zenith, the defeated broke into groups to discuss his words. There had been the odd man who thought he might ignore Túshānshì's earlier instruction, but the few were soon put in their place by the many. They were all hungry, filthy, and tired. Many had gut problems that meant excessive flatulence and repeated trips into the sparse vegetation. Dehydration was their biggest concern, although solutions were at hand as their victors delivered more and more water vessels. Notwithstanding their catastrophic defeat, the overwhelming emotion was one of hope. It was a long-term hope that most had not known in their entire lives.

Fifteen: The Aftermath

There was also a short-term hope: to hear Túshānshì speak to them again. Whatever chores she was to dish out, they were prepared for a life of hard labour to keep her happy and to hear her voice again.

The division of labour was conducted by a small council of the defeated in conjunction with Yú's wife. All booty was removed from the dead, whatever their rank, ranging from the jewelled jerkin of a lord to a simple stone axe from a child. The children's bodies were buried carefully in the now redundant foxholes, and the workers' bodies in a mass grave at the base of the downslope. At Yú's request, they cast their leaders' bodies into the river, each left with a single arrow in their back. Yú told them it would be a signal to a group he said was bringing food.

Another squad demolished the leeward half of the fort, which was used as firewood to prepare campfires for an evening meal. Yet another went off to bring the cooks into the fold. It was even more important to rescue and clean the cooking gear. Another band collected the discarded weaponry, creating a massive stockpile of armaments. The booty and the arms were all piled on carts. Only individuals with insufficient clothing were allowed to take items for themselves.

As the battle site cleared, it became evident that a circle had formed around one of the deceased, a circle of inattention, as the object at its centre was studiously ignored. They had feared him in life, and it seemed it was the case in death also. Chīyóu lay face down with a single arrow in the back of his neck. As none of the men of Táosì would go near him, it fell to members of the Xià clan to strip the body and relieve the corpse of its ornaments and weapons. The King's body was dragged to the top of a riverside mound, slightly north of the camp, and thankfully downwind. The widespread consensus was that the toppled king would feed the assembled buzzards and crows.

Before sundown, all that remained of Chīyóu were those bones too big for the birds to carry. When a loud call came from the south, the focus shifted away from the dissection of his body; it would never return.

Yú had been right about the message. Sauntering along the riverbank came a fur-clad individual. He appeared to lead a flock of sheep numbering more than anyone could count. When the sheep had gathered in the bowl, several more herders hove into view, dressed identically to the first.

105

They called themselves the Xīwǎ and sometimes the children of the Qíjiā, but there was little time for folks to get to know them as they were ushered into a meeting with Yú and a handful of the Xià. It was clear that the animals were either a gift or a trade. The intent was to feed the large assembly that night and to facilitate their journey back to Táosì.

The Xīwǎ were toasted repeatedly that evening. Many were interested in the Xīwǎ leader's name, Kànménrén. Depending on how you looked at it, it meant either the 'gatekeeper' or the 'gaoler'. It was fortunate that most interpreted it as the former.

For Girl, the most satisfying news from her father was that he had captured Hú and Xí. The pair had already been dispatched in the direction of Èrlǐtou. Kàn described the branding he had inflicted on his prisoners with some satisfaction. He had drawn the symbol in the dirt as he explained how it covered their backs.

Few saw the Xīwǎ herders slip off that evening; most were too absorbed in demolishing the sheep carcases. Those that did would have noticed they left with a bucket of bronze arrowheads and another of spearheads. It seemed a trifling price for the banquet that fed so many that night, and it might have crossed the minds of a few more astute individuals that the bronze weapons were merely a down payment for something much, much bigger.

Sixteen: The Transformation
Táosì, Shǎnxī
Year 83: Year of the Snake
Twenty-three days to summer solstice
29th May 1912 BCE

Táosì had changed.

It was not just that the cold northern winds had disappeared or that the frosts were now over. It was not that the sun had moved into that phase of providing comfort rather than the pallid orb of winter. It was not the light rains that now swept in every other day, replenishing the water butts and the irrigation channels. These were all cyclical occurrences.

Táosì had been turned inside out.

There were now animals grazing within the city walls, where there had once been a patchwork of graveyards, industrial areas, housing, the palace compound, and so forth. During the daytime, there was a peculiar absence of people. If one were to stand atop the walls and look outwards in any direction, it was clear where the people had gone and what had become of them. The population of Táosì, near its entirety, was occupied in the town's fields. Planted arable land now extended two thousand paces in all directions.

Seed stock had not dictated the limits to the planted fields, although these had been barely sufficient. They had been determined entirely by the amount of dung dug out of the town. It was a job that Hòutú had taken to organising with the enthusiasm of a young child.

For the first time in over fourteen years, Hòutú considered herself happy. Whilst shit-shovelling occupied much of her time, it was not her most important job. The observatory, now restored to a workable condition, meant her sightings had given her the confidence to dictate the planting times for the foxtail millet and wheat.

107

It was more challenging to determine what degradation of the night soil was acceptable before moving it to the fields. The people of Táosì had grown used to human effluent piled up next to their houses, and perhaps it offered them some resistance to the maladies that often seemed to reside in the waste. Transporting cart after cart of human waste required superhuman effort. On the return journeys, the wheeled contraptions brought in any potential animal fodder that had remained in a reasonable condition over the winter.

There had been no carts in Táosì for a lifetime, and the novelty value was extreme. Most were pulled by teams of people, many of whom had been enthusiastic initially. The excitement faded after a few days on the yoke, after which the volunteers would cast jealous stares at the two vehicles dragged by bullocks.

It was a new moon that night and the end of their exertions. The following week was allocated to rest, a concept as welcome as it was unexpected. It was Hòutú who would give the call for them to return from the fields for their holiday week. She idly fingered the bronze mirror she would use for the signal. One side of the disk was highly polished and reflective; the other displayed the symbol of the Motherland in bas-relief. It had been a gift from the townspeople to recognise imprisonment and sacrifice. Although she might shout at the top of her voice, it would not carry to the furthest fields, but the blink of reflected sunlight would do the job if the workers were alert.

The individuals toiling to complete their tidying up, weeding and the firming down of fertiliser did not have the label of workers. They were working, but they included all the members of Yú's clan. The boys who had fought against them bent their backs; most of the imprisoned females and their gaolers from the quarries made up the rest. All worked together with a common purpose. Amongst them, Yú and the master archer strained their backs as an example to others. Whilst there were divisions of labour, one did not afford any more status than another. Their efforts were for a common cause and the common good.

Hòutú turned her attention within the city. There, a few individuals tended the stock. Goats were corralled in the expanses of the graveyards, the pigs in the industrial area, and pheasants in a few scattered courtyards. The walls that had previously divided urban functions now kept the animals apart.

Far in the distance, she could make out the cattle grazing in the re-walled Altar of Earth, which was a far better use than it had previously served. Her next task was determining where all the cow manure would be stored. It would probably be best in the Zhong Liang Gully, which had the advantage of being on the leeward side of the town during summer and was already the location for depositing the daily nightsoil.

In the observatory grounds themselves, the recently introduced chickens pecked around. They were particularly fond of the area around Hòutú's mother's new grave. Hòutú had thought it was fitting to move her remains here. She felt the Lake Tài chickens would have made her mother smile. For a moment, she allowed a small fantasy from her homeland to bury the practical thoughts that had dominated every waking moment since Yú's arrival in the city.

It was always the same: swept off her feet by a strong, handsome, and caring man. Carried to her marital bed and swamped in an arousing, passionate embrace. Her hero, her lover, her husband, and the father of her unborn children. The vision gripped her, and her thighs and belly tightened in excitement. Then it was gone and replaced by Chīyóu's slobbering face and the thrusting genitals of too many paying visitors to her prison cave. She was unable even to recall the beautiful Niúláng and his gentle kiss. Too many moons had passed since then.

When they had opened her mother's earth tomb, little remained of her flesh, and her clothing proved to be no more than a bag of bones. There was little to mourn over. However, the lacquered staff had been buried with her, clear evidence that Hú and Xí had no idea how to use it or its significance. Unlike the body, the pole showed only slight deterioration, and it felt like it hummed in her hands.

The staff was more than significant, its value being far more practical than any layman might think. Used in conjunction with items from her cave, it was power. This staff had allowed her to accurately foretell the seasons using the gaps in the observatory walls. That Hú and Xí had understood the extent of the shamanic power was true. The pair failed to grasp that the power lay rooted in science rather than magic. The two men had attempted to overturn the order of the Sisterhood without any suitable replacement. It was odd, for they had always relied on the knowledge of natural lore residing within that body.

Without science, they depended upon captive shaman. Without captive shaman, they had no power. It was no wonder they had demanded the complete subjugation of women but further demonstrated their limited understanding if they believed they could force cooperation. Hú and Xí were only the latest in a long line; it was hoped that the only reason they might stand out would be that they proved to be the last of their kind.

Hòutú now knew why the pair had been spared, although it pained her that they still lived, even so. Her daughter's final prophesy had been incorrect, for they lived. A false prophecy brought no good to the Sisterhood's reputation; it was best if no one learned of it. She supposed she might accept that they were allowed to live if the Sisterhood could manipulate the two men as they intended. However, the very thought of it made her scars itch terribly.

To utilise the staff, Hòutú had to unearth the *bi* and *cóng*, which were kept buried in the sandpit where Tú had her writing lessons. The bi was a flat disk with carvings on either side and a hole through the centre. Her cóng was a more complex object, a roughly squared-off outer shape, this one taller than most, with a cylindrical inner tube, which tapered towards the centre but extended from top to bottom. It was a rare household that did not have a matching pair.

If every household had one, it did not mean that every family had any idea of what they were. And that had been the point. *Cóngs* and *bis* were the training shapes that jade artisans used for their apprenticeship; few were top-notch. On the other hand, Hòutú's *cóng* and *bi* were perfect, although they were pretty simple in design. It had become the ultimate tool in hiding; who would ever attempt to search for a single, specific grain in a field full of rice?

The observatory may not have been a work of art, as Tú had pointed out, but it was an accurate scientific tool. When placed in the central dais, the unique jade pieces and staff gave an accurate "eyepoint" to look through each of the gaps in the observatory. The northernmost sighting indicated the direction of sunrise at the summer solstice, and the southernmost slit at sunrise on the winter solstice. Nine further openings divided the year into twenty periods; these related directly to successful farming around the town. Nine days before, the last seeds had gone in. It would be time to switch from irrigation to drainage in ten days as the rains increased their intensity.

In addition, markings in the jade *bi* could be aligned on the *cóng* to forecast planetary positions. There were five keys: the observatory, the staff, the *cóng*, the *bi* and Hòutú. If all five keys were used correctly, they opened the skies to interpretation. If used in conjunction with news from the pigeons, the year's timetable could be adjusted for the practical considerations of weather and flooding, which were not always dependent upon the celestial objects. Even the great sun could occasionally be temporarily overpowered by a torrential weather system.

That was complacent thinking; it was silly of her. She had made a mistake; there were now six keys. Tú had joined the party and would soon replace her. Tú! She knew so much, but she knew so little. She was young; would she be able to keep the impudence of youth in check? When would she acquire some social skills to prevent her mouth from beating her brain in any race to respond? Was she ready? Hòutú knew the answer, and the answer was no.

Hòutú considered the seventh slot, the one that marked the spring equinox. That would have been the day before she and Tú came out of their cave, when the city had been abandoned, and they became ingloriously drunk. The final two blocks of the ancient structure had been added later than the others; they were slightly out of line but provided more finesse to the high season deadlines as the crops matured.

All the details of the astronomical farming calendar were consigned to memory. Even that could be regarded as incorrect; perhaps memories was a better term, as Tú also had perfect recall of the system. And that was the weakness. That is what had brought Táosì's agriculture to its knees. It was not just the failure of the stone monopoly but a failure to listen to those who held the information. Hòutú considered, not for the first time, that it should perhaps now be recorded if only to avoid charlatans such as Hú and Xí from making things up.

Across the fields to the city's north, Yú was the first to catch the flash from the bronze mirror. Like everyone else, he looked forward to the feasting and the first day of the holiday. He wiped his hands, toughened from six weeks in the fields, and called to those working with him. Smiles,

111

grins, and whoops of joy followed his call. The day had been a tidying-up exercise, not too much hard work, and most had eased up as they realised their tasks were all but completed.

Hòuyì, the master archer, waved from two fields over. He had been inspirational in selling the new concepts to his men. As the only part of Chīyóu's army that had remained undefeated, other than the cooks (although they preferred not to have it mentioned), the archers had always had the potential to upset the applecart. Being well-armed, having had many of their comrades perish at the Battle of Sanjiadiǎncūn and then losing what they had considered status were all factors capable of sparking a nascent rebellion. Hòuyì had worked them away from it.

Many of the archers were further afield right now and were combining their excellent prowess with the bow with a steep learning curve in pastoral management. Their task was to cull male animals for the pot and herd female goats, sheep, and deer back to the city; their greater success had been with the culling rather than the herding, but they were learning.

Falling into step with Yú as he strode from the fields was Bóyì. With absolute certainty, he had become the spokesman of the remaining boys. They admired his courage and his thoughtfulness. It was an admiration that Yú shared with the lads. Bóyì was of an age with Tú and had encouraged her to involve herself with more people, a task that could be likened to pulling a particularly obstinate snail from its shell. Together with Túshānshì, he had spent long nights in disguised discussion on various aspects of social etiquette, and although progress was slow, there was progress.

Surprisingly, for it seemed they had most to gain, the women of Táosì objected most to the changes. An inherent reticence, instilled by hundreds of years of persecution, had made it difficult for them to assume their expected equal roles. Túshānshì had spent many hours in meetings, trying to break down the barriers they constructed against progress, but the deep disquiet in the group meant there had been little success. Gradually, a few of the younger girls had been persuaded, although they were few, as female births had dropped precipitously in previous decades. At the bottom of more than a few postholes could be found the skeletons of girl children given to the gods rather than brought up in the wretched life that Táosì had offered a female.

Even after all Túshānshì's pleading, with carefully directed assistance from Hòutú, they had not been able to prevent the women from setting up and cooking that evening's meal. They simply could not escape the preconceptions that held them in servitude. As the women were the largest group in Táosì, they needed to have representation at the council meetings; so far, the best they had managed was for Hòutú to appoint a couple of wiser heads. However, it was with reluctance that they attended the meetings and never spoke.

There was to be a feast that night, although there was a severe food shortage. The great storage jars of grain had been depleted. All the seed stock was gone, planted for next autumn's harvest. While they were breeding stock as fast as possible, these things took time, especially for meat animals to come to size.

That evening, it had been the fate of Chīyóu's hunting dogs to come under the axe. There were fifty-odd scraggy animals, which had spent no time hunting and two months of eating every scrap they could get their jaws around. Even so, a single dog would feed ten at most. Two hundred dogs may have sufficed, but not fifty. Therefore, it was with some excitement that, as the people streamed back to town, they could spy a dust column rising in the west, about half the distance to the river. It was the keen-sighted Bóyì who reacted first.

"That's sheep! Yú, they'll eat the seedlings. We've got to stop them!"

"Easy, easy! They're not at the farmland yet; if we run and shout, we'll scare and scatter them. Best we get to the edge of the planted land and then form a funnel into the city. Let's do it! Nice and quiet." It seemed Yú had forestalled a big disaster, also ensuring mutton would be on the menu tonight until the familiar faces of a band of Xīwǎ hove into sight.

The lead rider drew level with Yú, reining in his horse.

"That's a thousand sheep there, Yú. Happy?" Kànménrén chuckled. "The last before autumn. Any more, and we'll go hungry. How's it going?" The Xīwǎ leader dismounted, walking alongside his business partner.

"It's good, Kàn, good. Everything is working out. Food is short, very short. We have a holiday feast today, so your timing is perfect."

"It's only what we agreed, Yú. They'll start to ask about these woolly gifts soon. You know you'll have to open up to them."

"The plan is for a meeting tomorrow. That's when it all comes out - when their bellies are full. Best if you were gone by then just in case there is any anger."

"Ah! You should be able to control that, Yú, a man with your smile. You and Túshānshì could persuade the gods to open the doors of heaven, even for me! Where's the problem?"

"Me and Túshānshì hail from Sìchuān."

"So?"

"Well, my friend, they're not always comfortable with outsiders up here, more than you might like to think."

"True! But if that's all—"

"No. The other problem is that I'm a man."

"Yes."

"Well, it's fine to be a man up here, but it is quite another thing when they think I am a man controlled by women!"

"Isn't every man? Remember that, Yú."

"I don't think they trust the Sisterhood, Kàn. Not really. They look at the slide in Táosì's fortunes and cannot help but feel the Sisterhood failed them. Perhaps they are right. Perhaps this plan will not work."

"If this plan does not work, Yú, it is more than you and I who will fail. Our children's futures will be gone, and their children's, into the damning mists of uncertainty."

"That might be the problem…some people do not want a certain future."

Seventeen: The Speech

Táosì, Shǎnxī: Palace Hall
Year 83: Year of the Snake
Twenty-two days to the summer solstice
30th May 1912 BCE

Last night's feast had been magnificent. Everyone had gathered in the palace compound, and some hundred cooking fires had warmed the evening air. The arrival of the massive number of sheep had provided unexpected work. Extracting over a hundred animals for the pot took time. Temporarily penning the remainder into the residential area took even longer. Such was the benefit that all had thrown their weight behind sorting the flock.

The gathering for the feast had allowed different groups to nominate their representatives for a council meeting. Yú had initially been keen to have everyone in the city attend but had the impracticalities spelt out to him. He knew how to work a big crowd, but there was too much information to be disseminated. The women closest to him had convinced him of the need to address an audience of representatives.

Those women were Túshānshì, Hòutú, Tú and Girl. It was the fourth of the group that concerned Yú most. He had known her since she was a babe in arms but had never heard her name. He had watched her involvement with the senior women grow week by week, month by month and year by year, but even they referred to her as "Girl" or "the girl". She mystified and entranced Yú. When she spoke, it was with quiet authority. Quite obviously, the other female advisors looked up to her. Who she was, he knew. What she was, he did not. Yú had no clear idea of her role and sometimes even forgot who her parents were. She was confusing.

Each group of twenty citizens had nominated two individuals, the logic behind this being that when they returned to their groups, one could correct if the other made a mistake. Now, some two hundred and fifty

115

people crammed into the palace hall for the first meeting of the representatives. They would have been in the palace yard if the entire population had been present. As a light rain fell, everyone took comfort in the roof, even if it had seen better days. Once again, the women had chosen to sit slightly apart from other groups, although it was clear that some members were now mixing more freely.

Their total numbers had swelled somewhat. Some deserters had returned, some women's groups had come down from the hills, and a few nearby hamlets had determined to throw in their lot with the new regime. Nearly all had quickly adapted to the new social system. Those who had not had left or were cast out, although that had only happened twice.

There was a long list in Yú's head, and he had asked his wife to prompt him if he missed something or took things in the wrong order. In addition to the list were the responses to questions, which were even more complex. His inner circle had tossed some ideas around about teaching him to read, but he had been unsure what they meant and had not listened to the details. Tonight's address was to stretch his abilities to the limit.

Yú climbed onto the flatbed of a cart, to speak. It was the same cart he had stood on after the Battle of Sanjiadiǎncūn. Rips from spear points were still evident, although a few had filled with excrement on the trip from the cesspits to the fields. The smell threw him for a moment; he should have had the cart cleaned. Rising to his full height and putting on his warmest smile, Yú commenced.

"Friends! We are—"

"Yú. A point of order." It was gloomy in the hall, and Yú strained as he swept his eyes across the gathered throng and through the smoky air.

"Here. It is us!" Two females had stood, an island peak surrounded only by those of their gender. One was younger, and the other ancient. "I am here to speak for those of us who were imprisoned in the quarry."

An unanticipated silence engulfed the hall. All heads turned; this was a first and a shock.

"I would speak to the meeting." The younger woman had a powerful voice.

"Please. Please come up here." Yú indicated the cart.

116

"No. What is to be said will be said from here, for this is our voice, not my own."

"I will sit." Yú flopped down on the cart bed, his speech temporarily forgotten. He focused on the speaker and listened intently.

"I speak for all of us. Us women," the younger woman continued. The older remained standing beside her. "Perhaps I speak for more than those surrounding me in this spot. We shall see. Perhaps I also speak for some of the men. We shall see. But first, I will speak the words of the lady next to me. We have all agreed that this shall be done."

The older of the two threw back her headscarf, revealing greying hair. It was clear she had seen the passage of many years. Her wrinkled face remained impassive. The younger woman adopted a more oratorial pose and commenced.

"Do you know how many times I have been raped? No?

"I lost count after two hundred. That was when I was half my age.

"Do you know how many homes I have been thrown out of? No?

"Too many to count. Each was taken once I had improved it.

"Do you know how many nights I have gone hungry? No.

"Most of the nights I have spent on this earth!

"Do you know how many children I have borne? No!

"Some ten children!

"Do you know how many of them still live? No!

"None! All were healthy. All should have lived." The younger woman raised her arms to use her fingers as counters.

"Four of my boys were killed by the lords who came before Chīyóu. Three girls, I buried beneath my house posts, having smothered them first. One girl reached near her teenage years when the Princes Hú and Xí summoned her; she never returned. Two more boys grew to adulthood and lost their lives in the Battle of Sanjiadiǎncūn."

The silence in the audience persisted, but there were nods of recognition amongst many of the women and children. Some of the men shook and hung their heads.

"I may have seen ten children come and go, but I have seen nearly seventy years pass me by. Mine has been a hard life. There has been no rest from the wickedness.

117

"That is my story," said the younger woman, indicating her partner, "That is her story. She asks you to look at her!"

The ageing woman turned her toothless face this way and that so all would recognise her before speaking herself. When she did, her voice was soft. She was short of breath, but still, it carried the fixated audience.

"I want so much more for you…there is no more for me. I will die before the next harvest. Little matters to me anymore. But it matters to you.

"I will say no more. But there is more to be said." The older woman was helped to a seated position by those around her. The younger of the two spoke again.

"Many women in this room could have spoken those words. Many! Now, I speak for us all. We all have our histories bottled up within our souls; for some, they will never be uncorked; we will die with our anger.

"We have listened to the ideals espoused by Yú. We have heard, and we have discussed them. There are admirable aspects to what he has outlined. We understand that Yú should be speaking now and outlining what may be all our futures. We know this is important.

"More than any of you, the women of Táosì have prayed for a better life and have actively worked to improve things here. We have failed. In only one respect have we succeeded, which is to be more united in our determination to make a better life.

"The result is that we were united in our misery.

"Then into our lives comes a new force, a young man, a man full of kindness, and the Xià, a group we admire before any other. A wonderful man and a beautiful people. Who would not wish to be a part of their idyllic future? Every one of us would wish it could be so.

"Yet, you must sense our reticence. Why are there doubts when it seems the future is golden? Why should we not rush headlong into this paradise on offer?

"It is this we are here to discuss. It is this that holds us back. It is this for which we need answers.

"Táosì has existed for hundreds of years. We all know the tales. It was a city of wealth, a city of fairness, and whilst it was certainly not a city of equality, for there were always them in the palace, them in those

118

big houses," she pointed westwards, "and us in the poor quarter!" Laughter erupted around the hall as the woman paused and smiled for the first time.

"Yes! That's you and me that it is - down in the poor quarter!"

Quite clearly, she had the absolute attention of all in the audience. Her voice was melodic and even captivating, and it was evident she had either a natural ability for public speaking or had been exceedingly well trained. It also became clear that she had an exceptional grasp of the reasons for the socio-economic factors that had led to the present situation.

"We understand that the decline in the stone monopoly has been a fundamental cause of Táosì's decline. A smaller population in the region has led to lesser demand for our tool production. Combine that with alternative products coming into the market, products over which we have no control, and it is completely understandable why things have slipped so badly."

Some of the younger members of the audience were becoming a little restless as she expounded on her theories, but the adults soon hushed them.

"When a society is faced with intolerable economic stresses, it is beholden on the leaders of that society to act. It is a given that they are responsible for finding ways to alleviate the miseries caused by a decline in a single industry. The kings and their nominated officers have signally failed in their responsibilities. There has been no replacement. There has been no consideration of trade deals that could have resulted in our being more successful in producing bronze." She paused to scan the faces.

"Instead…what have we had? I ask you, think, what have we had?

"Instead of proactive leadership, one that would have taken us down alternative routes, we have had an elite who have only protected their own concerns. I have grown poorer by the day. Most of you have become poorer, week by week, month by month, and year by year. This has persisted for longer than any of our lifetimes. We workers, who comprise the most significant percentage of the population, have suffered and suffered. During this time, few suffered more than us women, but it is relative. You men here, you boys, you have suffered too. Men! The only thing that makes you think you are not doing so badly is that you have done better than the women. Or so it seems.

"In terms of wealth and rights, men have been better off than women. But! But compare your state today to that of your fathers and grandfathers and their fathers. You, too, are poorer. Much poorer!

"There is only one group that maintained or even increased their wealth. One group that improved their status. Although that elevation perhaps only appeared to their eyes. A group that gave themselves more rights and did so by taking away ours.

"Are you aware that our leaders could rape, maim, and kill...at will? Are you aware they could rape, maim and kill without fear of punishment?

"There have been three sets of laws in this town:

"For one group, the only rule was they had to accept that anything, however terrible, could be done to them. The women!

"For another group, there were draconian rules to keep you in your place. The men!

"And finally, for the third group, there were no rules. No rules at all! You all know who that might be!

"Only one rule persisted, supposedly one to protect women, and that was the rule of fourteen. Just look at what that has done to us! It has been twisted against us so that women who would not wish to bring children into this degraded, debauched, and disgusting society are forced to try to do so every fourteen years as a means of self-protection. Why do you think so many women die in childbirth? They spend thirteen years giving themselves abortions and then hope to have a successful pregnancy. It doesn't work that way!

"And so, we were let down by our leaders. Is this not a reason to cast doubt on any male leader who might put his head above the parapet? And yet, we trust Yú. We trust him absolutely. He is a good man, a charming man, a kind man."

A sigh of relief rose from the assembly. It was a point on which all agreed. What was unclear was where this argument would go. As surely as the evil leadership had gone, so a new, saintly leadership had taken its place, and all the wrongs outlined in some detail would be righted. Undoubtedly, the problem was solved.

"I can see what you are thinking. And those thoughts are what we have been considering as well. Here is Yú, a good man who could convince anyone of anything. A man so good-looking, not one of us would not be happy for him to father our children or simply keep us warm at night!"

Laughter bounced around the hall. Seated on the cart, Yú blushed, his face dropped lower to avoid the stares. Túshānshì wrapped her arm around him protectively.

"So, if Yú is not the problem, what is?

"Well, there are two. The first is quite simple. It is the question of who will follow Yú when he has gone. No man lives forever; that much is clear.

"The second is extremely complicated, and I am afraid I will lose some of you. Please bear with me.

"There is another group in our society that wields some power. It is a group known to most of us women. It is a group about which some of you may have heard whispers. Unlike Yú, this group rarely puts its head above the parapet. Its highest profile may be seen with individuals you may have referred to as shaman." She pointed toward Hòutú, who sat with the womenfolk.

"Hòutú is a shaman, and her daughter Tú is trained to replace her. You have all seen her wisdom in the last few weeks. She has brought the observatory back to life. She has accurately forecast times for planting. She has supervised the much-needed fertilisation of our fields. Without her, we would still be in a mess, and undoubtedly, there would have been mass starvation over the coming winter season. As a shaman, she is a wonder!

"However, Hòutú is part of a bigger picture. She is one of the Sisterhood. It is the Sisterhood that has wielded covert power throughout the years. Much of their fight has been for good, of that there is no doubt. There is little doubt either that their intentions are honourable. Whilst we cannot argue their principles, what we can argue is their success." She paused, primarily to re-focus the crowd's attention.

"The point we wish to make…and make extremely clearly…is that the Sisterhood has failed!

"The Sisterhood has failed Táosì, they have failed women in society, and they have therefore failed our entire culture.

"If they were the force they claim to be, they would have prevented this decline. They would have ended the rapes. They would have stopped the deaths. They would have halted this rampant growth in inequality! Yet, they did not!

"You may ask how we know about the Sisterhood. You may ask how we know about the pigeon messages. You may ask how we know about their writing. Go on! Ask me?"

"How?" A single voice rose from the centre of the boy's group.

"How? Yes! How? I will tell you how!

"I was part of the Sisterhood. Several of the women here before you were part of the Sisterhood. You could say that we escaped the clutches of the Sisterhood!

"We left the Sisterhood because it was failing. We left the Sisterhood because it was misdirected. We left the Sisterhood because it did not protect us in our time of need. The Sisterhood is about the bigger picture; this we understand. However, the Sisterhood has forgotten that every big picture is made up of smaller ones, and I should point out that the smaller ones are falling apart.

"I am going to sit down in a moment. You have heard enough of my voice. Before I do, I will state the demands of the women gathered here. There are three of them:

"One. We accept Yú as our leader. However, we wish to ensure that his successor will be appointed by agreement from all of us. Inherent in this is that there will be an advisory council helping him make the right decisions. This brings me to:

"Two. We do not accept that the Sisterhood should form a majority on the leadership council. They may play a part but should be limited in their role. Implicit in this is a set of regulations, which leads me to:

"Three. There should be a set of rules which apply to everyone. These rules must be recorded and written down. It is beholden on us all to ensure that all can view and read them. For those unsure about the reading and writing parts of this, it will become apparent when you have been taught. Most significant in this third demand is that it makes it a requirement of the Sisterhood that they let go of their secrets; we should all be able to read, we should all be able to write, and we should all be able to use the farming observatory.

"When these demands are met, we will discuss the future. Yú, I apologise, but we will take no further part in your meeting tonight."

With that, she sat down. For a moment, there was silence before a ripple of applause began to jag out from the women's group. Like the approach of a fast-moving rain front, it gathered in volume, spreading to the entire assembled mass. Many applauded the speech's content. However, all praised the style and passion of its delivery. It had been an outrageous assault on their preconceptions and had them entranced.

As the applause diminished, the women gathered and rose to prepare to leave. Yú rose also.

"Stop. Stop, please, I beg you! Wait a moment." The women paused.

"I cannot thank you more for your contribution." Yú shook slightly. "Some of what you have said has horrified me. Some things scared me, and others I did not fully understand. Please appreciate that I cannot answer your questions right now; therefore, we will abandon our planned meeting. May we sit in this same group in three days, and I will try to answer your questions and demands? Meanwhile, I would encourage everyone to discuss what you have heard with the groups you represent. Let these words be heard widely and understood as fully as possible.

"Now…I do have a question. For the speaker. Yes, you. Please stand." Yú smiled broadly as the woman rose and stepped forward before her group.

"Well done, that was an amazing speech. What is your name?"

"May I answer with a question of my own?"

"You may!"

"What is her name?" The woman's arm and finger pointed ramrod straight at the girl tucked beside Túshānshì.

"But…my name is 'Girl'."

"Well, if that remains the case…then my name is 'Woman', and whilst you may have heard me roar, you have yet to feel my bite!"

Eighteen: The Secret Meeting

Táosì, Shǎnxī: Beneath the Palace Hall
Year 83: Year of the Snake
Twenty days to the summer solstice
1st June 1912 BCE

Girl was in a bind. She had successfully led Yú and Túshānshì back and forth and then led them to defeat Chīyóu at the Battle of Sānjiādiǎncūn. With Hòutú's assistance, she had reorganised Táosì and implemented a food programme. With her father's help, she had successfully arranged to relocate Hú and Xí. There was no doubt that life in Táosì was a hundred times better. That she was now facing defeat at the hands of the very people she had helped irked her beyond belief. Nothing had prepared her for this.

She felt alone. Her only confidantes were Hòutú and Tú, neither of whom had demonstrated disagreement with Woman's address three nights ago. In fact, they had actively applauded her speech. Girl questioned whether they could still be considered part of the Sisterhood.

With no one to ask, as both Grandmother and Mother were in transit, she was forced into making the decision alone. There were dilemmas within dilemmas. She could tell the truth about the Sisterhood's grander plans. She could partially explain the goals, keeping hidden the most sensitive parts of the scheme. She could stay quiet about the bigger picture.

In the first of these scenarios, she would have to reveal information that could assist the Lóngshān in disrupting or preventing the plan. In both of the last two, she would undoubtedly have to lose a degree of influence on the future of Táosì. She might even be exiled and lose all control. Although Táosì itself would lose its importance, the area it could control was crucial.

124

Eighteen: The Secret Meeting

Grandmother had been right about Girl; she was exceptionally intelligent. What she lacked was experience and someone to advise her. She needed wise counsel, and this need led her to a decision.

When Yú learned what they were asking for, he was worried. His wife had requested the meeting of a special council. His leading causes for concern were that such a group did not exist and would almost certainly not receive public support. She had been specific about the members, giving him further unease. If the group were to gather, it would be difficult to disguise. To date, all decisions had been made with much larger numbers, and he had already expressed reluctance in dealing with representative bodies. What was being proposed was an unrepresentative council. As far as Yú was concerned, he would prefer all Táosì to be present at all meetings to discuss all matters. He was aware that he received advice from smaller groups; however, as far as he was concerned, it was only through the acceptance of all that proposed policies should be adopted.

Yú had a secondary concern, one that was very personal. Although he gave the appearance of total confidence, he was periodically wracked by self-doubt. His public persona and ever-cheerful, positive outlook were little more than a mask, admittedly one he wore for most of his waking hours. Whilst he had no worries about his ability to put on a show, he suffered anxiety attacks regarding his actual ability to lead. If cracks appeared in his public support, he feared it might reflect in the bonhomie he had carefully cultivated. Yú knew he was an actor and knew he had been typecast. He did not believe in his ability to adapt to a less comfortable role.

An attempt to publicly bring together what amounted to a leadership council, without approval from the masses, could place him on a slippery slope, both public and personal. He desperately needed wise counsel, and the most intelligent head in town was Líng. It was his need for Líng that led him to accede to Túshānshì's request.

When the request to attend a secret meeting reached Woman in a message brought to her in great secrecy, her first reaction was a surge of pride. She was fully aware of the massive impact her speech had made. It would have been hard not to be as many had congratulated from dusk to dawn for two full days. Her second and more coherent thought was that they were attempting to circumvent those she had represented in her address. What matters should be kept from the women who had asked her to stand up for them? There were some serious issues to discuss; if not, a meeting would not be needed. That she was asked to speak to no one until after the meeting did provide her with an excuse; she would then be able to excuse her behaviour by revealing precisely what was said.

Unlike Yú, Woman was supremely confident in all her abilities, but like Yú, she thrived on attention. She enjoyed the company of others, the respect they offered her, and the applause for her successes. What Woman lacked was access to the bigger picture, and this, to a large extent, restricted her analysis. She needed information rather than wise counsel, and it was this need that led her to attend.

Beneath the palace hall was a chamber. The room's original design had been to fulfil the role it would take today and act as a multiple escape route. Of the assembled group, only Hòutú had known of the room's existence, and only she was aware of the four secret entrances. Two were at opposite ends of the palace grounds, one through a residence to the west of the palace and the fourth lay outside the city walls to the east.

Túshānshì had brought in Hòuyì and Bóyì. They entered from outside the city walls. Whilst the master archer took things in his stride, the boy had lost some confidence and seemed most concerned about his presence in such a gathering.

Hòutú had the responsibility for fetching Woman to the meeting. Hers was the most challenging assignment, and they had gone to some lengths to disguise their disappearance through a disused home. Whilst it was a route that Hòutú knew, both women were shocked by the contents of the house they passed through; it overflowed with every imaginable object of the finest craftsmanship, a veritable treasure trove—the same conclusion formed in both their minds. An exchange of glances said as clearly as day is day; this had been the home of Hú and Xí. No words were needed.

Yú and Girl entered from the northernmost palace tunnel, whilst Tú came in from the south. It would have been impossible for anyone to know the eight were meeting, and although Yú's disappearance with Girl may have raised the odd eyebrow, no one would have suspected him of being disloyal to Túshānshì.

Eight sat around a low stone table, a slab that seemed older than old, even older perhaps than the room. Intricate carvings ran around its edges, with leaves and branches real to the touch. It was the only piece of furniture; the participants knelt or sat on the earth floor. The circular room gave a new meaning to the term dimly lit; only a single torch remained alight; it flickered briefly, illuminating different sections of the crumbling and unadorned walls.

"This place always reminds me of my *yáodòng*!" Hòutú was the first to speak. "Except it's got four entrances, and I only had one."

"It's a lovely table." Hòuyì attempted to lighten the mood further. "I expect they were never able to get it out. It must have been lowered in before the ceiling was constructed. You know, I never knew this place existed."

"I suspect there were only two, other than myself and Chīyóu, who did know. Hú and Hum! Woman and I might have something to tell you about what those two had been up to. Yes, Woman?" Hòutú nudged her.

"Yes." Woman did not wish to continue that discussion whilst she was still waiting to hear the real reason for the meeting. "I am concerned that of the eight people here, I believe four are of the Sisterhood, and I was previously a member; this does not seem to reflect the request we made. This appears to be a secret meeting, one dominated by the Sisterhood. We asked for no more secrets from the Sisterhood. It was a simple request. Now I have made that point, could we get on with it, please?"

"I think only Girl can start this off. Girl?" Yú nodded towards Girl.

All sense of formality disappeared as Girl started to talk. She spoke to them in hushed tones and a manner that brought them into the plan rather than thrust it in their faces. Out of politeness, she made no mention of the efforts that the Sisterhood had gone to in ensuring Yú replaced Gǔn, nor did she explain their actions to pair him with Túshānshì. It was best to keep it impersonal.

127

"I heard the argument you put so eloquently. Not only did I listen to it, but I also understood it. Every bit of my heart feels for the suffering that has gone on in Táosì. In this respect, we agree we have failed you.

"However, I would like you to appreciate that circumstances in Táosì are replicated across Lóngshān lands. Women are raped, tortured, and killed across this land from here to the great sea in the east. Whilst our objective has been to help the women of Táosì, we feel this is more than a local issue. Our objective is to free women of the yoke they bear across all lands. And the burden, as in Táosì, has been imposed under the authority of the Lóngshān."

"I agree," Woman interjected, "But—"

"We intend to obliterate the Lóngshān culture within eight years." Girl paused to allow her avowal to sink in.

"It will be evident that the Sisterhood cannot do this alone. We are dependent on Gǔn in Èrlǐtou, on Yú and Túshānshì, who have acted for us in Mount Sōng and here in Shǎnxī. We have been dependent upon Hòutú, here in Táosì and Tú, who will take on her work. But we are also absolutely reliant on you three. Hòuyì, Bóyì and Woman. As citizens of the new Táosì, we depend on you and everyone here. Most of the people in this room are natural leaders who will ensure the defeat of the Lóngshān.

"I am now going to tell you some of the details of our plan. Túshānshì and Yú know much of this. Hòutú knows a little. The rest around this table know only of the plan to relocate. When I am done, we will decide how much of this detail should be revealed to the citizens of Táosì, for only then will you appreciate how important it is to keep the information from spreading."

Girl proceeded to outline the Sisterhood's intentions. She left nothing out. The immense scope of the preparation and the scale of the intended actions caused jaws to drop around the table.

"I think you will now understand the need for secrecy. I think you will appreciate the enormity of our commitment; hundreds of thousands, if not millions, will die. The suffering will make the difficulties you have faced here in Táosì pall—"

"Don't say into insignificance, for God's sake!" Woman bristled momentarily.

128

"No. You are right. I abhor your suffering. Every piece of the puzzle is significant; they are not insignificant.

"I am going to leave you with three questions.

"One. Are you all prepared to support our plan to obliterate the Lóngshān?

"Two. How much of this should we reveal to people in general?

"Three. Would you find it acceptable for the Sisterhood to occupy just one seat on the council of Táosì?

"If you prefer, I could leave while you discuss this."

There was silence around the table, a silence that persisted for longer than was comfortable. Finally, Hòuyì spoke.

"I think we need to start by using your real names." He indicated Girl and Woman. "Then…I, for one, would be happy for us all to remain around the table until we have resolved the answers to these questions. Yú, I apologise for speaking out of turn, but it seemed fit."

"There's no need, Hòuyì, no need to apologise. We are all equals." Yú glanced around the table. "Do we all agree with Hòuyì?"

There were nods of assent all around.

"It looks as if we have agreed on the first step. This will probably be a long night, but we cannot leave these issues unresolved. Yú has to address the people tomorrow, and we need agreement before that." Túshānshì appeared to be the most anxious contributor, although, to her left, Bóyì seemed dumbfounded.

As it turned out, the meeting concluded only a short while later. There was not only complete agreement but also an atmosphere of total commitment.

Nineteen: The Address

Táosì, Shǎnxī: Palace Hall
Year 83: Year of the Snake
Nineteen days to the summer solstice
2nd June 1912 BCE

Three days after his aborted speech, a sense of déjà vu haunted Yú.

The same representatives sat before him, as far as he could tell. Perhaps one or two had been changed; it was hard to know in a crowd of two hundred and fifty. In one respect, the group's composition had subtly altered because it seemed there was more integration than previously.

Yú's list of points was now a little more complex, and his prompt had changed. Instead of his wife, it was now Tú who sat close to him, ready to remind him if there was anything he had missed.

Once more, he stood on the same cart, noticing it was much cleaner. The pungent aroma had gone. Once more, he scanned the crowd, hoping that this time, there would be no immediate interruption to his prepared speech.

"Welcome. Welcome, all. We will resume from where we left off in a moment, but I have some important announcements in reaction to Woman's words.

"As many of you already know, Woman's name is Jīngfēi. She has asked that, henceforward, we all use her real name. Jīngfēi, would you please stand so that everyone might recognise you." She stood as the audience erupted into cheers.

"Thank you, Jīngfēi. Thank you.

"As you are aware, Jīngfēi asked, on your behalf, about the Sisterhood." Yú indicated to Girl that she should stand. Whilst it was a hushed response, there was audible disquiet amongst the assembly.

130

"The Sisterhood would like two things to be known. Firstly, that Girl's real name is Líng, and she should be addressed as such from now on. Secondly, they have requested that they be allowed only one seat on our council, a matter I wish to discuss with you next. The Sisterhood does not want to have undue influence on our affairs.

"Líng, please feel free to sit." As she did, loud muttering circulated the congregation. "I did say 'they have requested'; I did not say it was a given. In the end, it will be up to you."

Yú gathered himself to move on to the next stage.

"We need to have a council to truly represent your views. A council that you will appoint. I am suggesting a council of nine members, as it is impossible to conduct discussions even in this reduced group, let alone in a whole city meeting." Yú paused as seated neighbours briefly discussed the idea. After a short buzz, the noise died again.

"Obviously, you will have to put this to the people you represent, and they will have to organise representatives. I would ask you first to accept me as the chairman of this council. You will have every right to deny me this, and you will have every right to remove me from the position if your feelings change." There was another mumble from the gathering, but this time, one with a ring of positivity.

"The Sisterhood requests that you allow Tú to be their representative on the council." This last statement produced a much stronger reaction, not one of objection but one of shock. "Please allow me to continue. Remember, this is a request; it is in your hands to deny it.

"Further to this...further to this, I propose having the following representatives. A male and a female from the Xià clan." A few hands went up, and Yú dealt with them promptly. "I know that some of you want to speak, but—"

"Are we not all Xià now?" came a call.

"It's good to hear you saying that! I will change my words. A male and a female from those who came with me to Shǎnxī. Is that better?"

"Yes!" There was a chorus of approval.

"From the citizens who previously lived in Táosì, I would propose two women, one man, one girl and one boy. We will maintain the age of fourteen as the cut-off point." Again, there were mutterings from the crowd, although Yú felt they were not enough for him to halt proceedings.

131

"This might surprise you, but that was the easy bit!" Yú smiled broadly. "Now it becomes extremely complicated. If any of you want clarification of what I have said so far or what I am about to say, you will be able to come up and ask me or Jīngfēi or Túshānshì or Gir...Líng or Hòuyì or Hòutú or Bóyì or Tú." Again, the muttering commenced, but this time Yú waved it away. "These people are not your representatives; they are not in some position of power; they have not been proposed for the council...other than Tú and me. It is simply that I will not be able to answer all your queries, and each of them has memorised what I am saying today. They will not interpret; they will repeat my words.

"And so...the complicated bit.

"You have already been made aware of the plan to leave Táosì. I need to explain to you why you should leave your homes.

"Táosì was founded on the lithic industries, as Jīngfēi pointed out three days ago. The problem is that the age of stone is ending. Never again will Táosì resume its once supreme status. Secondly, as you are very aware, the soil degradation in this area has been terrible. We can only use so much nightsoil to maintain fertility and grow crops successfully. Thirdly, the wider environment is damaged, almost beyond repair. There is little wood for fuel and none for new buildings. Hunting is now a pastime for those who can travel for days; no game remains around here. Táosì is dead on its feet."

Yú allowed time for his points to sink in, although each had received nods of assent.

"And so...and so, we plan to move to Èrlǐtou. Let me point out the advantages.

"There is extremely fertile soil, and my father, Gǔn, has spent time preparing irrigated areas to feed a number almost ten times the current headcount of Táosì. Not only will we be able to grow millet and wheat, but we'll also be able to grow rice in vast quantities." At the mention of rice, the smiles broadened on many faces.

"To the south of Èrlǐtou, a mountain chain runs westwards from Mount Sōng. This area provides a supply of wood for building and fuel that is, to my mind, almost inexhaustible." Yú knelt for a moment, whispering to Tú. "What's next?" When she answered immediately, he stood again and threw himself into the next phase.

"One of the questions you will ask is about protection; it is already arranged. The tracks to the south and southeast are something of a mess. There are many refugees from Lake Tài, and many people are short of food. Indeed, they are not a threat; we would seek to help them, but that will be our most significant burden. The people from Lake Tài, the Liángzhǔ, have been terribly devastated.

"The routes southwest and west, along the Wèi River, are occupied by my kinsfolk, the people of Sìchuān. They are now your kinsfolk also. They will also secure a trade line for us, an important trade route. Those of you who have smelted bronze here will understand best. They are going to sell us their tin!"

"Yes!" An enormous cheer went up from a small group of men near the back, a group who had spent far too long smelting arsenical bronze and looked much older than their actual years.

"And this is going to interest you the most. It might be that some of you choose to join this group of people. They are good friends of mine; you have met some of them. Their leader is Kànménrén, and they are the Xīwǎ. They are the herders who have fed you more than once.

"We are going to give Táosì…no, not just Táosì…we are going to give the whole of Shǎnxī to the Xīwǎ!"

"Why? For sheep?" The man from the back repeated the phrase, "…For sheep?"

"Yes, for sheep, but also something far more important. The Xīwǎ will protect us from the north and west. They will also protect our copper mines at Xīwū. Sure, they are also keen to trade with us, which is an added advantage. Are you starting to imagine lamb and rice for dinner each week?" Yú smiled and licked his lips. "I am!"

There was undoubtedly interest amongst the gathered throng. No one was leaving, and all seemed intent on hearing Yú out, however long it took.

"You may have noticed that I excluded the east and northeast lands occupied by the Lóngshān. It is now that I must make an admission to you. There is a secret that I cannot share. It is a secret I will not talk about under any circumstances. You cannot ask this of those people I named earlier, for they do not know the secret either." It was the one lie Yú would tell, and he had to be convincing. "Only I and the senior

133

Sisterhood know of this secret. That means, of those here, only Líng and I. Whilst we will not reveal the secret, I will tell you why it is a secret."

If someone had dropped a stone needle, the sound would have resounded around the hall.

"We are going to obliterate the Lóngshān masters!" Cheering commenced. "Within eight years, we will reduce their diabolical culture to dust. We are going to–" Yú's voice was drowned by the hollering. Excitement shone from nearly every face in the room. Gradually, the roaring morphed into a chant. Quiet at first, it rose and rose in volume.

"We are Xià! We are Xià! We are Xià! We are Xià" Yú allowed the call to go on as long as possible. There were now faces crowded at every opening in the walls of the palace hall. The city wanted to know what was going on.

Yú raised his arms, and gradually the chant subsided.

"This secret. The secret I cannot tell you. Should it get into the hands of the Lóngshān, this secret would seriously disrupt our ability to fulfil our destiny. That is why it must remain what it is: a secret. I hope you understand.

"Hopefully, you will return to those you represent and relay all I have told you. I want to hold our first council meeting before Hòutú gets you back in the fields.

"Is it a deal?"

"Yes!" Two hundred and fifty people spoke one word with near-perfect timing before the cheering and chanting commenced again.

Yú dismounted the cart and leaned toward Tú. "How did I do?"

"You were wonderful...just wonderful." She could not keep the burning admiration from her smile, which was returned in full. As Yú moved on, she whispered, "Wonderful."

Both Túshānshì and Líng, looking on from a distance, did their best to smother their expressions. It was impossible to determine whether one was smiling and the other frowning, but they both pulled their hoods down to cover their reactions.

Twenty: The Rape

Táosì, Shǎnxī: Southwestern gate
Year 89: Year of the Pig
Eighteen days to the spring equinox
3rd March 1906 BCE

It had been nearly six years since the formation of the Táosì council. In that time, its members had remained unchanged. Not once had there been an attempt to replace one of the councillors. Eight of them now stood lined either side of the southwestern gate, but the ninth sat proudly on a two-wheeled cart; Bóyì would miss their next meeting.

To call it a gate was a misnomer. There was no longer any gate, and nothing opened or closed. The entranceway, deprived of its tree trunks and beams, had collapsed, and the towers now only resembled two piles of previously tamped earth. The roadway itself was in good condition and wholly cleared of rubble. On it, stretching into the distance, ahead of Bóyì's cart, was a wagon train. It comprised over one hundred vehicles, each pulled by two bullocks. Each transport was only half laden, and those loads were comprehensively strapped and covered, mainly to keep dust off as the chances of rain were small, but also to deter prying eyes. Upwards of five hundred men, women, and children accompanied the carts. There were the same number of happy, smiling faces.

Their destination was Èrlǐtou. Most of the carts and the majority of the passengers were leaving Táosì for good. Some drivers and riders were to return, as would their animals, but they were few.

It was Bóyì's first opportunity to lead one of the trains that had left Táosì at the same time in each of the last five years. He hoped to be asked to lead the final one, but that was a year off. He was no longer one of the boys; he was a young man in the prime of his life. Still, he oozed confidence, but it was never thought of as cockiness; his ever-ready smile

135

and willingness to help all made him one of the most admired individuals in Táosì.

As ever, their load consisted primarily of bronze and jade, although ten carts were devoted solely to provisions and camping equipment. Another ten carried spare parts, mainly for the carts, wheels, and axles. The bronze had been melted into ingots, ready to be reformed in Èrlǐtou when needed. There had been some discussions about the damage from the arsenic levels, but the bronze workers and Hòutú had all sworn it was only dangerous in the original ore smelting. Whilst the bronze had a clear, practical purpose, what was less clear were their intentions for the jade. After a few years, everyone knew there were only a few useful pieces. For most of the town, jade was simply decorative, but the Sisterhood was always keen to exaggerate its value. The only answer that anyone found acceptable was that to leave the jade in situ would attract robber barons from the Lóngshān; that was enough.

Protecting the column were thirty horsemen carrying fine shields, spears, and axes, with bows and quivers strapped across their backs. In the previous five years, they had only been bothered by small travelling bands of outlaws, who could easily be deterred by the armaments on display. If they were to meet a more extensive and organised force, the expectation was that everyone in the train of carts would be able to fire an arrow accurately. Each cart came equipped with four bows and four quivers, each containing ten arrows. If every one of the wagon train members considered themselves a farmer, then each considered themselves a bowman and potential warrior.

The carts were built entirely of wood re-purposed from the structures in Táosì. As each dwelling or workshop was gutted, the wooden posts, beams, and flooring usually came out last. In many cases, the structures then collapsed, which could make demolition a risky business. Most of the wood had been well preserved and ended up as components for the wagons; what was not became firewood. Due to the different shapes and sizes of the raw materials, each cart had a unique appearance. However, some fundamental standards applied to their construct.

Two years ago, they had experimented with larger carts, some with four wheels. Although these contraptions were practical on the flat, they broke up far too quickly when used in more arduous terrain. They also required four bullocks to pull them, which made the harnessing more difficult. The idea had been scrapped, but perhaps the technology could be used once more when they lived on the flatter lands around Èrlǐtou.

Everybody knew the wheels had a problem; they were solid and heavy. In addition, they took an enormous pounding from being the cart's only contact with the ground. The construction teams could only work with the technologies they had, although all were fully aware that some sort of spoked wheel would be a step forward, as would a metal rim. Bronze had been tried but was not strong enough.

If the wheels were a problem, then the axle was also. They were attached directly to the flatbed of the cart. The axle ends were carved into cylinders to accommodate the hole in the centre of the wheel. The wheel was fixed in place with a wooden wedge. A standardised design for the wheel and axle mechanism was essential as so many broke, and there was a constant need for replacements. The wagon train left Táosì only half full because there was an expectation that they would lose a minimum of half their fleet.

There was a single rectangular stone in the work yards of Táosì used for all the main measurements for cart construction. Its width provided the dimensions of the square flatbed, the length matched the axle, and its height was the diameter of the wheels. In addition, doubling the stone's length provided the measurement for the bullock shafts. To his enormous embarrassment, the three measures had been taken from Yú's body, from his feet to navel, feet to shoulder and feet to the top of his head. It is no wonder they were named 'Yú's body carts'. The mistakes and offcuts, re-purposed or sent to the fire store, were jokingly referred to as Yú's spare body parts. The first of the two names stuck; the second did not.

Completing the cart were detachable sideboards, and a tailboard was added, which prevented items from slipping off the flatbed. In front was a raised box, offering a crumb of comfort for the driver and a yoke for the bullocks.

When they started these trips, no one had been quite sure how Kànménrén had come up with so many bullocks at short notice. Rumours were that the first group had been rustled and brought across the mountains from Héběi. If so, it would have been a risky venture that could have caused disaster. Instead of investigating their loss properly, the Lóngshān continued to blame each other and fight amongst themselves. Many of the bullocks were hardened veterans of the trip; only a handful had died and needed replacement.

The journey had many inclines, both down and up. The bullock's loads became heavier as time passed, as items were offloaded onto fewer carts. The animals earned their fodder and were well-treated by their human companions.

To fill the carts year after year, Táosì was ripped apart.

It had started with abandoned homes and factories. Stone, bronze, and jade working had all but ceased, although a small bronze foundry continued working to meltdown items to produce the ingots. The workers there also repaired pots and pans, weapons, farm tools and so on as required. Most new items were acquired by looting rather than manufacture, although re-purposing was the preferred phrase, taking from the houses and graves of the rich to service the city's needs.

To demonstrate the extent of earlier misdeeds to the townspeople, the council threw open the home of Hú and Xí to all. A procession of fascinated citizens had taken several days to file through their rooms and the many secret chambers leading off them. When everyone had been sufficiently astonished, a team went in to strip the place, and a section of the palace hall was set aside to pile the loot into different categories.

The stash had been enormous, and the extent of the pair's philandering had been blatantly obvious when brought to light. The bronze alone had covered an area eight steps by eight, to the depth of half a man. The jade had occupied a smaller space, clothing another, and furniture took up a fourth. Once the house was stripped, a team ripped out all the supporting beams and wall posts; these eventually occupied an area larger than the bronze.

The council requested the townspeople re-visit the hoard to explain its future use. The bronze was melted down for ingots, and the jade was packed tightly in large wooden boxes. Clothing would be re-used, although the soothsayers' fashion choice meant there was not much take up. The recovered furniture and structural wood would be utilised to build the carts, and these had a special significance for all as everyone was invested in the migration.

For many months, a pottery slab hung on the wall above Hú and Xí's treasures, publicly displaying the first writing to be seen in the town. It clearly stated what the objects were and their intended use. The sign soon became the focus of the first reading lessons.

Soon after, another more prominent sign went up. It was under a shelter but open to all on the outside of the palace wall. It contained a short list of rules. This sign also became a tool for reading lessons, and Hòutú, Túshānshì and Líng had soon been instructing class after class in the magic of reading and writing. It had been an exciting process for the three women, for they found that not everyone could access reading successfully. A stubborn group of fifty or so steadfastly claimed they could not do it. It was even more interesting that most of them were male.

Repeatedly, Hú and Xí's residence was used as an example of how to gut a building. There were plenty on which to practice. There had been many empty homes, although none contained as much wealth as the soothsayers' dwelling. An interesting comparison was the home of Chīyóu, which was positively spartan by comparison. Most of the loot came from the homes of the elite, and there was little to be found elsewhere, with one exception. There was another group of homes that would prove to be enormously lucrative. These homes were not for the fainthearted because they were the homes of the dead.

The graveyards of the average man or woman contained almost nothing of worth and were left in peace. The graves of the rich were a different matter. Once again, it had been necessary to excavate an exemplar, display the grave goods in situ, and then display them again in the palace hall. It was not long before all the citizens became accomplished grave robbers.

Taking apart these tombs had proved a complex business; more than a few were booby-trapped. Many of the easiest to access had already been robbed, Hú and Xí being the prime suspects. Yú insisted that human remains be dealt with respectfully, even when divested of their property. However, in the already raided tombs, it was evident that earlier visitors had no such instructions. In some graves, skulls had been kicked from the bodies, and often their clothing was removed. The remains and any unwanted items had been shovelled into a corner. The new rule had been explicit: treat the remains as if they were your father or mother.

At the time of Bóyì's departure, there were very few tombs left to empty, very few bronze ingots remained for next year's final trip, and there was genuine concern there may be a shortage of wood for carts twelve months from now.

As the crowds waved goodbye and passed their best wishes to the departing horde, the remaining eight from the council strolled back together from the gate.

Fewer than four hundred souls remained in the town; they would nearly all be leaving on the last wagon train in a year's time. The council had made complex calculations about the population's needs and the demand for foodstuffs, storage, and housing. It was the same procedure used in the last three years. In each, they had been successful, always coming through with a small but sufficient surplus.

This year would be the last planting season. It was necessary to provide for the winter, but five hundred steps would reach the edge of the land to be planted with the fields now vastly reduced in size. The grain stored in previous years would meet many of their needs. It had been good to see wildlife returning, even if it meant the local deer now regularly attacked their crops. Some of the lands within the walls were turned back to arable production to protect against the problem.

At Yú's behest, the council had agreed it was time again for a meeting of the entire town. There were now few enough that they would fit in the palace hall, even if it were a bit of a squeeze. Yú had agreed with Kànménrén, and the Xīwǎ chief had once again timed his mobile meat delivery to perfection.

Whilst it was a special day with the wagon train leaving and a planned whole town meeting, Kàn seemed particularly excited about his visit. His wife and sons had been torn from him by the evil acts of Léigōng almost ten years ago. His focus on bringing up his daughter had consumed him since then, but now, as she came into her own, he had become intimate with a girl in Táosì. His visits had become more regular, and although no one was sure what was happening, many speculated. However, it was a complete surprise when Kàn approached Yú privately that evening and asked if he might marry Hòutú.

"Kàn, why are you asking me?" Yú was stunned. He was genuinely shocked, both at being asked and by the proposed marriage.

140

"It's up to you what you do…and up to Hòutú." He placed his arm across his friend's shoulder. "Why didn't you tell me before? Everyone's been joking about you hanging around like a little puppy and…and now this! Hòutú, eh? I thought she had gone back to her days as a virgin shaman. I–"

"But do you give your permission, Yú?"

"I said…I said, Kàn, it's not my permission to give. You're both free people. It's your choice. Do you think people in Táosì come to me each time they want to wed?"

"No…no…but I am Xīwǎ. She is now Xià. You are the leader of the Xià. I am an outsider."

"So, what does that make Girl…sorry…Líng? Is she Xià or Xīwǎ? She's your daughter, and she's part of the Xià. It's a long time since I said this to you, Kàn, but there's a lot of fear of strangers in these parts, and you seem to be displaying it most of all! We are all one, as far as I am concerned. All one!

"Purely on a technicality, and to satisfy you, I will give my permission, but that is between you and me. No one else. I don't want to make decisions people should make themselves."

"Yú, it is important you understand. You would be losing her. She will come with me. She wants to range the land after being cooped up for so long. She wants to ride horses and hunt and herd. She wants her freedom."

"Why isn't she telling me this, Kàn?"

"Yú, my friend, you may not understand this, but Hòutú, like everyone else, is a little scared of you. Not for what you have done or what you do but for what you have the power to do. Hòutú believed you might say no."

"I don't believe it!"

"It's true!"

"I want to see the pair of you together. Sort it out, Kàn. There are some aspects of our grander plan that your arrangements could well assist."

Twenty-one: The Affair

Táosì, Shǎnxī: Hòutú's Yáodòng
Year 89: Year of the Pig
The spring equinox
22nd March 1906 BCE

It had been a convenient venue. No one ever passed by, particularly after dark. Fundamentally, the structure remained the same, although softer bedding and warm blankets had replaced the original sparse furniture. Inside there was also a covered water butt and a small wooden chest containing *ròugān* and dried fruits, sealed so that local scavengers would not consume its contents.

Their affair had commenced some five years before, although the smouldering looks and suggestive comments went back half a year earlier. The result had seemed inevitable. Neither of them had ever reached the point of making a decision; the passion simply took control. It just happened: a matter of convenience, an opportunity when interested parties had been otherwise engaged, and an available bed. The arrangement to use the *yáodòng* had come later.

It was a space to which she was accustomed. No longer did it seem to be a cage that confined her. Instead, it was a secret place where she could indulge her fantasies with a man who wanted her with a passion that burned. She could spread her wings. In these moments, she felt no guilt and no remorse. The *yáodòng* was now her place of personal pleasure.

In the process, any innocence between them disappeared. The relationship may be covert, but for all that, it was becoming an all-consuming passion threatening the sanity of both. There were many unasked and unanswered questions, most involving their relationship with others and their respective roles in the plans of the Sisterhood. It had become clear things could not go on as they were.

142

However, the time had come to shed all thoughts of what was happening outside the cave. It was a time to forget the worries of everyday life and dismiss concerns of those to come. Before closing her eyes, she looked down momentarily to check her lover was ready, although she could feel everything was as it should be. He was working hard to please her, sweating and straining and thrusting himself higher and higher.

The touch of fingernails running upwards from her buttocks, then slowly and gently across her waistline and on and up towards her armpits, was precisely what she had taught him to do, and he had executed the move with precision timing. The moment her eyelids drooped, all conscious thought dissipated. Her inflamed organs tightened and descended further on her lover's erection. The waves crashing through her forced her back to arch, her arms to spread, and each finger straightened to the point of delicate agony. Her head thrown back, she groaned once, twice, and a third time before her back sprang like a bow, her head drooped forward, and her body shook. As she collapsed forward, she felt his fluid shooting inside her again and again and again before she lost count. She groaned as her tensions unwound and only momentarily felt hands caressing her breasts before she slid off her man, falling into semi-consciousness by his side.

It could have been moments, and it could have been hours; she had no idea. Drowsily she felt herself rolled, a newly stiffened penis pressing against her from behind. Their combined fluids made for a slippery penetration as he pushed deeper and deeper inside her. She squirmed with pleasure as he remained inside her, and his arms and legs wrapped themselves around her body. Sometimes, she had to request or prompt this pleasure, but today, he remembered it himself.

As Yú gently rocked back and forth inside her, Tú fell asleep.

It was not as if he had been dissatisfied with his wife. Túshānshì remained as beautiful as ever, cared for him wonderfully and never was a sharp word thrown in his direction. Yú still loved her deeply. However, at times, he had become irritated by her company, and in the bed he shared with Tú, he would often complain that he felt smothered in his wife's presence. It was a complaint he knew was unfounded.

From time to time, Yú considered his position and determined he should act to change things, but it never happened. He would not allow himself to admit that, to some extent, he was content with the arrangement. Sex was not an issue. He enjoyed himself with Tú and enjoyed himself with Túshānshì, although it was altogether different. His wife always went out of her way to please him, above all else, whereas it seemed Tú's priority was to please herself, allowing the fallout from her passion to be his greatest satisfaction. On many occasions, when bedding either woman, he had contemplated the three of them exploring their sensualities together in one bed. It was an idea that excited him to the point of frenzy but one that bent too many of the taboos he had brought with him through life—most of all, that his wife should not know.

Tú also thought about their circumstances. She came at the whole affair with a completely different perspective from Yú. She was single and had no personal need to keep the relationship hidden. There may be no need, but there was guilt, which took several forms. In terms of her friendship with Túshānshì, sometimes the pain would shoot through her, leaving her incapable of standing. What was she doing to one of her dearest friends? The thought of discovery turned her knees to jelly.

She feared what her mother might say. Whilst Hòutú was not particularly uptight about relationships, her daughter felt she might disown her if this thing got out. Their relationship was still close, but not close enough for Tú to feel she could confide in her. In fact, Tú believed that if she told her mother, the news would immediately be broadcast throughout the town; she might even suggest her expulsion.

The council would be horrified and would undoubtedly eject her. They were a close group, but not once had an intimate relationship developed between two of their members, other than the one she had with Yú. They would suspect complicity and feel threatened by a pairing that could become a power block. If that were not bad enough, there was the fact that she was the Sisterhood's representative on the council. If she were to lose her seat, they would lose access to decision-making in Táosì and possibly beyond.

If it terrified her that Túshānshì, her mother and the council might find out, she was petrified by what the Sisterhood might do. They were used to getting their way and did not look kindly on one of their own who might upset the apple cart. It was bad enough when one of them had lost control of someone outside the organisation; sparks had flown when Gǔn went his own way, and Mother had been unable to persuade him otherwise.

What Tú did not understand was the conflict. Since she was old enough to understand the concept, her mother had always told her she would have Yú's baby. As she understood, this was all part of the Sisterhood's grand plan. She had never fully understood the reasons and still had no idea how it would come to pass without suspicion; if she were terrified, she was also confused.

Unbeknown to Tú, Túshānshì had known about the affair from the start. She had gone out of her way to ensure there were no signs that either Yú or Tú might find out she knew. She had gone further and covered for them so others might not discover what was happening. She had spied on them on a couple of occasions, listening to them as they made love. She did so out of curiosity and to ensure they were both content; it seemed they were.

Túshānshì appeared to love Yú, of that there was no doubt; it was her life's purpose. She had been taken from her parents before she could remember and brought up by Sisterhood members who had raised her with one express intent. Her role was to guide Yú through the difficulties of founding the Motherland. Love and lust were an integral part of providing that guidance. It was a settled bond, not one to be unbalanced by something as petty as Yú having a relationship with another woman. Only a threat to the Motherland would cause imbalance. If she could control the situation, she was content. There was only one cause for concern, and it left her in something of a dilemma. She wanted a baby, and Yú wanted a baby. She also knew that Tú wanted Yú's baby, and the sisterhood wanted the same. For the first time, she felt a little uneasy about her role.

None of this was irreconcilable if it were not for the fact that Túshānshì's body stubbornly refused to allow her to fall pregnant. Tú was so uptight about being discovered that she would do anything to avoid having a child. A new balancing act was required. The Sisterhood had made it more than clear they expected a resolution. With a superiority complex that reminded Túshānshì of times before the creation of the charter of rules, the Sisterhood seemed convinced that Tú's son by Yú should become Yú's successor. The problem was that they wanted everyone to think he was Túshānshì's son. Nothing could have been more complicated, and she realised that her renowned powers of persuasion would be stretched to the absolute limit. Hòutú would not be around for much longer, which further complicated matters, although there might be advantages if she were not around to interfere.

As Túshānshì saw it, there were three options: to pretend she knew nothing of the affair and ask Tú to have a baby by Yú; admit to both that she knew of the matter and explain the requirement for a child; the third option was to admit to Tú alone that she was aware and persuade her to fall pregnant. In all three scenarios, dealing with the child's upbringing and the ongoing relationship between Tú and Yú would be difficult. She also wanted her marriage to come through unscathed so the Motherland would succeed. It was not easy.

The Sisterhood were aware of the circumstances, although Túshānshì believed their only source of information had been herself. Neither Líng nor Hòutú had expressed anything but surprise when she had told them, even if Hòutú seemed of the opinion that what had come to pass was as it should be. If Tú were to find out about her mother's understanding of the situation and the Sisterhood's involvement, it could go one of two ways. One would have been Tú's rejection of the Sisterhood, something the organisation found most undesirable. At the same time, the other would result in a calmer, less guilty lover, who might finally begin contributing to their grander plan.

Yú's belief that only those who had sat down in secret nearly six years before knew of the Sisterhood's master plan was somewhat erroneous. As far as he was concerned, eight individuals knew the details, even though only he and Líng were in on the secret publicly. In reality, whilst the eight were party to the plan to defeat the Lóngshān, none, other than senior members of the Sisterhood, knew of the longer-term intent, which effectively meant only Líng in Táosì and Mother in Èrlǐtou knew all the details. Whilst Túshānshì and Tú both realised that there was significance in the production of a child by Yú, neither of them was party to the bigger picture either. It was with this complex backdrop that Túshānshì made her decision alone and determined to speak to Tú first.

They were plucking chickens in the kitchen area of the palace. The birds were no longer regarded as the exotic meat they once had been but were still in demand. No one lived in the palace itself, but its kitchen had plenty of flat, raised surfaces and the best collections of sharp knives and functional pots anywhere in the city. Usually, several men and women worked in the area, but today, it was just Tú and Túshānshì.

"I think it's time I told you something, Tú." Túshānshì was almost conspiratorial in her approach. "I know more about you than you might think."

"Oh!" Tú feigned surprise whilst desperately trying to think what her friend would impart. "Now…what would that be? That I'm lefthanded!"

"No, Tú. I know that! I mean about you and Yú."

"What about Yú and me?"

"Don't be silly! About you two and your affair."

"Wha…" Tú's heart sank into the pit of her stomach.

"Now, don't get all funny. Don't let's get in a panic about this. I'm not upset, Tú. Really. I'm not mad at you. It's just there are a few things we need to sort out. If you were to carry on the way you're going, well…Someone could find out. It's best if we pre-empt any problems."

"I see." Tú did not actually see anything. She was too focused on trying to stop her hands from shaking. Tears began to streak down her face.

"I know what's been going on. I know for how long. I know where you now go with Yú regularly. The *yáodòng* was quite a clever choice. Does it still feel like home to you?"

"No…no…not really." Tú sobbed. "I'm sorry, Túshānshì. I'm so sorry. You must think I'm a dreadful person. You must think I've no respect for you. You must think I'm an animal." Tú put down the carcass she was preparing, placed her knife on the counter, and, still crying, pulled open her smock, baring her breasts. "If you want to take that knife and stab me through the heart right now…I will not stop you. Go ahead. I deserve nothing else."

"Tú, Tú, Tú! That is not what I want at all." Like her friend, she dropped the bird and her knife. Then, throwing her arms around Tú, she tried to comfort her. "We're friends. We're sisters. That will not change, Tú. I hope you're being silly if you think I would stick a knife in you!"

"What…what are you going to do? What are…What are we going to do?"

147

"We're going to talk, Tú, and we're going to sort something out."

"What about Yú?" Tú's expression was screwing up her face making it hard for her to speak. "What...what are you going to do about...him?"

"I want to ask you about that, Tú. We'll come to an agreement. We'll work out what we're going to do.

"Come, let's finish up here, and I'll get Yú to cook us up a feast. That gives me and you the chance to develop a strategy before either of us must speak to him. He's a better cook than either of us, so at least we can look forward to a good meal."

The two women cleaned up the workspace and carried the two dressed chickens to the cooking area, although Túshānshì did most of the work as Tú continued to sob. When they had finished, they left both birds in a pan sealed with a lid to keep the flies off. Leaving a message with one of the boys hanging around waiting for Yú, Túshānshì first found a jar of *jiu* and a couple of beakers, then indicated to Tú that she should follow her.

As Tú stumbled down the ramp to the secret chamber, she felt it might well be the slope into her tomb. Approaching the table made her think of the slab on which her grandmother's remains had been placed. Even the stool on which she sat seemed to be made of ice, although, as they talked, her body warmed somewhat.

Following a rather long sojourn together, it seemed they had reached an agreement. When they resurfaced, Tú had cleaned herself up to the extent she looked almost normal. The pair appeared to enjoy a cheerful meal with Yú, although his wife put a considerably better face on it than Tú. The decision had been that Túshānshì would talk to her husband later that night. It meant that Tú had to act her way through the meal. She was discomforted throughout, her mind in turmoil and still harbouring jealous thoughts that conflicted with her guilt. She would have loved to have been a fly on the wall in their bed-chamber. She would have loved to have taken Túshānshì's place in the bed, as long as it was not she who would have to tell Yú the game was up. All now rested with Túshānshì and her incredibly persuasive manner. Tú wondered what that mysterious art was.

148

Twenty-two: The Image

Táosì, Shǎnxī: Palace Hall
Year 89: Year of the Pig
The summer solstice
21st June 1906 BCE

There were upwards of thirty women circling the massive wooden structure located in the palace hall. It was Chīyóu's old table that was the centre of their attention. As it was a struggle for those at the back to see properly, some stood on hastily gathered chairs. If they were now silent, the excited expressions on their faces suggested they had not been for long. It was as though someone had temporarily placed the top on a pan of fiercely boiling rice and water; in moments, the lid would blow off.

A closer examination of the group would have revealed a few periodically closed their eyes. It was they who remembered being here some nineteen years before, although today, no one chose to ask what was going through their minds. However, every one of the women strained forward to see the spectacle unfolding in front of them. They had not been coerced into attending, but none could turn or walk away from the unfolding scene.

The hall had seen several temporary repairs in the last few years. Beams of sunlight no longer shafted to the floor. The source of the light cast on the table came only from a series of torches held in bronze stands. Even though individual torches flickered, with so many of them, the platform and its contents maintained a steady level of light. Around it, the flickering revealed the faces of the crowd, and behind them, there was only gloom.

The crowd huddled around the centrally lit point from where the flames emanated. If a visitor had walked in, not knowing what was happening, they would have the suspicion it was a witches' coven. The newcomer would have been unable to observe the focus of attention, just

149

as they would have been unable to see the walls. It was as if the scene floated in some mythical world.

Habitually, the hall was open to all; today, only women had been admitted, and there would be no other visitors, but there were two notable exceptions. Close to the table and in deep discussion were two males of the Xīwǎ tribe looking out of place. The scenario was not an everyday occurrence and was certainly not a typical gathering. The older women present recalled the intended double execution from decades previously and shivered silently, for the same two women lay on the table, mother and child. As before, the audience was once more here to be taught a lesson, albeit a somewhat different one.

The two men toyed with the tools of their trade, which lay at the end of the large table. There was a selection of sharp knives, needles and small clay bowls containing what appeared to be soot.

A young naked woman was centrally positioned on what had previously been Chīyóu's eating table. She was tied down by hemp ropes, encircling her wrists and ankles and running around the table's broad legs. She formed an imperfect cross. Two additional bindings extended across the table's width, the first across her pelvis and the second just above her breasts. In her mouth was a rectangular section of wood on which she could bite down.

The victim herself had some control over her fingers and toes. She could move her head from side to side and raise it from the table if she wished. She could see all those attending, other than those women positioned behind her head. She also had a clear view of the two men who intended to cut her.

Glancing sideways, she met her mother's eyes; for a second woman occupied the table's surface. The older female lay on the victim's right-hand side, although anyone could have mistaken them for sisters from their looks.

Like the trussed and immobile form, the second woman lay on her back. Like the victim, she was completely naked. Unlike the victim, she sported massive scarring on her abdomen, scarring that had been put there in this place while today's focus was still unborn and inside her.

Hòutú was not bound; she could have stood up and left at a moment's notice. She would not. In addition, she was not gagged and

150

could converse with her daughter, although it may well have been a one-way conversation.

"Are you sure you want to do this, Tú?"

The victim shook her head and pushed the gag from her mouth using her tongue.

"Yes, *Māma*, it's fine. I know it will hurt, but everything will be fine."

"These bindings are just like mine were. Are they essential?"

"They're not the same; there are fewer of them. I had one of the older ladies tell me about your bindings. Yours were much worse. These are to keep me still while these men work. They told me it was best to be absolutely still because it would hurt less, although I'm still trying to convince myself. They said they would have a break now and then, and I would be able to make myself more comfortable at those times." Tú looked deep into her mother's eyes. "Are you alright with this? It's a lot of people watching."

"That's why I asked you to keep the men out. It was...Well, to be honest, I didn't want them ogling me, or you for that matter! Besides, I will have to flaunt this time and time again when Kàn and I go on our tour, and I'm already bored with it. It will not be too bad for you, probably just the once."

Before arranging this day, they had engaged in lengthy discussions about replicating the Motherland symbol on Tú's body. Tú's mother had favoured a body paint, while Tú herself felt the scars should be made in the same fashion her mother's had been inflicted. Hòutú had been aghast. However, it had been impossible for her to dissuade her daughter, notwithstanding her detailed explanations about the infections, the agony of childbirth and the wounds opening again. Hòutú even stressed the perpetual itching that still bothered her, especially on damp days.

The one argument her mother could not use was the visual impact. The scars may have been disfiguring, but there was no doubt that the image on her body had a massive effect on all who saw it - the very reason that Tú felt she both wanted and needed the copy.

It had been Kàn himself who intervened. Having had night after night of Hòutú's wailing, he had suggested an entirely different approach.

He explained the tradition of marking people's bodies in the west and north. In Shǎnxī, it was primarily used on the faces of criminals, although it was occasionally also used by shaman. It was widely practised and regarded as high art in more remote areas. He explained that it would be possible to persuade some practitioners to put their skills to the test for such an ambitious project. He called the art *cìqīng*[13].

It had not taken long. Some western travellers had been passing through the south of the area. Once it was ascertained they had artists with them and that they had previous sound experience, Kàn's suggestion was taken on board by Hòutú, and she built a massive campaign directed at persuading Tú. It had not proved as difficult as she had thought it might. The deciding factor that ultimately tipped the scales was that the marking would be even more apparent than the scars on Hòutú's body. When she learned that the marks would eventually turn blue, Tú had resisted, but it had been a short-lived objection. Her only other issue was that Kàn's *cìqīng* team were both males, but once again, her protest faded relatively quickly. Tú promptly invited the artists to Táosì.

Now, just one week later, they lay together on the table. Looking over at her daughter, Hòutú's doubts had resurfaced.

"Are you sure you couldn't make do with paint?"

"No, *Māma*, I couldn't! I think they're about to start. Would you push the gag back in, please?"

Although she complied immediately, Hòutú did not consider the request something she wanted to do. Her presence on the table was not simply to reassure Tú. Her scar was to be the model from which the artists could work. As she lay on her back, she tightened her muscles, hoping that any slightly saggy areas would be more disguised. She was relieved to see the two men were wearing slight but comfortable smiles of reassurance. It seemed that only she was panicking.

"We're ready, Tú." The taller of the two men had a gentle, calming voice. "Are you?" In response to a brief nod from Tú, the second man spoke.

"Now...remember, we're doing the outline today. It will take some time, even with both of us working. We've got to finish this today,

---

[13] Tattooing.

however long it takes. When we're done…Well, when we've finished the outline, that's the worst bit over. Then we can take our time filling in the symbol." He turned to address the audience.

"Ladies. We are here to celebrate our skills and share them with you all. If you have any questions, would you save them until the end. Thank you."

Both men then rounded the table to look closely at Hòutú's scars, something she found uncomfortable. She felt objectified, even though neither man appeared to show any interest in anything but the wounds. Regaining their positions over Tú, one took up a bronze needle and the other a bowl of soot.

"Here we go."

Immediately, Tú wanted to scream. She felt her teeth would meet in the middle of the wooden block. She was unable to control the tightening of the muscles in her abdomen. The two artists had been aware of the likely reaction and had commenced their work in a location Tú was least likely to be able to move. Working close to her sternum meant Tú could look down her nose at them as they focused on the skin between her breasts.

Prick, prick, prick, prick, prick!

With each subsequent penetration of her skin, the pain grew less. Tú entered a state she had prepared herself for, neither sleep nor unconsciousness, but a nowhere land somewhere in between. She focussed on the parts of her body that seemed furthest from the pain and found herself idly considering her womb. It was something she had done before. She had tried at times to imagine being inside her heart, which, right now, was far too close to the action. Sometimes, it was her liver, but that felt quite uncomfortable at the moment, pressing hard on the table. She had no idea where they had got to with those needles; in fact, all external sensations had gone. Her mind remained in and around her womb. She then sensed something was different; something inside was not entirely her. As she began a mental count, a voice brought her around.

"We've finished for today. Well done. The outline of the *wénshēn*[14] is complete!" The artists turned to the assembled women, not

---

[14] Tattoo.

only to answer any questions they may have but to gratefully accept a drink. Tú turned towards her mother and spat the gagging wood out of her mouth.

"*Māma.*"

"Yes, *Bǎobǎo.*"

"*Māma*, I'm pregnant!"

Twenty-three: The Return
Táosì, Shǎnxī
Year 89: Year of the Pig
The autumn equinox
22nd September 1906 BCE

It was time for the autumn festival. The harvest was in, and although much reduced, it was more than sufficient to feed the citizens for their last winter in the city. It would even leave enough stock to hand some over to the Xīwǎ. It had been a good year, albeit one containing a few surprises. All looked forward to the final round of searching for and collecting the city's last remaining treasures.

It was also the date set for the celebration of the union of Kànménrén and Hòutú. They were to leave the following day, and rumour had it they were to spend their first months together in northern Shaanxi[15] and Níngxià. Although no one would have mentioned it publicly, the idea of enjoying the first months of their marriage in such bleak areas during winter confirmed to many that Hòutú had probably lost her mind during her long captivity. However, insanity or not, the result was an even bigger party than would have been justified by a successful harvest alone. Kàn had, of course, brought more sheep with him. This bunch were juicily fattened, most perfectly ready for the cooking pot.

Bóyì's return made it even more of a time for celebration. He had become even more popular over the years. His common sense, an ability to get on with anyone, and a permanent sunny smile were a winning combination. Only half the bullocks had made the reverse journey, but

---

[15] Shaanxi (Shǎnxī) has been left with this spelling and without accents to prevent confusion with the entirely separate province of Shānxī.

155

some were lightly loaded with saddlebags. Their contents were almost a gift from heaven. Rice.

Bóyì and his team also brought news. As Táosì's population had shrunk, that of Èrlǐtou had expanded. Friends and neighbours were temporarily separated, and it was time to catch up. People wanted to know about other newcomers and what they were contributing to their intended homeland. They also took an interest in the housing quality and the weather; both seemed better than in Shǎnxī. Concerning their friends and relatives, they asked who had taken key roles, who had fallen foul of the law, and who was bedding whom. All the fun gossip that keeps a community ticking over.

From a practical point of view, Gǔn's exploits in Èrlǐtou had been hugely successful; they were now producing surpluses above expectations. Notwithstanding the growing population there, the fields were more than capable of supplying the needs of all and were proving exceptionally fertile. The massive irrigation schemes had not failed them and seemed set to provide a pattern for further development. Gǔn's objectives had been to ensure they had at least one year's worth of basic foodstuffs in storage and that those stores could feed at least twenty thousand. That amounted to double the natural population, which would be attained once the remainder of Táosì's citizens joined them the following year.

Yú had promised them an escape from tyranny, he had pledged to the rule of law, and he had offered them greater prosperity. All three promises had been met, but another had not. Those still in Táosì were not yet enjoying the warmer climate; they would have to wait until they moved.

One person who had met each of the returnees from the cart teams was Tú. She had wanted to greet one individual particularly but was too shy to do so. Instead, she had gone down the whole line of carts, showing off her *wénshēn*.

Whilst there was widespread admiration for the body art, what was even more apparent was that she was pregnant. Several women jumping off the carts were prepared to feel her bump while they made rapid estimates of the likely time of conception. All concluded the pregnancy had commenced after they had left, which had the effect of removing several possible candidates for fatherhood.

Tú had not even considered she might be advertising her pregnancy, not for a moment. When the *wénshēn* was finally completed, she had displayed it to the town's remaining population some two months before. At that time, the fact that she was with child had been unapparent. It was weeks before that news had leaked out.

Tú's earlier display had resulted in one unintended effect. Yú had seemingly lost all interest in her. It was something that had disturbed her greatly. She missed the physical contact; she missed the sex, and she missed the danger. Admittedly, her focus had shifted somewhat, and what was growing inside her had begun to dominate her thoughts.

With a baby on the way, Tú wanted to ensure she did not have to bring up her child alone as her mother did. Only one man was on her mind, even if she was too timid to approach him directly. Her mother's earlier concerns about her social aptitude were proving prescient.

If everyone else appeared happy with their circumstances, it was clear that Bóyì was not. His cheerfulness had been evident on his immediate return, although there had seemed to be some underlying concerns. However, within hours of his unloading, a scowl and furrowed brow had overtaken his countenance.

Jīngfēi was the first to take him on one side for a chat.

"It looks like a dog just ate your dinner, and you knocked over your wine! What's up with you, lad?"

"It's just things."

"Things? Things? When you're thirteen, you can say it's just things! How old are you now, seventeen…eighteen? Whatever, you're not a boy anymore. You can't go around sulkily and say it's just things! Come on! Open up. We've been friends for near on…how many years is it? Oh, I don't know! What is there that you can't tell me?"

"You wouldn't understand!"

"Wouldn't understand…it's just things…you know, someone will get the idea you're trying to hide something. Just things…"

"Well…one's her." Bóyì waved in the general direction of quite a large group.

157

"Her? You're going to have to be a little more specific, Bóyì. Her? Who's her?"

"Tú."

"Tú? What's she done to you? Not put some kind of spell on you, has she? They can be a bit weird sometimes, those pigeon fanciers." Jīngfēi had adopted a jocular manner but could sense Bóyì was in some sort of crisis. "You and me...you and me are going to walk over to Háng's bar over there and get ourselves some beer. Come on. Come with me. If you don't look to it quickly, I'll make you pay."

Háng's beer was the best in town, brewed using yams and red wheat. In the last few years, barley was introduced into the crop rotation, becoming Háng's additional secret ingredient. Not only did it taste good, but the brew was also the least lumpy beer to be found north of Guófēng Mountain. It was almost possible to finish it without a spoon. Bóyì made short work of the first pitcher.

"Better? There's not a lot that can't be sorted with a few of Háng's beers. Another?" Jīngfēi's teasing eventually drew Bóyì into a smile.

"Better!" Bóyì scowled again, "Not really, you know, my face struggles with looking down. The beer may solve the facial muscle situation but hasn't sorted my heavy heart."

"So, Tú. Is it the *wénshēn*? No. Ah! It's the fact she's pregnant! What is she to you, Bóyì?"

"It's a long, long story, Jīngfēi. When I first met her, I helped her to settle in. You know, she was brought up in that poor cave. She was raised alone with her mother; she had no idea how to fit in. Over time, we just got closer and closer. I was going to ask her to marry me, but then...Then, a few years ago, she just started to blank me. I didn't understand. Perhaps I do now; I don't know. Who is it she finally bedded?"

"You don't know? Really?" Jīngfēi's eyebrows rose so high they were momentarily hidden by her shaggy fringe. "She's carrying Yú's child."

"Yú?"

"Yes, Yú. It's been very open. They didn't try to hide it."

"What about Túshānshì? What did she think?"

158

"Have you seen her?" A shake of the head met Jīngfēi's question. "She's pregnant as well."

"Yú?"

"No! Túshānshì!" Jīngfēi paused. "Ah! I see what you mean. Yes. It is Yú's baby. All three of them came out and announced it at the same time. It all seems a little weird. It seems that Túshānshì had been trying to have a child for ages. They say that Tú agreed with her to have a baby with Yú so he and Túshānshì could have a son, but as soon as the deed was done…Well! She fell pregnant also! That's the story, anyway. But I know better." Jīngfēi slid her forefinger down the side of her nose and winked.

"There's more?

"My sources tell me that Yú and Tú had been at it for a couple of years…that Túshānshì knew all about it…but did not let on and…when she finally confronted them, she insisted that Tú should have a baby for her. Come to think of it that would explain her going cool on you–"

"Shit!" The surprise on Bóyì's face briefly shaded his anger. "How come Yú ends up with two women, and I end up with none? It's not fair!"

"Life isn't fair; didn't your mother tell you that."

"I never knew my mother. Well, she left when I was five or six. I brought myself up on the streets. The first time anyone taught me how to do anything properly was when they taught me how to read and write."

"That might explain why you're shy around women."

"I'm not shy…I'm not!"

"How come you spent time trying to get off with Tú and…did you ever ask her?"

"No. I thought I'd wait."

"Well, that…Bóyì…is a bit shit, isn't it? You can't leave a woman waiting forever, especially someone like Tú, who hasn't got a clue. You needed to say something. You should have said something a long, long time ago."

"Mm…there are only three women I ever wanted. One was Túshānshì - taken! One was Tú - now taken! And the other–"

"Come on, who was the other?"

"You!"

159

"Me?"

"You."

Háng's Bar was a flexible creation. Positioned at a crossroads in the town, it mainly consisted of a series of stools. In the summer, the seating would be on the shady side of the street. In the winter, he would find a sunny spot for them. He always kept the pitchers of beer in the shade, and customers could refill their beakers and keep their own tally. If it were raining, the stools were moved under the semi-derelict roof of a partially demolished house. If it were cold, a fire would appear as if spontaneously. It was generally a popular spot, although they were the only two patrons this evening. The pair huddled closer as the sun went down; only Háng watched them, and then only out of mild curiosity.

Paying the bar owner was always entertaining because of its impossibility. For many, it was the high point of the evening. Bartering for the beer consumed was a complicated business in the ultimate cooperative. The beer had no price. There was no medium of exchange.

The city's deal with Háng was that he did not have to do other work if he maintained the bar and served drinks to those who needed them. His raw materials were supplied at no cost, and there was no shortage of equipment in the town. It was an arrangement that worked well, and the same system applied to those who worked at the smelters, the cleaners, the teachers and even the sex workers. If it was the case that someone felt that someone else might not be putting their back into their work, it was always possible to complain to the council. It had not happened. It was unstated if there was any complaint, although those most inclined to protest would have been the specialist workers. Sometimes, they felt undervalued.

As Bóyì and Jīngfēi rose to leave, Háng called over in their direction.

"I'm makin' that seven…or was it eight?"

"Eight, Háng…it was eight." Bóyì was reasonably convinced.

"Well…there's good news."

"What's the good news, Háng?" Jīngfēi called back.

"Those are on me…on the house…you two seems like you're deservin' it." Háng laughed.

Jīngfēi strolled over and kissed the barman on the forehead.

"Thank you, Háng. Thank you. Goodnight." Everyone knew that Háng wanted further reward, but no one knew what could be done. A kiss on the forehead was the best tip that came to mind.

Jīngfēi and Bóyì left the bar that evening and spent their first night together. Jīngfēi determined not to mention that Yú and Tú's relationship seemed to be over. She thought it for the best.

Notwithstanding the fact their romance commenced as an attempt on behalf of Jīngfēi to cheer up Bóyì, it persisted. Despite a substantial difference in their ages, they remained together through good times and bad, through happiness and sorrow, and despite all attempts of others to prise them apart.

Twenty-four: The State

Táosì, Shǎnxī: Palace Hall
Year 89: Year of the Pig
Eight days after the autumn equinox
30th September 1906 BCE

"These are my concerns about the situation in Èrlǐtou." Bóyì had the floor. He was the only one of the council members to have visited their future hometown and was heard with a significant degree of interest. Apart from everyone having aged a little and one of their members being heavily pregnant, it could have been a week since their founding meeting. Three-quarters of their people had been relocated in those intervening years; the council estimated that a higher proportion of transportable wealth had also gone.

"In the first place, we have to be worried about the way the Lóngshān have been scouting the Èrlǐtou area. It cannot be long until they persuade themselves to attack. The Sisterhood says that their presence in Ānyáng is having an effect, and they believe they can manufacture a situation whereby the Lóngshān warlords will set May of next year as a time to attack.

"It seems the Lóngshān kings have been meeting every two years. Apparently, their get-togethers have been somewhat fractious, although, in their last one, there was some suggestion that next year might be the preferred time to strike. It all fits together and suits our plans. Yú tells me the date also fits in with the grander plan, but only he can vouch for that of those present.

"I suppose my question is whether the Sisterhood can be trusted on this?" It was a query that caused Tú to bridle. As the organisation's only representative on the council, it was a dig clearly aimed at her.

"As Bóyì knows, I am not a party to all aspects of the grander plan. Only Yú or Líng can answer that question." It was becoming difficult

162

for those council members in the know to maintain a position they knew nothing of the Sisterhood's broader plans. Jīngfēi, Hòuyì, Bóyì and Tú were very well aware of the details, but it was still believed by the other council members that only Yú had comprehensive knowledge.

"The Sisterhood can be trusted." Yú was emphatic. "For now, we stick to our plan. The only available forecast is that the Lóngshān will be defeated. I trust the news they are supplying from the Lóngshān areas. I trust the information because Líng has given me regular updates.

"This means that for now, you have to trust me. I hope you can do that."

Although Yú's authority was still regarded as sound, his reputation at the council had slipped somewhat since the news had come out regarding his fathering Tú's child. The fact that she still sat next to him at the table caused some unease among the council members; a few were unaware of their falling out. The four who had not been party to Líng's explanation all those years ago suspected that it was likely that Tú, not only as a member of the Sisterhood but also having spent time in Yú's bed, knew more than she was letting on. However, it was not an argument that anyone wished to explore further.

"If there is anyone that does not have trust in me, please let me know." Yú looked around the table. "I know this is important. So far, everything has gone to plan. Everything promised has been delivered, and often earlier than expected. I think the only thing I can add to this discussion is that I firmly believe the Lóngshān will be eradicated by the end of next year."

There was no dissent, which allowed Bóyì to bring up his second point.

"My other concern is regarding the council in Èrlǐtou."

"What's going on there? It seems unlikely the council could be a problem." Yú expressed surprise.

"I'm afraid the council members say your father overrides their wishes. They say he's acting more like a ruler than a chairman. They say they are unhappy about this even though they know things will change once you arrive." Bóyì indicated Yú by nodding in his direction.

"My father is an old and stubborn man. I'm afraid that not only is he set in his ways, but my mother is as well. The two of them get together on most of their plans, as many ideas are my mother's as my father's. Neither of them likes to be contradicted. Do they accept that they will step down when we are all united? Have they anything to say about that?"

"Indeed, they have, Yú. While there, they asked me to attend a council meeting to give them an account of the situation in Táosì. When I had finished, they allowed me to stay on. There was quite a heated argument. It seemed it had to do with public space. Gǔn had become so obsessed with maximising the arable land that he had been forgetful...and I suppose that is the most polite word I can use...about land needed for other uses. Fundamentally, the people are asking for public spaces, and he is ignoring them.

"It seemed to me that the issue will die a natural death, as Gǔn has determined there is now enough land under the plough and that it will not be enlarged for this coming season. He seems content to perfect the irrigation systems rather than enlarge them further. Anyway, he stormed out of the meeting at that point. Your mother was not in attendance from the start."

"Typical! I hope he relaxes. He's a stubborn old man. If you had met my mother, you would know that standing up to her is almost impossible. He did just that when he decided to go to Mount Sōng. Talk about arguments. He wouldn't listen. He took sole charge of the Sìchuān group and began to 'rule' right then. It took my mother several years to get him back on track, and then she had to change her approach completely to get him to do what she wanted. There was no point telling him to do something anymore; it has to be much more subtle than that." Yú shook his head in exasperation.

"I suppose the council should talk to my mother first...I mean, she's on their council as the Sisterhood representative. Then, they need to find a way to talk to him that persuades rather than instructs. He can be painfully obstinate, yet he is not a bad person." Yú sighed. He had not seen his parents for over seven years and was inordinately fond of them despite their many faults.

"I think the problem goes deeper than that." Bóyì was clearly on less certain ground now. "I spoke to several members of the council after their meeting. It was almost a whole council meeting because your mother

164

and father were the only people who were not present. They are worried about succession."

"Succession?" Yú leaned forward, but there again, the entire council did as well. It was not an expression ever used in their meetings or in general discussions about how the Xià should organise themselves.

"Succession. I'll try and explain. They were united in their thoughts but came at me from all directions. I understand they wanted the council here to be aware of their views, and they most definitely wanted Yú to know." Bóyì ran a hand through his hair and caught Jīngfēi giving him a secretive smile. Before speaking, he had felt her foot run the length of his calf. He wasn't sure if it was to give him confidence or remind him to stand his ground. Jīngfēi had learned of his concerns a week before and had helped him prepare for today's meeting.

"What do they want us to know, Bóyì? Come on, what do they want me to know?"

"They realise they can cope with your father for the next few months. I told them during their full meeting that we intend to arrive shortly after the spring equinox. What they are concerned about is that…well…is that Gǔn seems to think that he will stand down then and–"

"Which is good, surely." Jīngfēi threw in support at the right time.

"Which is good…I agree. Exceptionally good. The trouble is what he seems to think he will be standing down for."

"And what would that be, Bóyì?" Hòuyì asked.

"They seem to think that Gǔn thinks that he will be stepping down so that his son will be king."

"No!" Yú laughed out loud. His genuine hilarity poured oil on what was becoming a serious concern around the table. Only Tú remained expressionless, although that was short-lived.

"Ow!" Eight faces swivelled toward Tú. "Ow! I think we just had a contribution from an extra council member." She said as a smile crept across her face. "The extra member just kicked me. Hard! It was the first time."

It was more than a simple reaction to a surprising kick inside. Many thoughts were going through Tú's mind, and, in truth, it was not the first kick she had felt. That had come earlier, just before they had taken their places. It was the main reason she had sat next to Yú. She desperately wanted him to give her some attention, and it seemed this might do the trick. It was a plan. Unfortunately, it was a plan that did not work.

"Let's take a short break, Yú. Some of us would like to give this a little more thought. May we?" Jīngfēi had been the first to stop smiling, and Tú's exclamation had provided the wake-up call she needed.

"Agreed." At Yú's remark, the women on the council surrounded Tú, although Jīngfēi chose to remain in her seat. She leaned toward Bóyì and whispered behind her hand before heading off to relieve herself. Yú remained seated, displaying not the slightest interest in the fuss surrounding Tú.

When they resumed, Yú completely ignored what had gone on and requested Bóyì be more specific.

"They did not say he had used the word 'king', but they suggested that was what he had implied. It goes a bit further than that, though."

"In what way?"

"It seems they believe that Gǔn believes that—"

"I'm getting a bit fed up with this 'they believe he believes' and 'they think, he thinks' stuff. When we add Bóyì into the equation, it becomes third-hand information." Hòuyì was exasperated. "It would be good to get the information from the horse's mouth."

"I think Bóyì is doing his best to repeat what he has heard." Jīngfēi leapt to his defence. "It's unfair to suggest he is distorting the information. What good would that do him?"

"We would not know, would we?" Tú's contribution shocked those present.

"Yes...we would! He has nothing to gain by—" Jīngfēi was interrupted by Yú.

"This is not the way to conduct a council meeting. Let's calm down.

"Bóyì, please continue." If lightning had arced from the eye of Jīngfēi into those of Tú, no one would have been surprised, although the pair seemed content to leave their verbal conflict for the moment.

"The council members believe that Gǔn wishes Èrlǐtou to become a kingdom. They believe he wants to proclaim himself as the founder. They believe that he will abdicate so that Yú will become king. They believe that Yú's son will follow him on the throne." Bóyì had finally spat

166

it out and finally relaxed. "That's all. Sorry about bringing this news, but I had to. They asked me to. I have now discharged their request. That's my job done."

"Thank you, Bóyì." Yú smiled. "I think it is time to tell you all part of that big secret." Once again, the other eight leaned forward, and sixteen elbows rested on the tabletop. None knew what he was about to say, even those who knew of the more detailed plan.

"There will be no king in Èrlǐtou! We are not set to repeat the errors of the Lóngshān!"

"That's hardly a secret, Yú." Hòuyì opined. "That's what we expect."

"It is." Yú maintained his cheerful expression. "There will be no king in Èrlǐtou because Èrlǐtou is not about to become a kingdom. This is a part of Sisterhood's plan that you may share with anyone you wish. Èrlǐtou will be a capital city but not of a kingdom. Èrlǐtou will become the capital city alright, but it will be the capital city of a new form of state. It will be the capital city of an empire! The Xià Empire!"

"And what, Yú, is an empire?" Jīngfēi asked first, breaking the astonished silence. Most of the others also seemed confused; it was not a term they had heard before.

"An empire, Jīngfēi, has a central Motherland, in this case, centred in Hénán, just south of the Yellow River. It has satellite states around it; in our case, this will mean my homeland of Sìchuān and the Wèi Valley and this area, Shǎnxī, led by Kànménrén. Eventually, we will add Jiāngsu as and when the people can return. In time, Héběi will come into the orbit once the Lóngshān rule has gone. A central Motherland surrounded by like-thinking states with fully supportive trade relations and a common desire to achieve peace and prosperity for all."

"That all sounds fine, Yú. It sounds perfect. So, you are telling us that this, er, empire, is the culmination of the Sisterhood's grand plan?" Huìān, one of the quieter council members, spoke up.

"Yes. I'm not going into any detail about how the Lóngshān will be beat−"

Finding her voice for the first time had emboldened her, and this time she interrupted Yú.

167

"What I really want to ask, Yú. What I think is most important to all of us…is…well…um…Who leads this empire thing?"

Twenty-five: The Births

Táosì, Shǎnxī: Yú's home
Year 89: Year of the Pig
Thirty-nine days after the winter solstice
29th January 1905 BCE

Whilst Yú may have had little time for Tú in the last few months, that did not mean he was not fully engaged in the result of her pregnancy. He did not like the image now adorning her body, and whilst supporting the cause, he did not like body art in any shape or form; for him, it was a massive turn-off. That Tú was less than distraught was due to her achieving her objective, her mission in life. Túshānshì ensured that Yú's relationship with his former lover had not broken down entirely and had planned that her friend should give birth in their own home.

When Tú's waters broke, Yú's wife first stepped in to assist, although it soon proved she also needed help. There was no shortage of advice. Túshānshì knew all the theoretical and technical aspects of birthing; after all, she was directly responsible for ensuring they would both give birth almost simultaneously through her knowledge of natural medicines. However, she was completely inexperienced as regards the act of giving birth, having spent more of her life sharpening weapons than on the art of midwifery.

In these odd circumstances, two of the more experienced sisters were given the run of Yú's home. They had spent a day or so ensuring they had everything they needed and knew where to find anything in an emergency. The loss of mothers and children at birth was still a significant issue; at least one in five resulted in the death of the baby, and perhaps one case in twenty, the mother's death. The odds significantly improved with the attendance of those who had seen it all before.

There were fundamental and practical issues that required the midwives' attention. Túshānshì had not given a thought to the fact that

169

birthing was a messy process and had intended to give birth on the bedding she used with Yú; that had caused peals of laughter to resound around the dwelling and ensured Túshānshì's face remained beetroot red for most of the morning. The experts quickly brought in cloths and covers that could be burned or boiled as required and extra straw to replace any that was soiled.

One of their biggest concerns was Túshānshì's age. She was in her mid-twenties, unusually old for a first baby. There was less concern over Tú. However, both women had come through the last nine months with no hiccups. The child that Tú was carrying seemed to be more than vigorous in the womb, Túshānshì's a little quieter. With everything seemingly on track, without ceremony, Yú was shown the door.

Outside, he had a cold and gruelling wait. He sat on the step, head in hand. There was no hiding the noises emanating from inside his house, and nothing he was permitted to do about it. By the time the lower groans and curses had given way to full-throated cries, rhythmic groaning, and the demands of the midwives to push, he moved a little further away to save himself from the apparent insanity. After what seemed like years, the women's moans subsided to near silence.

In what to many seemed an astounding coincidence, the two women gave birth within minutes of each other in adjacent rooms. The cry of the second child came only moments after that of the first. As if on cue, Háng sauntered by and offered Yú a swig from his bottle. It was gratefully accepted, as was the pat on the back.

Inside the home, each midwife went through a mental checklist, examining the babies and ensuring they were getting air. At this point, the mothers were advised of the gender of their offspring. A second checklist followed as they undertook another examination of the new mothers. During these checks, they counted up to eighty-eight, quite deliberately, quietly and slowly. However, on reaching the final number, it was shouted out loud as a blessing to the child. This particular count was a time-honoured ritual that no sane mother would have refused. It was considered the optimal period before the next stage of the procedure.

With the count finished and the midwives satisfied, it was time to cut the umbilical cords, a procedure that, by tradition, was left to the mothers themselves. A sharp bronze knife lay by each bed. Although the blade had a practical purpose, it was also partly ceremonial, with the mothers kissing the dagger before the problematic task of hacking through the cord. It was usual for the midwives to assist by squeezing the umbilicalis closed on either side of the cut. On occasions, such as when the mother was too weak, the midwives used the knives themselves, although this was not a preferred option. All too often, when the assistants had to raise the blade, it was to take drastic action and most likely, it would conclude in the death of either the mother or child. Mothers were invariably keen to handle the cutting themselves.

Whilst the midwives allowed the mothers to make the cut, the job of tying the knot and cleaning up the afterbirth fell to them. Before the newborn was loosely wrapped and handed to the mother, the cord was knotted as close as possible to the baby's tummy before sloshing the afterbirth into a waiting pottery vessel. Tú had asked that hers be given to Jīnxīng to eat; Túshānshì had no preference, so it was likely hers would go to the pigs.

With the new mothers holding their infants close to them, the two midwives met in the drainage area to clear up and get ready to wash the babies down. It was a time for them to compare notes. It seemed Tú's baby had been the more awkward of the two, having appeared to perform somersaults before assuming a head-down position. In Túshānshì's case, it was she who had been more problematic; the baby itself had exited almost perfectly, although the mother had undergone several panic attacks during the birth. The two midwives were delighted with their day's work, knowing that cleaning the new arrivals was the only remaining job. There was no expectation that this might prove to be a problem.

When one woman returned to Tú's room, she was faced with a dog on the bed, joyfully licking the baby's feet. As she approached, it turned and suddenly snarled at her, making her jump. It was an altogether different animal from the dog that had lain quietly throughout the birth. Tú managed to quiet the dog, but it continued to growl at the midwife as she carried the newborn through to the sluice room.

The second lady attended to Túshānshì. There was no dog to contend with, only a mother who did not want to let go of her baby. A minor wrestling match followed, which the midwife won, only because the new mother was in no condition to fight.

171

Now, the midwives had a little more to discuss since what had been relatively normal successful births had now come coated with the potential for a perfect yarn to arise. They took turns cleaning the infants, and only after they were thoroughly rinsed and dried did they stand back and look at them to compare. It proved to be a rather shocking experience. There were piles of soft cloth to dry the babies in the sluice area and another mound of towels to wrap them. There was no distinction between the wraps. It proved to be the first of a series of confusions.

Throughout the births, Yú had whiled away his time rather nervously. Sat on the outside step, he had been a picture of misery, his shivering only slightly lessened by the large throw he wore. It only worsened as time passed, which is when he moved away. Háng's intervention gave him the courage to knock on the door after he heard the cries from inside. The father was sternly told to leave, a message he received through the door, as it was unopened. Yú resumed his position, perched outside, yet only managed to control himself with difficulty. It was a while longer until they called him in. He managed to trip on the steps when he entered before rushing inside to be with his wife.

Túshānshì was weary and in more than a bit of pain but accepted his embrace willingly. She was excited for herself and her husband, but her overwhelming desire was to see the child, who was still in the sluice room.

"Go get the baby, Yú. Go on! They're out washing him."

"Him! It's a him! Are you sure?" Yú's concerned expression had broken into a wide grin. "It's a him! I mean a boy!"

"Yes, Yú, he's a boy. Now, see if they've cleaned him enough to bring him to me. Go!"

Yú immediately headed into the central area and ducked into the northern room. Inside were the two older women. Both turned as he entered. Behind them lay two newly bundled babies. Yú could probably have put names to the women if he had been in a more relaxed state of mind, although he failed utterly in these circumstances. Instead, he grabbed one and then the other, whirling them around and performing a little dance.

"Errr…please, may I have my son?"

"Yes, of course, Yú, but which son do you want first?"

172

"The first one, of course! Err…I mean mine. That is mine and Túshānshì's. Obviously, err…It's not that the other is unimportant, but…but my wife asked me to bring him in." Yú squeezed between the two ladies. Ah! Which one is he?"

If the two babies had been identical twins, they could not have resembled each other more. If Yú was flustered, then the two midwives were as well. When their silence had stretched out for a rather embarrassing period, the older woman reached across and picked up one of the boys.

"It's this one. This is your son, and he's Túshānshì's also. The other is yours and Tú's." She strained to exude confidence in her choice.

"Thank you!" Yú failed to notice the air of doubt in the room. Holding the one child tightly in his arms, he leaned forward, poking his face into that of the second child. It cried. "They're both beautiful. Thank you, thank you, thank you! Take that one in with Tú, please." With that, he turned and headed for the bed-chamber, where Túshānshì was impatiently waiting.

"Hand him to me, Yú. Gently. Put him on my breast. If he feeds early, it's always best. Come on."

"Here." Yú handed the baby carefully to his wife and dropped to one knee to share the moment at close quarters. "He's hardly beautiful, is he?"

"He is so, too! A beautiful baby. Our baby. He looks just like you, so if you think he's not beautiful, what does that say for you?" Túshānshì afforded herself a laugh, which she halted abruptly as her muscles objected to the mistreatment they had suffered in the previous hours. "It hurts, Yú, but look…it was worth it, wasn't it? Look! Our baby! What are we going to call him?"

"What about…what about…Yú?"

"I'm not calling him Yú! It's bad enough having one of you around the place!" Túshānshì pulled her husband closer and kissed him. "If you want to call him Yú, it's your choice, but don't be surprised if you end up with some confusing moments. How about Qí? Nice and short! I always thought my name was too much of a mouthful, but Qí is easy, and even you can write it down. Even if you have to do it slowly!"

Yú had been one of the more challenging students regarding reading and writing. When he had finally mastered the idea, everyone had thought he would speed up. He never had and was not particularly keen on mention of the subject. Only Túshānshì could get away with it.

"Qí it is. You know I would do anything for you. Qí. Qí. Qí. I'll get used to it!"

"Now, aren't you forgetting someone else?" Túshānshì nodded towards the next room.

"I…I don't really think I should go in there."

"Don't be silly; you have to. Tú's had your baby as well. It's not just me."

"I don't think…I don't think she would want me in there."

"Yú! Go in and see Tú. Now! The poor girl will be wondering what's up–"

"No, I'm not!" Tú stood at the door holding her newborn babe. "Here he is. Look." Tú moved over to the bed, sitting opposite to Yú. I came to show you, and I came to show his father. "I heard you deciding on a name just then. Qí. Is that right? If you're going to call your son Qí, would it be alright if I called mine Yú?" Tú smiled. "And just so we don't get confused, while he is still a young boy, we could call him Yútú! How does that sound?"

It did not sound good at all to Yú. Not good at all. He was fighting the urge to say something and hide his feelings; he began to look in more detail at the two babies. For the life of him, he could not tell them apart. His wife noticed a slight worried frown cross his face.

"And what's wrong with you? You should be pleased. Two perfect babies in one day, and both yours. No one could be unhappy." Túshānshì slapped his arm as she spoke.

"But…I can't tell them apart! I don't know which is Qí and which is Yútú. The thing is–"

"It's easy, Yú." Tú interrupted, "This one with me is Yútú. That one there with Túshānshì is Qí. We'll keep you sorted out, won't we!" She beamed at the babies one at a time.

"Why don't you leave us for a while, Yú? We need to get cleaned up. Yes, I know you think you came in after it was all over, but if you were to see the bedding right now, you would realise it is not something you would want to sleep in. The midwives will sort us out. Go! Go and have a few drinks to celebrate. Go on! Leave!"

As Yú reluctantly exited, Tú lay down next to Túshānshì, pulling Yútú onto her breast in a similar fashion to her friend.

"I know what he's saying, Tú." Yú's wife was the first to speak. "I can't tell them apart." Tú looked more closely at the two babies.

"No. I can't, either. We'll have to scrutinize them carefully to find a difference."

"We could, Tú, but does it matter?"

"Well…" It was the oddest thing her friend could have said. Tú expected alarms to set off in her head and heart, but there were none. "Well…I don't suppose it does. If it doesn't matter to me and it doesn't matter to you, then does it matter at all?"

"I don't know, Tú. I don't know. But it might matter to Yú, and it might matter to others. We don't know yet. Let's take it day by day. We could practise. Here…" She reached across, holding her child. "Take him. Go on. And give me yours."

It was a hesitant exchange, but within moments, both babies settled on different breasts.

"Look, he's feeding. He's taking milk from you, Tú."

"And look at you…the same. It's good! We can share the job!"

The pair held hands contentedly as their babies took their first meal. Both smiled at their children, although Túshānshì's expression was of arch-satisfaction. There were now several objectives Yú's wife had achieved. They had taken a long time, many years in the making, but the pieces were beginning to fall into place.

Twenty-six: The Arms Dealers

Shímǎo, Shaanxi
Year 89: Year of the Pig
Thirty-nine days after the winter solstice
29th January 1905 BCE

Hòutú and Kànménrén had never planned for theirs to be a party trip, but neither had they planned to freeze to death. The local people had a simple test to measure how cold it was outside. Three small beakers were left out: one of water, one of beer and one of wine.

If the water remained liquid, it was a warm day, and all were encouraged to be outside. The fact that the water had remained frozen since the first full moon after the autumn equinox demonstrated it had been an exceptionally long winter. This winter, nobody bothered looking at the water beaker anymore.

The beer had been frozen hard since the second full moon after the autumn equinox. If the beer froze, it was generally an indication that the younger children should stay indoors, apart from a short run around in the noon sun. Outside work was minimised for the adults, animals were brought inside each night, and the fire was permanently stoked.

When the wine froze, it usually indicated a cessation of all outdoor activities. However, as the wine beakers had been solid since the winter solstice, such an agenda had proved impossible. Bringing in fodder for the animals, firewood to keep the hearth permanently blazing and rescuing meat and fish from the ice houses were ongoing jobs. There was a strict rotation to take care of these tasks, followed assiduously and only altered if someone was too sick or had died.

It had been the same in every village they had visited, which now amounted to upwards of fifty; they had been on the road for ninety days. First, there were the greetings. As the trip progressed, the formalities reduced in length. News had got around about who they were and what they wanted. It mystified Hòutú how the word was spread, as no one seemed inclined to move further than a few paces from their hearths.

Then came the feasting and drinking. It was customary amongst these peoples, who were nomadic during the summer months, that greeting visitors with more food than it was possible to eat and more drink than it was possible to swallow was essential. Coping with the alcohol was quite different; in each of the fifty villages, there was a hangover the following morning. It was a testament to the hard work she and Kàn had spent travelling between the settlements that neither had gained any weight.

After the meal came the stories. In Shaanxi, it was customary for the guests to begin and end the tales; they alternated with their hosts between the two. Kàn was the better of the two at telling a yarn; these people were practically his own culture, and he knew what they expected. He always commenced with the Battle of Sanjiadiǎncūn. It was a detailed telling, and he always made it sound like he was in the thick of the action, even though he had been over a thousand paces downstream. The tale was gobbled up by all, followed by a myriad of questions, many going into detail that neither Kàn nor Hòutú could answer accurately.

The hosts would return the favour with a battle story of their own. These were bloody and graphic, although they amounted to little more than skirmishes. Often, they concluded with a redirection; 'if only the Lóngshān had been at the points of our spears' was a common refrain.

Hòutú was obliged to pitch in with their second story, which was a detailed account of her torture at the hands of Hú and Xí. For much of the tale, she depended on the descriptions given to her by her fellow sisters. Even twenty years on, much of her memory of the episode was still blocked. It did not mean that she did not lay on the pain, gore, and pure violence to the absolute maximum; after all, it was crucial to their theme. The point that drew most astonishment, and even anguish from the assembly, was when she told of Hú and Xí's intent that her mother was to have been the one that cut her open. It brought people to tears when she told them of her mother's subsequent execution.

It was the conclusion Hòutú dreaded most, for she had to reveal her scars on reaching the end of her tale. To do this as clinically as possible, she wore only her new bearskin robe, one that Kàn had gifted her for their wedding, and to her enormous relief, her new deerskin boots. She thought that if it had not been for the footwear, she would have died of cold each time she had to strip.

Once she had allowed the robe to drop to the floor, it was always time for an inspection. The women always came forward first; they were not at all shy about pinching, prodding, and asking questions. The children were second and more circumspect, sometimes asking a timid question but most times touching light as a feather, followed by quickly withdrawing their fingers.

Then came the men. It was the part that Hòutú hated most. They never touched her; not once had that happened in their village visits. It was the way that they looked at her body that disturbed her. They showed a clear interest in her scars and asked detailed questions about them. They wondered particularly about the different knives and how these had altered the scar patterning. One problem was that they crowded around her when they were asking questions. At these times, they obscured the view of their womenfolk. Sometimes, their gaze seemed more focused on her breasts than the scar. In one village, a man had kneeled to look intently at the bottom-most point of the wound, where it entered her pubic hair; it had been an intensely disturbing experience for her.

Hòutú had discussed the matter with Kàn, and they agreed. The underlying problems of the Lóngshān menfolk had not altogether disappeared. On the surface, what had occurred in Táosì had been replicated here in the northern Yellow River loop. Indeed, Shímǎo had fallen and fallen violently, the populace finally so sickened by the Lóngshān overlordship that they had brought it tumbling down. However, neither was convinced their achievements on the Fèn River and societal change in Èrlǐtou had penetrated male hearts and minds in these cold wastelands.

The nights did not finish with Hòutú displaying her scars. After their hosts' next story, Kàn would complete the evening by regaling them with a colourful account of the branding of Hú and Xí, something he had done himself. It was a tale everyone loved; it brought as many significant and sympathetic glances at Hòutú as it did cheers for Kàn.

The business was always conducted the following morning.

In nearly every home they had visited, they were afforded the privilege of sleeping next to the fire. Whilst this had the distinct advantage of keeping them warm, there were massive disadvantages. Firstly, it ensured they both stank of woodsmoke by the morning. More importantly, it guaranteed that even considering copulation would have to be regarded as a public act. Whatever they might have intended regarding their honeymoon trip, with the cold, the public stripping and the lack of sex, it had not entirely worked out to be as much fun as intended.

In the morning, Kàn would bring their sledge to the door of the communal dwelling. Only one sledge had to be hauled to each village. Kàn had his men positioning the loaded sledges across the countryside so that their final task of dragging them to each was not overly arduous. At each village, four people turned up, pulling a sledge; Kàn, Hòutú and two others rotated from a group of ever-willing assistants for each trip. Usually, their helpers were a couple, and Hòutú found chatting with another female during the day was welcoming.

Removing the trunk and bringing its load indoors was easy if the sledge had been under a shelter overnight. If it were exposed, there was a different story. On one occasion, snow the depth of a man piled atop the vehicle, which had hardened into ice. It had taken them a long time to offload and bring the gifts into the halls.

The gift for each village was the same: fifty bronze arrowheads, thirty bronze spear tips and three clay casting moulds for a knife, arrowhead and spearpoint. There was also a large sack of barley seed. The bulk bronze gifts had an immediate and obvious use and were welcomed warmly, as the people in these parts predominantly used stone. The use of the barley and the moulds required an explanation. Whilst Kàn expounded on using barley to make beer, Hòutú explained how they would, in time, be able to make bronze objects using the moulds.

It was made clear that the spearpoints and arrowheads were gifts, but it was also evident that further assistance with the art of brewing and bronze smelting was not. It was part of the deal.

The trade had changed as the season progressed. The pair had two requests on the first half of the trip; as the freeze set in, only the second remained necessary. In return for the new technologies, each village was to light a big fire on the new moon following the spring equinox. While a few realised the local impact of the fires, only Hòutú and Kàn understood their significance in the grander plan. However, they would be too geographically distant ever to have an opportunity to see its fruition. The pair had to be satisfied with their bit parts in the play, for they would never see the finale.

Now, they had finally returned to their starting point, Shímǎo. The full moon was due in just over a week. The last new moon had signalled the start of the new year festivities, but few in the villages had any cause to celebrate. However, in Shímǎo, there was most definitely a party atmosphere.

Like Táosì, the rape of Shímǎo was almost over. The few remaining people occupied the central terrace area; the outer and inner enclosures had been abandoned and stripped of anything useful. The pillage had been organised; a slide was constructed from the central area down to the Kuye River. Only unbreakable objects had been consigned to this ramp, mainly the wooden supports for structures and some of the larger stonework. Even so, some items were pulverised by the abrupt halt on the iced-up river after the two-in-one gradient.

Hòutú and Kàn had a guided tour, one which reminded her of taking Tú around Táosì for the first time. There was a significant difference; Táosì had been cold and empty. Shímǎo was crazily cold, windswept, and barren. It sat atop a hill, ensuring icy winds blew through them at every corner, and while the exercise kept them warm to some degree, Hòutú did wonder if it was worthwhile.

There was much to take in: A rectangular altar mound with sloping sides and a flat walled area at the top. A pond, square in shape and sizeable enough to swim in if it had not been frozen solid. At the fortress entrances were geometric patterns drawn on the walls, although these might have been deliberate damage from when the city eventually fell. Likewise, human faces appeared carved in the stone sections of rooms, but these had been defaced by the nomads when they stormed the citadel. The walls were more substantial than Táosì's, consisting of an outer and inner wall in addition to that around the central area. There was much more use of stone and little in the way of tamped earth fortifications.

Kàn had been here several times and spoke of its historic grandeur. For Hòutú, this was only her second visit; they had dropped in
180

briefly at the commencement of their circular tour of the Yellow River loop. In its present state, she found it difficult to appreciate the scale of the place and found tales of its previous wealth incomprehensible.

Against the inner wall, a collection of cleaned and dried bones caught her eye. There was one large pile and two smaller ones. Examination of a bone from the larger revealed it to be a sheep's scapulae. She had to ask about the second and third piles; the former she guessed to be of a large deer; it was the same shoulder bone, but the third pile had her guessing.

Hòutú mulled over the possible reasons as she stroked the flattest surface of the scapula. Looking at the others, she realised the one from the sheep was the smoothest. It was an odd bone to have chosen to keep. It almost seemed designed for some other purpose than keeping a sheep upright. It was a thought that would nag at her for months before she realised its potential re-purposing.

Their guide proved hesitant to reveal the identity of the bones in the third pile. As Hòutú turned a bone over in her hands, he finally admitted it was human.

"If this is the shoulder bone, where's the rest of the skeleton?" Kàn asked quite innocently.

"I don't know. I do know where the skulls are, though. We dug some out just last week. You know—"

Hòutú interrupted their guide. "Are these what I think they are? Are these the remains of the slaughtered girls? Really?"

"It's only some of 'em. There were hundreds and hundreds. It's what led to the war. It's why we finally kicked those Lóngshān bastards out. They kept stealing our daughters and then raping 'em and then killing 'em. They were real bastards, those lot."

"Show us the area where the skulls were." Kàn was demanding; it was not a request.

"They're all over. You can find 'em at almost any of the gateposts buried underneath. In fact, you can scratch the earth in most places and find bones. This city was built on bones, but mostly skulls. I think they usually fed the remains to the dogs, but they kept the skulls for some reason. I have no idea why they kept these shoulder bones. None. Really." Their guide was becoming agitated and tearful. He seemed desperate to avoid taking them to see a skull pit. Eventually, he pointed one out near the east gate and sent them on alone.

"I know all about the girls," said Hòutú, "but I didn't realise it was so many. How many did they kill to push the herders to rebel?"

"Who knows in all? They called for over two hundred the last time, and the herders let them take them. They took up arms when they got together and realised how many girls were gone." Kàn turned her, so their eyes met, and, with arms outstretched, he lightly held her shoulders, "You know, these people living in the wilds up here…Well. They don't always think too much about a child going missing. They're happy if they can bring one boy and one girl to adulthood. If others fall along the wayside, then that's quite normal. Too many girls aren't always a good thing for them. But, you know, I guess they came to the point where they could see there wouldn't be enough. It wasn't the slaughter they objected to as such; it was the shortage."

"That's disgusting!" Hòutú was absolutely horrified.

"It may be, but it's true."

"Will this place ever be civilised, Kàn?"

"What I think will happen is that someday, someone will build a big wall. It'll be like a sheep fence. The herders and all their wild ideas will be on the north side of the wall, and to the south will be the farmers and civilisation."

"But you're a herder, Kàn."

"I'm a herder through necessity. My people had to give up farming. We had to go on the move. It doesn't mean we don't want to settle down again. That's what Shǎnxī is all about. We'll herd and hunt until the land is fertile once more. We'll keep moving until the forests have grown back and the streams are clean. Then we will become farmers again, but I'll be long dead, and so will you. Until that time comes, you and me…well…we'll be herders and hunters. Like it or not."

"That doesn't mean we'll kill babies, does it?"

"I think we're getting a bit long in the tooth to be having babies to start with, let alone killing them." Kàn pulled her to him. "Let's not get all upset about what has gone. We must look to the future now; we've done our part. It is for others to move the process on. All we can do is hope that our contributions have been sufficient."

182

"Well…I gave them Tú–"
"And I gave them Líng!"
"Do you think it'll work, Kàn?"
"One day."

Twenty-seven: The Gambler

Táosì, Shǎnxī: Yú's home
Year 90: First day of the year of the Rat
Thirty-five days to the spring equinox
14th February 1905 BCE

Líng had permanently shed the moniker, Girl; it was only used now when she sat down with Grandmother and Mother for their annual meeting. She had been the only resident of Táosì to be selected for every migratory trip; she now knew the route well, both the outbound cart journey and the inbound march.

In all those years, she had never again backed such an outside bet as the Battle of Sanjiadiǎncūn. When she considered that night and the following morning, it always made her catch her breath or pause mid-step. Many nights of every year since then, her nightmares of losing that conflict had woken her. Líng considered winning the battle as her greatest triumph. She did manage to laugh about sitting under a cart whilst spears rained down. Even so, she remembered she had not even contributed to the distracting noises; hers had been a silent vigil, other than a whispered prayer that she would succeed.

Whatever she thought about her role in the triumph, Líng was not considered a hero in any sense. To a large extent, people had regarded her as a nuisance, which continued to be the case. Even as the Sisterhood's plans unfolded and the migrations to Èrlǐtou had strengthened, her role was never publicly understood. That it was only ten days before the final trek and the complete abandonment of Táosì was not particularly associated with her. It was as if the Sisterhood did not exist. Líng approved of the low profile.

What it did mean was that she was lonely. She met with Yú once a month, usually a day before the council meetings; she treasured that time. She had similar discussions with Túshānshì, Tú and until her

184

departure, those meetings had also included Hòutú. She also met those women who still allied themselves with the Sisterhood, although there were now only a handful, and they had little part in the ongoing processes. However, they did provide occasional strands of information.

One such titbit she had missed entirely was that Jīngfēi had fallen pregnant. It seemed as if this year would be full of births, planned and unplanned. The latest news did not concern her over much; she regarded it as peripheral to her plans. Bóyì had been over the moon at impending fatherhood and spent time trying to convert one of the carts to make it more comfortable for the future mother. Three months into a pregnancy was not an ideal time to undergo a four-week trek in a rickety wagon. Líng had suggested it would be better if Jīngfēi walked on the basis it would be better for her, but the expectant father would have none of it.

Indeed, two carts had already been prepared for women with babies, which included Tú and Túshānshì. If Hòutú had performed her responsibilities to the Sisterhood admirably, Líng could not say the same of the two younger women. Whilst Túshānshì had cooperated in getting Tú to reproduce with Yú, it had never been their intention that she become pregnant herself. Additionally, the last thing they wanted was for Tú to no longer be talking to Yú.

When Líng was first introduced to the babies, she was shocked by their similarities. Although the father may only be on distant terms with Tú, it did not prevent the two mothers from getting together whenever he was not around. Their children were not only difficult to tell apart when they were naked, but when wrapped in identical blankets and tightly bound, they could have been pupae from the same butterfly. What increased the surprise was that the two mothers' looks were so different. Whereas Tú was short and slim built, even wiry, Túshānshì was tall and even more voluptuous since childbirth. Yú's wife had maintained those attributes that made everyone stare at her when they saw her walk by, whilst Tú would not have stood out in a crowd.

If Líng felt a moment of sympathy for the drabber of the two, it soon dissipated when she considered her next task. It was necessary for her to be able to tell the babies apart. If going into battle some seven years before had given her victory against ridiculous odds, here was a situation where it was simply fifty-fifty. Not only did it have to be one child of only two candidates, but the odds could also be improved through observing the baby's interactions with their mothers. It appeared to be simple.

When Líng considered her successes and failures, there were some of each; outcomes had yet to be determined for others. One such that remained in the balance was Kàn and Hòutú. Allowing her father to take his new wife with him was a risk; after all, he was engineering their biggest lever in the planned downfall of the Lóngshān. She regarded her most successful gambles as the battle itself, getting a representative onto the council and having Túshānshì let Tú get pregnant by Yú. Her biggest failures were allowing Tú the *wénshēn*, simply because of Yú's immediate reaction to it, and in not preventing Túshānshì's pregnancy. Meeting Grandmother and Mother this last year meant she had not always been present when she should have been. When the cat was away, the mice always seemed to enjoy a bit of a party.

When Líng added everything up, she realised there was little gain from the experiences, although she had become better at predicting her mistakes. One of the babies was necessary, and one was not; her job was to know which of the two was paramount. She needed to be on a sound footing regarding identifying the babies; the task would become much more difficult when they left Táosì.

If that concerned Líng in the short term, she felt the reason the problem had arisen hid a bigger worry. Was it Túshānshì or Tú who was now pursuing a personal agenda? Were the pair operating outside the parameters set by the Sisterhood? If they were not in an alliance to confound the expectations of them, which one of the pair was pushing the boundaries? Líng suspected that it was Túshānshì who was pulling the strings but could not be sure about Tú's involvement. Hints had produced no answers, and direct questions were met with dismissive hilarity, but still, the outcomes were too critical for chance and error. What the Sisterhood wanted was Yú's son by Tú, but they wanted the whole world to believe the child was Túshānshì's own. The pair's actions were making an initially delicate scheme increasingly tricky.

What was confounding Líng most was the extent to which the two women actively shared their babies. The sharing was not only confined to cuddles and hugs; it extended to breastfeeding and cleaning them up.

Neither woman appeared to favour one child or the other, and neither pupa preferred one of the mothers. It was as if they were a single organism.

Líng had found it easy to slip into the role of short-term babysitter. Usually, if one mother wanted to slip off, the other would do the chores. If that extended to one breastfeeding two babies at once, that was what happened. Although neither mother would leave her child for long, Líng encouraged them to take a daily walk together to rebuild their strength in preparation for the long journey ahead. It was such a common-sense idea that both had jumped at it immediately. If nothing else, it was a chance to walk Jīnxīng. The only problem was that both wanted to take their babies to parade around the town and show them off. Líng had to put her foot down.

"You can't take them out in this temperature…they'll freeze!"

"Not if they're wrapped up." Tú held several blankets aloft.

"Not even with blankets. You'd be crazy."

"We may be crazy, but the babies will be nice and warm…you'll see." Túshānshì took one of the wraps from Tú and began to swaddle the infant she held.

"Besides," Tú added, "everyone wants to see them. Do you know what they're calling them? The Táosì Twins…"

"I know they're calling them the Táosì Twins…however inappropriate…but they'll be calling them the Táosì Twin corpses if you take them out in this. You should invite people around if you want to show them off."

"But we want everyone to see them! You can't get the whole town in—"

"You two are supposed to have had a Sisterhood education, and you're thinking about going out in this. I can't believe—"

"What's the Sisterhood got to do with this?" Túshānshì was suddenly quite serious. "My boy has nothing to do—"

"I meant that you are both trained to use some common sense and to have a modicum of medical knowledge. You do not want icy air in the lungs of a child not yet one moon old! Let alone two of them!"

"She has a point." Tú conceded. "You know—"

"I know she has a point. It's just…It's just I don't like being told what to do. That's all. I've been doing what I've been told to do all my

187

life, and I'm getting a little irritated by it." Túshānshì's pent-up steam was beginning to escape.

"Eh, Túsh! They're both asleep. Let's pop out now, walk around, invite a few people in, and we'll be back before lunchtime." Tú's calming words worked.

"Right. How many visitors for today, Tú?" Túshānshì asked.

"Three hundred! Let's go for it!"

"No! That's too many for the babies. What about ten?" Líng saw an opportunity, but the idea of visitors bringing their winter germs into the place was not appealing.

"It's a deal, Líng. Now. Do you mind looking after them?" Tú winked at Túshānshì. "No? Then we'll be off." Once Jīnxīng had been roused, she dragged her friend to the door. They both waved at the babies before slipping out.

It took Líng a moment or two to determine which baby to mark. It was evident to her that there was nothing to choose between them. One of the babies belonged to Tú, as to which one was anybody's guess. Determining how to make the mark was a decision she had made the week before.

It was the recollection of Tú's *wénshēn* that had finally given her the idea. She had a needle, soot, and plenty of rags to clean up blood spots. What she did not have was the faintest idea of how a baby might react to being pricked with a needle, where might be the place she could do so without causing excess bleeding, and where was the best place to keep it hidden from its mother, whoever that might be. Líng had determined to work backwards; once one child was marked, she could then work out who the mother was.

She knew that mothers tend to look almost everywhere on their child's skin, and only after long deliberation did she choose a point behind the ear, halfway down, just where it met the scalp. She was surprised at how minimal the blood loss was and how quickly it clotted. With some luck, the tiny scab and the blue mark it left would go unnoticed.

By the time Tú and Túshānshì returned, there was no sign of the soot, needle, or bloodstained cloth. Líng heaved a sigh of relief as she waved them goodbye.

It was two days later that her relief turned to total exasperation. On Líng's subsequent examination, it turned out that both babies sported an identical tiny blue mark behind each of their ears. The two mothers were playing with her.

Twenty-eight: The Departure

Táosì to Shāngyuǎncūn, Shǎnxī
Year 90: Year of the Rat
Twenty-one days to the spring equinox
28th February 1905 BCE

There was a sense of urgency about the departure. Several messages winged in by pigeons had urged haste. The goal was to have everyone settled in Èrlǐtou by the spring equinox. It was to be both a speedy and arduous journey.

A few had chosen to remain, although they amounted to no more than a handful. Their reasons were predominantly escapist, almost a frontier mentality, for Táosì, once a central hub to rival any, was no longer habitable. The last six months had been spent ensuring the infrastructure was damaged beyond repair, and the final few weeks ensured the destruction of the last remaining habitations. In the days before the departure, sleeping arrangements had become communal. The palace hall provided the final roofed space, and that was to be brought down by those staying behind.

The remainers knew what they were doing. Like the villagers visited by Kàn and Hòutú in the Yellow River loop, they were left with quantities of bronze arrowheads, spearheads and the three moulds. Additionally, they were given supplies of grains: millet, wheat, barley, and rice. They had no plans to farm, and the grains provided only an emergency food supply. Those staying behind planned to abandon a settled urban life for one of semi-nomadism. Large stocks would only weigh them down.

They were also left with love. There was no animosity between those going and staying, merely a sadness at the parting. It was early and dark, but a tiny group waved off the train of carts. Many were tearful and would momentarily step up to hug or kiss those on the wagons to whom they had been closest. 'Bring me some good skins!' had been a popular shout from those trekking away from the town, and 'I'll pay you well for some mutton in a few years!' The cries were a poor disguise. Most believed that they would not meet their comrades again.

If the destruction of Táosì was significant symbolically, it was even more important strategically. Although the city had lost its primary economic purpose, to have left it intact to rot naturally would have invited alternative occupations. The Sisterhood intended that Shǎnxī should act as a protection for Èrlǐtou, not to become a centre from which an attack could be mounted. There were routes from the east and north from which the Lóngshān could infiltrate the area - the last thing anyone needed was a surprise pincer movement. The Xià would have enough on their hands in the coming months even if all went to plan. If everything did not go smoothly, a Lóngshān occupation of Táosì would become a distinct possibility.

Therefore, the remainers' last task before moving to their chosen areas in the Fèn Valley was to disrupt the town's water supply. It amounted to little more than smashing channels, aiming to provide flood water with alternative exit routes. That simple step would undermine walls and carve the gullies deeper. The care that went into the demolition work was probably more thoughtful than the original design of the drainage and supply system. If those leaving for Èrlǐtou did not want Táosì to become a magnet for Lóngshān hordes, then it was doubly so for those who were to remain in the valley. All had seen what a power-hungry Lóngshān city could do to Shǎnxī, and there was no wish for a repeat of that situation.

The sixty wagons rolled out under the light of the full moon. Sunrise was still a while off. Little light was needed on the well-known tracks closer to Táosì as the going was easy. An early start substantially lengthened the distance they could travel on the first day. If the hour of departure had been carefully considered, then the date had been given even more thought. It was still cold in the Fèn Valley and would be colder still in the mountains, but the firm ground compensated for this. There had been minimal winter rain, and there was a need to reach the Yellow River before its waters began to rise.

Whether walking, riding or sitting atop the carts, there was not one of the party who did not glance back at the home they were now leaving for good. For so long, it had been a home of hatred, but in the last six years, it had become one of comradeship and brotherly love. Crumbling towers of tamped earth shone in the moonlight, giving it the appearance of a fairy castle on the horizon. As the city dropped out of sight behind them, they approached the fishing village on the river to collect a few more adventurers and their pre-loaded carts. The train did not pause; the newcomers simply joined in as it turned towards the south.

The first day's trek was flat, easy-going, and allowed the teams to find their pace. It was also a long day, and it was expected they would reach the foot of the escarpment at Shāngyuǎncūn before nightfall. They would make camp and plan the passage through the low pass to the south the following day. The pass would be the first experience of challenging terrain for many. The second day's march would only cover the distance a man could walk in an hour to ensure the train did not break up.

From their first overnight stop, it was only a short horse ride to the site of the Battle of Sānjiādiǎncūn and back. Túshānshì was keen to show Tú the location of the victory about which she had heard so much. As Bóyì considered it tempting fate for the two to go alone, he borrowed three horses so he could accompany them. Very publicly, he temporarily passed the leadership of the cart train over to a deputy before the three veered off to the west. When he had asked Jīngfēi about coming, she patiently explained that it might not be a good idea for her to get on a horse in her present state. Yú also declined when he learned Tú was going, and when Líng was asked, she seemed delighted that the two new mothers were shooting off for a while.

After an energetic gallop, which left them all breathless, it took little time to arrive at the riverbank.

"So, Bóyì, you were on the losing side?" Tú managed to smile wickedly between deep gulps of air.

"I thought you knew, Tú. The boys won the battle, even if we did lose!"

"We were positioned here. In a hole, covered in thorns." Túshānshì was more interested in explaining Yú's role on the day. "And where were you, Bóyì?"

"I came down around here. You can't tell anymore. It's overgrown. I think those thorn bushes you used must have rooted. You must remember. I have childhood friends buried under here."

"Sorry, Bóyì, I forgot. So, what about Yú?" Tú was excited in her attempt to relive the battle.

"Well…Yú and Túshānshì would have been there in the centre of the scarp. We must have passed almost straight over them; we didn't see them at all. We got to the base of the slope and were then ordered to spread out. It was all quite strange. All the little kids in front of us and the real soldiers at the back. We threw our first spears over the palisade; that's where it was." Bóyì pointed, making a circle with his finger. "It was like a competition to see who could throw furthest into it. Then we launched our second spears, and that was when it happened. We just heard arrow after arrow after arrow. It was like rain. So, we flattened ourselves on the ground."

"So, you didn't see anything else?" Tú asked.

"Ah. Some of us saw Hú and Xí escaping into the river and–"

"And then they were captured by Kàn! I can almost see it."

Tú closed her eyes, imagining the sounds and smells of the battlefield. Bóyì had pointed out the place where Hú and Xí had slipped off; she now superimposed her memories of the two men on the riverbank. The two dandies would have been unwilling to mess up their clothes, let alone jump into the icy water. She delighted in their discomfort and tried to picture their dishevelled state when Kàn had fished them out downstream. The whole scene was so real it was beginning to make her feel horny. The hairs on her arms were standing, her nipples had firmed, and without realising, she ground herself down harder on the horse's back. As she opened her eyes, there was only one thought.

"Bóyì, do you have any regrets about what happened or what has happened since?" Tú had pulled her mount up to his own so close their legs were touching. It was much more than simple flirting.

"No. No regrets. Other than my friends, of course. Everything Yú promised us that day has come true. I don't remember any father, but Yú is like a father to me, a good father, an exceptional father. No, I have no regrets."

"What about me, Bóyì? Do you have any regrets about me?" Tú leaned forward and whispered, firmly pressing her calf onto his own. She whispered so quietly that Túshānshì could not hear, and her mount hid the movement of her leg.

Bóyì met her eyes momentarily and, realising the danger, turned his steed before trotting away from her.

Back at the wagon halt, carts were drawn in a circle, the bullocks hobbled in grazing pasture, and fires were lit. To everyone's surprise, Háng brought one of the carts into the centre of the ring and began to open its carefully packed contents. He had been prevented from loading the large pitchers of beer, but no one had said anything about the smaller flagons in which he had a distilled brew made from yams. As there were four hundred thirsty people involved, each was limited to about half a beaker. Inevitably, the once fully laden wagon became empty very quickly.

Half a beaker of yam hooch was probably enough for anyone and possibly too much for the small children who got their hands on it. One staggered silently through the throng, and another repeatedly failed to stand on her head. It was the spur the trip needed: a party atmosphere to get them over the leaving and into the journey.

Nobody took any notice of Líng. She had avoided the wine and sat quietly with her two charges, Qí and Yútú. The two boys were probably weary themselves, having been carried throughout the day by their walking mothers, who had concluded the back of a wagon was not quite as comfortable as it might be. They were wrapped up and sleeping in massive bundles on the back of one of the carts.

Líng perched on the edge of the flatbed and called Jīnxīng over to her. The bitch responded immediately; she now regarded Líng as part of the family. When she tapped the flatbed, the animal leapt up, quickly sniffed the one sleeping infant, and then sniffed and licked the other before curling itself around its wrapped form. Líng sighed in relief. It mattered not that she could not tell the bairns apart; it mattered not that the mothers seemed unable to distinguish between the two. Now she was convinced that, with the help of the bitch, she would know which child was the one. A brief thought flitted through her head. Here was another life more important than her own; she would extend her babysitting duties to include the one with four legs.

The three riders returned shortly after the wine had run dry. For food, they had to content themselves with leftover gruel. When all had eaten, the council members assembled to hear Bóyì's explanation of the agenda for the following day.

"Tomorrow is our first preparation for the tougher sections…it's a very short day. The experienced cart drivers will double up with the new ones to help them, although we will not all leave at once. It's best if everyone walks except for the drivers."

"How long a walk is it?" Jīngfēi asked.

"About an hour if you walk quickly. It's pleasant, and the walking is easy. A tree-shaded valley with not much of a climb."

"Why all the fuss, then?" Yú asked.

"As I said…we need to get the drivers trained. They'll be crossing streams, taking on short, steep sections. There are a few downhill bits, all of that sort of stuff. These are minor hazards, but good leg work for the larger hazards they'll face. They have to learn, and this is the best place to—"

"Any chance of bandits?" Huìān interrupted.

"Yes. We don't expect any who'll take on the whole train, but they might take on stragglers or an advance party. Stay together. Yú can lead the horse riders to scout out the route. Yú, I'll send someone with you who knows the lie of the land.

"Does everyone understand?" There were nods around the campfire. "Any questions?" A chorus of negatives followed. "Right! Would you please let everyone else know what's going on. Then let's get some sleep. We begin to roll at sun-up. Be ready. I'm off to bed. Goodnight!"

After he left, there were a few shocked faces around the fire. It was only now beginning to sink in that Bóyì was in charge. Yú may be their council leader, but these were not issues they would debate and vote on. For however long they were on the trek, they did not have a council leader; they had a commander. Their commander expected everyone to do as they were told, when they were told, without the necessity for discussion. That he was willing to listen when there was an opportunity was positive; that his expectations extended to all, including Yú, his hero, simply astonished.

Twenty-nine: The Mountains

Xilěngkǒucūn to Yuanqù, Shănxī
Year 90: Year of the Rat
Eighteen days to the spring equinox
3rd March 1905 BCE

Bóyì had paired himself with Háng. The barman had been extremely nervous on the easier inclines on the second day, and now they were facing much worse. His empty flagons had been jettisoned, and his new load comprised more basic provisions for the journey; it ensured his cart became lighter as the trek went on and the going became trickier.

"They seem to go on forever!" Háng waved his hand at the vertiginous, conifer-clad mountains stretching around the horizon ahead of them. Only the crags closer to the peaks were bare of trees, and here, whereas snow lay in the crevasses, bare rocks were exposed where the wind had swept them clean. To the rear was the flatland. They faced the mountains, snowdrifts, and a severe uphill haul for the next few days.

"No, Háng, not forever. We'll not be climbing the mountains; we're going through a pass. We're not going far each day; the first day is–"

"Easy! Yes, you told me. It's easy! You told me last night, you told me this mornin', and you're tellin' me again. It doesn't look easy to me!"

"Look ahead." They seemed to be rattling along, but in reality, it was only a stiff walking pace. "See how this valley twists and turns between the mountains. Well, for three days, you're basically going to follow the valley. You could do it by yourself!" Bóyì laughed.

"Like hell!" Háng shouted as the cart's right wheel jarred over a rock, dropping suddenly and jarring the spines of both men. "That's what I'm talkin' about, these–"

197

"You have to avoid those rocks, Háng. Going over those is the best way to lose a wheel. You wouldn't want that now, would you?"

"I could do with a drink! I used to tell my ol' missus; it doesn't do no good to be farin' abroad without a shot or two. Trouble is I've none left."

Bóyì had dismounted and was walking alongside when another rock interfered with Háng's progress. Once again, it was the right wheel. It dropped the vehicle the length of a man's lower leg. With a tearing sound, followed by a loud crack, the axle snapped, and the cart lurched to one side. Although the sacks survived the drop, Háng was thrown into a patch of marshy grasses. If the barman had stayed where he was, he would have escaped the accident with minor personal embarrassment. It was unfortunate that instead, he rolled a few steps directly into a large stagnant and partly frozen pond. Swearing, he rose from the water covered in stinking mud from head to foot. There was no real damage done except to his pride.

"I hope your ol' missus advised you to bring a spare set of clothes with you!" Bóyì laughed before calling to those around him. "Someone wrap a blanket around him; he'll freeze otherwise.

"These carts here. Yes, you! These ten. Come to a halt, and we'll show you how to fix this." Bóyì commanded an immediate response. "Which one of you has the spare wheels and axles?" A hand went up at the back. "Right, dismount and gather around Háng's cart."

"But Háng's still there."

"Yes. You'll be helping him as well."

"That may be true…but he stinks!" Twenty laughing women and men gathered in a circle as Háng tried to clean himself.

Bóyì placed his arm protectively around the barman. "He may stink, but you will too when this is over! Come on, let's get this fixed.

"This wheel looks sound…no need to replace that. The axle is ruined. Look at the damage that rock caused. Now, look at the rock. That's what you've got to avoid. We can't afford to do this job too many times." He returned to his work, calling for a hammer and then brute strength when needed for the lifting tasks.

All were impressed at the speed and efficiency with which Bóyì fixed the cart. Three men helped with the lifting, and two women brought

198

the new axle; the remainder stood in awe as they learned how to do the job.

"...and that's it! Finished. Let's get these wagons rolling again!"

Over the next few days, time after time, there were breakdowns or simply carts getting stuck when the turns were too steep. On more than a few occasions, one of the bullocks stumbled so seriously that it had to be put out of its misery. Each time, Bóyì was at hand, organising, encouraging, and working his muscles to solve the problems. As the trek went on, his standing rose and rose.

On one of the straighter and more even sections, when there was time for a chat, Háng brought up the problems of running a bar.

"You see, Bóyì, it's not as easy as you might be thinkin'. Everyone thinks it's just a matter of makin' beer. However, that's the easy bit." He flicked the bullocks' arses with a pitifully small whip; they showed no response. "Well, you see, you've got to get the ingredients and, fair dues, I get them for free, but makin' beer is an art...it's a craft...I put all my skills and knowledge into makin' the best beer I can."

"And it's mighty good beer!" Bóyì smiled at what seemed to be the minor matter of how Háng organised his life.

"It is that. It is the best north of Mount Guófēng, even if I say so myself. But, but 'cause I am given the ingredients, then I can't be picky. Like, I must accept what I'm given. If I was a buyin' the ingredients, it'd be a different matter. Then I could select the best."

"I see your point, Háng, I see your point. So, you'd prefer to pay for your ingredients, then?"

"No, no...not like it is now. That'd not be fair. What are you thinkin'? Me payin' for ingredients and givin' the beer away! That makes no sense."

"It does not, Háng."

"You see...if I was paid for my beer, then I could pay for the ingredients. End result - everyone would get better beer. You see?"

"There's a minor problem with that system, Háng. How would people pay? How would you buy it? Will you sleep with the farmers so they pay you in barley, wheat, or yams? The way we worked it in Táosì is that you got off doing the farming jobs and got free ingredients if you made beer and gave people somewhere to sit. It's the same system with the bronze smelters or the whores; it's give and take. It's a community system; no one pays for anything. It all seemed to work. Look at everyone. Six years of taking Táosì apart, and everyone's happy."

"That may be so, young man, but it'll not work for much longer. I agree with you; takin' apart Táosì was the job. The one and only job. Everythin' else was per..peri…"

"Peripheral." Bóyì stepped in. "So, you don't think we can transfer that system to Èrlǐtou?"

"Èrlǐtou won't be no bleedin' commune…not like Táosì became. Everyone's going to start lookin' out for 'emselves. Everyone's gonna want a piece of the pie. You know, it's difficult gettin' a piece of the pie when there ain't no pie." Háng peered at Bóyì. "That's what I'm thinkin' anyhow."

"I do see your point, Háng, I–"

"Whether you see the point or not, right now, is not the issue. It's whether you see the point when we've been a year or two in Èrlǐtou. I'd be bettin' they've come up with somethin' already." Háng sucked in a deep breath. He was coming to his point. "It's just that you're on the council. You've got the ear of Yú. It might be up to you to get things done. What d'you think?"

"I will think about it, Háng. What you're talking about, though, is complicated. You seem to be asking for a method of exchange or a means of paying for something without barter. It's not something I know anything about. Nothing. I'll have to ask someone."

"Well…you'd better ask the right person!"

"I'm not sure there is a right person. What you're talking about is different. What you're talking about would make a big change to how we live our lives. I think Háng that you're talking about societal change, and I reckon that you, as a barman, know much more about society than someone like me who is just on the council."

"You may be right, Bóyì. You may be right. Let's talk about it again sometime." Háng refocussed on the track ahead as the going became more difficult. From that moment, Bóyì felt a worry begin to niggle him, one that would not go away.

The third day after Háng's cart had broken its axle, they fetched up at an overnight halt at the top of the col. Although they had been rolling up the pass for some time, the concentration required by all had meant they had not necessarily had time to look around. The scenery was awe-inspiring. Rolling forested slopes ran in every direction, the hills undulating into the distance seemingly without end. The track was still clear, although light snow flurries swept around them.

Nobody had ridden on the carts except the drivers for the last three days, but the walking, whilst uphill, had not been arduous. Even so, an early halt was gladly accepted as it would mean time to butcher and cook the fallen bullocks. There was also a simple burial to attend to; one of the young children had become ill and died unexpectedly. Bóyì found this sad, but to have come so far with only one fatality and no severe injuries was very satisfying. His priority was for the entire party; it was Yú who headed off with the deceased girl's mother and father to help them dig a grave. Arms draped over their shoulders, he offered as much comfort as possible. It seemed the cold alone had carried off the baby. There were no other indications of illness.

There was not enough space to arrange a circle of carts. Instead, they positioned themselves just off the track under the vast cedars. Once they were all set up and fires had been started, for the first time since the trek had begun, Bóyì called them together for a mass meeting.

There was good shelter from the wind and snow amongst the trees. Even so, Bóyì had to holler so that everyone could hear.

"The first thing is…well done! This is the highest point on the whole journey." There was a resounding cheer. "The next few days are all downhill…downhill to the Yellow River! Now. I don't want you to think that downhill is easier than uphill because sometimes it's harder. I'll be speaking to all the drivers about that separately." He paused for a moment. "Isn't it beautiful? Look around you."

"Yes, it's beautiful but a mite cold!" A shout from the crowd.

"It is cold, which is why I've brought you this." Bóyì turned to the cart behind him, pulling back the cover and extracting a single flask. His audience groaned.

"That'll not go far, Bóyì!"

"No, Mài, it would not. That's why there are another ninety-nine bottles on this cart. They're all for you, and they're all for tonight!" If the

201

cheer had been loud before, it was now tumultuous. Bóyì had to wave them to silence.

"Noise is good. Noise is terrific. There are bears and wolves out in these woods, and we don't want any of the youngsters wandering off. Make a lot of noise, and it will keep them away."

"What…the kids?"

"No, the…Sorry, you're joshing, aren't you? I want you all to say a big thank you to Háng because he made this spirit, although he had no idea, no idea at all, that I was bringing it with us. I had to keep it hidden from him! Where is he?" Háng waved over the group. "Cheers, Háng!

"Now, take care. Get a big meal in you, and…stay safe!"

A great deal of private analysis was applied to Bóyì's performance. Over the last week, he had proved himself. Yú was considering him in a new light as a future leader. Tú looked wistfully at him repeatedly and at Jīngfēi's pregnancy; she wondered what lever might separate them. Túshānshì appeared confused; would the timing of her son's coming of age be too late? Jīngfēi simply hugged her partner, then eyed him proudly all evening, making plans for the night ahead.

Thirty: The Crossing

Yínyánxiáng, Shǎnxī
Year 90: Year of the Rat
Eleven days to the spring equinox
10th March 1905 BCE

There was bright sunshine. Tiny clouds scudded across the skies, but the day was set fair. After the mountains, it was a relief to feel some warmth. Driving sleet had accompanied them for much of the previous few days. Today was the opportunity to dry some clothes.

It had been downhill most of the way, and it was now more than evident they had reached the bottom. Directly across their path lay the Yellow River. It appeared shrivelled. To the west were immense sand flats, with meandering waterways interlaced between them. The flow was so slow; it seemed like a young child could splash her way across, paddling through the channels and dancing across the sandbanks.

To the east, the river narrowed and entered a much steeper-sided valley, almost a gorge. The flow was faster there, although not the raging torrent many had expected. It seemed as if the best opportunity would be down there, where they could run a rope across; the bullock carts were undoubtedly weighty enough to manage the current.

Therefore, it was met with some surprise when Bóyì indicated they would cross directly between the Yellow River's two polarised characters. A distinct line appeared running across the river, from northwest to southeast. On the upstream side, the waters were calm, appearing almost still; a short vertical wall of the river showered from the ledge to the downstream side.

In all, they had lost ten carts, although stripping them for spare parts had taken the space previously occupied by the provisions already consumed. Bóyì was happy that, other than the single child, no lives had

203

been lost. They now had a few bullocks to spare, which would add to their food stocks for the latter part of the journey.

Yú and Bóyì stood together on a boulder, raising them the height of two men above the waters and one above the stationary cart train.

"See that peak to the southeast. We're heading directly toward that." Bóyì pointed at the mountain that towered above the far bank.

"What? We're going up that?"

"No!" Bóyì laughed. "No! Once we're over the river, we can skirt along the south bank for about half a day; then, we turn south. We go over the mountains where they're much lower than that one.

"This is where we cross."

"Here, Bóyì? It would seem easier upstream. It's shallow there. Or downstream, where it's narrow. Why here?" Yú was perplexed, as were all on the caravan other than those who had made the trip before.

"Firstly, if you try to get the carts across over the sand flats, you'll soon find out that the sand is a lot like mud…the wheels will dig in, and you'll be stuck. If that happens, the cart must be unloaded and the contents carried. Then, the bullocks must be led across. Then, if you're lucky, you get ten men to pull the cart out. If you're lucky."

"Ah! So, what about downstream?"

"It looks like a good possibility, but you'll find that the water is much deeper in the centre of the channel than you think. The bullocks would end up swimming, and it would become impossible to keep the carts on the rope. The animals would drown."

"How do you know this, Bóyì?" Yú was genuinely fascinated. "And what's so good about this wide stretch with what I can only describe as a waterfall…however little it is?"

Bóyì flushed, his face reddening alarmingly.

"I said the same as you last year. We had a bit of time, so they let me try. I got the cart stuck in the mud upstream. It had to be offloaded. We saved the bullocks but not the cart." He paused for breath.

"Did they let you cross down here?"

"They did, but only me…no cart, load, or bullocks."

"And the result?"

"I almost drowned!" Turning, Bóyì proceeded to point out the ledge across the river. "What you have here is a band of hard, flat rock.

It's been smoothed by the river. The little fall you see is where the water drops over the edge of the hard rock. The sand is piled up on the upstream side. It leaves a track about four paces wide, just wide enough for the carts as long as they leave a body width on the downstream side. Now, that's the dangerous job. The best way to do this is to have someone walk alongside the left-hand side of the cart. If they feel they're being pushed over the edge, they shout extremely loudly to the driver–"

"And if the gap is getting too big?"

"They shout extremely loudly to the driver!"

"When do we get started?"

"Hang on, Yú, it's not just the river that's dangerous. Other people know about this crossing point. From here, downriver as far as…I'm told as far as Shandong…in fact anywhere north of the river, that's Lóngshān controlled."

"Even this far west?"

"Well, I doubt they'd come this far, except perhaps a patrol of some sort. You know what it's been like; you've heard the reports. We don't know what they might do to prepare for an attack. Better safe than sorry."

"True, true. Anything else?"

"Bandits!"

"Bandits? Here? It seems so peaceful. I thought we'd see the bandits in the hills. Up there, perhaps. Not down here."

"Huh! They wait on the northern side and attack there while the crossing continues. That means we will get most of the people across first, then some of the carts. We must do one at a time just in case one gets stuck. There's nowhere to turn around. That means–"

"I guess that means we must leave a heavy guard on this bank until everything is over."

"You're right. A heavy guard."

Bóyì led the pedestrians across. As soon as he reached solid land on the far bank, he doubled back, recrossing the river to escort the first carts across. It proved easier than expected, the icy water barely covering the ankles of the adults, who carried the youngest children whilst the older ones clung grimly to their parent's hands.

Unusually, Bóyì had chosen Yú to drive the first cart. He had not been one of the regular drivers, although he had done a few stints. As the wheels entered the water, the bullocks leaned forward to drink.

"Let them, Yú, let them drink. That way, they'll not want to stop when you're halfway." He turned to those still on the northern bank. "Are you all watching? Closely now. Closely. Don't stop watching until we're over." Yú flicked his whip, and the bullocks lurched forward.

"Easy now, Yú. Easy."

Yú kept the cart on the expected line for around a hundred paces. About halfway, the vehicle began to veer to the left, squeezing Bóyì for room and pushing him towards the falling water.

"Right a bit, Yú, right a bit!" The cart straightened and then veered too far over. "Now left! Now. Straight. Straight!"

"It's a bit harder than it looks, Bóyì! Why did you pick me instead of one of the normal drivers?"

"Ha!" Bóyì laughed loudly. "I knew if I picked you, everyone would want to be able to say that they could do what Yú can do. Besides, what are the carts called? Yú's body carts. They're all hoping they don't see Yú's body parts and…Now! Right…just a bit! Good! And they will see your body parts if you keep doing that!"

"So, you didn't pick me for my driving ability?"

"No chance!" Bóyì beamed. "That's it, Yú…you've done it. Easy as you pull over those rocks and park up on that flat area over there. Go as far as you can; we've got to get all the carts up there before we move on. I'm off back over the other side. See you later."

When the sun began to fall over the mountains to the west, Bóyì called a halt. Thirty carts had crossed. They had lost one of the bullocks, which slipped, fell over the ledge, and failed to right itself before being tugged into faster-moving water. Fortunately, the boy leading it had had the sense to cut the tether and to let go of the rope before he, too, was pulled in.

That night, there were two camps. The main body on the southern bank left twenty carts, forty drivers and guides, and thirty guards, accompanied by their horses on the northern bank.

The smaller party had pulled the carts into a defensive ring and set up an area where the bullocks could feed and drink. It was a beautiful spot. The moon was full, and the sky clear. The river babbled as bats swooped across its waters. Across the heavens, the stars shone like diamonds.

In both camps, guards were posted, although there were no disturbances other than the odd howl of a distant wolf. Therefore, it was some surprise that they woke to a drab and damp dawn, although that was not as much a surprise as the river's changed state.

The previous day, it had run relatively clear; now, it was a deep brown. If yesterday's pedestrians had only just had their ankles wetted, it was clear the level had risen to reach an adult's knee today. The gentle babbling had gone; the river now had a much more forceful rush, slapping across the rocks on the northern bank. Of the southern bank, nothing was visible. Then, while they peered into the fog, the bandits struck.

An arrow thudded into the back of one of the female drivers. She had been trying to make out the ledge extending across the river. She toppled forward, clutching her chest where the arrow's tip had exited. Rolling into the turgid waters downstream of the falls, her body was quickly swept away.

Most of the camp was already up and about. Most had come to the water's edge to look at what they faced. Their weapons, and in some cases their clothes, were back with the carts. As the realisation set in, they turned, sprinting towards the camp. The sprint ended almost before it had begun, coming to an abrupt halt where they faced a line of bowmen with strings taut and loaded.

It was a stand-off. Over sixty Xià faced fewer than twenty archers. A direct charge would have brought a Xià victory, although as many as a third of their number might perish. There was no natural leader amongst them; Bóyì, his deputy and Yú had spent the night on the southern bank. No one had been appointed to a commanding role, and it appeared that no one would volunteer for the position. Several mistakes had already been made. Nervousness grew.

To the surprise of all, Líng stepped forward, her arms raised as she called to the bandits.

"Do you have a leader?"

A short discussion followed amongst the bandits, and an ageing man pushed his way to the front.

"I am the leader."

"Can we talk?"

"If no one else moves…yes…we can talk."

"Right. Wait, please." Líng turned to the men on either side of her and whispered. "If this doesn't work, rush them. You know you'll win; it'll just be a matter of how many are lost. One of you…you…yes, you. Watch me for any signals."

With that, she strode out of their line and moved off forty paces upstream. The bandit's leader followed. When they were out of earshot, Líng spoke quietly.

"What's your name?"

"Hán. My name's Hán. You?"

"Líng."

"Right, Líng, are you really in charge?" She nodded, and after a moment's surprised delay, Hán asked, "Right, what's the deal?"

"Well, it looks like we would crush you in this fight. We lose maybe twenty, whereas you lose everyone. It doesn't seem much of a deal is needed."

"What you say is true." He looked directly into her eyes. "I think you have much more to lose than we do. We have nothing; you have much. You have friends, and I, well, I do not. I have them." Hán waved in the direction of his men. "They're not friends, and they're not even friends with each other. They're just a bunch of desperate outlaws."

"Outlaws from where?"

"Well…the Lóngshān chased us into these mountains after we escaped from Jìyuán. That's four day's hard march from here, out that way, to the east. We–"

"Stop. I think we have a trade. Are your group all males?"

"Yes."

"We need to talk, and we cannot have this lot standing ready for a fight while we talk; mistakes happen. How would you trust us?"

"Give us one of them carts, with four of your men, and pile it full of food and some weapons. We'll take off into the forest, and I'll return with four of my men for you to hold. Tell your team not to try to enter the forest; they'll be ambushed. Is it a deal?"

"Deal." They shook hands.

"I'll be back at midday." Hán smiled at Líng. "It's sometimes best not to fight. True?"

"True!"

When Líng returned, she instructed two men and two women to go and load up a cart. All the way, they had arrows pointed directly at their heads. Very soon, it was harnessed, the hostages leading away the bullocks. Once they had covered half the distance to the forest, Hán signalled to his group, and they silently filed after it.

The river fog had cleared. It was essential to get the carts rolling and to pass a message to Yú and Bóyì. As it turned out, both men had come back over the river before the third cart set out. The water conditions were becoming more difficult as the day wore on.

It took a little persuasion, but ultimately, all the outlaws chose to join the Xià cart train. They were all farmers at heart; they had little interest in fighting and had not enjoyed their time living off the land and dodging their pursuers. Líng had led the discussions, focusing on increased safety, free farmland in Èrlìtou and the seemingly ever-present gender imbalance. In Hán's group, it seemed they were evenly split as to which of the three was the deciding factor, but they were unanimous in their desire to join the cart train.

Yú and Bóyì only announced their roles as the increasingly relaxed negotiations ended. However, Bóyì insisted that there should be an apology to the friends of the fallen woman; it was swiftly agreed on.

By the time the meeting was over, only the bandits, a single cart and the three Xià negotiators were left to cross. The river had run higher still. While all made it over, the wagon was swept away with its animals. The driver and guide just managed to leap aside, clutching at the rope that had finally been positioned to guide them over.

As well as being drenched and cold, they had gained twenty men and lost a cart full of provisions. It was fortuitous that the plan left them one more day before they resumed their trek.

Yú took the opportunity to sit down with Bóyì.

"Why did the river rise, Bóyì?"

"There was more water, Yú."

"I know there was more water. That's obvious, but what caused the rise?"

209

"I thought you were the water guy?"

"Not really. My father knows a bit, but I'm not sure he could answer this one."

"From what I hear, there are two main rivers involved here, the Yellow River itself and the Wèi River. You know the Wèi Valley, don't you?"

"Yes." Yú nodded. "It flows into the Yellow River at the big turn…near Huáyīn. What about it?"

"Well, we better hope this extra water comes out of the Wèi River."

"Ah! Got it! It's too early for the Yellow River to be rising. We wouldn't want that at all. We could do without either rising just yet. It'll mess things up a bit."

"A bit?" Bóyì whisked a fly off his gruel. "You could say."

To everyone's satisfaction, the river returned to its previous calm the following day. As they followed the southern bank downstream, it became clear the level was also dropping. There were a few members of the cart train who kept their fingers tightly crossed. Perhaps it had just been a few local showers. The alternative did not bear thinking about.

Thirty-one: The Viewpoint

Near Zhàishàngcūn, Shaanxi
Year 90: Year of the Rat
Eight days after the spring equinox
29th March 1905 BCE

There was no pigeon post. There were no visitors either. There would be no news other than that which they observed themselves. The closest settlement was a stiff walk across the mountain behind the cave, a journey only worth contemplating if they were to run short of food or water. It was unlikely.

Kànménrén had spent a long time working out where they should spend their time and had picked wisely. After the strains and stresses of the winter, they had indulged in a leisurely journey. They left from Shímǎo, down the Tūwéi River and onto the Yellow River itself. The sledge journey had not been arduous, although it was to Hòutú's shame that she had done little to provide locomotive force. Only in those areas where it had been necessary to pull the sledge over obstacles had she needed to apply her strength.

Both rivers were frozen hard, and the conditions ideal for sledging. A hand's depth of snow had provided the much-needed traction for Kàn's boots. They had reached their destination two days before the new moon, the deadline they had specified on their winter tour. Their final day's journey on the great river suggested that a significant thaw may be commencing.

They had now been in the cave for seven days. Whilst it could not be called a *yáodòng,* it had many natural features that were an improvement over any manufactured space Hòutú had previously stayed. One huge advantage was that the rock was not weak loess but a much harder sandstone. While making notches in the cave wall was relatively easy, it did not crumble like loess and was structurally sound. To the rear

211

of the cave, some ten paces into the rock face, there was a natural funnel in the ceiling; it meant they could have a fire burning throughout the night without choking to death. The entrance to the cave was so small it was necessary to duck to enter, but once inside, the roof arched upwards, making it possible to stand. To the one side, close to the rear hearth, was a ledge that may well have been designed for two people to sleep. It had become their bed after they had covered it with dried mosses, grasses, and furs.

Hòutú and Kàn had discussed the comforts of the cave at length. Kàn claimed it was entirely natural, whereas Hòutú believed humans had a hand in its design. Her argument was supported when they found the bones of a young child buried in a deep scrape towards the rear. The remains were old and dry, crumbling as she touched them. They may have been there for hundreds if not thousands of years. They had respectfully reburied them and regarded their presence in the cave as protective, as had probably been the original intent.

Outside the entrance was a wide ledge, some five paces deep and ten across. Once again, nature or human ingenuity had provided a perfectly protected area for a fire, with a shelf of rock blocking the northern end of the terrace and deflecting the icy northern winds. To top it all, there was the panoramic view.

Directly below, at the bottom of a steep slope, lay the Yellow River, still white and silent in its late winter slumber. Their temporary home sat above a gigantic meander. Upstream, the great river appeared from the northwest. Downstream, it disappeared from view as it swung to the southwest, then west, before resuming its southbound course once more. Their balcony, being at the bend's apex, maximised the channel length they could observe.

Directly across the frozen waters were stands of larch, aspen and white birch, all now showing the first signs of budding, intermittent swathes of green beginning to tinge the bleak branches. There were fewer trees in the drier and more exposed areas, with low scrub interspersed with shrubs taking precedence. The terrain on the far bank rose less steeply than on their side of the river, topping out as low hills, a plateau to all intents and purposes, but one bisected by run-off which had scored the area, somewhat like the cuts of a butcher's knife through a block of hard fat.

It was an idyllic place for a belated honeymoon with plentiful fish from ice holes, game from the surrounding woodland, and easy access to ice, which they melted for water.

With a week of waiting and no apparent change to the river, it finally turned out to be the time she had wanted. The daylight hours may have seen bursts of activity on the hunting and cooking front, but the long nights were full of joyous play, heavenly sensuality, and the time to tell each other stories. At last, they began to get to know each other.

Hòutú's relationship with Kàn had not commenced as a love affair; it had started life as an instruction. The Sisterhood had seen the need, and Hòutú had fulfilled it. To begin with, she hated the role, but as she grew into her position, she first found it acceptable, then agreeable. It had now reached the point where she did not want to be parted from the man. She realised now that she would disobey if instructed to do something other than remain with Kàn.

It was mid-afternoon, and they both sat contentedly on the lip of their ledge, feet dangling over the scree slope. Each held a beaker of *fénjiǔ* liquor[16], which they sipped cautiously. The fénjiǔ burned Hòutú's throat in a manner that warned anyone consuming it that extreme care should be applied. Kàn had traded a few remaining arrow points for several pitchers of the stuff in the closest village of Qìkǒuzhèn. It had taken him a whole day to get there and back, and his load was significantly heavier on the return journey.

"So, Kàn, where did you get the idea from?"

"I made it up."

"What, you're telling me this has not been done before?"

"Well, I guess it may have been done on a small scale, you know, for individual villages, but I've never heard it being done on a large scale."

"And you told the Sisterhood about this when?"

"Years ago. The idea just came to me, like in a dream. I thought to start with that they might want to use it on Héjīn or Yúlíngzhèn or even

---

[16] An extremely strong liquor made in northern China from the seeds of sorghum.

Sānménxiá because, you know, they were all Lóngshān outposts. I even wondered about Shímǎo, but that wouldn't have worked."

"Is it going to work now?"

"Well, I never thought the plan would involve the lower Yellow River. You know, it must have taken someone exceptionally clever to calculate if it would work."

"There is someone. They have someone, Kàn. It's your daughter, Líng!"

"Ah…she's clever, alright. She doesn't tell me much, though, only bits.

"You see, Hòutú, the reason we're sat right here isn't just this beautiful cave. It's the Qiūshuǐ River down there," he pointed to the south and then swept his arm northwards, "and the two rivers joining just up around that bend. If it's going to happen, this is where it will start. Right here.

"You saw it. You saw it at the mouth of the Tūwéi River. They all did their jobs on the new moon. They were competing with themselves to see who could get the furthest, never mind any dodgy ice.

"You know that I got it wrong, don't you?"

"How did you get it wrong, Kàn?" Hòutú had heard the story before, but with a couple of *fenjuis*, Kàn's inclination was to ramble and repeat himself. It was a habit she had once endured but now felt somewhat endearing.

"I asked them to light fires on the ice. You know, to melt it. They laughed at me. I'd had this idea for years, and it always involved fires on the ice, and they just laughed at me. Do you know what they said? You know what they said? They said the ice would melt and put the fire out. They told me they could build fires on the ice that would not melt the ice, but that was hardly the point, was it? We wanted a fire that would melt the ice.

"It wasn't entirely my idea. This guy, this guy, you know, I can't remember his name now. Well, he said to use stones. That's what he said - hot stones. So, you know what they did? Do you know?"

"Tell me, Kàn."

"They…he said to light the fires at the side of the river, big fires. He said to use the fires to heat those big round stones, you know, the really big ones you find along the river, anything bigger than a man's head. Then he said, have your fires on a slight slope of greenwood, cos that won't burn so easy, you see, with a ramp down to the water. You know, after an hour or so, those rocks are so hot. Then you roll 'em down the ramp onto the ice and have someone with a big stick pushing them further onto the river. Got to be careful, though…"

"Yes. What's next?"

"More stones. You can do ten or eleven loads of stones during a day. They–"

"No, I mean, what happens on the ice?"

"Well, those stones roll pretty well, but eventually, they start to dig in. They make a deep hole and get stuck if the ice is thick. If the ice is thinner, they go through it with a lovely plop!

"You know…they have to be careful. One foot in the wrong place, and…splosh! An almost immediate icy death. These people…these people are used to such conditions; they are used to noticing the first signs of a thaw. They know when to take care. Good people.

"You know, we saw it on the Tūwéi River! And…and they didn't just do it for one day; they got up and did it the next, once on the Tūwéi and once on the Yellow River itself. It wouldn't surprise me if they're still doing it, you know, it's like a winter sport for them, and it keeps them warm. If–"

"Kàn. Kàn! Look!"

The Great River and its tributaries had always been prone to icing up. The local peoples often encouraged the process, as somewhat ironically, it made fishing easier. During the winter, Kàn had encouraged them to make more of the ice dams. No one would ever know whether the human interference had been entirely necessary, but the rivers had frozen harder than the oldest could remember.

The reversal of the process was simply to hasten nature's progress. It had taken much effort and a massive leap of faith to prepare, for none of those involved fully understood why they were undertaking such a task. The objective of their actions was understood, but not how their actions would lead to their goal. However, a deal was a deal; if their three tasks were to be rewarded with better weapons, better beer, and

215

finally be rid of the Lóngshān warlords, who was to worry how it would be achieved?

"I think we might have got upwards of two hundred villages involved in the end. You know—"

"Kàn, I said…look!"

Kàn raised his eyes from his beaker and peered across the river. There was a strange noise, a groaning, then a very explicit crack.

"Kàn! There!"

In the gathering gloom, they squinted towards the frozen waters. The sounds had come from the north. Then, without warning, one massive sheet tore from its neighbour and momentarily stood vertically. The sharp retort reached them a second later and then echoed off the far bank.

Upon their arrival, Kàn had laid a line of rocks across the river ice. It extended from in front of the cave over to the far bank. Without snow, they had remained exposed. No longer was the line straight. It swept away from them in a half-circle, the rocks at the centre having shifted furthest downstream.

"Well." There was no need for more; the single quiet word summed up her feelings.

"I think, Hòutú…I think it might be time for another drink." Kàn threw his arms around her, almost wrestling her to the ground. "First, I'm going to kiss you." He did. "Then we're going to get this pitcher here and finish it. What do you say?"

They finally called it a day as the full moon began to set. It was late. Much to Hòutú's disappointment, it was the first night they did not have sex in a week. Kàn had some trouble finding the bed, let alone an erection. She made do with lying in his arms as he snored loudly.

The following morning, they rose belatedly and not in the best of states. A whole new vista presented itself. The great river was alive and moving. There were visible streams of open water churning against the ice floes. Large slabs were now floating downstream quicker than a walking pace. It took their dulled minds a moment or two to take it all in.

"Is this too quick, Kàn? Is it happening too quickly?"

Kàn rubbed his bleary eyes. "No…shouldn't be…it'll get blocked further down. You see, that's the idea. Get it moving as much as possible, but leave the final ice dams. Then, when it's built up enough pressure, the

216

last ones will all come tumbling down, and all this water will have only one place to go."

"Where's that?"

"Downhill, of course, love, downhill! All the way to Hénán!

Thirty-two: The Warlords

The King's Palace Hall, Ānyáng, Hénán
Year 90: Year of the Rat
Eight days after the spring equinox
29th March 1905 BCE

At roughly the same time as Hòutú and Kàn were finishing off their pitcher of *fénjiǔ*, the tenth flagon of precisely the same spirit was emptied in King Léigōng's hall. It was to the immense irritation of the king that his fellow sovereigns now only seemed content when consuming his best liquor. Stocks were running low, and no one seemed to be able to source it any longer. He momentarily considered whether he should take a raiding party west, not only to secure a supply but also to bring back a few men who could make the stuff properly.

As his eyes swept around the table, he tried to recall the names and faces of those absent; it wasn't easy. He had some problems remembering the names of those who were there. They had held such meetings every two years since the first, although they had decided the situation was becoming intolerable the previous year and should wait only one year until the next. Here they were; they had reached the tipping point and were considering taking more serious collective action.

In the very first meeting, they had lost Yúntóng from Kāifēng. At the second, the king of Niujiaogang had gone missing; at the third, Gǔchéngzhài had failed to appear. The situation was clear; there was now no one around the table coming from the south of the great river. No one. There was still no news from Shímǎo out west, but of Táosì and Sānménxiá, Léigōng had first-hand information of their fall.

It was unsurprising that those present were becoming nervous. Léigōng clearly remembered the irritating and overconfident king from northern Shandong, even if his name escaped him. For two meetings

218

running, he had repeatedly asked, 'What will I lose in Chéngzǐyá?' Now, he was pleading for action. At that very moment, the King of Qīchéng was speaking. He was panicked - of that, there was no doubt. Only the King of Xīnxiāng seemed more desperate. Even Fēngbō in the distant east was pushing for immediate collective action.

By now, they had almost become accustomed to sitting together, although fighting between their states had not come to an end. At least they had agreed to keep their disputes to late spring and early summer so as not to interfere with the harvests. The argument that regular battles kept their men fighting fit had been trashed because so many of their best troops died each time.

If there was agreement about the need for action, there was none on what that action should be. Léigōng had expected this to be the case and, fearing the meeting would end in acrimony, planned to bring his secret weapons to the table. To do so, he needed to make an introduction that would stun them into silence. He stood up.

To date, in their meetings, the only reason for anyone to rise was to fetch more food, or more likely drink, or to relieve themselves at the far end of the hall. The problem with having so many kings around one table was that no one was quite sure of the required etiquette. Certainly, no one had stood up to speak, and even more certainly, no one had banged on the table with his fist. Even so, everybody knew slamming a fist on a table was improper if directed at a king. What saved Léigōng was that the others believed his fist coming down was directed at any monarch other than himself. The comical result was that everyone fell silent, expecting a brawl to erupt between Léigōng and any ruler other than themselves.

"You sit there, and you talk and talk and talk. Then you drink and drink and drink. After that, you talk some more. You never, ever, ever reach an agreement!

"I want you to listen very, very hard. The west is lost. Shǎnxī and Shaanxi. The south is lost. Everything south of the Yellow River. The city-states closest to the river are expecting attacks on a daily basis. This has happened in fewer than ten years. If we wait another year, what else will have gone?"

"Ānyáng might f—"

"Shut up!" Léigōng silenced Fēngbō, who initially rose to contest him before falling back in his seat shamefaced as the irritation of others became apparent. "I can give you a list, in the likely order: Wǔzhì, Jiāozuò, Xīnxiāng, Měngzhuàng, Qīchéng, Huaxian, Xunxian, Púyáng…I could go on, but a few more down the list is Ānyáng. And after Ānyáng come the Shandong cities, then all the way up to the Bohai Sea."

There was significant and concerned muttering around the table, particularly as the Ānyáng king had deliberately mentioned places of direct personal interest to them individually. Léigōng gave himself a mental pat on the back for managing to recite the list he had memorised, lifted a beaker, and took a quick swig before continuing.

"That is what will happen if we do not act together. The longer this is left, the stronger they will become, and the harder they will be to fight."

"But they're fucking farmers!" The King of Xiànxiàn believed he was furthest away from the problem. "How many farmers does it take to beat an army? Thousands. That's what it takes. Thous—"

"You are right, of course; they are farmers. Do you know how many farmers it takes to beat your army? How many crack troops do you have? Sixty, seventy, a hundred? No! Well, I'll tell you a story.

"I have first-hand information from Shǎnxī. It's a bit dated, but I will bring before you two witnesses who were at the Battle of Sanjiadiǎncūn. Old King Chīyóu, I say old, but I should, in all honesty, say dead. He took two thousand to the battle; over a hundred were crack troops. He faced a force of two hundred. Not two hundred soldiers but two hundred men and women. He lost. It seems they were farmers. They call themselves the Xià, and they are no longer in Shǎnxī. Where do you think they are? Where?" Léigōng looked around at their faces and realised he had them spellbound. "Where do you think they are?"

"Come on, Léigōng, if you know, just tell us." The King of Jiāozuò had more reason than most to be concerned.

"They're about three days to the southwest of your city." He allowed it to sink in. "When these…Xià defeated King Chīyóu; they were about three days southwest of Táosì. So, let's have a little less talk about fucking farmers. Táosì was more powerful than any one of us. Shímǎo even more so if it has indeed been lost.

"Now! Will you allow me to bring two people into the room? They are here to help. They were at the battle when Táosì fell."

A murmur of agreement swept around the room. It was as if, at that moment, the kings had finally reached a collective and unanimous decision.

"Let them in." The agreement came from several mouths.

King Léigōng rarely opened a door and had never opened a door in company before. It was a strange experience for him. Even stranger was the sight that met him when he opened it. Standing a full ten paces away were Hú and Xí, who had dolled themselves up for the evening. They were arguing. Each wore matching black silk robes patterned with silver stars and belted with silver rope. Long sleeves swept the floor, and on their heads were black pointed caps sporting the same design of the cosmos. Their beards had been tightly twisted and waxed into semicircles to meet their extended moustaches. It appeared as if they had blackened the upper parts of their faces around the eyes, contrasting starkly with the dead white jowls. Frozen and stunned by the apparitions before him, it was a moment until he found his voice.

"I see you've dressed for the occasion?"

"Yes…yes…yes, we have," stuttered Hú.

"Indeed, my lord, it seemed appropriate," Xí answered.

"And what were you discussing?"

"We were trying to establish what we should call a group of kings, my lord. That is if you are to allow us to address them." Xí bowed deeply.

"Is…is…majesties alright?"

"You can call them women for all I care. Get in here!"

The pair followed the king into the room, bowing deeply at each step. They had plenty of experience dealing with a single monarch but were overawed by having thirteen in a room at one time.

"May I introduce Princes Hú and Xí." A titter had passed around the group. "Princes Hú and Xí survived the battle when Táosì fell. While working under King Chīyóu, they trained themselves in the magic arts. They replaced the female soothsayers in the city of Táosì. They tell me that only Chīyóu's stubbornness led to his losing the battle."

"He always was a bit stupid that Chīyóu. Can't think why they didn't get rid of him years before." Fēngbō alone thought his remark was amusing.

"These two fled south, disguising themselves. They followed the Yellow River, then came northwards and eventually found themselves here. They are the ones who brought me the news of Sānménxiá.

"They have now been with me for some years. They have more than earned their keep. Let me tell you of some of their successful prophecies.

"One. They correctly forecast the moon changing to a completely red colour when it was at its fullest. It was blood red!

"Two. They forecast that Gǔchéngzhài would fall. Who was missing from our next meeting? Correct! The King of Gǔchéngzhài!

"Three. They prophesied the drought last year, telling almost half a year in advance that the summer rains would fail. And tell me, did it rain? It did not!

"Now. You might look at them and," Léigōng turned to Hú and Xí, "And think that they may be a bit...crazy...but there's no point ignoring them just because they look stupid; they seem to have the knack of getting things right.

"Let us hear what they have to say about the future. Princes?"

"My lords. I...I...I can tell you now that frogs and turtles will appear this very night in the palace pool. They...they...they have been absent for many, many years, I believe."

"Léigōng, send someone to look for my ancestors' sakes!" The King of Xiànxiàn hollered.

Léigōng found himself opening a door for the second time that evening, this time to shout to bring a servant running.

"He'll come back with the news in a moment."

"My lords, while we are waiting...while we are waiting, we have another prophecy for this evening." Xí was eager to speak, "We believe there is a spy in our midst! We will uncover that individual!"

The second prophecy was met with incredulity and a barrage of indignant voices. They were interrupted, however, by the appearance of an excited servant at the door. Momentarily, the suspicion fell on the poor lad until Léigōng asked him to speak out.

222

"My Lords, there's hundreds and hundreds of frogs in the palace pond and turtles too. Some of the turtles are eating the frogs." The boy hurried his words, which spilt out as if they were falling down a flight of stairs. Kùàimǎ had once again ensured the two men appeared to be the real deal.

"Right. Go, boy." Léigōng pushed him out of the door. "That cesspit of a pond has not had life in it for years. Now, if you're going to get upset about someone being a spy, then just think about that first prophecy."

The group eyed each other nervously and visibly edged their chairs away from their closest neighbours.

"So, princes, you say there is a spy in the room." Léigōng took back control.

"Yes, my lord," Xí replied confidently.

"We...we...we did not say it was one of you kin...maje...excellencies," Hú added. "But...but...but there is a spy. We...we...we will find the spy and reveal the identity at the end."

"Now, we get down to real business. Princes, would you tell us your prophecies for our little skirmish with these, er, Xià farmers?"

"We will, my lord." Xí forged ahead. "We prophesy that the Lóngshān lords will control the lands north of the Yellow River after the battle!"

"All of them?" Fēngbō asked.

"All...all...all of them." Hú continued. "We...we...we also prophesy that a river will wash away the sins of the Lóngshān kings so they may be at peace with their ancestors."

"What sins is he talking about?" The king of Xiànxiàn looked perplexed. "What do you mean by sins? Is he talking about killing and such? And when you say, 'at peace with our ancestors', what does that mean?"

"It is not for us to know what the prophecy might refer to." Xí was on the defensive and somewhat concerned for his own life. "We just know that a river will wash away the sins of the Lóngshān kings so they may be at peace with their ancestors."

"If…if…if I may guess, Your Majesty, I would say it means so that your ancestors will be happy with you, not that you would be dead with them." Hú pulled them out of the hole.

"The…the…the final prophecy is the most important. Xí?"

"On the new moon after the next new moon, the sun will shine bright, and the Xià will be slain."

"This…this…will be the day for the battle: there will be no fog, no rain, and it will be dry for your horses."

"The battle will be on the Yellow River, a day's march south of Jiāozuò."

"M…M…Many will run away to the south."

"That sounds pretty clear. Is that it?" Léigōng asked, almost politely.

"We…we…we also have a suggestion. It is not a prophecy."

"Please, go ahead."

"We would recommend that your troops wear thick leather armour across their backs." Xí completed. Whilst he was concerned about their safety, after his experience at Sanjiadiǎncūn, he also wanted to ensure the branding he and Hú had received remained undisclosed.

Their suggestion was met with derision by all. Laughter erupted around the table.

"But then they'll run away!"

"Stupid idea!"

"We want them facing the enemy, not looking the other way!"

"How are we expected to change everyone's armour when they need it in…in what? Forty-odd days?"

"It's impossible!"

"And unnecessary!"

"Idiots. They should stick to prophecies and leave the advice to us!"

"Let's focus on the prophecies." Léigōng had to raise his voice to quieten the gathering. "Let's hear from Xīnxiāng."

"I think it best to hear from Jiāozuò; he's closer to it than I."

"We are close to the river, about a day's walk. We don't often head south; usually, it's too wet. The area floods a lot, but right now, it's dry. Solid. Good for troops and good for horses. I've heard about some activity along the northern bank of the river, but I haven't had the numbers to risk investigating."

"We'll talk numbers in a moment, King Jiāozuò. Still, it sounds as if we'll be on good ground. Don't want to get stuck in any mud so close to that river." Léigōng was feeling pleased it was all coming together. "Is anyone disagreeing about the place and date?" He looked at each face around the table. "No. Alright. Let's talk numbers."

As might have been expected, when they added up how many men-at-arms they had between them, there were far fewer than if one had listened to the bragging and boasting of previous years or even hours. In all, the Lóngshān could put out fewer than a thousand well-equipped and trained soldiers and only if the remote city-states could mobilise quickly enough. Far more guesswork went into the numbers of auxiliaries they might hope to bring, who would essentially be unwilling farmers armed only with stone hoes and axes.

Thirty-three: The Spy

The King's Palace Hall, Ānyáng, Hénán
Year 90: Year of the Rat
Eight days after the spring equinox
29th March 1905 BCE

It was dark in the cabinet; since noon, she had lay there, totally still. There was little room to move, which meant regular cramping in her calves that made her want to cry out. It had been silent until the meeting commenced, although once they got going the volume became louder and louder. It was as if all the room's occupants were trying to talk over each other, and it was not easy to pick up on any single discussion. Regularly, those present would visit the cabinet she lay in, pouring beakers of *fénjiǔ*, breaking off pieces of bread or scooping *ròugān* onto their plates. An irritant was the regular dripping of spilt wine, kissing her neck and trickling into her cleavage. However, no one bothered to open the doors to the cabinet; all that was needed was on view.

She drifted in and out of their discussions, waiting for the entrance of the pair who would cement their plans. Hú and Xí. Would they rise to the occasion? The thought allowed her mind to drift back over the previous year.

She had been undercover for nine months, going by several names. In her latest reincarnation, she was simply *Āyí* Feng,[17] although the girls in Ānyáng routinely called her *Mǎ*[18]. Having left Èrlǐtou and the company of Mother and Girl the previous June, she had been unable to talk to anyone completely openly since then. It had been a difficult period in which she had felt lonelier than at any other time of her life.

---

[17] Āyí can mean aunty, grandmother or refer to a home help.
[18] Horse.

Grandmother was now deep in Lóngshān territory. Ānyáng was the city from which the cancer had spread. Moreover, she was surrounded by those leaders who had encouraged the cancer to thrive.

She had traced the same circuit as in previous years. She followed a list of contacts, each burned into her memory. In every village, town or city, her story was the same. To the public, she was a vagrant, not quite right in the head, but nevertheless harmless, someone who encouraged sympathy rather than rejection. Her fallback story had always been that she was trying to find a distant family member to care for her. With this being her fifth such tour, people had begun to recognise her. The only solution to their probing had been to feign even greater madness.

To the members of the Sisterhood, her visits were more than necessary; she provided their lifeline, their very reason to live. Each willingly stepped in to care for the vagrant for a day or two, sharing scarce food and risking everything. She could only talk plainly to them behind closed doors, but even on this last trip, she could still not reveal the whole truth. Each host knew she was a sister, though none knew she was their supreme leader, and none could be told the details of the grand plan. All she could do was feed them the information they needed and offer advice on what aspects of that information they should share with the local people—in this respect, the last year had been more crucial than those preceding.

She always advised her agents of a few key triggers but pointed out that they would ideally be asked to respond to a rumour. It may be a rumour that they had started themselves but that the questioner would have no idea their queries were directed at the original source of the information. She considered it ideal if several mouths and several months separated the source from the feedback; she called it "Whispers".

It meant spreading layer after layer of minutiae and surreptitiously prompting the unsuspecting public to build coherent arguments. Sometimes, conclusions may be seen as too extreme to discuss, and fearing punishment from others, people often found Sisterhood members more approachable, for they were the most trusted members of their societies.

They were not trusted as members of the Sisterhood, for the mere mention of that name in areas controlled by the Lóngshān could bring

227

death to entire communities. They were respected because they were wise women, although some were still in their teens. They were Sisterhood only to her and the few contacts they each kept in nearby towns. There were no pigeon fanciers in the remaining Lóngshān lands; it was simply too dangerous.

Her messages were different depending on the nature of the settlement; there was a geographical divide. The common thread was the timing and two independent events. The first one to look out for would be the soldiers' departure. The second would occur in the heavens, an extreme event. Other than the information that these would occur in order, the only other fix was that they would occur between the two new moons after the spring equinox. Both were triggers for action. The fact was the populace needed to know what that action should be. The problem was that the public could not keep a secret for long. Everything was in the timing.

Grandmother had not been appointed to her position because she glossed over details; she was a stickler for it. She knew that every community was different and that the sisters in those communities knew their patches better than she ever could. She had put her life in their hands, simultaneously thrusting into those same hands responsibility for disseminating the information.

It was up to her foot soldiers to determine how quickly they could spread a plan of action. Most importantly, who would need to know before the first event, for an upset at that point might cause a complete breakdown. They required the kings and their lackeys well out of the way before word spread more widely. Who could you trust? There were many desperate people out there. For some, earning a crumb of recognition from their lords might lead them to betrayal. Invariably, the number of people who could be trusted was fewer than her sisters had first thought. Grandmother had spent much of her time discussing real friendship and confidentiality pacts.

In the last year, she had effectively fomented the basis of a social uprising. She offered a platform whereby it could succeed and be conducted with minimal possible risk. As she looked back, she had delivered a panacea, although it had always been difficult for her charges to see through the inherent risks. The 'what if?' argument was raised time and time again.

"What if the soldiers don't go?"
"What if they find out?"
"What if I'm tortured?"
"What if? What if? What if?"

When the time came and, where the circumstances allowed, she had instructed them to take over their towns. In some places, however, it was more difficult. Over the last few decades, the plains had dried out, and the population had yet to recover from the two centuries of cold weather. People had moved to the lower lands where there was better moisture retention and greater crop yields. There were abandoned villages on higher ground, while those in the lowlands had been reoccupied or new settlements established. Grandmother planted the seed that the process might need to be reversed. Another point, repeatedly hammered home, was to maximise food stocks; it was a difficult proposition after a year of drought.

Her mind returned to the present momentarily when the cabinet in which she lay tilted alarmingly before crashing back to the floor. She cursed herself for losing concentration. It seemed one of those present had leant too hard when reaching for another flagon. Fortunately, the racket appeared to have covered up any sounds her body had made as it slid backwards on the shelf. Listening intently for a moment, it was only when she heard the sound of feet shuffling away that she could relapse into her daydream.

Ānyáng had always been different. Her team here were specialists. Although she had visited the city in years gone past, she had not lodged with them, for she would not have been allowed. Yĕmă, Măjié and Kùàimă worked in the home of Hú and Xí.

The Sisterhood had concluded years before that Ānyáng would not fall as the other city-states might. Here, there had been no instruction to plot rebellion. The city was the Lóngshān warlords' meeting place, and, as such, it was much more important than just another centre to be overthrown. The palace here would not only provide information to the Sisterhood, but it was also the ideal setting for disseminating covert information. Hú and Xí would unknowingly pay back what had been invested in them when Kànménrén had spared their lives in Shănxī.

Grandmother had feared for the three women over the years. Kùàimǎ had been kept in a cell almost permanently. Admittedly, she had been fed and watered, but she was only allowed out when her two gaolers needed a prophecy. To them, she was their pet witch and the source of their authority. They kept her a secret from all outside the home. Other than being held captive, the two men did not ill-treat her; she was too important to them. Every prophecy she had made came to pass. Hú and Xí could dine out on the successes they claimed as their own.

Yěmǎ and Mǎjié were not prisoners, although their lives were infinitely worse. For the Sisterhood, if Kùàimǎ was the mouthpiece, the other two were the messengers who had passed information to the oracle. To Hú and Xí, they were domestic slaves. Physical abuse was an everyday occurrence; both girls were permanently bruised and had suffered broken limbs, ribs, and fingers. Yěmǎ had lost her sight in one eye and Mǎjié her hearing on one side. The mental abuse was constant, but they both managed to ride through it.

Grandmother's biggest concern was the sexual abuse that had now been ongoing for five years. It was not their fear of Hú and Xí that stopped them from walking away, but their loyalty to the Sisterhood. She struggled to believe they had each maintained that loyalty while being repeatedly bound, raped, and sodomised, often by the two men simultaneously. They were in a desperate situation, although it would come to an end that night. The last thing they had asked of her, just hours before, was that they be allowed to torture and kill Hú and Xí. It was with infinite sadness that their request had been declined. They were good girls. They would obey. They had become the lever that would ensure this horrific edifice would come tumbling down, and the rewards would be much more than simple revenge on their current masters.

Only one month before, Grandmother had carved the symbol of the Motherland on her left breast. It had been painful. She had left it late, as the possibility of exposure as she crisscrossed the lands had been too great. As the wound had healed, she moved closer to Ānyáng. At the same time, Kùàimǎ began her prophesy about a spy in the palace. Hú and Xí loved it. The credit they would be given for unearthing a spy! They fantasised about it.

230

When Yěmǎ and Majie turned up dragging a madwoman off the street, it provoked more than excitement. When they ripped off her tunic, and the Motherland symbol became apparent, their masters were ecstatic. It sealed the deal when it was clear the woman was prepared to do anything in return for a few meals. In addition, she also provided Hú and Xí greater variety in their beds after they had confined themselves to their two slaves for years.

As Kùàimǎ tightened the prophecy, the plan began to take shape. The spy was to be discovered in the warlords' meeting. She would be exposed and beaten, then tortured for information by Hú and Xí. The following day, in front of the whole town, her execution would be by strangulation. Not a single aspect of the plan had come from the two men, although they had no realisation this was the case, and they had even been unable to see through the delayed execution as a ruse for escape.

When Grandmother heard the announcement introducing Hú and Xí and the accompanying laughter, it immediately brought her back to the present.

She sighed happily when the kings reached an agreement as regards the date and the location. She grinned widely when they laughed at the suggestion of better body armour. She almost laughed out loud when they came up with fewer than a thousand trained troops. However, the expression on her face changed instantly when she heard Hú speak again.

"Your…your…your majesties. Please. We mentioned a spy."

"Your majesties!" Xí's voice was louder and attracted the attention of all. "We mentioned a spy."

There was some nervous shuffling. Not one of the kings gathered here had been entirely discreet over the last six years. Each of them had a gnawing suspicion that fingers may be pointed in his direction.

"It…it…it is a woman." The sigh of relief that passed around the table was more than noticeable.

"She will be exposed and beaten tonight." Xí smiled. There was a round of fists banging on the table.

"We…we…we will torture her overnight for information. We suspect she may be a wi…wi…witch!" The fists were hammering again, although there were a few sharp intakes of breath and a little more uncertainty. None of them liked the idea of a witch in their midst.

"Your majesties, we are used to dealing with witches and such…we…we…will not allow her to cast her spells," Xí reassured.

"And the final part of the prophecy is that tomorrow, she will be publicly strangled to death in front of all the townspeople!"

"And…and…and your majesties…if you would care to watch."

"So…where is this witch?" Léigōng was a little irritated that he had known nothing of this before the meeting. "Come on! Where is she? I see no hiding place!"

"Tha…tha…that sire we know not. Simply that she is here, she may be invisible."

"Well, that would be a little inconvenient for you, wouldn't it!" Fēngbō was more than a little sceptical. "Maybe she's in this cabinet. Let's take a look!" He opened the lower doors and crouched before jumping back like a startled rabbit. "Shit! There's a witch in there!"

Grandmother was dragged from her hiding place by the same two men who had put her there hours before. They stood her up and roughly turned her face from side to side to ensure all had seen her clearly.

"Your majesties, we are looking for the mark. All these witches carry a mark." Xí's act was triumphal.

"It…it…it may be hidden, Prince Xí. We will disrobe her!" Hú ripped the cheap tunic from the neck downwards.

"And there it is! Look at this!" Hú held her right breast in an ever-tightening grip, pulling it forward with its owner stumbling behind it. "The mark! This is the mark of the Sisterhood witches. We have foiled their plot! Look at the mark!"

They flung Grandmother to the floor.

"I…I…I would invite you to beat her! Perhaps one kick each would suffice. But, please, your majesties, not her head; we need her to talk through torture.

Every man in the room took turns delivering a ferocious kick to Grandmother's body. Her stomach, breasts, thighs, and side were all the targets of heavy boots. She counted. It seemed some must have gone twice. Momentarily, she wondered why they had not attacked her feet before she felt them crushed by the weight of someone standing on them. The idea that she must live until she could pass on the information was foremost on her mind, but the men in the room were doing everything they could to foil her plan. Grandmother was not scared of dying, nor was she frightened of pain. What she feared was failure. There had been a short respite, but then a blow to her lower back finally caused something inside her to give. The second heavy blow to the same spot pushed her into unconsciousness.

While the kings continued to celebrate, Grandmother was dragged unceremoniously and semi-naked from the palace hall by two guards, who left her on the floor of Hú and Xí's home. Before Yěmǎ and Mǎjié could tend to her wounds, the two princes returned demanding drinks. It was what everyone had expected and prepared for; unknowingly, they consumed the sleeping draughts before they had even sat down. After pretending to fuss with them briefly, the two girls could return their focus to Grandmother.

"Girls! Success!" She was groggy, but her voice was commanding. "It's done. Free Kùàimǎ. Now!" She groaned in pain, writhing, before adopting a foetal position.

When the three women were all kneeling around her, she spoke again.

"You will take all four horses…I will not be coming, but a spare might be useful." Her words came in short bursts, breathing restricted by ribs that had punctured her lung. "Ride for Èrlǐtou…Cross the great river near Wēnxiàn." Blood was now oozing from her mouth with each gulp of air. "This will take you a week…maybe more…Split up if threatened. One of you must…must get the message through."

"What about you?" Kùàimǎ's voice was soft.

"I'm dying…No doubt about it." She attempted a smile. "I think they kicked hell…out of my liver…it felt like it burst…Lungs…no good…aargh!"

"No!" Yěmǎ was distraught.

"Yes…Too late to worry…The message…You must all memorise this…Promise."

"Promise." The three breathed the word together.

"This is it…Place…agreed. Date…agreed. One thousand…crack troops…And…Remember Hú and Xí's scars. That's it." She inhaled deeply, her face cracking with pain. "I'll say it one more time…Place…agreed.   Date…agreed.   A   thousand   crack troops…Remember Hú and Xí's scars…Say it back to me."

"Place – agreed. Date – agreed. One thousand crack troops. Remember Hú and Xí's scars," they chorused in unison.

"Now…No fuss…Give me…a very, very big drink…the same stuff… you gave those two. Then you leave…Immediately…Ladies…you must ride as if you are fire horses." Her last smile widened through a mask of blood; it was beautiful.

Kùàimǎ pushed a few soft rags under Grandmother's head whilst Mǎjié helped her down the sleeping draught. She was out in seconds. Each of the three kissed her. She was dead before the third kiss.

"Goodnight, Mǎ." Not one of the three bore anything but love for the woman who had put them through five years of torture.

Thirty-four: The New Town
Èrlǐtou, Hénán
Year 90: Year of the Rat
Twenty-two days after the spring equinox
12ᵗʰ April 1905 BCE

As the newcomers quickly found out, Èrlǐtou was somewhat different from the images they had conjured up, both before and during the journey. It was undoubtedly organised. The people looked healthy, their farms neat and manicured, and their food animals were remarkably plump. There was an air of settled domestication, quite different from the atmosphere they had come to know in Táosì in the last few years. Although everything worked, there was little in the way of excitement, and nothing to stimulate. It seemed the population was satisfied, perhaps even content, but it could not really be described as particularly happy.

What seemed to be physically missing was any functional or distinct town centre. There certainly was a centre; this consisted of a series of overlarge granaries, a bronze foundry, and a carpentry area. It was a large compound, occupying the equivalent space of some of forty farms, surrounded by a tamped earth wall. It lay centrally on the settlement's east-west and north-south axes, although these were not precisely aligned, much to everyone's annoyance. Gǔn's excuse was that the key crossing points of the two rivers were not north-south aligned. He had simply linked the two with his central avenue. The only other building in the compound, in the northernmost section, was Gǔn's house, attached to which was the *huìyì shì*[19], a large room with various public uses.

The compound was a significant irritant to Gǔn. Because it took up many farming blocks, he had needed to divert the irrigation ditches,

---

[19] Meeting room.

235

which had laughingly become known as the *huángjiā hé*[20], around its outer walls, likewise with the roads. His perfectly misaligned grid of north-south streets was uninterrupted, one passing through the compound's north and south gates. However, the east-west tracks had to dog-leg around the area; this imperfection sometimes drove Gǔn to near madness.

Each farm consisted of a square allocation of land, each side being one hundred and twenty strides in length. Along two of its sides ran irrigation ditches and, on the other two, cart tracks. A home stood in each corner of each farm, and even these were standardised. Standing in a fenced compound, some twenty paces square, the house was single-storey and rectangular, occupying half of the fenced area. No one in Èrlǐtou could look enviously at his neighbour's land, for it was identical in every way to his own.

Only the crops varied from farm to farm. Seed stock was maintained centrally, consisting of millet, rice, soybean, wheat, and barley, although the farmers could grow additional crops to supplement their diets. The farms were in groups of four, with cooperative planting and harvesting encouraged. Neighbours could rotate their cropping, which meant a colourful patchwork existed at different times in the growing season.

Even the equipment was standardised. Each farm was issued with two axes, two hoes, four knives, five spear tips and twenty arrowheads, all made of bronze. Each group of four farms had a bullock, a plough, a cart, and a bronze plough blade. At harvest's end, the bronze was replaced with refurbished tools from the foundry, and taxes were paid.

Taxation was heavy, at one-third of each farm's produce, but it was never a matter of contention. The centrally maintained revenue was used to feed the non-farm workers, keep a reserve in case of drought or famine, and act as seed stock, which would be issued on request and at no cost before the planting season. A relief system existed for those whose farming had failed, a process that had been instigated several times. The taxes were not considered onerous because of the level of protection they offered the citizens.

---

[20] Royal river.

The massive grid was nearly perfect in many respects, except where it met the Luòhé River to the north and the Yī River to the south. Here, the farms had been reduced in size slightly as the resident farmers had easy access to the abundant river fish. These plots were snapped up by those who had lived on the banks of the Fèn River. Some Jiāngsu migrants joined them; they had been swamp-dwellers for decades. The fishing farms had their own representative on the council and somewhat different schedules for paying their dues.

In all, there were four thousand family farms, one hundred from east to west and forty from north to south. The growing problem was that a trip to the centre and back could eat up a whole day for those who lived furthest east or west.

It had taken a genius to work out the implications of Èrlǐtou's location; this was the Sisterhood's prime contribution to the project. A bowl surrounded by mountains, with enough fertile land to expand onto as much as fifty times the area currently under the plough. Indeed, Gǔn had irrigation schemes already in place to take the settlement up to ten thousand farms and then on to fifteen thousand, which was only using land within the confines of the two rivers. Taking the next step and moving outside the confines of the Luòhé and Yī could mean as many as one hundred and fifty thousand farms. Everyone understood the potential. The knowledge that their children's children would be able to move onto farmland in a beautiful, safe, and fertile setting was the prime cause for the general sense of satisfaction.

The twin-rivered valley had been abandoned after disastrous floods over a lifetime ago. No one other than the Sisterhood had been prepared to risk a re-run. At their insistence, the design of Gǔn's waterworks was for flood prevention and irrigation. On both the rivers Luòhé and Yī, right opposite the extraction points for irrigation, emergency sluice gates had been constructed to take flood water to the areas north and south of the paired rivers. No one ever argued about the design and efficiency of the scheme; it worked, and it worked well.

Fundamentally, Gǔn's construct was idyllic for farmers who only wanted to farm. Perfect for those who had little interest in anything else. Of course, such people were in short supply. The majority view in Èrlǐtou was that the town, if that is what it could be called, was boring. The atmosphere was mind-numbingly so for the more recent newcomers with their wilder experiences.

It was the non-farming workforce that both created and warped Gǔn's idealised vision. He needed the makers of carts and ploughs. He was dependent on the bronze smelters. It was necessary to employ people in the granaries and for general administration. Keeping the town ticking were the irrigation and roadmaking engineers. Gǔn prioritised farming and the creation of new farmland above everything else; he had engineered a new culture but had little idea how to administer it successfully. To him, those peripheral aspects of life were irrelevance; his work was his life, his life was his work, and he was obsessive.

The idea of each farm contributing a labour pool was another idea that had been derived from one of the earlier meetings of the Sisterhood's high command. Nüxi, Gǔn's wife and Yú's mother, was tasked with persuading Gǔn to adopt the idea. Each farm had to contribute one hundred days of labour each year to cooperative projects, in addition to the third of its harvest entering the city coffers. The labour arrangement provided Gǔn with his much-needed workforce, and the harvest tax enabled the town to hold almost two years' essential food supply.

Nüxi was fond of saying, "I see Gǔn in the distance, perhaps three or four times a year when his work brings him closer to the house." It was not entirely true because Gǔn and Nüxi were typically assiduous in attending the council meetings every new moon. It was not that Gǔn enjoyed the council meetings or even regarded them as necessary. Still, he wielded a veto, and without his presence, the council might introduce ideas that conflicted with his plans for the farms and the water. He allowed nothing that might contradict his grand design.

Gǔn's considerable successes in providing new farms for thousands had allowed him the leeway to override all and sundry. In this regard, time was now running out. Notwithstanding the general level of well-being, he would have been forcibly deposed if it had not been for his required work on the Yellow River, which had meant he had been absent for much of the previous winter. His position was such that he could not be removed, which proved a significant irritant to many. Gǔn's obsession was grinding and ceaseless; he had annoyed many. However, some factors had prevented rebellion, one being the knowledge that Yú would soon be with them and the second being that the Lóngshān needed a good hiding to keep them from upsetting the applecart.

Today's council meeting was unusual in that it combined the members of the council from Táosì with those from Èrlĭtou. Some had not met each other before, as several had been with the refugee groups coming from Jiăngsu and Shandong. If they had looked forward to having the time to get to know each other, they were sorely disappointed.

"Excuse me!" Gǔn's voice rang out in the *huìyì shì*. "Quiet, please!" He was unused to a council with over twenty present, and bringing them to order took longer than usual. In the centre of the room were four tables. Gǔn had dragged them together so all could sit in some semblance of order without anyone having to defer position to anyone else.

"A welcome to all. A special welcome to those of you who have recently arrived from Táosì. We have all heard about your journey and how it was expertly led. I want to congratulate Bóyì on bringing the expedition home to Èrlĭtou with such great success. Well done, Bóyì! Give him a round of applause." The cheering and clapping gave the Èrlĭtou members the time to express surprise to each other that Gǔn had been so upbeat; usually, he was a grumpy and reluctant chair.

"I think that you all know it is within our rules that the council can be suspended for a period of two moons. This may be done at the command of the council leader." There was an irritated hum around the tables. "However, I do not intend to command anything. I will ask you to vote on the issue at my son's request." The humming quieted at the mention of Yú. "I would like to invite Yú to address our combined meeting and explain why he would like to suspend the council. Yú, please go ahead."

"Hello, everyone!" Yú stood. His confidence and demeanour soared when he faced a slightly larger group. As he glanced around, he saw warming smiles from those new to him and encouraging grins from those who knew him well. He was back in his element.

"So…you'd like to know why I want to take all the power away from you? Yes?" Laughs greeted his opening remark. "Well…here goes!

"We have a place to live here. We have a place for our children, their children, and great-grandchildren to live. Sure, it needs some

239

changes." He looked directly at the council chair. "My father, Gǔn, was asked to provide the fabric to build a great community. He was never asked to build that community. I know, and he also knows, that changes are needed here in Èrlǐtou." A sigh of relief passed around the table. "But that was not his job. It is not my job. It is going to become your job." Yú paused to let the idea sink in.

"On this basis, we would like to ask the Èrlǐtou council to have a vote. This vote would not include those from Táosì. We, and by we, I mean my father and me, are proposing new council elections." The group was hushed. "We are proposing that the new council elections should take place on the new moon after next."

"Why not the next new moon?" A call went out from a woman at the end of the table. "The sooner, the better!"

"Ah…well. There is going to be a minor problem thirty days from now. Let's call it a clash of interests or perhaps a conflict with appointments. Put it this way: many people will not be around on the next new moon. You're called Cháng, aren't you? Sorry, we haven't met. Hi, Cháng!"

"Hi!" Slightly red-faced, she nodded her head.

"Thank you, Cháng. I will be addressing your question a bit later." Yú paused to gather his thoughts. "In the poll, all council positions will be up for election. A position will not be reserved for my father—" There was instant bedlam. "There will not be a—"

"Order!" Gǔn broke in. "Quiet now! Hear him out!"

"There will not be a position reserved for my father. There will not be a position reserved for me." A collective gasp followed this. "And there will not be a position reserved for the Sisterhood."

The resulting noise was not so easy to quell. It was quite a time before Yú was able to resume.

"I will reiterate. There will be no reserved positions on the council. None."

"Does that mean we cannot vote for you?" Bóyì chimed in this time.

"I believe I am right in saying that the rules in Èrlǐtou are like those we had in Táosì. Anyone over the age of fourteen may stand for election. Anyone! That means that my father, Gǔn, Líng, who is not here,

240

Nüxi or myself or Cháng," he smiled again in her direction, "are all able to stand for election...if we so wish." A raucous cheer went around the table. "However...and they have given their permission for me to say this...my mother and father will not be standing in any future election...I don't think you realise how much these last six years have worn them out."

The noise levels rose again.

"Order!" Gǔn was on his feet. "Order! We will adjourn so that everyone can gather their thoughts. We will resume as the sun sets. Do not be late." With that, he sat down wearily, with the air of a man who had worked himself to a standstill.

"Thank you, son." a whispered aside to Yú. "Thank you."

"Yes, it was time." Nüxi broke in. "Any longer, and we might have been lynched!" She stroked her son's head adoringly.

As the sun set on a momentous day, the evening was just about to become more interesting.

"Order!" Gǔn re-started proceedings. "First, may we vote on holding new elections on the new moon after next. Please - just the Èrlǐtou council members." He pointed at each councillor as he counted. "Good! That's unanimous!

"Moving on. Yú, would you please explain your plans between now and then?"

"I would like you to listen very carefully. I am going to ask you to suspend the current council. I hope you will agree. If you disagree, I will go ahead with most of these plans anyway because they are to ensure your future safety." There were a few mutterings amongst the Èrlǐtou councillors but total silence amongst those from Táosì.

"I want to appoint an emergency war council to make executive decisions for the next two months." The noise levels began to rise again rapidly. "Hush! Wait! Hear me out. The emergency council will make no decisions concerning Èrlǐtou or the lands bounded by the rivers Yī and Luòhé. For day-to-day administration of the town, I will ask my mother to step in to adjudicate."

Nüxi was popular. With Gǔn out of the picture, she was considered fair in the extreme; it was a popular suggestion.

"We are about to fight and defeat the Lóngshān." Yú had to halt as the gathering now erupted into a wild state. Once again, it was an extended interlude; once again, he gathered his thoughts. As the pandemonium diminished, he recommenced.

"I asked you to listen carefully. Please do. This will not be compulsory; we will ask for volunteers to fight, including anyone aged fourteen or over.

"I will lead the war council. Its members will be Líng, Bóyì, Gǔn and, it has been recommended to me, Cháng and Yuán from the Èrlǐtou council. However, you will have to accept that this is a war council. The members will advise; they will not vote. For we are going to war, and you need a war leader in times of war. That is my job, and I promise I will not disappoint you."

This time, there was no muttering or discussion; there was simply cheering. Yú allowed it to continue for longer than was necessary.

"Order!" Gǔn broke in. "Order. We will have a vote. This includes all of you, except that mutt that seems to have crept in at the rear." Everyone turned to laugh at the animal curled next to the door. It was Gǔn's dog.

"Please raise your hands if you agree to Nüxi running Èrlǐtou for two months, the formation of a war council, its leader being Yú, and its members being Líng, Bóyì, Cháng, Yuán and myself. If there are any dissenters, we will hold separate votes on each." Once again, Gǔn pointed at each councillor as he counted.

"That's unanimous! This council is stood down. Nüxi, you to oversee Èrlǐtou. Yú, I believe the war council will meet immediately. Should we conclude?" Yú nodded. "Yes, it is. Thank you, everybody. Goodnight!"

Thirty-five: The Council of War
Èrlĭtou, Hénán
Year 90: Year of the Rat
Twenty-two days after the spring equinox
12th April 1905 BCE

"I would first like to introduce you to three women who have just arrived in town." Yú commenced the meeting without the customary formalities. "Then we will introduce ourselves.

"You will notice I have appointed a woman to tend the door. Cháng and Yuán, you know her and will know that she is completely deaf; the rest of you may not. She is instructed to sit facing away from us while we are in session. Bóyì has brought in four men to watch this building from each side. They will sit far enough away that they cannot hear but close enough to observe if anyone else approaches.

"No information is to leave this room without my express permission. Is that understood?"

There was affirmation from the other five around the table.

"No one is to come into this room without my express permission. Is that understood?" Again, there were nods around the table. "I want to hear you say 'Agreed', please!"

"Agreed, Yú." They were as one.

Yú strode to the door, tapped the doorkeeper on the shoulder and beckoned across the yard. Within moments, three cloaked women arrived. They were ushered into the hall and seated in the closest vacant chairs.

"These ladies are Kùaimă, Yĕmă and Măjié. They have brought information for us. They have not passed this message to anyone outside this room and have sworn not to do so. I will let them tell their own story."

"We have ridden from Ānyáng." Kùaimă commenced and paused momentarily as one or two in the room gasped. "We have been undercover for five years in that city. We have been working for a woman that we

243

knew as *Mǎ*, although Yú tells us that she was also known as Grandmoth—"

"You say was - is she dead?" Líng interjected.

"I'm afraid so," Yěmǎ answered. "We helped her. She was horribly injured."

"You know what this means?" Líng directed the question at Yú.

"I do. I'm sorry. You're in charge of the Sisterhood now, Líng.

"Ladies, please carry on."

"It's quite simple, really." Mǎjié took on the story. "We have a simple message, although it is not necessarily clear. It is this, 'Place – agreed. Date – agreed. One thousand crack troops. Remember Hú and Xí's scars.' That's it. That's the message."

"We don't really understand it, apart from the 'crack troops' bit." Kùaimǎ followed up. "I think she should have added 'on horses', but she was in a bad way."

"Yes, we all agree, it should have been 'Place – agreed. Date – agreed. One thousand crack troops - on horses. Then remember Hú and Xí's scars."

Yěmǎ whispered. "We can tell you about Hú and Xí's scars. Huge. Right across their backs. It looked like they had once been tortured."

"And they deserved it!" Yěmǎ looked wounded. "Twice over! The bastards! The marks were the same as the one *Mǎ* cut on her breast. Like this." She outlined the symbol of the Motherland on the table.

"Thank you, ladies. I think Líng would like to speak to the three of you later if you don't mind. Is that alright?" The three nodded. "Is there anything else before you go?"

"Yes." All three spoke at once before Kùaimǎ took the lead. "Yes. We want to be there, all three of us."

"Where?" Yú asked.

"At the battle, of course!"

After the agreement, they were all smiles, and Yú saw them out before resuming his place at the table.

"Well, father, that's a relief!" Yú beamed at Gǔn. "All that work over the winter will count! Now, we can plan our battle! Are you up for it, Líng?"

There were those around the table who knew a little, those who knew nothing, and three who knew everything. Yú, Gǔn and Líng brought the others up to speed on the details. Gǔn initiated proceedings.

"I've been working on the Yellow River over the winter months. We could only do preparatory work while the river was high, but since the winter solstice, it has been possible to work flat out.

"The reason is that we needed the river to be as low as possible. We had some assistance. Upstream on the Èěrduōsī Loop, Kànménrén and Hòutú worked with the local people to ensure the river froze as hard as possible. Since the spring equinox, they have worked just as hard to reverse that process and persuade the river to thaw. In the Wèi valley, the kinsfolk of Yú and myself have spent the winter trying to keep as much of Wèi River as possible out of its regular channels, which slows it down. Here around Èrlǐtou, we have done the same. You may have noticed the flooding on the northern bank of the Luòhé and the southern bank of the Yī River. That has been deliberate. We have slowed the flow of the Yellow River to a trickle.

"The objective was to ensure the Yellow River was as low as possible in the year's first four lunar cycles. This enabled us to create a dam in Xíngyáng, some three day's walk to the east. It was also to help us prepare a diversionary channel a short walk further downstream. That was the work many of those undertook on their hundred days of service, which is why they went missing for long periods.

"The dam is of tamped earth and clay, fortified by a few rocks and tree trunks here and there. It cannot withstand the Yellow River for long. We have already had to find spillways for some of the water so it will not breach too soon. On the other hand, the diversionary channel is constructed from rock broken off the cliffs over the river at Mùméngōu. We expect this to hold up for many years.

"I think, Yú, I have given away the 'place' the three girls talked about; my apologies."

"May I interrupt?" Yuán asked, receiving an affirmative nod from Yú. "You say a diversionary channel?"

"Yes."

"You're planning to divert the Yellow River?"

"Yes."

"Fucking hell! That is one big, big river. So, you're planning to divert it. Where?"

"Oh. All the way. I have it in mind that the river will no longer enter the sea in Jiǎngsu. I hope we can persuade it to pass through Lóngshān lands and flood into the Bohai Sea."

"Gǔn, I've always thought of you as one crazy old man, but that's...that's..." Yuán stuttered to a halt.

"It would take about a month to walk from the old river mouth to the one we hope for." Yú assisted. "What you might not know, Yuán, is that...hang on, you're from Jiǎngsu...I don't suppose you remember what it was like before. Before the floods?" Yuán shook his head. "Well, before my father was born, the Yellow River used to flow to the north of Mount Tai. Then there was disastrous flooding, and, just east of Kāifēng, the great river spilt its southern banks and cut a new route through Jiǎngsu. With that and the Yangtze flooding as well, it was a disaster. That's why your people came north. So, what we are trying to do, is to return the Yellow River to its more usual northern route."

"What caused the river to move all those years ago?" Yuán was impressed.

"Who knows? Fate. The gods. This is not a question we asked ourselves." Gǔn answered.

"And...and this time. It won't be the fates or any gods. What you're telling me right here and right now is that it will be you?" Yuán extended his arm towards Gǔn.

"Yes. That's the way it will be." Gǔn was quietly spoken. Yuán had never admired Yú's father, but he now viewed him with new eyes and something close to a feeling of reverence.

"Let's move on. Father, would you continue, please."

"Where was I? Er..."

"At the dam." Líng helped.

"So, the dam is designed to hold back as much water as we can, but it will not be a great deal. When we collapse it, the Lóngshān army will not get washed away in one go. It's designed to hold enough water to hit the diversionary wall forcefully but not enough to break it. The flow should be deflected to the north rather than the usual channel to the east. It will make conditions to the north of the river quite difficult to manage."

"You're going to collapse your own dam?" Yuán was awestruck.

"Correct. The dam is designed to be collapsed.

"The extra flow built up by the ice dams will hopefully not hit us for a week or more after the battle. I say hopefully because if it comes early...Well! Then we have a real problem. If it comes on time, it will then follow the channel that water from the collapsing dam created.

"My only problem at this stage is caring for the dam. Because it is designed to collapse quickly, at a moment's notice, it is a delicate structure. Generally, the Yellow River does not like delicate structures. I will spend the next month at the dam with some of my best engineers and fifty labourers. Yú tells me it would help if those labourers were also archers, but primarily, I need people who can shift dirt quickly."

"Thank you, father. Líng, may I pass this over to you, please."

"The Sisterhood has been planning this longer than I have been alive. This is all part of our grander plan. Gǔn has explained about the place. Yú will explain how the battle will be fought. I am going to explain the date and the personnel required.

"On the next new moon, something will happen to the sun. None of us has ever experienced this sort of thing, as it has not happened in our lifetimes. However, shortly before noon, the moon's disk will creep across the face of the sun. It will make the day much darker and go on for some time. It is a natural process that occurs repeatedly, but only once, or never, in a lifetime. The Sisterhood has recorded such instances over hundreds of years and has forecast it will happen next month. I am confident it will.

"There is a big problem. Those who do not know it is going to happen will be scared. Terrified! They may well try to hide. This is what we want to happen to the Lóngshān forces. Our people must know it will occur and feel confident in its outcome.

"Therefore, we will tell our people only the day before. At the same time, the news will be shared with the citizens remaining in Èrlǐtou, but not before. This is the reason we need Nüxi in charge of Èrlǐtou. We cannot afford this information to leak out."

"How sure are you that this is going to happen?" Bóyì asked.

"Certain. Absolutely certain." Líng was not confident but had a backup plan if the sun remained unchallenged. "It will happen...on that day…just before noon! Our plans revolve around this as surely as the earth moves around the sun. We—"

"You mean as the sun revolves around the earth," Bóyì interjected.

"I know what I said. We can discuss that later, which brings me to the second half of the timing. Because of our chosen location, the Lóngshān will likely request a parlay before the battle. In fact, we have our pet soothsayers, Hú and Xí, who have been prompted to suggest just such a thing. It is pretty standard when they fight between themselves. It is almost regarded as gentlemanly conduct! Anyway, what they actually want to do is to have a better look at the battle site. They will typically send a group of eight, which is thought of as lucky, and they will be unarmed.

"We will suggest Tú, Túshānshì and me from the Sisterhood, but would request Kùàimǎ, Yěmǎ and Mǎjié, the women you met tonight, are with us. In addition, Jīngfēi, I'm sure Bóyì can get her to volunteer, and Mài if you can ride, would you like to be with us? That would be eight."

"I've just noticed…I might be foolish, but isn't that eight women," Yuán pondered, "facing eight males? All serious soldiers and possibly several of the Lóngshān kings? Is that wise?"

"You are not stupid, Yuán. You would not be sitting here if you were. It's quite deliberate. When assessing our forces, they will come into it with all their usual preconceptions. We will ensure that to them, we look weak."

"Who, the Lóngshān delegation?" Bóyì was quickly trying to take it all in.

"No. We want them to think our own forces are weak. They think we're a bunch of farmers. They think we'll fight with pitchforks. It'll just confuse them more if our delegation is all female. They think of women as weak; they think of women as slaves; they think they can do with us what they want. To them, this will be perceived as a serious weakness. It will be especially so when I tell them I am our battle leader."

"But Yú is!" Bóyì was shaking his head.

"No…I am not, Bóyì. It will be Líng." Yú clarified. "It was Líng who planned and executed the Battle of Sānjiādiǎncūn…every bit of it. I might be good at motivation, but she is the brains behind the tactics. Líng,

248

I will be happy to address the men and women at arms if you wish, but I am even happier that you are in charge of the battle."

"Allow me to continue, please." Líng indicated a slight irritation. "We will then apply our magic! Of course, I have never performed magic in my life, and I believe that none of our eight representatives has, but it will appear to be magic to the lords of Lóngshān."

"What will this magic consist of?" Mài asked.

"We'll get Hú and Xí to take their tunics off. We're going to have them reveal the symbols on their backs. To make the point sink in, we'll have Tú show the same symbol emblazoned across her body. We'll have the three of them in a line, all three displaying their loyalty to the Motherland!

"I am hoping. I am hoping, more than anything else, that they choose to leave those two curs with us when they return to their armies. I will allow Kùàimǎ, Yěmǎ and Mǎjié to deal with them as they wish!

"However, to return to the point. We will ask if they have a weather prophecy for the rest of the day. They do. They have been told it will be bright, sunny, and fine, which is Hú and Xí's prophesy. They also believe it will be dry underfoot.

"We will counter that the sun is about to be eaten by a dragon. That it will go very dark; that it will be wet. They will, of course, believe we are talking absolute nonsense and return to their men to share the joke. It is then that the timing is crucial.

"We will have observers looking at the sun. Not directly, of course, as it would blind them. They will use finely cut jade discs, so finely cut they are translucent. The watchers will be able to see the first moment the moon cuts across the sun, which will give us plenty of time before the Lóngshān observe it."

"And that is where I come in." Yú took over. "We will have a line of troops across the battlefield. They will look like farmers and be armed like farmers. The only addition will be that they will all carry horse spears to the site of the expected charge; they will set these across a gap. The diversionary boulders are on one side of the gap, and behind them, completely out of sight, will be archers. The levee has been artificially extended to the north on the other side of the gap. Behind that, again completely hidden, will be more archers." He smiled. "It seems the

Lóngshān have yet to realise the effectiveness of the bow and arrow; they seem to think battles must be won on the battlefield with a series of one-to-one fights! They're seriously deluded and outdated!

"Our signal will be drums. The drums will start rolling as soon as we spot the shading of the sun. The drums will change to a single beat when the Lóngshān begin to charge; then, they will begin a double beat to indicate that our spearmen should flee. They will all be pointing at the sun in alarm. This will focus the attackers on the sun, to the south, when, directly to the west, the same double beat will signal for Gǔn to do his stuff, collapsing the dam."

"Líng? Yú? Sorry, I'm not clear who to address here." Bóyì was confused.

"Bóyì, think of the cart drive. Who was in charge?"

"Me…ah! Got it!"

"Right…I'm the chair of the emergency council. Got it?" All heads nodded. "And Líng is in charge of the battle. Got that?"

"So…now I know who to ask." Bóyì looked more comfortable. "Aren't we in danger of overkill here?"

Thirty-six: The Greatest Fears

Èrlĭtou, Xíngyáng & Jiāozuò, Hénán
Year 90: Year of the Rat
Forty-four days after the spring equinox
4th May 1905 BCE

Líng was now probably the most confident general of her time; it was quite a reverse from the Battle of Sanjiadiăncūn. Her job was complete if everything went to plan. There were backup scenarios for each section of the battlefield, and each had a commander. Only a catastrophic reverse would mean she might have to emerge from beneath the cart she had once again planned as her base.

Túshānshì was to act as her runner, but it was unlikely she would be able to pass messages any further than Yú and his archers. Tú would remain with her also, but she would be taking care of any messages that needed to be sent by pigeon. Líng hoped that only one would be required. A series of emergency mirror signals had been established, and spotters appointed to ensure they were noticed.

Everything, Líng believed, was in the planning. Forget better weaponry, forget that the opposition had well-trained and battle-hardened troops and forget individual heroics; these things were irrelevant. Preparation for any encounter was essential. The key elements were planning supplies, planning positions, and planning precise timings. However, overriding all this was to know your enemy. Líng had an excellent idea of her enemy and their likely strategies. She also knew they had no idea whatsoever of her own.

Líng's greatest fear was also one of the Xià's greatest strengths. She was scared that when she proclaimed herself the Xià leader during the parlay, the Lóngshān warlords would laugh at her. However, it was a fear she had brought under control, knowing that being laughed at ultimately helped their cause.

*

Nüxi was more than content to be running Èrlǐtou. The only aspect she found disagreeable had been the order to dispatch her pigeons to parts far and wide. She was not worried about their return journeys; she expected her brood to make those flights successfully.

She was most concerned for the male pigeons. They had gone westwards, being dropped off with her sisters upstream along the Yellow River. Their sole purpose was to deliver messages to her about the flood surges due within the next month. Their outbound journey on the backs of horses worried her most. Pigeons did not particularly like horses and did not enjoy bumping around. The riders would also probably have little liking for pigeons, for although she had rehabilitated the bird's reputation in Èrlǐtou, old prejudices died hard. Nüxi had spent several days with the riders, ensuring their understanding of pigeon care and the importance of diet. Although they had all sworn to defend the birds with their lives, Nüxi was still unsure. She spoke to them again before they left, each bird with its purpose-built cage strapped to a rider's back.

In the other direction, she had another team of riders prepared to relay any incoming and pertinent information from Èrlǐtou to Xíngyáng. Their job was to carry messages, not pigeons, so she had selected those least taken by her avian crew. Nüxi had little concern for the female pigeons going eastwards. For a start, Tú was caring for them. They were all going to Xíngyáng; their purpose was to bring messages to Èrlǐtou regarding the build-up to the battle and the conflict itself.

The news that Grandmother had died saddened her; she had been a close colleague. However, it was also irritating because, in a moment, Girl leapfrogged her into a position of command. It had been Grandmother's final decision in their last meeting, inevitable but still hard to take. Nüxi was an organiser, a listener and, except for the Mount Sōng debacle, had exerted a vice-like control over Gǔn; she had done her job. It was a role that Nüxi knew Túshānshì would have to step into as Èrlǐtou entered its next phase of development, and she passed over the baton.

Nüxi's greatest fear was that she would receive messages from the battle site advising her that the Lóngshān army had won and that she should prepare for an attack. The only backup plan the Sisterhood had for

252

that eventuality was a rapid retreat and a chaotic escape. She did not wish for the life of a refugee again and feared for her husband and son.

*

Gǔn was more than well aware of the fundamental water problem; it always went downhill. If this were a problem, it was also a property that could be advantageous. His life's goal had been to reverse the laws of nature and persuade water to flow upwards. To date, his most significant success was the invention of the *hùdǒu*[21], which took two men or animals pulling in opposite directions to raise a wooden bucket of water. He was still attempting to apply his understanding of the wheel to the conundrum but kept coming unstuck. It was perplexing. He could make water force a wheel to rotate but could not find the means to lift the stuff. In truth, Yǔ's father, whilst not a particularly intelligent man, was one of the first to comprehend the laws of gravity. Over the last ten years every day of his life had been devoted to water.

It had been a wrench to abandon his irrigation and drainage schemes in Èrlǐtou, but he understood the importance and the reasoning behind his current projects. Only when Yǔ pointed out that Lóngshān control of Èrlǐtou would devastate the water systems he had created had he finally been persuaded. Gǔn's prime reason for contributing to the war effort was to protect his work, and a distant second was that he desired fame for his son.

At this point, a mere week before the likely battle, Gǔn was entirely focused on his dam. He was not as confident as everyone else that a clash would occur when and where they said it would. As an eternal pessimist, he believed his work here on the barrage would be wasted. His work on the diversion a short walk downstream was over. Even with the added impetus of the released dam water, he was confident of the efficacy of that structure, for it was made of boulders too large for a winter flow to dislodge. However, his overriding doubt was that the river would not behave as the Sisterhood believed it would. The Yellow River was a temperamental beast, and Gǔn's inclination was that it might loop itself

---

[21] An ancient Chinese device used in irrigation.

back southwards, re-joining its previous course. In contrast, the Sisterhood believed it could be tamed and would adopt a new north-easterly route.

Gǔn had been unable to survey the hoped-for river channel. The area had been in Lóngshān hands forever; only the Sisterhood's spies had managed access. Notwithstanding his long and lasting relationship with Nüxi, he had developed a distinct apathy towards the organisation over time.

Today, as he would for the next seven days, Gǔn monitored the water behind the dam. Only so many actions were open to him if the levels were to rise too fast. There were two zones on either side of the confluence where the Yīluò River[22] emptied into the great river. Artificial levees had been built around these so that if flooded, they would take some pressure off the dam. Indeed, the larger of the two was finished, and the second would be complete within days.

Further upstream, near Jili, he had built a sluice that would take water out of the river, dumping it onto the flood plain south of the town. The Jili option was risky as it could cause the entire Yellow River to divert at that point, which would not help them in the forthcoming battle. It also had the disadvantage of being a day's horse ride away; its implementation was an issue.

Gǔn's final mechanism to defend the dam was the dam itself. The whole structure was constructed to collapse; that was its purpose. On the uppermost part of the dam were two points where brute force would cause tree trunks to give way, weakening the earth wall and allowing the river's natural erosive powers to do the rest. There was a proper spillway, expertly built using earthenware pipes, and a reusable sluice; the only problem being that it was untested. The water levels behind the dam were only now reaching sufficient depth. As a last resort, Gǔn could release water into the existing bed of the river. However, the risk of prompting an early collapse was considerable and would result in a water channel through the battle site before the conflict. Neither of these downsides was considered desirable.

---

[22] The Yīluò River is formed where the Luòhé and Yī Rivers meet, just east of Èrlǐtou.

Gǔn's greatest fear was of the dam collapsing too early. He made ten daily trips, crossing back and forth to check its integrity from every angle and in minuscule detail.

*

Bóyì oversaw the line of women and men who would be facing the enemy directly. It was hard to tell whose role was the most nerve-wracking, but this was undoubtedly the most dangerous for those on the ground. Troops in the centre faced the highest risk, not only from their opponents but also from the floodwaters that Gǔn would unleash on them.

Much of Bóyì's team preparation had been on sprint training. The fastest would be those occupying the centre of the line. He had also worked with them on using a triangular shield devised explicitly for this purpose. It was an idea he had tossed around with Líng and Yú, going through circular and square shapes before settling on the stability of the triangle. Just before the troops ran from the battlefield, in apparent fear and confusion as the sun was eaten, it was their job to turn the triangular shields.

Each shield had a bronze loop screwed into one of its corners. An extended spear or pike threaded through the loop, with its end embedded in the earth. Only the shield would be seen with the spear lying on the ground. When it was rotated, the spear, now at the apex, extended upwards toward the enemy. Great care had to be taken that the blunt end remained firmly embedded. To the enemy, what had once seemed to be a harmless serrated shield wall would become a mass of points level with a horse's chest. Bóyì hoped that the spear points might not be visible to the horses with the darkening skies. They would see the gaps in the triangles as perfect places to jump through the wall. To enhance the deception, he had ordered all the spear points be covered with a thin layer of mud to prevent them from reflecting whatever sunlight there might be.

Bóyì's greatest fear was that the floodwaters would reach his men before they could enact their strategy. A delay might also prevent them from circling to back up Yú's archers. He planned to place himself in the very centre of the line.

*

Yú was in control of the archers. The bow carriers split into two groups; old Hòuyì, a former master archer, had been wheeled out to supervise those embedded in the diversionary rocks. Yú, himself, would be situated on the western flank, protected by the extended levee. The two groups were critical to the action and expected to see more of it than most others.

Their training regime had focussed on the time needed to take their shots. After a few initial volleys, the plan focused on exposed individuals, so tracking was a concern. That these would mainly be back shots was obvious, but Yú was as interested in those horsemen who started to find the ground was not to their steeds' liking. The archers numbered some three hundred, divided equally between the two positions. They were chosen specifically for their hunting experience, although their number was augmented by some who had accompanied Yú at the Battle of Sanjiādiǎncūn. The archers' units were each allocated a specific area of the battle site, making them less likely to aim at the same targets. Much of their firepower would be directed at cavalry held up by the shield wall.

Yú's greatest fear was that his father's scheme would not back up his firepower. Whereas the odds looked good if conditions on the field became boggy, if it remained dry, there might be problems.

*

Tú was beginning to hate the Xíngyáng area; it offered little to her. She had been somewhat irritated that her primary role seemed to be confined to a few minutes at the start of the final day. Whilst six of the eight women on the parlay team would be joining the small group of Xià cavalry, and Líng herself would be taking control, Tú alone appeared without a specific job. Admittedly, she was not a fighter and would have two babies to care for, but it irritated her.

She had volunteered to look after the pigeons, for which Nüxi had been eternally grateful. She had taken turns atop the cliffs, splitting rocks and watching them tumble onto the riverbed below. Nights spent around the campfires with the labourers and troops had been somewhat entertaining, and she added to this by playing a few magic tricks her mother had taught her. Whilst the babies had slept, she had made food and sharpened arrowheads to keep herself busy.

Tú's greatest fear was that she was simply a walking symbol. Once the prelude to this battle was over, she would become an irrelevance. To a large extent, her position in Èrlǐtou and that of her son was beholden to Túshānshì. Her role there was unclear. More and more, it was a relationship that was bringing her some discomfort.

It was a relief when Líng took her on one side and asked her if she would be willing to undertake a piece of counterespionage. The archers had picked up on a young man who seemed decidedly out of place. He was undoubtedly a fine archer, but it was unclear from where he came. The concern was such that his training was allocated to a specially formed unit. This group was kept well away from all tactical planning and out of sight of Gǔn's dam.

Yú had reported the man to Líng, suspecting him of spying for the Lóngshān. He had gone further and recommended that the man be given false information to take back with him if he left. Yú's involvement had not ended there, for he had gone a whole step further, suggesting that Tú be the active agent in duping the man.

Tú was extremely uncomfortable with Yú's intervention. Her annoyance was exacerbated as it was only months since she and Yú had been lovers and even less time since the birth of their child. Now, the fact he was suggesting she undertook the job as a sexual encounter did not go down at all well.

It was not that Tú minded sleeping with the enemy; in fact, the prospect enthralled her. What annoyed her was Yú. She agreed to the role, not out of her loyalty to the Xià or the Sisterhood, but hoping she would hurt the Xià leader. She was determined to hump the poor bastard senseless and ensure it was as public as possible.

Thirty-seven: The Supreme Commanders

Jiāozuò, Hénán
Year 90: Year of the Rat
Forty-three days to the summer solstice
10th May 1905 BCE

All the monarchs, even those who had lost internal battles in the previous year, considered themselves capable of commanding the Lóngshān army. It had proved a nightmare for Léigōng to establish that they needed a single commander and then ensure he was the man to fill that role. Their arguments had almost come to blows.

Although all of them knew the need for a single commander, all recognised that if this were to happen, the odds of them commanding the army were minimal. They eventually came to some compromise in that they were determined to recognise a single leader, albeit they would each take on the title of Supreme Commander. It was a consensus that would at least allow them bragging rights when they returned home.

To achieve the controlling position, Léigōng had found it necessary to threaten to withdraw his troops from the army. His was the most significant contingent and, from casual appearances, seemed to be the best armed. None of the others was happy to submit to the Ānyáng leader's threats, although equally, they would have been extremely unhappy to see the army considerably depleted. Consequently, Léigōng was now going by the title of 'Supreme Commander in Charge'.

Léigōng and his army had been holed up in Jiāozuò, which he considered a dump, for a week. As the days dragged on and more units joined them, the place was now hosting nearly two thousand men, putting enormous pressure on its resources. He had personally evicted a family from its home to find a suitable bed for the night, and he was aware that the situation was repeated across the small town. The meetings of the

258

monarchs grew larger as the week progressed until two nights ago, all had been present. It was only then that the command situation was agreed upon.

At the previous night's meeting, Léigōng had once again dragged out Hú and Xí. They were not quite as resplendent as when first introduced to the gathering. Once again, they repeated their mantra, although, after pressure from their king, they omitted the section about washing away sins. Léigōng had insisted that only Xí speak and that he would add a line after each section. Xí was close to shaking as he stood in front of those gathered.

"On the day after tomorrow, there will be a battle on the Yellow River, a day's march south of Jiāozuò."

"Well, that bit's clear then," Léigōng spoke to the meeting as deferentially as his new position allowed him to. "We know where it is. We've had some scouts out, and it's quite clear they have a small army bivouacked down there. Probably a thousand or so. From the reports, they look and smell like farmers. Xí, continue."

"There will be no fog, no rain, and it will be dry for your horses."

"And…look at the weather. There has certainly been no fog nor rain, and the ground is rock hard." Léigōng smiled at the assembly. "But we need to make sure and get closer. I will call for a parlay before the battle so that we can make sure of our ground. The messenger sent to set up the parlay will approach their lines even closer than we will. He'll bring back a report as well. Xí?"

"The sun will shine bright, and Xià will be slain."

"Well, I think these are both obvious points. If there's no rain or fog, it's hardly surprising that the sun will shine. If we fight the Xià, it is unsurprising that many of them will die. Xí, more."

"Many will run away to the south."

"They'd have to be stupid if they ran to the north now, wouldn't they? Come on! The important one!"

"The Lóngshān lords will control all the lands north of the Yellow River."

"Xí, the only thing I don't like about this is it doesn't mention us controlling the lands south of the Yellow River."

"My…my—"

259

"Shut up, Hú! I want an answer from Xí!"

"On the other hand, my lord, it does not mention that the Lóngshān will not control the lands south of the Yellow River," Xí hedged. "Prophecies can be notoriously vague."

"Yet in all other ways, the prophecy is so precise? Why is that?" As usual, Fēngbō was the first to break in.

"My...my—"

"Shut up, Hú! Xí, answer!"

"Of this, we are unsure, my lords. The prophecies come from both the souls of our ancestors and those of our great-grandchildren, who are as yet unborn, so it is possible that they do not observe everything." It was a more comprehensive answer than any had expected and took a while to digest. In the silence, Xí congratulated himself for the nonsense he had made up on the spur of the moment. It seemed this job was getting easier for him and more challenging for Hú. Perhaps it was time his friend lost his stutter.

"What?" The King of Chéngzǐyá broke the silence. "I'm not sure I understand."

"He means that..." Fēngbō paused, "He means that prophecies are accurate but cannot be completely comprehensive. Yes. That's what he means."

"I wish someone had told me that years ago!" The King of Wǔzhì opined. "Might have saved a lot of fucking guesswork!"

"And right now, King Wǔzhì, we are trying to minimise the guesswork for the battle. Let us concern ourselves about further conquests later." Léigōng was becoming more confident that he could rely on those gathered to listen to him. He did have an ongoing concern that their troops might not. "May I outline my...sorry...our plans?"

There were low murmurs, although nothing that constituted a rebellion.

"Tomorrow, we leave this shi...apologies, King Jiāozuò, this town and move our forces southwards. There is an abandoned farmhouse there that goes by the name of Dōngliǔcūn, and although I have no idea why someone should wish to give a name to the place, that is what the King of Wǔzhì's scouts call it. It is they that will lead the column."

"And we are to overnight there?" Fēngbō asked.

"We will."

"What about food?" the King of Púyáng looked concerned.

"Well. Most of us have brought our own. Is that not the case?" Léigōng enquired of the group. It was clear from the shaking heads that little consideration had been given to this matter.

"Right. Here is an instruction. Get orders to your men to gather enough food for two nights. Do it now."

"But there's–" The King of Jiāozuò was rightly concerned about his town's food stocks. He was rudely interrupted.

"This is war, Jiāozuò. War!" Léigōng stared hard. "We'll resume this meeting in Dōngliǔcūn, tomorrow evening, the eve of the battle! We set off at dawn. I will see you then."

With that, Léigōng walked out. He was utterly oblivious that he had sent thirteen sections of his army to fight over food resources that might not be enough for a quarter of that number. After a moment of indecision, Hú and Xí followed him to the house he had appropriated. When he entered, the king beckoned for them to join him.

"I don't know if this has occurred to you two, but on a technical basis, if I am running the whole army, you two will be in charge of my forces." Léigōng lay down on a narrow and uncomfortable bench.

"Why?" Xí asked plaintively, palms outspread.

"Seniority. That's why. Now, what I don't want is you interfering with Captain Cóng. He's really in charge, and the men will follow him. However, I want you two to be properly dressed for battle."

"With...with...with armour?"

"Yes! With...with...with fucking armour. And you can stop that fake stuttering. If you don't, I will kill you. And I will kill you very unpleasantly."

"Yes, my lord." Hú's stutter disappeared instantly.

"Both of you, properly dressed for war. None of those magic outfits you like so much."

"May we ask if we may wear our cloaks," Hú enquired.

"Of course, you can wear cloaks, but plain cloaks! It'll be cold overnight; that's what the cloaks are for. You can't wear them when you're fighting. Got it? I don't want any embarrassment coming my way. None!"

"Is that it, my lord?" Xí very much wanted to depart hurriedly.

"No, it is not. Both of you are coming with me on the parlay team. I want to know if those farmers' witches are up to anything. It seems to me you'll be the first two who can spot any shenanigans. They're bound to bring one of those Sisterhood cows with them to parlay; they have their noses in everything."

When Hú and Xí finally left Léigōng, they hurried to the small barn they had made their own for the stay in Jiāozuò. When they finally sat down with a strong drink, Léigōng's remarks seemed to be sinking in.

"It's bad enough we've got to go to the battlefield," Hú whined. "But to have to go along for the parlay as well—"

"It's worse than that, Hú. He wants us...us...to take a full part in the battle also. You heard him, 'What I do want is that you two are properly dressed for battle.' It's ridiculous!"

"We got away last time."

"We did. We got away because it was dark. Remember, though, we only got a short way. Bloody Kànménrén!" Xí scratched his back. The wounds left by Kàn still bothered him daily. "In this battle...it's going to be bright daylight—"

"And we're surrounded by the king's forces—"

"And they're surrounded by the rest of the army!"

"If we're going to get away, then we need to do it before the day of the battle. Let us go now." Hú verged on shaking earlier but was now trembling at the thought of involvement in the battle.

"It'll probably be better tomorrow night, Hú. Safer. You've seen it out there; everyone's running around after food."

"That's why it would be best now. We take advantage of the confusion."

"I think we would be taken advantage of if we tried to ride through that lot! Remember, we'll not be showing anything to identify us. We'll get robbed before we can go a hundred paces."

"True." Hú rubbed his beard frantically. "But tomorrow...tomorrow everyone will be in their units...much more orderly... the trouble is, then we'll stand out like a sore thumb."

"Yes, but they'll be sleeping, won't they? That's the time to go. We bribe one of the guards to have our horses ready and—"

"Look, this depends on where we're going to go. Are you sure *Gojoseon*[23] is right for us?" Hú was still unconvinced by Xí's ultimate target. "It seems a long way."

"It's simple…we can't stay in Lóngshān lands if we run from this. That takes out all the land north of the Yellow River. We certainly can't move to Xià lands, and that takes out everything to the south. If you want to go west–"

"That's just too barbaric…no!"

"So, we go to *Gojoseon*."

"By land, or do we try to get a boat?"

"You know I hate boats, Hú. We'll have the horses. I'm told there's an easy route through the mountains. My source said we could get there before winter. Anyway, if we come out of the mountains, it will add to our mystique."

"Why?"

"From what I hear, the locals in *Gojoseon* are extremely superstitious. They believe they're descended from this man called Dangun and–"

"So what? I don't care if–"

"Let me finish, Hú. They believe they're all descended from this man called Dangun and that he was the child of a god and a female bear! They're crazy people! Anyone who can believe a story about a man mating with a bear must be as mad as mad can be. If they believe that, they'll believe anything, which means they'll believe in us. We just expand on our witch story—"

"Stop…stop! I'll go. Do we have enough to see us there?" The pair had switched from hoarding bronze and jade, knowing they may have to execute a swift exit at some time. Their more recent pastime had been trading for or simply stealing gold. The ill-gotten gains lay strapped inside concealed bags stitched into their cloaks.

"Hú! We have enough. We'll cast fortunes for people on the way to keep us fed. We should arrive in *Gojoseon* well-fed, still rich and before winter. You'll see!"

---

[23] Ancient Korea.

Whether Hú would see or not was going to be highly dependent upon the actions of another. It would not be the actions of Xí, nor would it be the actions of the young boy who had spent several hours kneeling outside their window. It would be entirely dependent upon the actions of Léigōng, towards whom the young boy was now sprinting.

Thirty-eight: The Parlay

Dōngliǔcūn & Xíngyáng, Hénán
Year 90: Year of the Rat
Forty-one days to the summer solstice
12th May 1905 BCE

It had been a chaotic evening; the monarchs were all trying to sort out the mess in one way or another. The meeting plans were abandoned. Once again, there had been inter-state fighting as their armies vied for the best land, driest firewood, and every scrap of food. It had been a pitch-black night. Initially, the darkness had quietened the men sooner than expected; it was a while before random thefts and retributions sparked them into life again. It was a process that continued throughout those dark, moonless hours.

The previous morning, Léigōng had succeeded in getting them all to start the journey from Jiāozuò on time, so he believed the same level of promptness might occur if he called the monarchs together for a morning meeting. It was dawn, and he waited impatiently.

Eventually, as they arrived, Léigōng counted them in. By now, he thought of them only by the cities they represented; they had ceased to be individuals. Wǔzhì and Jiāozuò were first, which was probably to be expected, as they had the most to lose and would lose it quickly if events did not go as expected. Creeping in sheepishly and last was Chéngzǐyá, a king whose state was further from the action than most. It left one short.

"Good morning, gentlemen. Do any of you know of the whereabouts of the king of Dōngyíng?"

"Ah. You mean, Fēngbó. Yes, I do." Chéngzǐyá did not appear excited to be adding a contribution.

"Well, where is he?"

"It seems he and his men slipped off in the middle of the night." Chéngzǐyá shuffled from foot to foot. "He came to see me before he went. He—"

"What the fuck is he up to?"

"Well, he wanted me to join him. He said...He said this was a nightmare. He said he'd rather not have anything to do with it. He said that we, he and I, were far away from all this, and it didn't make any sense to him. And he said he was hungry." Chéngzǐyá concluded with a smile, which was probably not the best expression to be wearing and finishing with an attempt at humour riled Léigōng further.

"Hungry! Hungry! I'll give him fucking hungry!" Léigōng stared at the eleven kings before him, eyeballing them individually. "When we've beaten this bunch...this bunch of fucking farmers...then we're going to head east and knock some sense into fucking Fēngbō. Is it agreed? I said, is it agreed?"

There was a subdued affirmative; most managed little more than to nod their heads; no one had considered the possibility of a second campaign.

"Moving on. That leaves twelve of us. After the last few nights, well days and nights, we dare not mix our men. I want as wide a front as possible. The horses will scare them." Léigōng was down to specific tactics at last. Everyone was attentive. So, we have four units across and three deep. What's the smallest unit?"

"I believe mine," Wǔzhì chimed in. "I've only sixty on horseback."

"Right...so each unit will be thirty horses wide. That means, Wǔzhì, you've only got two ranks, but it'll have to do. Most will have three, my own, four. If we're going to charge them, I'm sorry, when we charge them, they'll have a shield wall."

"Where is this information coming from?" The King of Qīchéng looked sceptical.

"Jiāozuò, do you want to tell him? It was your agent."

"Thank you, Ānyáng." Jiāozuò's use of the city name riled Léigōng enormously, but there was little he could say when he was doing the same himself. "We sent a spy into their camp about ten days ago. The man we sent, Liú, is a good archer, and they put him in one of their crack

266

squads. It seems their archers will all be trying to come up behind us. They'll be on foot, with no cover. Now, he reckons that if we keep pushing forward, the archers will not get into range, and they'll waste their arrows. When we finish with the farmers, we can then come back for the archers, who'll only have their short axes left and—"

"So, we push forward and through their shield wall," Léigōng interrupted. "But there's more, is there not?"

"Oh yes, there is! Liú got lucky in more ways than one! He spent the last two nights fucking this Xià bint." There were laughs around the table and more than a few suggestive comments. "Well, it seems like she was one of the higher-ups in their place. She had this massive mark right across her front, from between her tits to her pussy and right across her stomach; the mark of the Sisterhood."

"He screwed a fucking witch! On my father's grave! The man'll never walk straight again. She'll have infested his balls!"

"Don't you mean 'infected'?"

"No, man. I. N. F. E. S. T. E. D! Infested! She'll have filled his balls with little witches. You shouldn't let them near you—"

"Enough! I agree it has entertainment value, but we have important issues at hand here. Jiāozuò, continue."

"Thank you, Ānyáng. You should see Liú; he can hardly walk right now! Apparently, she was the sort who liked to spend half the night humping and then half the night talking."

"If any bitch spent half the night talking with me, I'd have her tongue cut out!" Měngzhuàng spluttered.

"And then what? Then you'd only have half as much fun when she was sucking your d—" Qīchéng broke in laughing but was brought to an abrupt halt.

"Listen! It was then in bed that she let slip some secrets. They've only got about five hundred men with pikes and axes. Liú saw himself that their archers only numbered thirty or so. And they're not all men; more than half are women.

"Their big plan is to stop us at the shield wall, throw spears at us and have the archers attack us from behind. It seems they are using the same tactics they used against King Chīyóu of Táosì. Moreover, they're praying for fog or rain to help them. Even more exciting is that many of them plan on running away, including this whore he bedded.

"It gets better. You know their supposed platoon of crack troops?" Jiāozuò held up his fingers. "They have just three! Not three platoons. They have just three crack troops!"

"At this rate, Jiāozuò, I'm not going to have to fire these guys up at all. We're going to be fighting a bunch of women! Hah!" Léigōng smiled. "I still want to have a parley, to check out the battlefield; although it may not be necessary with the information we have, I have another reason.

"Fēngbō may have done a runner, but within my unit, I had two men trying to do the same. I've had them bound since last night. With your permission, gentlemen, I would like them to be amongst the eight who go to parlay. I want to make an example of them. Jiāozuò and Wǔzhì should come as well, as they're more acquainted with the local area. May I have three other volunteers?

"Thank you. I think Qīchéng, Púyáng and Xīnxiāng were first. Thank you, all. I'll now send a messenger requesting a parlay. Could the parlay team be horsed up soon? Could the fighting units be ready in formation by mid-morning? I hope you'll all be keen to let Fēngbō know what he missed!"

The messenger was back before the parlay party were readied. It was proving somewhat difficult to persuade Hú and Xí to mount up. Finally, they were lifted onto their steeds. Not only were they reluctant, but they were also unusually heavy. Léigōng was about to insist they remove their cloaks, but he gave the order to move forward, realising it would mean further delay.

As they departed, the units behind them were gathering for the march. It would take the army an hour to reach the intended battlefield. At this point, Léigōng realised he had not told his fellow kings where the infantry would be positioned and had to call out for a messenger.

"Tell them we'll use the infantry to block these bloody archers. They'll all go at the back—the same formation as the riders, four units across and three deep. If anyone's going to get an arrow in the back, it can be them. Tell you what. Have the final ranks walk backwards. Make sure that message gets to all the unit commanders."

268

When the parlay team approached the battlefield, the army was a line of dust behind them on the northern horizon. None of the eight chose to look in that direction; the view in front of them commanded their complete attention. Léigōng had to adjust. It may have been a shock, but he was here for a reason.

Behind the enemy's parlay team, a low rise extended to the east and west, although directly behind them was flatter land. A rock structure could be seen behind the eastern rise, although it looked haphazard and unimportant. What was important was that the ground underfoot was firm and ideal for the horses. From the dust thrown up by the Xià mounts, it appeared that conditions did not change further to the south. It was a little hard to see, but he could just make out a low shield wall on the flat land behind their parlay team. He was satisfied that everything was as it should be, and his attention snapped back to the eight Xià representatives.

All but one wore leather body armour like his own; the odd one out wore a long black cloak, which seemed a bit silly as the hot sun beat down on the arid plain. It appeared they all had two arms and two legs and were all unarmed, although that was where the similarities with his team of eight finished. As they drew their steeds up abreast, not ten paces from their enemy's matching line, Léigōng's eight men were faced by eight Xià females. Each woman lined up directly facing a member of the Lóngshān team, locking a hard stare in place. It was somewhat unnerving. It took a moment or two before the Ānyáng king could speak.

"Er...who is your leader?" The rider who had been eyeballing him nudged her horse a step forward.

"I am. I am Grandmother."

"Grand...grandmother...but you are young?" Léigōng stuttered. He was having enormous difficulty trying to hold together a discussion. To the best of his knowledge, the last two-way communication with a woman he had engaged in was with his own grandmother, which was only shortly before he killed her. However, the rules of parlay were strict and must be honoured. He had to swallow his pride even to continue to listen.

"True. If you like, you may call me Líng. Who are you?"

"I..." Léigōng was also completely unused to anyone asking who he was; they were expected to know. "I am...er–"

"Come on! Do you know who you are or not?" Líng realised there was an opportunity to demean the man with little danger to her or her parlay team.

"I am King Léigōng…King of Ānyáng. I am the leader of this army."

"Well, Léigōng, may we agree on the signal to commence battle?" Líng was riding her luck on this one. She had heard from Hòuyì that before the Lóngshān fight amongst themselves, there was always a signal, but she had no idea if it was true or not. It was times like this when she wished the previous Grandmother were by her side; she would have known.

"Yes. A signal. You will become the loser, so what would be your choice of signal for our attack?" Léigōng's back stiffened as his look of disdain returned.

"Perhaps three flashes from a plate?" She referred to the shiny bronze mirror used to send light signals.

"Three flashes are agreed."

"Tell me, Léigōng! You have met me before?"

"No…no, I do not believe so. Why would I remember a farmer? I mean, a farmer's wife who seems to have found some body armour and is far too brazen for her own good?"

"Oh, but you have indeed. I believe I was hiding in your cabinet. I believe that your henchmen killed me."

"She's a witch, my lord," Hú whispered.

"So…you are dead, yet you lead these…these farmers?" Léigōng was unsure of his ground. "We'll have to kill you again. But by the way. You don't look anything like the woman from the cabinet. She was older, although it has to be said, a great deal more attractive!" He sneered.

"He told you…she's a witch, my lord!" Xí was louder.

"So, maybe I'm a witch. What do you think?" Líng wheeled her horse through a circle so they could see her from all sides. "Don't witches make prophecies? I forget myself. I prophesize that you will watch our dragon devour your sun. I prophesize that you will walk on water. I prophesize you will meet the same end as my brothers and mother."

"You're no witch! Complete nonsense! Dragons, walking on water, even these two idiots don't come up with that sort of rubbish! You'll be telling me next that you dried up the Yellow River!" Léigōng

270

sneered again. "Where is the river, by the way? It seems strangely absent?"

"Perhaps you're right. Perhaps I did make the river go away. What do they say?" She pointed at Hú and Xí. "What comes around goes around? If I made it disappear, maybe I can make it reappear!"

"Hah! Gobbledygook! Bring on a proper witch!"

"I can show you a proper witch, alright. Tú! Tú, step forward, won't you."

Tú pressed her mount to move three steps in front of the line of women. She allowed her hood and cloak to slip to the ground as she did so. She had worried about this moment for weeks. Those little runs of fat that had not entirely firmed up after childbirth irritated the most. Instead of the stage fright she expected, she experienced a surge of raw power running through her.

"Argh!" It was unclear whether the noise had emitted from Hú or Xí; both were looking green and trying as hard as they might to look anywhere other than at the naked horsewoman.

"A *wénshēn*, that is all it is. Hú, Xí, it is a *wénshēn*." Léigōng exasperation was clear to all.

"It may be a *wénshēn*, sire, but it is her mother's scar, not hers. She is truly a witch!" Xí covered his eyes.

"A witch who…" Hú tried to speak but could not.

"A witch with a secret or two!" Tú finally spoke. "King Léigōng, what is this symbol?"

"Are you testing me? It is the symbol of the Sisterhood."

"No, it is not." Tú grinned; her confidence had flowed back, and she cared not whether her body was perfect. "You think it symbolises the Sisterhood because you are ignorant. This!" she traced both hands across the marks on her body. "This is the symbol of the Motherland! We fight for the Motherland today, not for the Sisterhood. Agreed, my sisters?"

"Agreed!" They shouted as one.

"And today…today you will fight the Motherland, you will fight the Xià, you will fight this symbol!" Tú paused. "But I think you should ask yourself if you are not already part of the Motherland. Perhaps some of you are." She moved her steed closer to the men and began to circle the group. The immense power her nakedness had given her was only growing as she stopped behind the mounts of Hú and Xí. "What would you think if I asked these two grovelling idiots to dismount, step forward and cast off their cloaks?

"Well? What's your answer?"

"I think we could arrange that." Léigōng had to twist as Tú reappeared at the other end of their line.

"Well…go on then! Do it!" Tú returned to her position in front of the men. However, now she was more than halfway between the two lines.

Léigōng signalled Hú and Xí to dismount, which they did slowly and with the utmost reluctance. Even when ordered, they would not step forward. Wǔzhì and Jiāozuò had to press their horses into the men's behinds, nudging them towards Tú before reversing their steeds to their places in line.

"And their cloaks?" Tú insisted, but the two men failed to respond. Their king's direct order was ignored. "I have two women here who can help them to disrobe. Yěmǎ, Mǎjié, I'm sure you've done this before. Would you help these two with their cloaks, please?"

The pair dropped from their mounts, crossing over to Hú and Xí. It took only seconds before the two men recognised them; both their jaws dropped. In the blink of an eye, they were on them and had each ripped a cloak away. Hú and Xí may have been wearing armour as requested, but it did not cover their backs, just like the rest of the army.

Tú also dismounted, positioning herself slightly in front of Hú and Xí. As Mǎjié and Yěmǎ forced the two men to their knees, she stood flaunting her nakedness, the symbol on her torso matching those now exposed on their backs. Directly in front of him, Léigōng's view consisted of three of those most hated signs of the Sisterhood, the Motherland, or whatever they might call it.

"I think, Mister Léigōng, that you have two of our members in your midst." Tú laughed. "May we have them back, please?"

Léigōng's countenance changed completely. He had turned the colour of beetroot and was unable to speak. He turned his horse and began to trot away.

"Wait!" Jiāozuò requested Líng and moved after Léigōng. He was back almost instantly. "He says that…er… 'you can keep those two fuckers, and he's going to kill every fucking one of you before the fucking

272

sun goes down.' My apologies for using such language in a parlay, but that's what he said."

"Good!" As Líng smiled, so did all the other women. "Don't forget…please take their horses. We'll drag these two back to our lines. We'll take their cloaks. We must keep them warm, mustn't we? Ladies, what do we say?"

"The best of luck, boys!" A chorus of wishes followed the five men as they followed Léigōng. Hú and Xí remained kneeling, unsure what life's next turn might serve them.

Thirty-nine: The Battle for the Yellow River

Xíngyáng, Hénán
Year 90: Year of the Rat
Forty-one days to the summer solstice
12th May 1905 BCE

Hú and Xí were hauled back to the shield wall. They had stumbled behind the horses of Yěmǎ and Mǎjié, sometimes falling and being dragged before they were able to regain their feet. The pair now looked as if they had died and returned from hell.

The two women had no pity. Eliciting help from a couple who were driving in spear butts, they soon had the two men on their backs, pegged out, and spreadeagled on the ground. Not only were they out in the fearsome sun, but they were also only a few paces away from the northern side of the shield wall. If heat stroke did not get them first, the hooves of the Lóngshān cavalry should ensure their lives would end that day. Mǎjié and Yěmǎ were about to congratulate themselves on a job well done when Yěmǎ realised something was missing.

"Oh!" She whined, "No one can see they love the Motherland! They're lying on the symbols."

"Well, Yěmǎ, that's easy enough to sort out!" Mǎjié pulled her knife from her belt once more. "Let's just give them a matching one on their fronts!" She knelt and gestured to her friend to do the same. "Here we go…not too deep…"

Hú screamed, followed shortly by Xí, as Yěmǎ followed her friend's example and her blade cut into the second man's torso.

"Does it hurt, Prince Hú?" Mǎjié laughed.

"Prince Xí! What a fine picture we have carved!" Yěmǎ stood back to view her completed work. When Mǎjié joined her, they hugged tightly, waved to the two men and left without looking back.

The pair were now re-purposed and would join the archers stationed with Hòuyì; their position would give them a delicious vantage point to observe the final moments of their erstwhile masters.

To the north, Léigōng had spread the news to all in his army; for once, he even remembered the auxiliaries. It was clear the great river had dried up; he had heard of such a thing happening years before, and it could only assist his horse. They were fighting a bunch of women who believed they had a pet dragon to help them. They were fighting farmers who thought everyone was going to get wet. The farmers' wives were going to kill everyone with ploughshares. The news went around like wildfire, just in time to raise the men's morale, which had been sinking lower and lower as their rations had reduced. Their supreme leader's visage brightened when he realised the men around him were all smiles.

Tucked beside her cart, Líng was even more than content with the way the parlay went. To her, the most significant success had been to get Léigōng to agree to a starting signal. It felt a little stupid; this was war, whereas a starting signal seemed like something from a boys' game. Perhaps that was what they were playing. If Léigōng were as good as his word, of which she had some doubts, it did mean she could wait for the optimum moment before allowing the Lóngshān to charge. If the Ānyáng king provided one unwanted variable, so did her knowledge of the heavens. Léigōng had agreed on a signal; likewise, her older sisters had passed down the information about the sun. What if Léigōng reneged? What if her sisters had made an error? What if she, Líng or Grandmother, whatever, was simply not good enough?

Her doubts were exacerbated when she saw the massed phalanx kicking up an enormous dust plume. How many? She was told fewer than a thousand on horse and a thousand or more on foot. Was the information correct? What if she had got it wrong? What she saw looked like a vast number of men headed directly for her and the Xià defences.

Líng's most significant quality was her ability to instil confidence in a few. She had no idea how this might be done for the Xià army or the Xià people as a whole; that was a business left to others. Yú, Bóyì, Túshānshì, even Jīngfēi, they could rouse a whole city if they needed. Her job had been to ensure the motivators were fired up. They were.

Líng had detailed twelve soldiers to be dotted around the battlefield; their sole focus was on the sun. They were under strict instructions not to use the flimsy jade disks to look directly at the solar disc; if they did, there might well be several blind warriors walking home to Èrlǐtou. Each was issued with an extended jade *cóng* with a fine central hole. By positioning the film of jade on the top of the *cóng,* they could align it with the sun and cast an image on the ground. She had shown them how to clear a smooth, flat area, so the image itself would be sharp and had demonstrated throwing a perfect image of the sun on the ground. As soon as one of them believed they saw any reduction in the glowing disk, they would seek confirmation from those closest. If they agreed, they would flash a plate signal to her base. Of course, Líng had her own *cóng* and film; she would not rely entirely on others.

When three signals came in, one after the other, she checked the image cast by her equipment. She asked Tú to look but was unconvinced. Desperate, she turned to the sun, viewing it directly through the fine jade film. It was confirmed, but the decision left her with blurred vision for many months.

"Tú, it's happening. It's really happening. Don't look at the sun. It's happening!" Líng was almost screaming with joy, but tears poured down her face.

"Are you alright? Líng. Líng! Are you alright?"

"I'm alive. Isn't that enough? Start the rolling drums! Come on! Get them going. Drums rolling! Now! Now we count!"

The two women counted slowly to a thousand. It was a complete guess as to whether it would suffice. All that mattered was that by the time the Lóngshān charged, they would know the eclipse had commenced, but the Lóngshān would not. When they completed the count, Líng indicated that Tú should have Bóyì send the three flashes to Léigōng. When three flashes were returned, the battle should commence.

Léigōng had been waiting impatiently, "That's it! We're off! Come on, lads. Let's go!" He was more fired up than ever, consumed by blood lust. "Get those units moving! Now! Let's kill some witches!"

It was not a perfect start, but the stragglers caught up as there were over a thousand paces of ground to cover. By the time they were at full gallop, all the units were together as a formation. Surprisingly, it had become a terrifyingly coordinated cavalry charge. Seemingly, nothing could stand in its way.

The cavalry could not hear the drums and certainly did not notice the change to a single repeated beat. If they had, it would have been meaningless. When their charge had covered half the ground towards the shield wall, the drums began to sound a loud double beat. The riders were still oblivious.

Back at the dam, the double beat gave the signal for Gǔn to get to work. His role was so essential that the message was also flashed to him, although the drumbeat would have sufficed. Twenty strongmen began to swing heavy stone mallets at the ends of key tree trunks. At first, it was sweaty and unrewarding, but it became both sweaty and dangerous within moments. The engineering was such that the break-up was rapid when the dam began its collapse. Gǔn and his labourers had to sprint from the two breach points, pulling each other upwards to reach the safety of the levees. Lying there, trying to catch his breath, Gǔn's first thought was for the purpose-built spillway; it was a beautiful construction that had never been used; it now faced destruction.

The same double beat was the trigger for Bóyì's shield team to roll the triangular shields and sprint for the safety of the higher ground. A couple of his team struggled to align their spears; Bóyì had to halt his progress to persuade them to leave it. The hardest thing to do was also the most mundane, waving at the sun and looking horrified. The display aimed not at the cavalry but the foot soldiers marching behind them. As the horseback riders continued to charge, the foot soldiers behind began to waver.

Both Hú and Xí could feel the growing thunder of the speeding steeds. They were too petrified to scream. Then, suddenly, the thunder was all around them. Hú took a hoof directly on his thigh and felt the bone crack. Xí's arm was crushed. Wave after wave of horses passed over them without making further contact. Around them, they could hear the screams of animals and the curses of riders falling as the charge met the spears, but it seemed most had cleared the barrier as the cacophony began to diminish.

Hú lay groaning, oblivious to anything. Xí listened carefully, for two sounds were terrifying him. One he could place, the noise of horses returning, which frightened him beyond belief, but the other seemed out of place, almost unearthly. He tried to identify it and failed. As the returning charge met the barriers again, they became entangled with those who had fallen on the first pass. Around them was mayhem. When Hú groaned again, Xí had the strangest sensation; it seemed his back was wet. Throwing his head from side to side, it seemed a flow of yellow mud was passing through. Hú stilled his thrashing enough to speak again.

"I was wondering where the river was." As the flow deepened, they proved to be his last words. Unable to lever themselves from the ground, both men struggled to breathe and began to drown slowly in the slick mud.

Kùàimǎ, Mǎjié and Yěmǎ had not failed in their task as archers. They had waited patiently behind the rocks in the diversionary barrier and had held fire until half of the Lóngshān cavalry had passed them. On Hòuyì's signal, they aimed at the backs of the passing cavalrymen. All three scored hits, as did many of their fellow archers. As the cavalry passed the shield barrier, the whole unit lowered their bows; their range was compromised. There was to be a brief respite, which allowed the girls to pick out the targets of their own personal enmity. The three laughed at the two men's evident discomfort, more than happy to finish them off later if necessary.

Kùàimǎ glanced northwards and had to bring her friends' attention to the unfolding scene. The foot soldiers had halted; in fact, they had stopped dead. Hands raised, shielding their eyes and pointing southwards, up high in the sky. Although the horizon towards which they marched was obscured by dust, the sun hung above it, basking them in intense heat.

If it had been possible to paint a picture of fear, this is the picture that would have been painted. The whole scenario lasted no longer than it would have taken to count to ten, and then, as a body, the entire foot troop ran. It was not an orderly sprint. It was a terrified, random, dog-eat-dog fight to get out of something so unknown that it was impossible to understand where to escape. A few quickly buried themselves under rocks and bushes, perhaps realising there was nowhere to run. Most simply ran away, directly away from a sun slowly being eaten alive. Quite simply, they believed it to be the end of the world.

Líng's orders had been explicit. All the cavalrymen should die, no matter what the circumstance. She had been equally clear that the infantrymen should be allowed to live unless they engaged in combat; they were not here through choice. The Xià archers fired not a single arrow at the departing foot soldiers.

From Bóyì's vantage point, although he could see both sides of the shield wall, the infantry was out of sight; he had no idea they were fleeing. On the northern side of the barrier, probably a fifth of their cavalry was unhorsed and struggling with injured animals. However, it was the southern side of the wall that drew his attention. The ground appeared to be moving, and those horsemen still mounted were turning.

Bóyì had never believed the trick with the dam would work. What he was observing now appeared to confirm his instinct. Not until he turned fully and stared at the structure itself did he realise his scepticism was misplaced. Two huge cracks had appeared in the dam wall, through which twin geysers spouted. It seemed they were the cause of the apparent movement of the earth. A flow, not a handspan's depth, had filled the once empty channel, but it was deepening, the flow increasing rapidly. The cracks widened as he looked back upstream, and the geysers began to rip the whole dam to pieces. Massive tree trunks tossed in the waters like twigs. The once horizontal line made by the top of the structure slumped into an alarming dipping curve. It seemed every drop of the great river was heading towards him. To Bóyì, it appeared as if a mouth had opened and vomit gushed forth.

Bóyì moved his troop further up the bank, clear of the rising waters. By the time the greater flow came level with them, it was little more than waist-deep. They were well out of harm's way. Not so the Lóngshān cavalrymen.

Half of them had managed to jump their mounts back over the shield wall, but many became further entangled with their fellows who had fallen earlier. They were coming under increasing attack from the archers, biding their time and picking off the most exposed. The others were grouping to try to scale the levee directly under the nose of Bóyì's spear throwers. Again, it was a matter of waiting, allowing them to come closer and closer, and then picking a target. Killing ants was more difficult.

When Léigōng had jumped the shield wall, he knew men were falling around him. Finally, he understood that it was not a group of peasants who had put together the Xià tactics. Both their archers' positions and their wall's construct appeared well-considered. However, most of his force was over, and he could fully engage in hunting down those who had run from their positions, leaving the shields. It was difficult, for they had turned up slopes that the horses were finding impossible. There was no reason to panic. The foot soldiers should appear soon, and they could deal with the mopping-up exercise.

Léigōng pulled his mount to attention to look around. It was an unwise choice. As soon as he did, an arrow embedded itself in the back of his right shoulder. The impact caused his steed to pull around, leaving him staring directly at something he could not fully comprehend. It appeared that two dragons had opened their mouths through a wall, and thick yellow blood was gushing forth. He recalled the prophecies about dry conditions and glanced at the sun. Was that a cloud passing? It suddenly seemed awfully dark.

Momentarily, he shrugged off the atmospheric conditions. Breaking the arrow's shaft was excruciatingly painful; the tip would have to remain in the wound. Even so, he made a quick assessment of his cavalry. They seemed fewer than before, and those remaining were struggling in mud that became deeper by the second. As he turned his horse, he found he had the same problem.

It was only a little time before the pieces fell into place. The water around his steed was coming from that wall to the west. Just a little liquid was turning the once-firm earth into a bog. He glanced back at the sun and decided that was the least of his worries. Léigōng called the retreat.

It was what Yú and his archers had been awaiting. Much of the cavalry had been out of range on the first pass. His archers had picked off a few, but not as many as Hòuyì's team on the rock wall. Now Léigōng's return route was much closer, as the Lóngshān cavalry tried to avoid the deeper waters sweeping against the rocks. The horses were down to little more than a walking pace as shot after shot buried itself in the backs of the horsemen. One after another, they tumbled into the deepening water.

As Yú took a break, Líng and Tú joined him on the levee wall. The eclipse was attaining its greatest magnitude, and to all intents and

280

purposes, it seemed as if dusk had arrived early. Those of the Lóngshān unfortunate enough to look directly at the solar phenomena were left with the impression that a big bite had been taken from the sun's disk, which was followed by partial blindness. They became sitting ducks, an image that became more apt as the river ponded beneath their feet.

"This is like target practice! It's too easy!"

"Yú, it might be easy now, but a lot of hard work went into it. Their problem," Líng pointed at the enemy, "is that they did not put the hard work into the planning. One day, Yú, we should write down how to plan a battle. We could call it 'Rules for War' or 'The Art of Winning' or something like that."

"You know I don't write well, Líng. Don't be mean."

"I don't think she's being mean, Yú," Tú smiled, "I think she's being complimentary."

"Now. What's going on here?" Líng pointed at dismounted men being helped up the bank by Xià archers. "It's far better not to do that. Much better to kill them immediately, not to help them and have to kill them later. I'll end up doing this myself if I must! Yú, sort them out! Every single one of them dead, please. Ah, but who is that? Is that Léigōng?" Líng dropped her *cóng* and headed down the bank, grabbing a dagger from a surprised archer as she passed.

The man kneeling in the mud was held firmly by two of Yú's troops. Líng positioned herself directly in front of him.

"Surprised, Léigōng?" Líng sneered.

"I did wonder where the river was. How did you do it, witch?"

"Look at the sun." Less than half its disk was now visible. "Do you know when that last happened?" He shook his head. "I do. It was fifty-four years ago. Have you heard of planning? No? Well, we beat you because of planning. Do you know when that planning started? No? That would be before your mother's mother's mother was born. Now! Look at the sun.

"Tú! Tú! Come here!" Tú followed Líng's example as she slid down the slope, appearing with a dagger raised. "Tú, stop! I don't want you to kill him! Cut his armour off. Cut his clothes off. Now!"

It took two more men to hold Léigōng still as Tú's dagger sliced through the back bindings of his armour and the battle shorts he wore. The king now kneeled naked, surrounded by the debris of his clothing.

"You said you did not know me. You lied. We had met before, but I escaped. However, it was not before you made me watch what you did to my mother and brothers. And so, King Léigōng. I have a score to settle on behalf of my father and me. Do you remember Kànménrén? Do you? Do you remember what you did to his wife, my mother? Perhaps not. Let me show you."

A small group had gathered around the king and his captors. Not one had ever seen Líng raise her voice, let alone raise a dagger.

"Well…this! This is how you started on my mother." Líng took his left nipple between finger and thumb before slicing it clean off. Léigōng screamed and struggled against his captors as she repeated the process on the right.

"Pull him backwards…tip him backwards!" Líng ordered. "And this! This, King Léigōng, this is how you started on my brothers!" Grasping his genitals in one fist, she brought the knife down again, but it took a sawing motion to achieve separation. Once again, Léigōng screamed, although its register altered and ended as a gurgle.

"Now…we don't want you blacking out now, do we? Ah! What did you do in these circumstances?" Líng turned to the gathering crowd. "Water! Water in his face! Now!"

Líng circled around the fallen king as bowls of water were splashed over him. Settling herself behind him, her knife arm thrown over his shoulder, she dragged the point of the dagger from gaping wound to gaping wound until she reached his groin, where she thrust it hard, several times, in the direction of his bladder.

"Tú? What is the last thing you think this bastard should see? Perhaps our dragon's teeth around the sun? Perhaps…Tú? What do you think?" Tú shook her head before realisation.

"The symbol!"

"Yes, the symbol. Now, please!"

It took a few moments for Tú to remove her body armour. She then stood naked and posed in front of the vanquished king. Líng remained behind him although she had risen from her crouch.

282

"Hold his head still! Make him look! Make him look at the Motherland! This is for my mother and my brothers but is from my father. I also act on behalf of Grandmother. You should thank your gods that I do not believe in long-winded torture! Look at it!"

As Léigōng's head was raised again, Líng took the weapon in two hands and drove it vertically through the top of his head. She did so with such force its hilt met with the king's skull. It was the first and last time she used a knife in anger.

Leaving the bronze dagger firmly embedded, she placed a foot on the back of the dead man, shoving him face down in the mud.

"That...well...that was for Grandmother!"

Forty: The Final Summit
Xíngyáng, Hénán
Year 90: Year of the Rat
Forty-one days to the summer solstice
12th May 1905 BCE

There was still mopping up going on. The eclipse's maximum had come and gone. As the earth lightened once more, a grisly scene presented itself. Most other killings were not performed with the flourish that Líng had demonstrated so willingly on Léigōng. For the most part, it was a matter of waiting for unhorsed cavalrymen to drag themselves out of the mudflow and then, with little fight left in them, slitting their throats. Few enjoyed the process, although three went about their work more enthusiastically than Líng had demonstrated.

However, when the killings diminished around the levee breach, Mǎjié, Yěmǎ, and Kùaimǎ took to their horses and went in search of the Lóngshān who had been swept further onto the plain. The Fire Horse Three was a name now widely known and one they enjoyed; the Xià would now see how ruthless they could be.

"Remember, only the cavalrymen! If you find any of the farmers, just send them packing!" Líng shouted after them, although their blood lust was such her words would likely go unheeded. "And take a cart with you! Remember armour and weapons! Strip them!"

The three were not only engaged in collecting valuable trophies, but each also carried a hessian bag. For each man they stripped, they collected a more personal trophy. They planned a tally later in the day and were not overly concerned whether their victim's penis was removed before or after his neck was slit.

The maimed bodies of Hú and Xí had been the first they had sought, and they were more than upset to find they had already died. Unable to take further retribution on the men who had mistreated them for

284

years, it was now their intent to humiliate their corpses by amputating their manhood. A game had been devised over their former masters' blooded groins; Mǎjié, Yěmǎ and Kùàimǎ would take scalps but not from the heads of the dead and dying men. They had a plan for the loser, the one of them scoring the fewest amputations. The one with the least severed appendages would have to fry and eat one around the campfire later. The competition became fierce.

The instructions were to leave all Lóngshān bodies where they lay, for the river would wash them away. That may have been the intention, but the muddy flow would not move them far for the time being. The vultures arrived when the men were stripped, feasting on their unseeing eyes and any open wounds. Each man attended to by the Fire Horse Three could easily be identified from a distance, as a large raptor would have its hooked bill buried in the groin of the corpse. The girls' reputation grew as more blood and gore adhered to their clothes and coloured any bare skin. By the time they returned from the slaughter, their appearance was monstrous.

Líng's hair was matted with the blood of Léigōng. She had returned to the corpse for her dagger, and it had initially proved a struggle to remove it. Levering the blade back and forth had meant more blood, brains, and pieces of skull cracking. For the first time in her life, she had been physically involved in an action she had masterminded. The smell of death pervaded her clothing, and she could taste the blood and brains smeared around her lips. However, there was little time to savour the moment.

"Yú!" She called over, indicating she wanted a private talk, and then she turned to his ex-lover. "Tú! Send off the pigeon to Nüxi. You know the message. Just the one, mind, we'll be taking the others with us."

Líng scrambled back up the levee slope and sat cross-legged, just out of sight of the melee below. While she waited, she could still watch the antics of the three girls and the vultures that followed their every move in the distance. It was carnage. When Yú joined her, she finally smiled.

"I was serious about writing all this down. It seems there are two aspects to all this, er, war stuff. The planning and the motivation. One day, Yú, one day."

"You seem to forget I have a job to do." Yú returned her smile and momentarily caught her hand in his own. She did not release the grip; he did.

"You forget, you're unemployed! As soon as the war council has been disbanded, which to my mind will be as soon as you get this lot back to Èrlǐtou, you have no job!"

"What do you mean? When 'you' get back to Èrlǐtou? What about you?"

"I'll be leaving, Yú. Tomorrow morning or possibly later today. It depends on that." Líng pointed at the mudflow oozing through the gap in the levee wall. "We had a rider come in while you were still fighting. Nüxi has news from Sānménxiá; apparently, the waters are rising dramatically. It seems we finished this little job just in time."

"Planning and motivation, you say! What about luck?"

"Yú, Yú, Yú! Luck? Hòutú came through for us. If the waters had come earlier, well, we would have adapted. If they had come later, we would still have won. The dam did its job. Your father did his job. Hòutú and my father primed these floodwaters. They were going to come sooner or later. You can see now that the diversionary channel held the first onslaught; from now on, any further flow will follow it. Day after day, it will become greater and greater. If we had to face the extreme viciousness of the Yellow River in full force right at the start, we could never have diverted it. But we knew all this. Look." Líng pointed at waters heading slowly northwards, almost a sedate trickle. "You can see where the waters will swing eastwards. What you cannot see is where they will curl back. You cannot see where they will return to a northbound route.

"And that is why I must go, for that is the direction I am headed."

"North?"

"Yes…to Ānyáng."

"Ānyáng?"

"There is unfinished business there for Mǎjié, Yěmǎ and Kùaimǎ; they will join me. I need time and space. I need to think. It will also assist me in being someplace where the vestiges of the Lóngshān culture cling as I try to map the future."

"You'll be soothsaying?"

286

"Yú! I know you do not believe that rubbish! I'll be trying to work out how the new dynamics will change the Motherland. I'll be trying to identify the difference between stumbling blocks and barriers. I'll be trying to create devices to break down the barriers or even build tracks around them. The stumbling blocks will be left to the Xià to deal with, and that…that means you!"

"So, we both have jobs th–" Yú was interrupted.

"Sorry, I forgot something. We found many small pieces of gold in the cloaks of Hú and Xí. I plan to take them with us. Èrlǐtou doesn't need gold."

"That's true, but…but we need you in Èrlǐtou."

"Yú, I believe you misunderstand the role of the Sisterhood. When things get out of hand, as they had with the Lóngshān, the Sisterhood will work out how to collapse that system." Líng waved her arms over the plains stretching north and east. "That is what we have done. We have made a correction."

"You call this a 'correction'?"

"Yes. It is not the role of the Sisterhood to run things. If we did, then we would be involved in everything. Remember Jīngfēi's speech in Táosì. Remember, she complained the Sisterhood had not protected the women. She was right; we had not. We were focused on the bigger picture, and the bigger picture includes men and women. We needed to make a massive correction so that you and I do mean you, can run things as they should be run."

"So…you're planning the next correction? When do you think that might be?"

"This last one took several hundred years…the next…it may be the same."

"But you're planning it now?"

"Yes, we will start. And for the next few centuries, it's down to Yú!"

Yú's brow wrinkled.

"That's not really the case. My mother is in Èrlǐtou, and my wife is in Èrlǐtou; they are both Sisterhood."

"No, Yú, they are not. They are no longer. It is my decision, and they have been retired."

287

"What about Tú?"

"Ah!" Líng's gaze had been scanning the horizon since he had pulled his hand away; now, she looked directly into his eyes.

"Tú will be coming with me...and your son. The chance is you will never see them again. That, Yú, is the bad news."

"But..."

"No. If you are going to show you can lead the Xià, you need to be without the Sisterhood, and that includes Tú. She would be extremely dangerous in Èrlǐtou. If I could take Túshānshì as well, I would, but I cannot. This is how it will be."

"You said that you did not want to run things."

"I did."

"Isn't this running things?"

"It's the last act. After this, it will be down to you. I am removing as many obstacles to your success as I can. That is all."

"Do they all know?"

"The women coming with me know. Your mother and your wife are probably working it out right now. Yú, I want you to be careful. Nüxi will go quietly with your father. You can have them work on the irrigation and flood control far west of Èrlǐtou. They'll love it." She paused for a moment, deep in thought, "I'm taking some of Nüxi's pigeons...you'll have to apologise to her for me. Now. Túshānshì is a different matter and one you are going to have to learn to cope with."

"But...but she's always been behind me."

"No, Yú. For a time. For a time, she was for the Sisterhood, but now. Now, I think she has different ambitions. Be careful; she can still wrap you around her little finger." She placed a hand on his bare shoulder.

"I think the business end of this little meeting is ending." As Líng spoke, tears welled in her eyes, little rivulets clearing blood from her face. "Are we agreed?"

"Well, you've left me a lot to—"

"We are agreed. Now, this is personal." Líng shuffled over slightly and moved her arm around his neck. She kissed Yú's cheek.

"Yú...this has been so hard for me. I have had to stand aside and watch you with Túshānshì. Then, I had to encourage your relationship with Tú. I had to persuade both women to have your babies. I have

288

observed your skills and your shortcomings. I have done all this for the greater good." Tears were now streaming down her face. "All this time, Yú…all this time, I have felt deeply about you. I have not touched. I have not spoken of it. This might seem strange to you, but I'm deeply affected by you."

"Er…" Yú's face softened, but he had no words of reply.

"It's true. I can't even do anything now. I must go away. However, I want you to make me a promise."

"Of course, if–"

"This will be from the heart, Yú."

"Of course, I–"

"Promise me, Yú…promise me that if things go wrong…for you…that you'll find me. I'll be waiting for you. I'm keeping myself for you. I don't want any other man. I will wait for you."

"If you–"

"Be quiet. Listen. There will be a storm, not rains and floods, but a storm, nevertheless. Things will go wrong. When they do, when you can cope no longer, you are to come to me. I will be your shelter. There is a place. It is a hidden valley in a hidden valley. It is a secret. It is a secret I share with my father. It is not far. It is in Shǎnxī, on the Qin River, a day's walk northwest of Duànshìzhèn. You will have never heard of these places; they are well hidden. It is where I will go when I step down. I will be there in ten years. From that point on, I will be there; I'll be there as your shelter from the storm. Come for me then."

Yú had extended his hand once more, and Líng took it firmly in both sets of bloodied fingers. He allowed his eyes to drift over the woman he had worked with for so long. She was a mess, her face and hair were a mess, she smelled, and she was covered in gore. Something inside of him leapt, something that ever afterwards never seemed to return to its original place. Their eyes met once more.

"I promise."

The moment lasted only seconds before she stood and pulled herself clear.

"Good! Qin River. Duànshìzhèn. Hidden valley. Ten years on. Don't forget. I'll see you there, Yú." Líng turned away, throwing the remaining words over her shoulder.

"I will protect you! Farewell!"
Then she was gone.

Chinese Whispers Book II

Mothers

(1905 - 1886 BCE)

Chinese Whispers - Mothers follows the fortunes of many of the characters from the first book.

Yú, Túshānshì, and their son Qí struggle to come to terms with managing the Xià empire from Èrlǐtou. What will be the price of failure?

Bóyì and Jīngfēi, as they learn about politics and the fickleness of democracy in the Xià capital. Will imprisonment and torture finally pull them apart?

Hòutú and Kànménrén, as they discover a new passion and purpose in life, sharing it with youngsters hidden in a wilderness area of Shǎnxī. Will they create a future dynasty of scholars?

Líng, Tú and the fire horse three holed up in Ānyáng as they come to understand the difficulty of life and love in a defeated culture. Are they able to escape their misdeeds? In what direction will Líng's planning take the Sisterhood in the next generation and the forthcoming centuries?

291

Archaeological Evidence, History & Myth

Although my story is entirely fictional, the settings, events and some characters are based on hard evidence, some academic hypotheses and Chinese mythology. It is quite a mix. Below, I have outlined some of the background information.

Pigeon Post

Some argue that Neanderthals first domesticated the pigeon. Indeed, it was one of the first birds to have fallen under the spell of humankind, well before the chicken. Ancient Mesopotamian and Egyptian records show it had already been domesticated before 3,000 BCE and was used as a messenger. I have written that they were used in China a thousand years later. However, the earliest hard evidence of the Chinese using pigeons to carry messages comes from the Suí Dynasty (581-618 CE).

Writing

There is proof of writing from the Shāng Dynasty, but this comes later than the events depicted in the book. However, there is a widespread belief amongst archaeologists and historians that a more primitive written form must have preceded the complex Shang oracle bone writings. Evidence presented by Paola Demattè in "The Origins of Chinese Writing: the Neolithic Evidence" shows that the earliest forms may have been discovered in Táosì. I speculate that writing had been around for much longer but that the medium on which it was written, such as sand or cloth, is subject to such degradation that it is unlikely we will ever know the truth. One of archaeology's biggest problems concerns what has not been found rather than what has been found.

Solar Eclipse

There was a solar eclipse in China on 12th May 1905 BCE, confirmed by NASA and Moonblink. Initially, I wrote about it as a total eclipse, but due to the location of the Battle of the Yellow River, it was likely only partial, and I amended the story. As to the more precise timing of the eclipse, there is a margin for error. In the story, it occurs around lunchtime!

The Destruction of Taosi

There is no doubt that Táosì suffered vertiginous decline and deliberate destruction. He Nu writes about this in his paper, "Táosì: An archaeological example of urbanization as a political center in prehistoric China". There is also evidence that it was restored at one point, although it did not seem to last long. I speculated that the collapse in the lithic economy may have been the cause, although this was probably only contributory. There was widespread and deliberate destruction, which could have been caused by an enemy or its populace; whatever, it made the settlement uninhabitable.

When I visited Táosì, there was little to see. Today, there is a reconstruction of the observatory, and some old walls and gullies are in evidence, along with some loess caves.

The Destruction of Shímǎo

I have been selective in my use of the facts regarding Shímǎo. It was a significant centre, one of the biggest in China at the time. Read Zhouyong Sun's account, "Shímǎo: A Stone-Walled Settlement of the 2nd Millennium BC in Northern China". The town was likely abandoned around 1800 BCE due to the drying climate, but it was probably not sacked, as I have suggested. However, many sacrificial skulls were found in the ruins, mainly those of young girls. It is not stretching the imagination too much to suggest that some of their parents may have objected and rebelled.

293

The Changing Course of the Lower Reaches of the Yellow River

The Yellow River (Huáng hé) has changed course many times. Evidence for this may be found in the work of Professor Vivian Forbes, "Yellow River Changing Course". Whether there were any significant changes in the period covered by the book is much harder to prove because of the lack of records. We do not know. Many of the changes from 602 BCE were caused wholly or partly by human activity. My dating a course change to 1905 BCE was solely to link it to the solar eclipse of the same year. It is something that could have happened.

The Neolithic Bronze Age Horizon

The commencement of the bronze age was of extreme importance. A spin-off effect led to civilisation, writing, government, etc. Generally, the transition is considered akin to the start of the Communications Age (the times we live in today), whereas the reality was very different. Today, there are twice as many mobile phones globally as people; cell phones only became commercially available in 1983. As the Neolithic ended, this was not the case with bronze and copper objects; people continued to use stone as a tool for thousands of years, and in some parts of the world, they still do.

I have postulated that bronze was initially used for agricultural purposes but was withdrawn by warlords seeking to arm their troops. For thousands of years, peasants did not generally have access to metals for farming.

Named Characters in the Story

My good friend, Ian, the first reader of this book, suggested that a list of names and roles might be helpful. Here it is, compiled in alphabetical order. I have also included the character's gender, as I am aware that many Chinese names do not readily identify gender. The character's role is the one they had when they first appear in the story; I have not added later changes as this might ruin the tale!

In addition, many of the characters' names have some significance in terms of Chinese myths and legends or a particular meaning in Chinese languages. Where there is a relevant connection, I have identified the source of the name.

Bóyì (m)	A boy drafted into King Chīyóu's army.	In mythology, Bó Yì was an important minister in Yú the Great's government and the planned successor.
Cháng (f)	An Èrlǐtou council member.	A common Chinese name, it can also mean constantly.
Chīyóu (m)	Lóngshān King of Táosì.	An ancient Chinese deity with horns on his head, known as the god of war.
Girl (Líng) (f)	Kànménrén's daughter – number three in the Sisterhood.	A common Chinese name, but it can also mean clever.
Grandmother (Mǎ or Āyí Feng) (f)	Leader of the Sisterhood.	Mǎ can mean horse. She was born in the year of the horse under the fire sign, hence the Fire Horse Three. Women born in such a year are maritally cursed in Japanese culture.

295

Gǔn (m)	Father of Yú and leader of the Èrlǐtou settlement.	In mythology, Gǔn was Yú, the Great's father, and he failed to prevent flooding.
Hán (m)	The leader of a bandit gang.	A common Chinese name, it can also mean poor.
Háng (m)	A barman.	A common Chinese name, it can also mean a professional.
Hòutú (f)	Long-term captive of King Chīyóu, mother of Tú.	An ancient Chinese deity, an Earth Goddess.
Hòuyì (m)	The master archer in King Chīyóu's army.	An ancient Chinese deity who became human. He was renowned as the best archer.
Hú (m)	Soothsayer to King Chīyóu.	In mythology, Hú and Xí: the drunken astrologers who fail to forecast a solar eclipse and are beheaded by the emperor.
Hu Zu (m)	One of Hòutú's old pigeons.	
Huìān	A Taosi council member.	A Chinese name, but it can also mean drab.
Jīngfēi (f)	A militant citizen of Táosì.	A Chinese name, but it can also mean to go off like a rocket.
Jīnxīng (f)	A stray bitch adopted as Tú's pet.	Named after the planet Venus.
Kùàimǎ (f)	An undercover Sisterhood agent, one of the Fire Horse Three.	This name means clever horse.
Léigōng (m)	Lóngshān King of Ānyáng.	The name of the Chinese god of thunder.
Líng (Girl) (f)	Kànménrén's daughter, number three in the Sisterhood.	A common Chinese name, but it can also mean clever.

Liú (m)	A Lóngshān spy.	A common Chinese name, but it can also mean to disseminate.
Lord Fēngbō (m)	Lóngshān King of Dōngyíng.	An ancient Chinese deity known as the Wind Master.
Mài (f)	A Taosi council member.	A Chinese name, but it can also mean to take a step.
Mǎjié (f)	An undercover Sisterhood agent, one of the Fire Horse Three.	This name means horse hero.
Mother (Nüxi) (f)	Gǔn's wife and Yú's mother – number two in the Sisterhood.	In mythology, Nüxi was Yú, the Great's mother.
Niúláng (m)	Father of Tú.	In mythology, Niúláng looked after cattle and fell in love with the fairy, Zhi Nü. It is a famous love story. I changed this, so he partnered with Hòutú, Zhi Nü's daughter.
Nüxi (Mother) (f)	Gǔn's wife and Yú's mother, number two in the Sisterhood	In mythology, Nüxi was Yú, the Great's mother.
Qí (m)	Túshānshì and Yú's son.	In mythology, Qí was Yú the Great's son, although not his chosen successor.
Tú (f)	Daughter of Hòutú and Niúláng, also a long-term captive of King Chīyóu.	A common Chinese name, it can also mean to be a believer.
Túshānshì (f)	Yu's wife.	In mythology, Túshānshì was Yú, the Great's wife.
Xí (m)	Soothsayer to King Chīyóu.	In mythology, Hú and Xí are drunken astrologers who fail to forecast a solar eclipse and are beheaded by the emperor.

Yěmǎ (f)	An undercover Sisterhood agent, one of the Fire Horse Three.	This name means feral horse.
Yú (m) –	Leader of the Xià tribe, husband of Túshānshì.	In mythology, Yú was the first Xià emperor.
Yú Shi (m)	Lóngshān King of Chéngzǐyá.	In mythology, Yú Shi was the god of rain.
Yuán (m)	An Erlitou council member.	A common Chinese name, it can also mean a member.
Yúntóng (m)	Lóngshān King of Kāifēng.	In mythology, Yúntóng was an assistant to Léigōng and was responsible for cloud creation.
Xí (m)	Soothsayer to King Chīyóu.	In mythology, Hú and Xí are drunken astrologers who fail to forecast a solar eclipse and are beheaded by the emperor.
Yútú (m)	Tú and Yú's son.	A made-up name combining the names of his parents.
Zhi Nü (f)	Mother of Hòutú.	In mythology, Zhi Nü fell in love with the Niúláng. It is a famous love story. I changed this so that Niúláng partnered with Hòutú, Zhi Nü's daughter.

Sources

This short bibliography includes written sources for this book and the subsequent novel. Digital sources can be accessed at the link below; I have tried to document my sources of information accurately but find that putting these into print form is tricky.

As this research took place over some thirteen years, a few sources may have slipped through the cracks. If this is the case, I apologise.

Maps - The Times Comprehensive Atlas of the World, National Geographic Atlas of China, Atlas of China Kunyu Publishing Co. Ltd., Google Earth, and Google Maps.

General History and Archaeology –
New Perspectives on China's Past: Chinese Archaeology in the Twentieth Century – Xiaoneng Yang
The Archaeology of China – Li Liu & Xingcan Chen
Illustrated History: China – Patricia Buckley Ebrey
The Cambridge History of Ancient China – Michael Loewe & Edward L. Shaughnessy
Banpo Matriarchal Society – Banpo Museum
The Institute of Archaeology Chinese Academy of Social Sciences, various papers - He Nu

A complete list of websites used can be found on my website at **https://www.markwhitworth.rocks/post/chinese-whispers-sources-for-sisters-mothers**

Printed in Great Britain
by Amazon

40670935R00179